THE DURIAN EFFECT

This is a fictional memoir. Except where supported by the public record, any resemblance to persons living or deceased is coincidental. Names, places and historical events are products of the author's imagination, or used fictitiously. It's grammatically and politically incorrect in parts. Phonetically and typographically inconsistent too.

There are numerous literary, film and musical references. Effort has been made to attribute non-original, appurtenant material to allochthonous sources, including but not limited to Dante Alighieri, Woody Allen, Martin Amis, Aristotle, Lester Bangs, Jean-Jacques Beineix, Bernardo Bertolucci, David Bowie, The Byrds, David Byrne, James M Cain, Albert Camus, Neneh Cherry, Arthur C Clarke, The Clash, Jonathan Coleman, Samuel Taylor Coleridge, Joseph Conrad, Francis Ford Coppola, Jim Crace, Wes Craven, Crowded House, Descartes, Neil Diamond, Philip K Dick, Bob Dylan, James Ellroy, Neil Gaiman, William Golding, Woody Guthrie, Nick Hornby, Hunters & Collectors,, Chris Isaak, Matt Johnson, Janis Joplin, Kierkegaard, Martin Luther King, Darlene Love, George Lucas, Lydia Lunch, David Mamet, Midnight Oil, John Milius, Roger Miller, Van Morrison, Mike Myers, Willie Nelson, Nirvana, Chuck Palahniuk, George S Patton, Mark Peploe, Nicholas Pileggi, Python (Monty), Queen, Radiohead, Lou Reed, REM, Rimbaud, Smokey Robertson, The Rolling Stones, Isabella Rossellini, Mario Savio, Martin Scorcese, Ridley Scott, Ebbe Roe Smith, Phil Spector, Patrick Suskind, Talking Heads, Quentin Tarrantino, James Taylor, Paul Theroux, Robert Towne, Richard Tunbridge, Urge Overkill, U2, The Vapours, Kurt Vonnegut, Irvine Welsh, Oscar Wilde. Those omitted, misrepresented, desiring changes or formal acknowledgement should contact the publisher to ensure correct information is printed in subsequent editions.

Published by O GROUP LTD

FIRST EDITION OCTOBER 2003
SECOND E-DITION AUGUST 2015

ISBN 988972631-9

Written and directed by Richard Tong.

Comments, enquiries and information?
ogroup.com.hk

Also by Richard Tong

ME & MY POTATO

The misadventures of Jack So

BITCH ON HEAT

SAYONARA BITCH

SECOND EDITION

THE DURIAN EFFECT

An oriental oddyssey of epic distortion.

RICHARD TONG

THE DURIAN EFFECT

PRELUDE

Where am I?
In the People's Republic of China.
Why did you stop me?
You are a criminal. You must be judged.

We believe men are born good. We believe the only way to change is to discover the truth and look at it in the face. That is why you are here. You will begin by writing the story of your lives and by confessing your crimes. Your salvation will lie entirely in the attitude you take. I advise you to be frank and sincere. Otherwise things can still go very badly for you.

- The Last Emperor

ONE PART

I is another. Rimbaud

1. YEAR OF THE GOAT

I HAD NEVER BEEN ASSAULTED BEFORE. Not really. I'd been hit. Punched. Spend as much time in bars as I had and it was inevitable. People were always getting upset about something. Anything. They'd drag you into their grievances. Alcohol, the great social stimulant and enabler. Play a season of Australian Rules Football and you're bound to encounter some unnecessary roughness. A bit of the don't-argue. Late tackles. Professional fouls. Trips. A push in the back. Hip and shoulder bumps. A shirtfront or two. Collared. Clothes-lined. Cleaned up. Ironed out. It even sounds like a common domestic activity. All part of the game, in sport and in life.

C'est la vie.

I'd been abused, verbally. Emotionally. Hasn't everyone? Although I was born unto a little more pain and trouble than most.

I came into the world with a double hernia. Later, as an infant, I was scolded and scalded. When I was learning to walk. I pulled a boiling pot of pea soup off the stove and onto my face. The burns were so bad my mother had to carry me on her hip for twelve weeks. Every time she put me down to sleep I'd roll over, popping the blisters and peeling the scabs. The sequela of that encounter were barely noticeable, now. A lazy pea-soup eye after a few drinks and propensity to shed skin in summer. Others scars ran deeper.

In my early teens I was manhandled too. Intimately. Sexually. That was a little harder to deal with but, like Holden Caufield said, I don't feel like going into it now, if you want to know the truth.

The simple is truth is I'd never been on the receiving end of anything like *this* before. As complete, all-consuming, relentless and reorientating. Even the time I was ambushed by The Angriest Man In The World paled in comparison.

I was travelling that night as well. Hitch-hiking. Seeking automotive comfort from strangers, so to speak. A popular, albeit random *modus operandi* in a more civilized age. Although, with retrospective clairvoyance, not quite as civilized as my romantic vision of it. I guess I had delusions of Kerouac. On The Road. The Dharma Bums. It was late, in the 80s. Stirling Highway wasn't really a highway but, in suburban West Australia, it was about as close as they'd got to building one. Or needing one. Traffic was light. A dark sedan approached and slowed.

It stopped. The driver opened his door. He walked toward me. At me. There was purpose in his steps. It was one of those moments absolutely packed with possibilities. I smiled at him and the impending prospects. A ride. A smoke. Banter. I was about to welcome them all with a cordial G'day. How're you doing?

The words never made it out.

One punch smashed them back into my head.

He hit me so hard my grandma died.

I crumbled into a defensive foetal heap and braced for the torrent of blows that were sure to follow. I waited. And waited. In the vacuum of violence blood rushed past my ears. Dots flashed in my eyes. Cars dashed by my carcass. It was in this pregnant pause I gave birth to a vague notion that all was not as it should be with my nose and cheekbones. My dial was taking on Picasso-like qualities. Split lips, after all, tell no lies. The gospel was written in blood on my face, fingers and the pavement beneath.

I peaked over my hands as the sedan retreated into the night.

No doubt it was my mullet's fault. My ten-dollar haircut. A bit off the front. Short at the sides. Long at the back. The type of quiff favoured by Ziggy Stardust and antipodal musicians, sportsmen and soap stars. I'd fashioned mine after half the members of INXS, with a side-order of Bono. It was considered by many to be the reigning heavyweight champion of mullets. Of course this was five or six years BC. Before Cyrus. Billy Ray Cyrus. He of Achy Breaky Heart and super-duper shagpile. A lot of people resented mullets in the same way they would come to resent Billy Ray. They didn't understand them. They felt threatened by them. It wasn't just a hairstyle, it was a lifestyle. A state of mind. A statement. It held a curious, indefinable power. It was a gift and a curse.

With great mullet comes great responsibility.

My assailant clearly had severe mullet issues. Mullophobia. Maybe he'd been abandoned by one as a child. Violated by one. It was hard to come back from the mortification of those experiences. Trust me. They can change you. Whatever the source of his chagrin, he exorcised his demons with extreme prejudice. Nonetheless, I can say with the confidence that comes from a majestic bonce of hair that, compared to *this*, the beating he meted was a mere blip on the ECG of physical incursions.

This was different.

I'd walked into this of my own volition. It was an all-out, balls-out assault. On the senses. On mind and body. Relentless. I was surrounded and set upon. Screamed at and slapped. Blinded. Poked and punched. Knocked down and walked over, for years. It lifted me up, tossed me around and turned me inside out.

I didn't land on Hong Kong. No. Hong Kong landed on me.

It was all over me like a cheap suit from the mean streets of Tsim Sha Tsui. It was, to coin a phrase, a complete bastard.

In that way, I guess, we were perfectly suited to each other.

I was a bit of a bastard too. A young bastard. A naive, ignorant bastard. A grumpy bastard. An unlucky bastard. Shit just seemed to happen around me. To me. I was a catalyst for major uh-oh. An agent of disaster. An isotope of doom. A freak magnet. Some would say it was my own fault, that I was a stupid bastard. A weird bastard. A rude bastard. Moody bastard. More often than not I was an honest bastard. Categorically. Biblically. Like Freddy Krueger, the bastard son of one hundred maniacs. Give or take a dozen maniacs. I was the rebuffed by-product of interracial rumpo. Plucked from the shallow end of a Sino gene pool, adopted by Anglo Saxons at an age too early to remember and raised as a white suburban male. In sun-drenched Australia the only real clue to my pedigree, my mixed blessing as mother often referred to it in times of doubt and playground bullying, was something about the eyes. Pea soup could only account for so much. It was more obvious in family photos.

One of these things is not like the others.

All I knew about Asia was what I'd seen in movies. The only taste of the Orient I'd had, apart from a couple of spring rolls and some fried rice at The Sunflower, was an afternoon exploring the exotic borders of Naomi Chan and discovering the good things on offer there.

I was the alternative poster child for young Australia. The bronzed Aussie that didn't have blonde hair and blue eyes. I was Richard. I was Dick.

I was Melon.

You don't choose a nickname. The nickname chooses you. And mine plumped for me in the backyard, under the pergola, at the patio table.

Kurtis, Blutarsky, Alby Mangles and Chuck Norris were there. Celebrating a birthday. Lisa Bonet's, I think. She made the world a better place. How we worshipped her and envied Doctor Huxtable. My mother came to join us. She brought a photo album, as mothers are sometimes want to do when they're menopausal. Peer groups thrive on these scenarios. There's nothing like the prospect of a little ritual humiliation to bring people closer together. Sure enough, as we flipped through the pages of my life, one thing was becoming abundantly clear. A part of my anatomy had no changed since birth. And, landing on a lithograph of me at nine months, the table erupted.

Jesus Christ! Look at the size of that thing! What the fuck is that?

It was my head.

It's a fucking watermelon!

No wonder you were born with a double hernia. You probably got it trying to lift that!

There was no denying. It did look enormous. Was it an optical illusion brought about by an aberration of light, or some kind of forced perspective? No one knew. Did I came into the world with a disproportionately large head, or suffer an unfortunate forceps accident at birth? No one cared. Mothers are no help in those situations. Their memories are selective. All their children are beautiful, with or without elephantiasis. For the rest of the day I was Watermelonhead.

Shut up, Watermelonhead. Hey Watermelonhead! Grab a few beers. Got any smokes, Watermelonhead?

By the end of the week I'd been reduced to Melonhead. By the end of the month I was Melon. Mel. Meloso. Melonoma. Mélangé. Depending on how you felt about the whole brevity thing.

So long, Melon.

I had no idea what was waiting for me in The Pearl Of The Orient. As the aircraft banked over Hong Kong I recalled a passage from Rendezvous With Rama. The bit where Arthur C Clarke went on about encounters between two cultures invariably meeting with disastrous consequences, for one or both parties. He cited Pizzaro and the Incas. Peary and the Japanese. Europe and Africa. I thought of the English and Australian Aboriginals. North Americans and practically everyone else. Punks and Hippies. Mods and Rockers. Arthur C Clarke and Sri Lankan boys.

What about the Chinese and me?

Some might say I was already an example of the disastrous consequences resulting from cultural collisions. An accident waiting to happen, again.

I'd flown four times in my twenty years on this earth. Melbourne and back. New Zealand and back. And there I was blasting from one British Colony straight into another. Two years after that guy stood in front of the tank in Tiananmen Square. A few months after CNN and George Bush had won the media war in Iraq.

Me, with my pathetic suitcase, $4,800 and a mild sense of foreboding. Me, descending into Hong Kong. Kai Tak. The airstrip on the harbour, in the middle of the city.

The plane turned late and low.

Gliding between clusters of concrete blocks, the small window afforded brief glimpses into incredible chunks of humanity. Breakfasts were being eaten, ties straightened, children herded and clothes hung. Six years before The Handover. The Hand-off. The Takeover. The Do-over. The Great Chinese

Take-away, as t-shirts would proclaim the approaching return to sovereignty.

There I was, arriving. Like so many before me, with romantic notions of The East. Getting back to my roots. Me, the misinformed, misguided, misplaced, misogynist. Touching down in Beijing's Backyard. Taxiing along the banks of the Fragrant Harbour.

Was that the sweet smell of success, or the stench of excess?

It was the 1.5 million litres of raw sewage being pumped into it that day. It was The Nullah. The long, thin stretch of stagnant muck that had once been water. It separated the runway from a freeway, and men from their senses.

What the hell is that? said Bob Hope.

Smells like shit, Bob.

I know it's shit, but what did they do to it?

I disembarked and began my own Long March toward an unknown fate. I tried to look like I did it for a living. The international traveller. The gentleman gadabout. I fooled no one. The Qantas Tours hand-carry was a dead give-away. The fathead abroad. I stood in line. Got processed. A visa. A three-month stamp of approval. The frosted glass doors retracted. Hong Kong got its first glimpse of me.

Arrivals.

It was quite a turnout. Bigger than I was expecting. More than I was used to. Not a bad crowd for my first overseas gig. Although they weren't a very happy bunch. I didn't know a lot about airports but wasn't there supposed to be looks of quiet excitement and anticipation? It seemed they were all waiting for a feared relative. The aunty from hell. Maybe they were.

Outside, it was red taxis as far as the eye could see. I stood in the queue with my globe-trotting brothers and sisters. All of us thinking the same thing.

So, this is where the Nissan Cedrics come to die.

A battered door flung open with automated ease. I settled into the back seat and addressed the driver, using my most polite, mellow, radio-friendly tones.

Old Peak Road?

Huh?

Old. Peak. Road.

He stared vacantly into the rear-view mirror. I responded in the traditional manner. I shouted. This would make me easier to understand. Volume would succeed where content had failed.

Old! Peak! Road!

The communication barrier remained unbroken. He wasn't deaf. He was Chinese. This was probably one of the reasons I'd been told to take a shuttle bus to a hotel on The Island. Get a cab from there, I was instructed. The drivers knew the area.

Wrongway Feldman looked at me like I held the answers to life's mysteries. I rooted around my luggage for the piece of paper I'd prepared in anticipation of this situation. I gave him the name of the hotel.

Furama?

Wrongway smiled. He gave a grunt of recognition and we made passage into the morning traffic. The morning traffic jam. Ingested. Absorbed. Another red platelet shunted into a massive vehicular artery. The AM radio pumped talkback exchanges in foreign tongues.

I took stock of my driver's attire and station.

Wrongway was wearing a black beret, aviator sunglasses, leather driving gloves and army fatigues. His steering wheel had been converted into one of those small, sporty ones. Such things would strike fear into seasoned commuters but, then and there, it just seemed a tad excessive. Particularly for a non-combat vehicle incapable of pushing 60kph, in a demilitarized zone.

Children poured out from Tetra Pak buildings. They were dressed in crispy white, starched uniforms. Like Sta Prest lemmings they streamed into the chasm of public education.

Through the carotid tunnel we went. Atrium, tricuspid, ventricle. Out of the black, into the blue.

The financial heart of Metropolis loomed large. Gotham rose around me. Towered over me. Uncommon structures, straight out of Star Wars. Blade Runner. Audacious statements. A hundred architects screaming fuck-you at the same time. Their neon mastheads waiting to cut through the night from atop glass, concrete and steel.

Motorola. Sharp. Bond. Nissin. Canon. Carlsberg. Siemens. Sanyo. Panasonic. Furama. Olympus. Samsung. Ford. Nikon.

Frama Hotel!

My bag and I were dumped on the pavement and eagerly corralled by a bellboy. I tried to explain I wasn't staying there. I needed someone to point the driver in the right direction. It took ten minutes, three people and a doorman besplendid in top hat and tails to get me on my way, again.

Restart. Reset. Reload. Old Peak Road. Mid-levels.

There it was, appropriately, halfway up Mount Olympus. Victoria Peak. It dominated The Island and the city that dwelled beneath. Thousands of apartment blocks clung to its ridges and sought succour in its shadow. One day these towers would surely slide off their perches into the harbour. They were unimaginative, rectangular blocks of domesticity, at odds with the commercial giants below. Clad in all-weather tiles, replete with mould in the grouting. A combination of humidity and harbour gave The Island the subtle whiff of public pool washrooms. *Eau de Toilette*. It's not you, it's me. A dab behind the ears will drive the boys crazy.

Oh Peak Road. Ninety-five dollar.

Money. The other reason I'd been told to take the shuttle bus. I was now $4,705 away from being broke.

I stood before a small cluster of apartments, six storeys high. Once upon a time, before they were boxed in and dwarfed by their surrounds, they would've savoured harbour views. Now they were remarkable for their lack of stature. Their humility. Kowtowing to lofty, brazen neighbours.

I picked up my bag. Walked past a Mercedes. And another. And another. Two more. A Lexus. A Rolls Royce. A lonely looking Toyota Corolla. I stopped at the convertible BMW and stooped to collect a set of keys from behind the rear wheel. A friend of a friend's friend had left them there. Four degrees of separation. I was to stay with her for a few weeks, or so. Until I found my feet.

Sarah.

My single point of contact in a city of millions. She had left a note. She was at work. I was to go upstairs and make myself at home. She would see me when she got home that night.

The apartment was big, by anyone's standards. Huge, by Hong Kong's. That musky odour of rising damp permeated inside too. Only it was slightly woodier. Dryer. A dehumidifier was sucking litres of water from the air at bells two, four and six. I changed into my other pair of jeans and white t-shirt. I went out. No map. No idea. Just out. Around. And down. Past a small Botanical Garden. Into the city.

I saw a ten year-old girl enthusiastically displaying a pager to her classmates. Farther down, a double-decker bus had met with a mini-bus. It had been rear-ended by a truck hauling butane. Dozens gathered. Surveying the damage. Playing the blame game. Traffic built. Tensions grew. Tempers flared. Horns blared. People smoked.

Honk if you love Hongkers.

In other news... a 65 year-old woman is taken by a shark... A schoolboy, made to bark like a dog in front of classmates because he lied about eating someone else's lunch, goes back to his 34th floor apartment and jumps out the window... Misunderstanding a request to bathe the baby after doing a load of washing, a Filipino maid puts the infant in the washing machine and

drowns her... A 60 year-old man stabs another man in an argument over a
parking space... The corpse of a 10 year-old girl is stolen from a grave and
married to a dead bachelor.

HONG KONG, 6.3 MILLION WAYS TO DIE and counting. Central was awash with suits and lined with glossy, perfect images. Scant signs of Buddhism, Taoism, Confucianism or Maoism here. Materialism was the dominant religion. Consumerism was running rampant. There were shops the likes of which I'd never seen. Money dripped off people and it seemed to me they had little regard for anything outside the accumulation of it.

What did they do? Where were they going? And why did they have such appalling dental work?

An aged Indian security guard sat in a chair at the front of a jewellery shop, with a shotgun. Its butt rested on the pavement. He rested his chin over the end of the barrel, while he napped.

Two doors up, another guard stood out the front of a bank. Shotgun in hand. Double-barrelled. Double-take. He's cross-eyed. Hell of a guy to have on your side in a gunfight.

Further on, an old man was lifting a large, cane basket out the back of a truck. The sinewy tendons of his arms were wrapped around its belly, hugging it to his chest. The bottom of the basket gave way. Kilos of offal flumped to the sidewalk. Bloated intestines, kidneys, livers, stomachs and all the other inside bits of animals slid down his legs. He pondered the roadkill for a moment. Placed the basket on the ground and, using the sandals on his feet, attempted to push the offal back into the cane carcass. He picked it up and carried it into a restaurant. Dinner is served. What's the Blue Plate Special?

Forget it, Jake. It's Chinatown.

I was hungry but not ready for local cuisine. I went into a hamburger joint. Hardees. Burger King. Jollibee. Whatever. A lardy, middle-aged American was remonstrating with the manager. The hot dog he'd ordered didn't look like the one in the picture behind the counter. It was like that scene in Falling Down. Life imitating art. He wanted to know where the lettuce was. The mustard. The relish. And the onion.

Poster for display only. Advertisement. Not served that way.

My Team Member was Teddy and Teddy was in need of a good dermatologist. I'd always maintained there was a correlation between the skin condition of staff and the price of the food they serve.

Teddy was Exhibit A.

I walked out. Right into some stinky tofu. The Bill Of Rights had just been introduced that week and this was the first infringement upon it. An old man stood behind his variation on the in-flight beverage trolley. Where an insipid chardonnay or robust Cabernet Sauvignon would normally reside there was a giant wok. It bubbled with oil and tofu. Not trendy, nouveau tofu. *Tofeau.* Not TV tofu. This stuff would've made an egg-fart feel welcome. I took what I considered to be my last breath on earth. And hit The Hut.

Pizza Hut. My first meal in Asia.

Surprisingly, the majority of Huttians were not eating pizza. They were engaged in a bizarre ritual that involved stacking salad into small bowls. The free salad bar was a one-shot deal and they were getting their money's worth. Carrot and celery sticks were inserted vertically, to extend the side of the bowl. They lined the extensions with lettuce leaves. This tripled the size and cubic volume of the container. Having failed the prerequisite bowl-buttressing units at college, I settled for pizza.

$4,600 to go.

On Victoria Harbour a vendor of a different genus was selling spiky, green, organic footballs from a cart. Durians. I knew nothing about them but I could tell they were ripe. In the realm of the senses, to encounter durian, stinky tofu and The Nullah in one day was as brutal as introductions got.

A man in a kaftan approached me. Indian. Pakistani. He could've been Turkish for all I knew. He told me I had lucky eyes. He could see it. I was a lucky man. To prove it he asked me to name a flower. Like an idiot I said what 99% of idiots would have said. Rose. He opened the palm of his hand. There was a small ball of paper. He unwrapped it. Rose, it said. Amazing. He repeated how lucky I was and asked if I would present alms.

A donation, Sir. To keep your luck.

Not wanting to start an international incident, and keen to keep holding onto this mysterious luck that had come into my possession, I gingerly pulled out my wallet and withdrew a hundred dollar note. Before I could ask if he had any change he snapped it out of my hand.

Now you will be very lucky indeed, Sir. Yes, very lucky indeed.

Not as lucky as you, I thought. I was going to say chrysanthemum.

$4,500. At this rate I would be broke by sundown. I made a hasty retreat up the hill to my lodgings.

It was 7:30 when Sarah flung open the door and greeted the groggy stranger on her couch like a favourite relative. She was short, slim and fit. Like an aerobics instructor in a power suit. She led me down to the car and drove us to the top of Mount Olympus. We dined opposite that spot where Jean-

Claude Van Damme did his pre-fight exercises in Bloodsport, looking down on the city that Ridley Scott built.

Sarah was a big, swinging-dick lawyer, power-packed into a tight frame. A throw cushion to be tossed with caution. She told me there were no rules of engagement in Hong Kong. It was every man for himself, and every woman was on her own. Success was random, a common but unpredictable occurrence. There was no quintessential experience. It was different for everyone. I would hate it, or I would love it. Eventually I would hate to admit I loved it, or I would love to say I hated it. Still, it could be very good to me, like it had been to her. Like the toxic durians I'd encountered earlier, that hailed from foreign ports, Hong Kong might adopt me as one of its own too. Beneath that coarse exterior and noxious odour was a bittersweet flesh, a mélange of caramel, banana, onions and mustard gas. It was an acquired taste. And just one of a constant barrage of challenges the city would throw at me. It was a sensory, corporeal and cerebral obstacle course. I'd learn new definitions of patience. My ways would not be the ways of others. I'd have to get used to it, or go crazy trying. I was welcome to stay with her as long as I wanted. It was a generous, although somewhat disingenuous offer.

When AJ arrived, she was welcome too.

AJ was my girlfriend. Or, rather, I'd been AJ's boyfriend for just over a year. Among other things, she had the distinction of being one of the few girls I'd ever really pursued. Actively, over a prolonged period. I'd had other girlfriends, not many, but they'd just seemed to happen. I'd never had to make much of an effort, or cared enough to give one. In that regard I guess I was a bit of a lucky bastard. Or a lazy bastard. I could never be accused of enjoying first-mover advantage. If I was Han Solo I would've let Greedo shoot first. Suffice to say, relationships did not come easy to me.

AJ was different, but no different.

I'd known her for a while, and thought about her for an eternity. Her best friend was my best friend's sister. Three degrees of separation. Two and a half. I'd seen a photo of her on his fridge door. Once. That was all it took. The first time I met her was at Kurt's place too. I came back from ogling her on the icebox to find her sitting in the living room. We watched a movie together.

Colours.

There's two bulls standing on top of a mountain. The younger one says to the older one: Hey pop, let's say we run down there and fuck one of them cows. The older one says: No son. Lets walk down and fuck 'em all.

It was just me and her that afternoon. Chewing the scenery. Robert Duvall, Sean Penn and the others all faded into the background.

You don't wanna get laid, man. It leads to kissing and pretty soon you gotta talk to 'em.

Over the years I'd made discreet inquiries. So many discreet inquiries, in fact, it was common knowledge that I was mad for her. The mere sight of her enervated me. And terrified me. I was reduced to a blushing, mumbling schoolboy of terminal uncoolness.

When Kurtis told me AJ had finished with her longtime boyfriend, it was the window of opportunity I'd been waiting to open and wanting to crawl through for ages. I even broke up with my girlfriend to clear the way.

The first time I called upon her there'd been an accident. A family tragedy. She was home but her father said she wasn't up to seeing anyone. He'd tell her I called. Over the next few weeks I went to her door regularly. Each time I was met by a different member of her family. Each time I was told she wasn't around, or she was resting. She didn't want to see anyone. Our paths would cross, from time to time. In the bar I managed. At Kurt's. On the street. Her deep, dark eyes were always tinged with sadness. Each time I saw her I fell into them. And fell for them. Again. I took to calling on her. Again. Members of her family would greet me, this time with smiles of recognition. They were amused by my persistence. In the end they were the ones who persuaded her to go out with me, on a date. They told her to give me a chance. They told her to get me off their doorstep. I was making the place look untidy.

I phoned.

I asked her out for dinner. She said okay. She said okay. Jesus. Now what? I asked what she felt like. Chinese? she replied cautiously, like it was the ironic answer to the $64,000 question. Maybe it was. I didn't really eat Chinese food. She probably guessed that. My silence spoke volumes.

Do you like Chinese?

I love it, I lied.

Not the greatest foundation for a relationship, I know, but I was on unfamiliar territory and breaking new ground. There wasn't a lot of wriggle-room. It's not like it was a bold-faced, deal-breaker.

Was it?

I could clear up any misunderstanding later.

Couldn't I?

It's not that I didn't like Chinese food, or had a discriminatory aversion to it. I just didn't have a great deal of experience with it or know much about it. Chinese food was rarely on my table. I'd eaten fried rice every now and then, as long as it didn't have shrimp in it. Lemon chicken. I'd tried satay beef which, technically, is not Chinese but it was part of The Sunflower's menu. Spring rolls.

Did sesame seed buns count? That was about it. My diet was quite traditional. Palaeolithic. Cro-magnon. Meat and two veg. That type of thing. I didn't eat seafood. Not even a prawn cracker.

I took AJ to The Sunflower.

It didn't matter where we went. She was out, with me. It didn't matter what we ate. AJ was there, with me. Eight inches away. I encouraged her to order. She suggested garlic prawns.

Garlic prawns. I tried to sound enthusiastic. Great.

AJ was a vegetarian. Sort of. White meat was okay. Seafood. Chicken. A bit of bacon. By that description half the people I knew were vegetarians. It made me half-vegetarian but I was willing to convert, completely, for her.

Capellanus said love was an inborn suffering, derived from the sight or an excessive meditation upon the beauty of the opposite sex. That it caused one to wish, above all things, for the embraces of the other and, by common desire, to carry out all love's precepts in their embrace.

I was dying to get into those precepts.

Who knew when that dinner would finish, or where it would end? I just knew it was more than a meal, or a date. It was an omen. A sign from God, assuming God was more than an abstract concept. AJ was ethereal. Magnificent, in every possible way. Smart. Smarter than me. Too smart to be with me, some would say. Beautiful. Long brown hair. Long brown legs. Deep brown eyes. Brown is not an easy colour to wear. She carried it off in her sleep. Without even trying. AJ could make a brown paper bag and a hessian sack look good. The way she said Oh! just before she dropped things was pretty special too.

It was AJ, and my desire for her precepts, which planted the Hong Kong seed and set this journey in sinuous motion.

We were living together, house-sitting, while her parents were away. Two wonderful, balmy, languid months. One night, as she slipped naked from the pool, she told me she was planning a trip to Hong Kong or Singapore, to work.

Really? Me too!

I had no idea what I was going to do after the diplomas were handed out at the Academy Of Performing Arts. Hong Kong sounded exciting. A trailblazing, maverick thing to do. Even if it was just for a few months, on the way to somewhere else. It fitted perfectly with the rock 'n roll approach to life I'd been cultivating. It was the perfect getaway. We could escape the trauma of the past. Restart. Reset. Reload. Re-invent. It didn't worry me that, geographically, I had no idea where Hong Kong was or that I didn't know anyone there. It just sounded like a cool thing to do because it was what *she* was going to do. It was a wing and a dare. Like most of my privileged generation I considered myself infallible. Immortal. The future was irrelevant. I lived in The Now. All I had to do was get to Hong Kong, wait for AJ to arrive and everything would be okay.

Wouldn't it?

It is not in the stars to hold our destiny but in ourselves.

Whatever destiny held in the cards for me, Fate was playing them close to her chest. Day after day I awoke and searched the papers, fruitlessly, for opportunities.Money was always in the headlines.

World's Biggest Cash Robbery.

Three gunmen were reported to have held up a security van and absconded with $167 million. The boyfriend of the clerk at the security company was arrested and released. Unreliable and contradictory evidence. Soon after, newspapers began referring her lover as Big Spender. This tended to suggest, despite unreliable and contradictory evidence, he was probably the man behind the raid.

I was down to $2,700, with 85 days left on my Tourist Visa to find a job.

I called the local TV station. TVB. The Pearl. The person I needed to speak to was on holiday. I'd have to call back in a couple of weeks. Looking out the sixth floor window, I saw an old man below. Washing cars.

Maybe I could do that?

Sarah said most people already had someone like that old guy, if not that very same old guy, to wash their cars. It was not the type of job expats did. The pay was lousy. Still, she'd have a word to the man who washed her car, and the other cars, at her office.

I met Mr Miyagi two days later. He gave me a job, or Sarah paid him to employ me. I never found out. Wax on, wax off. Five days a week. Ten in the morning until three in the afternoon. I washed cars. Wax on, wax off.

In other news... the owner of a stolen car had left his mobile phone in it. He called. A young man answered. Was there was any chance he could get his car back? It was already on its way to China. In a few hours it would belong to someone else. Could he have his briefcase back? It contained important documents, worthless to anyone else but quite valuable to him. A courier delivered the briefcase to his office the next day.

I WAS SUPPOSED TO CLEAN A LEXUS, except it wasn't there. It had been stolen. The police said it was probably in China already. Smuggled aboard one of those long, thin boats with 400 horsepower engines. There was very little anyone could do. This car, however, belonged to a well-connected lawyer.

He knew people.

The Lawyer told these people his problem. They asked for his license plate number and the colour of the car. Two days later his Lexus was back in the parking lot. Vacuumed, washed and waxed. There was a note, apologising for the inconvenience. Should he have any problems with the automobile, or want another one, they would only be too pleased to help.

I'd never had much luck with cars.

In just five years I'd rolled a Toyota Land Cruiser, smashed in the front of my father's Ford, lost my license for doing 110 in an 80 zone, and wrapped Kurt's car around a lamppost. I'd left the keys to grandma's 1967 Morris in the ignition one night and it got stolen. I'd even backed AJ's car into a Jaguar. That had cost her father his no-claim bonus. If the HK Department Of Motor Vehicles had known any of this maybe they wouldn't have made it so easy for me to get a license. As it was the only test I had to pass was one of patience. 45 minutes later, and $600 lighter, I was ready to roll in whatever Mr Miyagi let me get my hands on.

I walked into the basement of an apartment block, to clean a BMW. 5-series. Three young men were standing behind it. They turned as I approached and, in a panic, grabbed me. They bundled me into the trunk and slammed it shut. That's it, I thought, the next time I see daylight I'll be in China, or on a very fast boat to it. Fortunately, the commotion disturbed a napping security guard and they took off when he came to investigate. I guess the trunk wasn't big enough for two of us. When the police asked me to describe the assailants all I could give them was the fact they were Chinese which, in Hong Kong, was not much help.

My days in car maintenance were over. I threw in the *chamois*. There had to be more to life than Turtle Wax.

Mr Miyagi, as you might imagine, was gutted. He'd have to find someone else to work for $100 a day.

On the way home I passed one of those sidewalk restaurants. *Dai pai dong*. A table had been cordoned off by the police. The scene of a crime. From the look of the flattened yellow ducks hanging in the window, and stench coming from within, someone should've been charged with something. There was, however, blood on the pavement. Chalk marks and a broken clay pot.

The restaurant had a history of noise complaints, late at night, from residents in the flats above. One had taken his protest to the next level. To the 18th floor. He dropped a pot plant from it, onto an unsuspecting diner. Lights out.

In other news... a man whose sons refused to let him live with them threw kerosene around the living room. And lit it... A woman ordered her son-in-law to vacate the family home and he bludgeoned her to death with a brick... A 72 year-old man fell from a rooftop, after suffering 30 hammer blows to the head. Police couldn't decide whether it was suicide or murder, even after finding a bloodstained hammer and pillows in the apartment he shared with two others. He could have hit himself in the head, 30 times, while lying in bed, face down, then crawled to the roof, without leaving any blood on the steps, climbed over a wire fence and jumped.

A NEW RADIO STATION was going to air. Having logged a few hours on community airwaves, during my college days, I thought I could blag my way into a job there.

I caught a double-decker bus to the interview.

Two seats at the front had hot pink upholstery. For the handicapped? Women? Handicapped women? It was part of a promotion. The current queen of soft porn had parked her petite frame and DD breasts in seats just like them, on other buses in the fleet. Men had been known to fight over them. The seats, that is. Her breasts too, presumably. It was a PR event unlike any other and a roaring success. Her warp was as good as her weft. None thought it strange that a 62-inch woman had 42-inch snokes. Sarah had a television that occupied more 3-dimensional space and pounds per square inch.

It was 30+ degrees outside, with 98% humidity. Inside was a dry five degrees, with high wind-chill factor. Hong Kong was having a steamy, sadomasochistic affair with air-conditioning.

It still is.

FM Select wished I'd been to see them a few weeks before, when they were hiring. They'd keep my demo tape and CV on file, for future reference. I had the rare quality of actually being qualified for a job in radio. The restaurant downstairs is hiring, quipped a DJ. If you're desperate.

I was.

The manager wasn't too happy with my inability to converse in Cantonese, but 30% of his customers were *gweilo* anyway. Foreigners, expatriates and miscellaneous tourists. I could bridge the gap between them and the rest of his staff. Work my way up to a management position. He gave me a job, pushing the *dim sum* trolley at lunch time. Eleven to three. Seven days a week. $800.

Things were looking up.

I inadvertently caused a demarcation dispute on my first day. Trolley-pushing was the domain of ancient warrior women. You had to be 85 or over to take the wheels. Fortunately, someone had started a rumour that I was the manager's nephew and the Mamazonians let me live.

I was familiar with Chinese food, as a concept. In the broader sense. As a visual entity. *Chinese* Chinese food, however, was a different basket altogether. I could recognise spring rolls, steamed rice and vegetables. It didn't worry me that lettuce was being steamed and smothered in oyster sauce. Where was the sweet and sour pork and the chicken *chow mein*? The beef and black bean? Fried rice? Didn't Chinese people eat Chinese food? Offal, as I'd learned, was thick on the ground. I found it hard to reconcile how people of such wealth dined on what I considered to be poor-man's food. The stuff others threw out. Much of it drowning in thick, impenetrable sauces to disguise it.

Where had all the good bits gone?

The rest of the animal was there. The extremities. The entrails. The fat. Chicken feet. Duck tongue. Fish balls. I didn't even know fish had testicles and now I was stuck with a mental Polaroid of them swimming around without them. What kind of fish had gonads the size of golf balls anyway? Congealed pig blood. Cow intestine. Deep fried cow intestine. Surely deep-frying would fry the goodness right out of them.

Forget it, Jake. It's Chinatown.

Over the border it was even more spectacular. They had dog stew. Pickled monkey brain. Rat kebab. In fact, anything rat was considered to be the duck's guts. What did that make the duck's guts? Braised rat. Satay rat. Rat casserole. Black-pepper rat. Fried rat with raccoon. Rat consommé. Rat restaurateurs were contributing to the new China, apparently. Getting rid of pests and enriching the peasants.

In other news... the China Morticians Association sued a writer who said a restaurant was selling steamed buns stuffed with flesh cut from the buttocks and thighs of corpses. The reputation of crematorium workers, already the victims of society's prejudice, had been further damaged, contributing to a crisis in confidence in cremation, making the already difficult cremation reform harder to carry out... Restaurants in one Mainland village were lacing food with opium, to make it habit-forming and generate repeat business.

THE TROLLEY TROLLS had developed a sure-fire way of getting customers to leave tips. As diners departed the women would look down and see what kind of gratuity had been left on the table. Then they would announce it, to the restaurant.

Table 10! $20 tip! Table 37! $15 tip! Table 3! $10 tip!

Regulars, aware of this and keen to leave with heads held high, would be sure to leave a noble amount. Those not used to the practice, or encountering it for the first time, would feel the eyes of the world upon them, judging them. If they left small change they would never make the same mistake again.

One afternoon, a local businessman and his associates got up to leave. Table 12! $1 tip! The entire restaurant stopped to stare. Embarrassment turned to anger. He went back to his table. And repossessed his coin.

Table 11! Taking back $1 tip!

I was fired at the end of the week. For stealing egg tarts, they said. The manager mumbled something about a pre-97 localization policy but I knew the truth. The trolls had it in for me from day one.

Sarah was out when I slumped home. A late meeting. I tried watching TV. A rerun of LA Law. I put on REM's Out Of Time and wrote a letter to Kurtis telling him how awesome everything was. I put on a load of washing. I plugged in the machine and pushed the button.

All the lights went out.

It was dark. Really dark. The great wall of buildings around us meant illumination was limited to a thin shard of light, stealing through the living room window. I went out the front door and down the stairs, in search of residents with a torch and the number of an electrician. A small, wary Indian woman on the third floor passed one of each through the latched door and security grate.

Love thy neighbour.

I returned to the black hole of Calcutta and made a call. Then waited in the dark for about seven and a half weeks, until Mr Lo, the electrician, arrived.

He took a quick walk about the apartment, located the fuse box, flicked a switch and, lo, there was light. I'd tripped the circuit-breaker when I turned on the washing machine. For this piece of information Mr Lo took 600 of my dwindling dollars. I didn't care.

AJ was on her way.

I could see my light come shining, from the West unto the East.

Arrivals.

She looked tired and nervous as she scanned the masses for a familiar face. I was standing up the back, waving a little Australian flag. Brandishing a solitary red rose.

Why does everyone looked so pissed-off? she asked. What did you do?

The taxi driver attempted a land speed record on our journey home, while I talked at a million miles an hour. About how great everything was. How fantastic it would be. AJ's eyes darted between mine and the back of the driver's head, in abject terror, as he rode the accelerator and the brake. Often at the same time.

Don't worry. You'll get used to it.

We got home and made love like clumsy sea-otters. It was probably the most heterosexual action Sarah's walls had seen or heard in a long time.

Sarah was not the first gay person I'd met but she was the first who didn't keep it behind closed doors. Or in a closet. There were guys I'd gone to school with who turned out to be gay, but they weren't gay when I knew them.

Were they?

There was that doctor at The Clinic. If he wasn't gay he ticked a few of the boxes. Or did he debase me impurely for shits and giggles? Just because he could. Maybe he was only a perverted, vulturous cunt. Whatever. Like I said, I don't really feel like going into it now, if you want to know the truth.

Truth is Sarah had a lot of butch, girl friends. They all wore sensible shoes and played golf. They'd regularly take off on golf weekends. I knew what this was code for with a lot of males. Was it the same for she-males? In the month I'd been boarding with her I'd never seen her enjoying the company of a man, not even a company man. Mind you, I'd never seen her in her underwear either. Yet, once AJ arrived, that's all she ever seemed to wear around the house.

The first time they met was on Sunday morning.

AJ and I were going to get breakfast and take a walk through Central. Sarah paraded out of her room, in camisole and briefs. She seemed surprised to see us. To see AJ.

Oh. I forgot you were coming.

She stuck her hand out and pushed her breasts up, like she was working for the bus company. This was not an uncommon response to AJ. A lot of dudes also sucked in their guts and puffed up their chests when encountering her. I'd been guilty of it too. The two of them made introductory small-talk and laughed, like girls do. I invited Sarah to join us. She declined. She said she catch up with AJ later.

We walked down the hill to Post '97. A cafe in the heart of Lan Kwai Fong. The drinking district conveniently located just behind the financial district. I'd never been to Central on a Sunday. Most of the buildings and many of the luxury boutiques were closed.

And yet every available space was occupied.

There must have been almost 84,618 people there. Sitting, standing, lying and walking around. Toting enormous red-white-and-blue striped, hessian bags. Cooks. Cleaners. Catholics. It was the all-singing, all-dancing, all-smiling Filipino backbone of the city. All speaking at speed in the sing-song, bubbly tones of Tagalog. They had one day a week to catch up with each other, if they were lucky, and they weren't going to waste it. Three city blocks gurgled with chatter. People swapped photos, took photos and posed for photos. They ate. They opened streetside salons and cut hair. Painted nails. Prayers were said and hymns were sung. Impromptu gospel shows. Can I get a witness? Alleluia. Amen to that. Teams performed synchronised dance moves. Line dancing. On the road. On the footpath. Anywhere. Everywhere.

Billy Ray would've loved it.

AJ wanted to know why people from the Philippines were Filipinos, and not Philippinos, or Filippinos. Phuck knows, I said. I'll try to phind out.

Sarah was on the phone when we got home. Sports bra, Lycra shorts. It was a good look, although it did make me feel a little uncomfortable. They just walked in, she said down the line, and passed the handpiece to me. She had a lovely chat about something with AJ while I spoke to Dougal, from The Magic Roundabout.

Dougal's mother had been speaking to my mother. Dougal and I were first cousins, twice removed, on my father's side. He was hosting a dinner on Thursday night. We were invited. Brian, Ermintrude, Dylan Florence, Mr Rusty and Zebidee would be there too.

Boing!

The room had all the ambience an obligatory get together that distant relatives feel duty-bound to organise. Those of us who weren't related were not among Dougal's nearest and dearest acquaintances. You don't expose people you really care about to such encounters. What if your first cousin turns out to be a plonker and has to be thrice removed?

AJ and I were passed around the room and left in a corner with Basil, Paul and Rosalie. They were also from Western Australia. Apparently this is what people who have flown 6,000km from Perth like to do. Hang out with people from Perth. Unfortunately, geographical dislocation was about all we had in common. We feigned interest in Dougal's collection of bronze statues.

Actually, Richard, they're not statues. They're castings. Bronze castings.

Starting to feel like social outcasts, AJ and I expressed a deep admiration for the predatory lines of the large panther casting and the chary mien of the stork casting. The critical mass of the elephant casting. The atavistic percipience of the bronzed Australian aboriginal.

Our noble savage cast his ironic gaze over post-modern colonists more fazed than he to be flung this far from The Fatal Shore.

Terror Australis.

Conversation was a distant continent. Insight and advice thin on the ground. I did, however, discover that it would be easier for AJ to find work than for me. She had a British Passport. It granted her Right Of Abode and pretty much guaranteed her a job. No work permits or employment visas for her.

I had no so such rights.

Australians had to be sponsored, which meant finding a champion for your cause in an environment where the path of least resistance was the preferred route. A potential flatmate was screened, despite Sarah's insistence we were to cohabit with her for as long as AJ wanted. Phone numbers were exchanged. Old Mr McHenry knew someone at the TV station. The possibility of a little voice-over work might present itself.

Thai and Indian food was ordered in. Swift lessons in piquancy were dished out. Small but lethal chilies sucked oxygen from the room. My mouth became a cauterized wound. AJ inquired after my health and the tears on my cheeks. I told her I was just happy to have added two cuisines to my culinary repertoire, regardless of their hostility.

Sensory experiences piled themselves one atop the other.

There was a remarkable sight for more eyes as The Leviathan prepared to make his way across the room. It took multiple attempts, from different angles and points of leverage, to extract himself from the lounge chair. Or rather, to remove the chair from his Kyber Pass. Waylon's efforts became the elephant in the room. Inching forward, across the seat, attempting to escape the arms of his captor. Every gain in territory announced by the squeak of leather under duress. He tipped his cetacean centre of gravity over the leading edge of the Hindu Kushion and sank to one knee. Then braced himself for the final push north with a burst of air from his blowhole.

It was only upon his rising that the enormity of the challenge Waylon wrestled with became self-evident. His buttocks, along with The Great Wall and fires in the Amazonian rainforest, were one of three man-made objects that could be seen from space.

They were not of this earth.

Staggering in their proportion, they were the glutes of Zeus. When displeased, he could surely hurl bolts of lightning from between them. Omnipotent. Omnipresent. They resounded across the room, threatening to destroy all in their path and leaving silence in their wake. The buffet table trembled. Dougal could've bronzed them, although he'd need to corner the copper market first.

Body-horror of a different breed that dominated conversation for the remainder of the night.

Bikini pageants were big business and there was no shortage of Suzies pouring themselves into swimsuits. Finalists were guaranteed more than a contractual fifteen minutes of fame. Particularly if they were prepared to shed a little modesty. There were TV and film appearances to cash in on. Soft porn. Not to mention the dating circuit. Contestants could be rented out like videos at Blockbuster. One man, operating under about four aliases, had convinced a number of pageanteers to perform a litany of lascivious acts. Beauties And The Beast, it had been dubbed by the dailies. He lured them to hotel rooms with promises of credit cards, film roles, watches and cash. He took photos *in flagrante* and painted the girls into more lewd corners. He promised to send prurient pictures to the papers if they didn't comply.

Hongky Heff ended up getting kicked in the tabloids and pulled into court on charges of blackmail, fraud and over-exposure in an undeveloped area.

To protect their identities in court, the women were monikered Miss A, B, C, D and E. The witness box, so to speak, was cloaked in mystery. Testimony was given from behind a black curtain. A precaution rendered somewhat moot when their agents released alpha-numerical publicity shots to the media. The only thing worse than being talked about, it seemed, was not being talked about. Or being mistaken for someone else.

The evening came to a premature end when Dougal revealed his organ. Sitting behind his Hammond he tickled a selection of Supertramp songs from the ivories. Dreamer. Breakfast in America. Logical Song. Bloody Well Right.

The meal gave an encore performance eight hours later.

My body went sub-continental and I had my first biological reaction to Asian food. Delhi Belly. Bangkok Bum. Tied intestines. It was terrible timing.

I had interviews to attend and jobs to secure.

The temperature sat at 38 degrees, with humidity pushing 100%. I'd made the mistake of wearing a wool suit. Actually, I'd made the mistake of buying it first. Wearing it was the price I had to pay. All the elements were falling into place. Irritable bowel syndrome. Uncomfortable clothes. Important appointment. A 45-minute journey into unfamiliar territory. Disaster was inevitable.

85% of the population lived less than a three-minute walk from the Mass Transit Railway. It shifted 66 million people a month, with ruthless efficiency. Every day, 2.2 million were packed into the MTR's subterranean steel casing, loaded into the breach and shot through the city. I knew nothing of other railways but I knew this had to be the most effective, efficient transportation network in the world.

On one of my first sorties, a small crowd had gathered at one end of the carriage. Arriving at the next station, six passengers carried a comatose man from the train to the platform. Medi-vac, sans stretcher. They placed him on the concrete. Then stepped back onto the train. Almost as an afterthought a woman rushed out and placed a briefcase beside him. Not that he would be needing it, not where he was going. The door closed. The train departed. The whole thing had taken about 35 seconds.

Ruthless efficiency, however, was in short supply on this day. For the first time in sixteen years the MTR broke down. 2,200,001 people were majorly inconvenienced.

I was suddenly, cataclysmically, incapacitated.

Trapped beneath the harbour, for 35 minutes. In a wool suit. An unnecessary evil twisting and turning in my stomach. The carriage rapidly running out of air. I began to sweat. The fibres itched. A woman in the corner was carrying a colostomy bag. Carrying it like a shopping bag, in a shopping bag. Her colostomy bag. Her half full colostomy bag. The tube ran between the lower buttons of her shirt. My stomach contracted.

I wished for a colostomy bag of my own.

The next stop was not where I had planned to alight but, I figured, if 85% of the population lived nearby there had to be a toilet somewhere. A hotel. A shopping mall. Something ablutionary.

Ascending into no-man's-land I soon learned why they say the road to hell is paved with assumptions. There was nothing remotely hospitable to be found and I lacked the intestinal fortitude to go searching. I ran back to the train and held myself together as best I could.

Kurtis had told me that the best way to stave off a soiling, and keep the goods at bay, was to squeeze your testicles. It was somewhat effective, although people were soon looking sideways at me and shuffling to the rear of the carriage. Backing away. Avoiding eye contact.

I was an hour and a half late for my interview.

Nature called upon me once again. I asked to freshen up and was ushered down a hallway to another hallway. There was half an inch of something on the floor to splash through. I entered the washroom. The stalls had no doors but I was in no position to complain. A security guard entered as I sat in contemplation. He didn't even bother to wade over to the urinal. He just spent his penny, adding to the unholy cocktail on the floor, like I wasn't even there.

Forget it, Jake. It's Chinatown.

The interview was a piece of piss, to coin a phrase. I was asked about my time at the West Australian Academy Of Performing Arts.

Was that the one Mel Gibson went to?

Yes! I lied.

She had me read some promo scripts. Then sent me on my way. She'd call if she had anything for me to do.

I got back on the train and went to meet Jimmy Marlboro. His last name wasn't Marlboro. People just called him Mr Marlboro because he was the guy who said Marlboro! at the end of Marlboro commercials.

He asked me to do a porno movie.

I wouldn't have to act, per se. He didn't want me to appear in one. He wanted me to read. To dub. To be a voice in one. Little did he know that for $1,200 I would've done almost anything, or anyone.

I had to get to Sha Tin, in the New Territories. The studio was near the Chinese University, on Chung Chi Road. If got lost I should just ask someone the way to Ponytail Road, he said. It was named after an illegal immigrant who jumped from a train there in the mid-50s. She got her ticket punched when her ponytail got caught in the door and ripped off her face. Her ghost was said to appear in the area from time to time.

Mind the platform gap indeed.

By the time I got to the studio it was late in the evening. Every available corner was occupied by women. They huddled beneath blankets. Filipinas. They'd been there for eight hours, giggling and moaning their way through the reels at semi-erotic points in the plot.

Just us, the cameras and those wonderful people out there in the dark.

I was to be the voice of Mr Johnson. He was the tennis coach at a summer camp for nubile semi-professionals. I could tell they were semi-professional because they were always bending over to tie their shoelaces and they didn't do their stretches properly. They had a very laissez-faire attitude to training. Many struggled with their uniforms. I don't know a lot about tennis but I'm pretty sure what they were wearing wasn't even close to regulation attire. The scenario had a whiff of *déjà vu* about it but I couldn't place the scent.

What else smelled like overripe fruit?

Mr Johnson would say things like Have you seen my balls? Nice forehand grip. Bend your knees a little. Change your approach, get lower. Out? Really? I think it's in. What a great set. Would you like to play mixed doubles? The entendres were intoxicating.

Sexy Tennis School premiered a few weeks later at Category III cinemas across the territory.

Category III meant Adults Only. Category III cinemas specialized in these type of art films. Taking a leaf out of Deng's book they had also implemented an Open Door Policy. Although theirs seemed more geared to local perverts than foreign investment.

AJ and I took in a matinee.

It wasn't exactly a full house but what they lacked in numbers they made up for with enthusiasm. Many rocked back and forth in their seats to the deft comedic beats of my nuanced delivery and dulcet tones. Some gave me a standing ovation or, as AJ referred to it, masturbated furiously. For her it was quite surreal. Hearing my voice in someone else's mouth. Listening to me having intercourse with another. For me it was more a case of art imitating life. A cinematic metaphor of the detachment I'd come to associate with sexual encounters. Like they were happening to someone else and I was just a one of Norma Desmond's wonderful people out there in the dark.

All right Mr DeMille, I'm ready for my close up!

From that night on there were times when life would imitate art. AJ would summon Mr Johnson to the bedroom, for private lessons.

40-love.

Mr Marlboro called a few days later. Someone was looking for a *gweilo* to do a voice-over in Mong Kok. A part of Kowloon that said, in no uncertain terms, you're not in Kansas anymore. It was one of the most densely populated places on the planet. 350 people per square meter. Half of them prostitutes and drug dealers. The other half sold dodgy computer software, discount electrical goods and pirate videos. I didn't realise there was such a huge demand for videos about pirates. Most of it was adult entertainment.

Pirate porn. Rated Arrr!

At the studio I was met by a conservatively dressed young woman. She had only booked the recording booth for an hour. The documentary I had to narrate was 40 minutes long. There was no time to familiarise myself with the material, run through the script and rehearse.

The footage started like an educational program. A brief history of China. Then it changed tack. There were images of churches. Religious gatherings. It was a call for missionaries to do God's work in China. This, along with my dalliances in the porn industry, would no doubt see me damned for all eternity.

An elderly man entered the studio. He waved me out of the booth and suggested I take a break. A few minutes later I was asked if I could speak with an American accent. The technician started to roll the tape back to the beginning of the film but was told there wasn't time to start again.

Just pick up where we left off.

God, as we are often reminded, works in mysterious ways. If he didn't care for continuity, neither did I.

We were blessed with good fortune in the immediate aftermath of my descent from Mong Kok's Mountain Of Transfiguration.

AJ was annointed Office Coordinator of a globe-straddling property company.

I became the voice of Lucky Strike cigarettes. This either made me Richard Lucky Strike. Mr Lucky. Or just Striker, depending on how you are with the whole brevity thing. There are many ways to say those two words. Lucky Strike. And no matter how many iterations or intonations you think there are, there is always one more.

LUCKY Strike! Lucky STRIKE! Luckee Striiiike!

This gig would make me famous. I would not be able to walk the streets of China unmolested. I'd be invited to host beauty pageants, open shopping malls, start motor races, call the lucky draw at annual dinners, and hand out prizes at primary schools. Such was the cult of nicotine. Deng Xiao Ping was never without a dart. Cigarettes were the one thing everyone could afford. For a carton of smokes anyone would pretty much do anything. There wasn't much I wouldn't do either.

A few days later Jimmy asked if I wanted to appear in a video.

I'd had quite a bit of on-camera experience from my years at The Academy. Hosting programmes. Presenting segments. I'd done five pilot episodes of a children's television show. A couple of TV commercials and a fashion catalogue. Still, I wasn't sure if I was ready to appear in the kind of videos I imagined Jimmy producing. I'd been told dubbing porn and voice-overs for cigarettes were gateway drugs to more hard-core pursuits. My degeneration into depravity had begun. The pundits would be proven right. Jimmy must have sensed the hesitation in my voice. He quickly clarified the nature of the shoot.

Karaoke video.

I was familiar with karaoke bars. The fad was beginning to take off in Australia. Music played, sans lyrics. Words scrolled across the blue screen of a monitor. You sang along. In this part of the world it was an Olympic sport. It had also been enhanced. Augmented. Corrupted. There were bars where you could perform a duet with a special friend, as it were. She would accompany you. Play the flute, so to speak. Were karaoke videos, like pirate porno, the next stage in adult entertainment? Erotic musicals where people did more than whistle while they worked? Despite his reassurances, anything was possible in Jimmy's video dungeon. Good money was being offered. I decided to see how he would make me earn it. Everyone starts in the mail room, after all. And you can't go wrong with a trade.

I arrived at a house in Kowloon Tong (no relation). It was an old, by-the-hour love-motel. Of course it was. What else would you shoot karaoke porn videos in? They corralled me and caked me in make-up.

The green room was filled with an equally green cross-section of society. All the major demographics were represented. The newly weds. The old couple. The kids. The Japanese tourist. The fat, ageing paedophile. I was a young German who was to fall in love with the blonde tour guide. I had no problems with my part, per se. I was a professional and would do my best to be convincing in my role. I just wasn't sure how I would handle, shall we say, an ensemble piece.

I gave discreet voice to my concerns with the producer and was somewhat relieved to learn that karaoke videos had nothing to do with blue balladry and off-colour choruses. We were making the videos that played under the music and scrolling type. She could, however, put me in touch with someone if I was interested in more exploitative entertainment and could carry a tune.

Our musical menagerie was packed onto a bus and shipped off to classic Hong Kong locations. The Peak. By the harbour. Jumbo, the giant floating restaurant. Stanley Market. We wandered about like tourists. Pointing at things. Other tourists, mostly. This gave it a somewhat existential vibe. I made eyes at the blonde tour guide, as per The Director's instruction. We would, presumably, consummate our relationship in some allegorical manner at a later date. The footage garnered would be edited together and accompanied by a tune. Something Cantonese and, more than likely, something about the vagaries of love.

Once again I was to be a detached observer of my experience. Emotions curtailed and contained, unable to penetrate the fourth wall of existence.

I chose to play my character with a little edge. Blue Velvet's Dennis Hopper meets The Deer Hunter's Christopher Walken. The tour guide said it scared her. My lovelorn look gave me the countenance of a serial killer, she said. I didn't care. According to the producer my love would go unrequited. Blondie was going to fall for a backpacker two songs later. No doubt she would go somewhere off-camera to fornicate with him. It wasn't the first time I had been betrayed by someone close to me.

It wouldn't be the last.

I got home late, just in time to scare AJ half to death. Not because I was still inhabiting my character, as good Method actors do. I hadn't removed my makeup. It had dried out. There were huge cracks in the veneer of my face.

In other news... after arguing with her daughter, an 88 year-old woman jumped to her death from their fourteenth floor apartment... A dead dog, thrown from the twelfth floor, knocked a policeman off his motorbike... A child was killed when a black vinyl couch dropped on him from a great height... A 13 year old boy became so excited watching a football match on TV he fell off the couch. And out his fifth floor window.

I OPENED THE APARTMENT WINDOWS to let in some fresh air. And forgot to close them when I left the house. When I returned in the evening there was a thin film of black crap on every horizontal surface. Tables. Books. The top of the refrigerator. Beds. Arms of the couch. Cushions. Clothes folded on the ironing board. The toilet seat. Everything. I'd also forgotten to empty the dehumidifier. In my absence it had tried to suck all the moisture out of the colony. It overflowed. The floor was now covered in a thick carbon-based paste. Sarah was furious. So was AJ. I didn't blame them. I was pretty pissed-off about it myself.

Who knew air had so much shit floating around in it?

There was pollution of all shades, some more deadly than others. Peril rained from above in new and exciting ways. Beer bottles, bags of garbage, wardrobes and even the occasional severed head were tossed from windows. I got hit by an errant can of tuna once. Dolphin friendly it may have been but it left a briny stain upon my shirt and basted me with the unmistakable stench of near-death.

Throwing stuff from windows was not unique to Hong Kong. Italians had been hurling objects d'art from above since time immemorial. On New Year's Eve. It was an out-with-the-old gesture. Everyone knew to stay indoors for that fifteen minutes after midnight. Mind you, unless they were renting in the Tower Of Pisa, Italians seldom lived more than five stories above the ground. Their evictions rarely had time to reach terminal velocity.

Hong Kong just took it to a bold new level.

The tea lady in AJ's office was burning joss sticks outside her apartment block one evening. To bring good luck to her tenement. A bag of concrete fell or was thrown from a neighbouring building site. And killed her.

Little old ladies could be pretty lethal too. Particularly when it was raining. Or even when it wasn't. They needed protection from the sun. All the elements, apparently. You never knew when they were going to pop their brollies. Being so diminutive in stature they could have your eye out before they knew what hit you. Not that it seemed to matter. Their concern for others was the same as their awareness. Nil. I preferred to let my smile be my umbrella.

They cared even less for that.

Hot on the heels of my audio-visual trifecta I was invited to TV City. Home of The Pearl, Hong Kong's number one English television channel. There was only two. Still, first was better than last and, considering less than 10% of the population had English as a first language, supply clearly outstripped demand.

TV City wasn't really a city but it sounded better than TV Suburb. It was also among the 15% of things not within a five-minute walk of the MTR. My journey to the land of smoke and mirrors included a half-hour bus ride.

As I disembarked the old woman in front of me opened her umbrella. The nylon rim brushed my eye. It began to weep uncontrollably and was still doing so when I was met by the Director of English Programming.

What happen to your eye?

I showed her my reel. A few on-camera interviews. Some news anchoring. I played a tape of station breaks and segments from my radio show. She got me to write and voice a promo for a movie. Three Men And A Baby. She thanked me for coming in and said she'd be in touch soon. I could only hope she didn't frequent any karaoke bars or Category III cinemas during her decision-making deliberations.

On the other hand, maybe that would work in my favour.

The following Thursday a young woman phoned. Winnie. She was a producer at TVB and wanted me to be in Tsim Sha Tsui tomorrow morning. 8am. I was going to do a segment for Eye On Hong Kong. A magazine program that ran in the evenings. It was called a magazine program because most nights you'd be better off reading a magazine than watching it.

Not any more.

Eye On Hong Kong with Tong would be different. I'd start by taking viewers on a tour de farce of the newly opened Science Museum. Then interview a local artist at the vanguard of the new cultural revolution. It was a little odd, to be honest. No introductions. No talk of money. Just turn up, she said. You'll be on television.

I did. And I was.

At the end of the day I met a fellow intrepid reporter, Rob. He took me to the pub. He told me he used to sell jewellery and heard the station was looking for someone to host a show. He'd always wanted to be on television and now he was. I told him I actually had a background in television. He said I was probably overqualified for it. Two years of formal training and actual experience made me a veteran of broadcasting by local standards.

Rob invited me to join his touch-rugby team.

They played on Saturday, at Happy Valley Racetrack. It sounded like an opportunity to meet some people, a few of which would be related to the industry I was trying to infiltrate. Unless, of course, touch-rugby was code for something else. It could've been.

Nothing in Hong Kong was what it seemed.

Saturday was 37 degrees, with a barmy 110% humidity. Teams were positioned over the centre of the racetrack. 20,000 spectators sat in the stands. I'd never played rugby, or touch-rugby, but it didn't seem to matter. From what I could see neither had anyone on our team. Most of our opponents, unfortunately, were a little more seasoned.

We got our cans kicked into touch all over the ground.

I took possession of the ball at one point and charged up the field. The crowd went mad. Fuelled by the adoration of thousands, and eager to impress them all, I ran.

What are your legs? Springs, steel springs.

What are they gonna do? Hurl me down the track.

How fast can you run? As fast as a leopard.

Like all sporting glory, my moment in the sun was short-lived. It was here, like Napoleon at Waterloo, I met my Gallipoli. Touch-rugby was something of a misnomer. Despite being a non-contact version of the traditional game, with taps substituting for tackles, three assassins came out of nowhere. They touched me with great intent and ferocity. They buried me. The crowd cheered. And cheered. It went on. And on. Like Romans baying for blood at the colosseum it seemed the longer I lay prone the more they rejoiced. I picked myself up.

All went quiet.

Turned out the crowd wasn't there for the rugby. They were there for the horseracing that was being broadcast on the giant screen in the middle of the track. They weren't on their feet for me. It was the finish of Race 5 at Sha Tin that had them up and about.

Rob dragged us to The Kings Arms, for the obligatory post-match deconstruction of our game-plan. With a few glasses of Dutch courage under our belts we would also work on a winning strategy for next week. Not-losing was about the best strategy I could come up with.

I got legless at The King's Arms.

They sent me home after seven and a half pints of ale. Not only was I drunk, I was nursing a mild case of sunstroke. I threw up for fifteen minutes and crawled into bed.

Rugby was hell but the life of a television personality wasn't too bad.

The Pearl were pleased with my on-camera work and offered a full time position. $6,000 a month. This was a little above the average wage, for locals.

I felt it was a little beneath my station. A bit low, for someone like me. You know, an expat. They said I'd be entitled to a review after the customary twelve-month period. This would result in a pay raise of up to 10% which meant, next year, I could be earning a princely $6,600 a month.

I didn't get a chance to accept, reject or negotiate the offer.

The discussion, like the position vacant, was made redundant when they asked for my ID card. They wanted to photocopy it, for their records.

ID card?

They asked for my passport. To get a copy of my work permit.

Work permit?

Thus ended my career in television. Not with a bang but with a whimper, from me. My golden era of touch-rugby went the same way. The Pearl didn't sponsor employees, even though it was a business that needed people with English as a first language. It would have been quite easy for them to do so. The oversupply of FILTH, however, meant it was as avoidable as it was unnecessary.

Failed In London Try Hongkong.

The FILTH was a contingent of Brits who made up a good percentage of Hong Kong's expatriate community. Like AJ and Sarah they had Right Of Abode. I guess this made them FILTH by default. In the same way AJ being a kind-of vegetarian made me kind-of vegetarian too. The same association, however, did not apply to antipodeans when it came to visas and work permits. Those of us not On Her Majesty's Service required them. I knew this. I just didn't think it would be difficult to wangle one. Particularly under such legitimate auspices. No one else seemed to have problems securing them. The immigration department was rumoured to be reasonably accommodating. I just had to find a company that wasn't adverse to a little extra paperwork. Until then, I would have to return to the trade I knew best.

Bars.

Lan Kwai Fong was the best place for that. The drinking district. Two streets. 30 bars and clubs. A dozen restaurants. The omnipresent stench of cat's piss. Home to the biggest and meanest rats ever to crawl out of the gutter. Rodents that knew no fear. They'd walk by, casually, stop, sit up, wink at you and spit through broken teeth. Then raise a rickety paw in a suggestive manner. They mingled freely with the *gweilos*, and locals that related or aspired to the culture of booze, on the cobbled streets of Lang Kwai Fong.

The Gweilo Ghetto.

The first three or four places I went to weren't hiring. Although they weren't put off by my lack of work permit either. Most people, a manager told me, did a Macau-run when their tourist visa expired. This meant taking a ferry to the nearby Portuguese enclave of Macau. It was only an hour away. Upon re-entry to Hong Kong you were issued another Tourist Visa and granted another three months to try your luck.

I went to Post 97. Got hired on the spot. 50 hours a week. 200 a month. $4,000 plus tips. Meals included. It wasn't brilliant money but it would have to do. Besides, AJ had a good job and was earning nice money. Sarah refused to accept rent. And I wasn't going to be doing this for long anyway.

Was I?

I had the eternal optimism of ignorance and a good feeling about Hong Kong. It was the right place to be.

The manager took me to Mecca. A small bar and restaurant with a Middle-eastern theme. I was introduced to an Englishman, an American, a Tunisian, an Israeli, two Filipinas and some guy from Sydney. If this sounds like the introduction to a joke it's because it kind of was.

I had to wear a uniform that consisted of red pantaloons and a white lace-trimmed shirt, tied off by a rainbow-coloured silk sash.

The American, with typical read-my-lips bravado, was on a personal mission to convince us all that Appetite For Destruction was the bitching-est album ever. I'd heard a few tracks and could see where he might be coming from but everyone else wanted to hear Seal. Over and over again. And again. Then Nirvana arrived and I was forced to enter into an unholy alliance with the American infidel. This was something else. I also had it on good authority that The Gipper partied with Michael Hutchence, lead singer of tonsorialy splendid Australian band INXS. Maybe we'd all get together one weekend, for a meeting of the mullets. We could call it Mulletstock.

Business at the front. Party at the back.

The Israeli would constantly remind us of his days with Mossad. Any doubts as to the veracity of his claims were quickly resolved. He'd kick us in the testicles. No matter how much warning he gave us, or how well we prepared, he would whack us in the whiblins at will.

The Australian, the other Australian, was somewhat shiny of face and spoke in a way that made everything sound like a question. His voice went up at the end of each sentence.

Sorry I'm late? Two drinks for table five? I'm going home now?

The little guy from Tunisia was awarded instant cult status because a lot of Star Wars had been filmed there. He also claimed to be best friends with a Jawa. His parents knew a couple of Tuscan Raiders. Sand People. He spent half his childhood asking his Uncle Owen if he could go into Tosche Station to pick up some power converters.

The Brit was disarmingly, enthusiastically English. He was well up for it, he was, and having it large. He wore a fluoro tracksuit to the shops on Sunday and made other British people uncomfortable. I liked him.

My domain was the bar. All eighteen square feet of it. The others worked the floor. Eight low tables. No chairs. Just cushions. It was going for an opium den cum rock-the-casbah vibe. Patrons were flush. Tips were great. $500 to $800 a night. Each. After 11pm it became a small nightclub. A bit of a scene. Some of the customers worked in advertising, or related fields.

Advertising.

Hang on a minute, I thought. Advertising is TV. Newspapers and magazines. Radio. I could do that. I'd already done some of that. Sort of.

One of my Mecca irregulars worked in the business. He looked a little like the bastard child of John Lovitz and Robbie Coltrane. He came in Wednesdays or Thursdays for dinner, and sometimes early on a Friday for a drink. I asked him which advertising agencies would be likely to hire someone relatively inexperienced. Someone like me. At the lower end of the food chain.

A lot, apparently. According to him most of the people in them didn't know what they were doing either.

I called dozens of Managing Directors, Creative Directors and Account Directors. They were polite but not much help. They weren't hiring at the moment. They were looking for more experienced people, or inexperienced women. The usual battery of rejections. One guy asked what part of the business I wanted to be in.

Any part, please.

I didn't know a lot about advertising and he could probably tell. He was just too nice or too lonely to break off the call. He asked me what I wanted to do.

Anything, I replied.

He explained some of the options available. Creative Department. Account Servicing. Media. I thought the Creative Department sounded cool. Coming up with ads and stuff. I also thought I could handle a job in Account Servicing. I was good with people and liked strategies and stuff. I was surprised he hadn't heard of my winning strategy for touch-rugby.

Not-losing.

Perhaps you should give it a bit more thought, he suggested. Get back to me when you've made up your mind.

I spent the next two weeks thinking about it. Forgetting about it. I became a creature of the night instead. Finishing work at two or three in the morning. Then going out with the United Nations of Mecca. I'd get home around six or seven. Just as AJ and Sarah were going to work.

Hi.

Bye.

With the exception of Sunday, the only time I saw AJ was if she came by the bar. On her way out. Friday and Saturday night, often with Sarah in tow. She'd say hello. I'd make her a drink and ask her what she'd been doing. She'd ask me what I'd been doing and we'd all have a laugh at my uniform's expense.

AJ and Sarah were becoming close.

They went to see Kenny G and Paul Simon. Not at the same time and not because either of them were particularly fond of the MOR legends. They went because Hong Kong was relatively starved for things like rock concerts and other loose approximations of contemporary culture.

Sometimes you just had to jump on whatever came by.

I made sporadic calls to ad agencies and decided I'd be better suited to the Creative Department. I could be a Copywriter. The alternative was Art Director. This was not really an option. My graphic nous and drawing skills would not be out of place in the Paleolithic caves of Lascaux.

My lack of tangible experience was proving to be a problem. I couldn't get a foot in the door long enough to secure an interview. On the occasion I did manage to meet with someone, the issue of work permits would surface and promptly slam it shut. AJ suggested the best way to overcome the problem would be to eliminate it. If no one was going to help me get a work permit I should just get one myself. Start my own business.

I could employ me.

Kurt's mum had a company that made corporate documentaries and safety films in Perth. I could open an office for them in Hong Kong. With a little embellishment my CV would make me a worthy candidate for the venture. Certainly Hong Kong would benefit from it. A quick look at any building site confirmed that regard for personal safety was dangerously low. People swung around on bamboo scaffolding, 40-storeys high, without safety harnesses. Hard hats appeared to be optional. There were slip-on sneakers where steel-capped boots should be. Newspapers were littered with reports of industrial accidents. Fires. Fatal falling objects. Electrocutions. It might end up being more than a front for my hidden agenda. There could even been a few dollars in it.

Adair Films was established in honour of Red Adair, ballsy capper of burning oil wells. It played off the daring nature of my gambit.

Two weeks of legwork, paper shuffling an ping-ponging between government departments was all it took to register the company. With that behind me I could to submit an application for a work visa to the Department Of Immigration. It wasn't common practice to issue permits while the applicant was still in the territory, on a tourist visa. It was, however, done from time to time. I'd get an answer within three months. I told my case officer I only had a month or so left on my current visa. She said not to worry. Once the application had been made I was permitted to stay while it was processed. I just wasn't allowed to work. Officially. All I needed was an Extension Of Stay, readily obtained on the floor above.

All I had to do was stand in line, for three hours.

Lines were an important part of daily life. Lines for buses. Taxis. Films. Thelma And Louise. Silence Of The Lambs. Dances With Wolves. There were lines at the supermarket. Lines of people. Lines of traffic. And, sometimes, a couple of lines of marching powder to get us through double-shifts at Mecca.

I became part of the establishment in Lan Kwai Fong.

With notoriety came an expanding footprint of bars and clubs where I would be looked after. I was obliged, in return, to look after others when they came into my bar. It was one of the unwritten rules of The Barman's Code.

AJ broadened her horizons too, independently of mine. No big surprise. We moved in such different circles and time zones. In much the same way as I became a product of my environment she became part of hers.

It was a world I'd gain entry to on those rare nights I wasn't working.

She'd take me to parties and, invariably, we'd get herded into little expatriate comfort zones. Support groups. Petite Perth. Mini Manchester. Little LA. They were populated by people who thought they were living overseas. They weren't, of course. They were just working there. The more they tried to make it feel like home, the more they'd end up missing it. What was the point of that? I wanted this. All of it. Or even just a piece of it. This strange and addictive fruit.

Hong Kong.

AJ came into Mecca with some people she'd recently met. After the mandatory pantaloon jokes I found out one of the guys had a spare room in his apartment. AJ and I were going to move into this apartment. His apartment. His name was Daemon.

He was from Perth.

There was to be no discussion, with me. The decision had been made. AJ was self-sufficient and upwardly mobile. I was just moving with her. Mind you, if my work permit didn't come through soon, Vietnamese refugees wouldn't be the only ones unwillingly repatriated.

I had to borrow $4000 from my parents to cover the first month's rent.

Sarah thought it was a mistake for AJ to be moving out so soon. I kind of agreed with her. She seemed sad to see us go. To see AJ go. It was like watching the end of Casablanca. AJ playing Bergman to Sarah's Bogart. They parted knowing they'd always have Old Peak Road.

There'd always be a bed for AJ at Sarah's.

Daemon's apartment was in the Western District of The Island. It sat atop The Stairway To Hell. This was five times longer and steeper than the stairs in The Exorcist. We would draw straws, or play paper-scissors-rock, to see who'd have to climb them when we needed something from the shops.

There was a bonus for making it back without suffering a stroke.

For $8000 a month we got two rooms. One was big enough for a double bed and little else. The other barely had room for a single bed. It became a closet to house our collective couture.

Daemon got me some part-time work at his company. A small, dodgy company fronted by a small, dodgy man. He had me collect addresses for a mailing list. I'd work the bar at night and walk The Island by day, recording names of streets and buildings and writing down apartment numbers. I'm sure it was possible to purchase a database with that kind of information on it but small, dodgy Australians thought that was a waste of money. Why buy a mailing list when you could make your own mailing list, and sell it to others? I didn't mind. I got paid reasonably well for doing very little. I got to see The Island, street by street. I got a tan. I got to fantasise about all the bored housewives on The Peak that would see me walking in the sun, muscles rippling, and invite me in for afternoon tea. Maybe a swim in the pool. I could rub lotion on them. I got to see how an awful lot of people lived, how a lot of awful people lived and how a lot of people lived awfully.

I got to see a million letter boxes and a shit load of mail.

There were letters addressed to Friend Li, Psyche Chin and Satan Yuen. Submarine Wong. Humble Bee Kwok. Camel Lau. Pinnochio Leung. Polyester Chan. Microchip and Innately Ng. Migraine Tsui. Milky Lau. Money Ting. At AJ's company there was Hardon Lee and Abracadabra Chan. One of the girls was Idot. Apparently Idot was trying to think of a name that sounded smart. One of her friends suggested Idot because she was not an idiot. When I thought about that it made perfect sense, and none at all. The phone company had a Silicon Cheng and Wing Wong. Tadpole Wang was at the Water Supplies Department on Blue Pool Road. Ronald worked at McDonald's. No, really. There was an Italian restaurant where all the staff were Chinese but had names like Luigi and Giovanni. There was Kitty Chow. Acne Chan. Nausea Tsoi. The daughter of a biologist at the university was called Chlorophyll Yip. There was Winky, Pinky and Kinki. Windy. Kellog. Cyclops Wong. Snake Fang. Swastika Leung. Fanny Chew. I even heard rumours of a Fanny Pong and, given there's a whiff of truth to every rumour, I could believe it. Gucci Ip. Tequila Fung. Hippo Lai. A dog named Ah-tak.

Her mind is Tiffany-twisted, she got the Mercedes bends.

Daemon invited us to go junking. This was an expat tradition which consisted of hiring the most unseaworthy vessel imaginable, a junk, and taking to the high seas.

There are over 240 islands in the territory which, technically, should be enough to earn it archipelago status. One of these was home to The Frog and Toad. A public house of ill-repute, infamous for hosting the annual Mud Olympics. This was also a bit of a misnomer, as the Mud Olympics are not officially sanctioned by the IOC. If it were, there would be gold medals for their barbecue ribs and tolerance of drunken expatriates.

We rolled out of the harbour, towards ports unknown, with people unknown. A motley crew of inebriates lead by Captain Underpants. Neither AJ nor I caught his real name. He earned his commission when he stripped down to his tighty-whiteys as we rounded the heads. No one knew why or seemed surprised that he had. Perhaps it was all part of the junking ritual. He also had the unattractive habit of sitting with his knees apart. Wide apart. His cargo would spill from the hold as we rode the swell. No doubt the purple pustules, clinging like barnacles to the keel of his thighs, benefited from their exposure to the sea air.

His First Mate was a man of infinite jest and wisdom. Alas, poor Yorrick, also spoke with a wisp. And the most Engwish of accents. An odd combination for someone so Chinese in appearance. I asked what school he'd been to in the UK. He said he'd never been to Engwand. He went to school in Hong Kong. His accent had been acquired from James Bond movies.

Every time we tried to relocate to another part of the boat, Yorrick would come with us. To the galley. To the bow. On the sundeck. There he was.

Down below, another of our able seamen proudly claimed to have been thrown in the brig for assaulting a taxi driver.

Sexually? I asked, immediately regretting my attempt at naval humour.

Bruiser decked me with a glance and went on to explain how he had thought the cabbie was taking him for a ride. Showing him the long way home.

Just when I thought the afternoon couldn't get any more Lynchian, he invited us all to a Twin Peaks party. Something about him suggested he wasn't the type of man you could just walk away from. Not without incurring some kind of penalty. Immediately, or 20 years down the track. We allowed him to monopolise us for the remainder of the trip to The Toad with his theory on who killed Laura Palmer and a nonstop quote-a-thon of his favourite moments from the series.

One chance out, between two worlds, fire walk with me.

We eventually dropped anchor and it was time to storm the beach.

A sampan pulled alongside. It ferried us ashore and we assembled on the sand. Captain Underpants led through the scrub. Across a rice paddy. James Brown blared from somewhere. I looked to the sky, expecting to find a squadron of choppers on the horizon. The air thick with the smell of victory and Wagner's Ride Of The Valkyries. All I needed was for our fearless leader to trip a landmine. Please. Or a rag-tag platoon of US servicemen to stumble out of the swamp. As it was, a three-storey concrete block rose from the reeds.

Welcome to the The Frog And Toad. Home of the Mud Olympigs!

The IOC must have been onto them about the misappropriation of the Olympic name. You could see where a stroke of the brush had changed the OLYMPICS to OLYMPIGS. They were probably still drunkenly patting themselves on the back about how clever the pun was and how it actually made the name better.

The roof of the building was furnished with long trestle tables and chairs, like Ikea's forgotten children. There was little to protect us from the anger of afternoon sun. Women took refuge beneath deteriorating beach umbrellas. Men found shelter in large jugs of beer. A stunning presentation of ribs and chicken ensued. Large prawns followed closely behind.

I don't know how you feel about this shrimp but, if you eat it, you'll never have to prove your courage in any other way.

Conversation became comparisons of arrival dates in Hong Kong, occupations, residences, and things found or not found in local the supermarket. Us and Them. Some recalled their weird encounters with Them. I wondered if they were any weirder than this encounter with Us. And so it went.

Blah, blah, blah.

Toward the end of the blahfternoon, The King of The Toad held court. He was a bourbon-toting raconteur. He offered shots of Jack Daniels to anyone foolish enough to accept such a challenge after consuming ten litres of beer, a side of ribs and eighteen toxic shrimp from the South China Sea.

Captain Underpants, who had thankfully dressed for dinner, rose to the occasion. He saw the proprietor's goodwill as a personal affront to his drinking prowess. Half a dozen shots later he lay sprawled on the beach, painting the sand with a bespoke cocktail of ribs, prawns, bourbon and beer. Two of the shrimp still appeared be alive. Of course, there was some residual corn, a carrot and, bizarrely, one unbroken Pringle. A lone chip in the dip. The rest of us were left to ponder that along with our predicament.

Mr Sampan was gone.

The junk lay anchored 100 meters offshore and, with Captain Underpants out of commission, someone had to swim out to the boat and return with the dinghy tethered to the stem of the mothership. Against the tide, and AJ's better judgement, I volunteered. Diving in where angels feared to tread.

Fifty meters out, I stopped to get my bearings.

I wiped what I thought was seaweed from my face. Except it wasn't seaweed. I was in the middle of a small oil slick. My hair was thick with black goo. And there was good chance my mouth held more than salt water. Still, I had to press on.

Alcoholics were depending on me.

I pulled myself onto the deck a called up the Captain. The groggy master and commander appeared from below. He was reluctant to issue me a smile, let alone a towel. I cleaned up as best I could. Still, I looked like one of those Exxon-Valdez birds on CNN and felt like a Gulf War pelican. Playing Gilligan to his Skipper, we managed to unhitch the dinghy and bring the rest of our crew aboard.

The trip back to Victoria Harbour was rough.

Heaving drunks attempting to navigate the gangways only made it slightly more interesting than the trip out. Yorrick garbled on, like a drunk James Bond with a speech impediment. Bruiser threw beer bottles at passing container ships. AJ and I observed it all from a relatively safe spot on the bow. We quietly vowed to avoid large groups of expatriates whenever possible and expose ourselves to things more local in nature. Even if that meant looking like tourists in karaoke video.

Up ahead in the distance, I saw a shimmering light,

One evening we ventured over to Tsim Sha Tsui. Kowloon. Mong Kok. The famous Temple Street Market. I'd never seen anything quite like the Chinese Opera on display there. The costumes. The painted faces. The sounds. Chris De Burgh warbling meets alley cats on heat. There was stall after stall of tourist fodder. Cheap souvenirs. Dildos. Lighters disguised as guns. Blankets of ethnic crap covered any remaining space on the pavement. Outdoor restaurants offered all kinds of seafood, offal with rare strains of cholera, typhoid and hepatitis.

In the centre of it all, The Snakeman.

He was the mother of all showmen. The Jimmy Swaggert of serpents. All shapes and sizes, alive and slithering. The crowd encircled him. He picked up a long snake, three feet if it was an inch. He heaved it around and addressed the masses. Something-something something. He picked up a short, pointed blade and placed it at the belly of the snake. Then made a small incision. He squeezed a small, Tylenol-sized sac from within and placed it in a small bowl.

Gall bladder? Thyroid? Pancreas? Testicle?

He raised the bowl and showed it to four or five couples. Then grabbed another snake from the basket. Again he held it up and, again, he placed his incision-maker to its belly. Another sac of something was removed, put in the bowl, and shown to the same four or five couples.

For his next trick he produced a cobra. Poisonous or not it made no difference. A cobra is a cobra. He placed it on top of the cage. It reared. He bent down and put his face a foot from it. The snake lunged. We gasped. He pulled away unharmed. He tapped the cobra on the head. It went after his hand. We gasped again. He puckered up and moved in to kiss it. He pulled away just as it struck out. We gasped. He snatched it from the box. He held it just below the head and waved it around. Then surgically removed another Bladdenol. He made another pass of the crowd with his bowl of magic, stopping at two couples. Challenging the men. Just as it was all getting a bit repetitive he made a fourth dip into Snake Central and withdrew a five-footer. He stretched it out. He raised it to his lips. I thought he was going to kiss it.

He put the reptile's head in his mouth. And bit it clean off.

He spat it out as if it were chewing tobacco. And inverted the wriggling body. Straightened it out over the bowl. Blood poured from the place where its head used to be, onto the sacs.

He approached one of the couples and offered them the potion. They declined. He walked back to the centre of the group and began the sale of the century. The tone of his voice and leer in his face suggested he was no longer attempting to politely off-load his product. He would goad someone into buying it. Appeal to their pride. Attack their ego. Question their manhood. Eventually he managed to bully one man into drinking it, for $800. It was probably one of those love potions that improve a man's virility. AJ suggested I make a small investment. I pretended not to know what she was talking about.

$800 was about the sum of my net worth.

AJ had landed a better job and more money. I was digging myself into debt and making a little bunker of depression to go with it. Calls to agencies had failed to secure anything of note. A little freelance writing. Direct mail for Alitalia and IBM. Yet there was no sign of anything permanent. Only the prospect of a lifetime in service of the hospitality industry.

Strung out in The Orient.

I had to borrow another $4,000 from my parents to pay the rent. I wasn't living extravagantly but my meagre income meant even subsistence living was beyond my means.

I didn't resent the success of others, not really. It was just that in a city where people were defined by what they did, and everywhere you turned there were images to remind you of what you should be enjoying, it was easy to feel inadequate. To become jaded and cynical.

I got the nod of approval from Immigration, eventually.

Things were looking up, for a while. On the same day I went to collect my work permit I secured an interview with MTV. For a youth-targeting, music-based enterprise I was surprised at how little they seemed to know about popular tunesmithery.

Is that Ice-T?

Dunno.

What do you think of that new REM?

Haven't heard it.

They told me I was overqualified for the job. This was probably just a polite way of saying I was undercool. Or maybe they really were looking for a Production Assistant who didn't know anything about production.

Daemon's brother arrived unannounced.

AJ gave him our other room to camp in.

I continued my daily pilgrimages to Mecca. With every shift it was starting to feel more like a job. Like work. Like something I had to do. Not something I did until something better came along. It no longer amused me to ask couples fornicating on cushions if they would mind waiting until they got home. It was harder to shrug off the slings and arrows of the madding crowds as I waded through them in my crazy Arabian Knights outfit.

Even Melvis was starting to piss me off.

The Cantonese Elvis. Melvis. A thin facsimile of the Vegas-era King. White jumpsuit. Rhinestones. Tassels. It wasn't a bad effort. Even if, upon closer inspection, the sideburns were fake and the quiff was a wig.

As the nights bored on, and wore me down, I came home later and later. Or earlier and earlier, depending on how AJ looked at it. My skin became pasty and anaemic. Daemon took to calling me Lestat, after the new-wave vampire in Anne Rice's novels.

And then things got weird.

I was seconded to work the bar next to Mecca. A pickup joint and drug exchange for the terminally groovy. Expensive local women. American Born Chinese. Wealthy Middle-eastern males. FILTH. Gweilos. All trying their luck, with the odds stacked in disappointment's favour.

It was a nice reprieve from my pantalooned life.

The Princess sat across the room, at a table in the corner. Long hair. Narrow slashes for eyes. Cherry lips. Pouty mouth. Her tiny frame was packaged in designer goods. High maintenance. The short, horrendously permed man in the loud shirt that sat opposite her would testify to that. He sported one of those ridiculous Versace shirts. Gold paisley swirls splashed around black and white checks. They weren't much of a couple, to be honest.

They just sat there, nursing cocktails.

I was hustling drinks to all and sundry. Working my way down the bar. I accidentally made eye-contact with her. The Princess smiled. I averted my eyes and went back to serving a customer. Moments later her curly companion stood before me. He'd had a few too many snake-blood cocktails. He accused me of looking at his girlfriend.

Sure, I had. Just not in the way he was implying.

I pretended not to know what he was talking about. I apologised if there had been any misunderstanding. Looking over his shoulder, I could see The Princess watching the exchange with royal interest. She was smiling like the cat that got the cream. Versace warned me. And walked off.

I tried to go about my business but it was pointless now. I was doomed. If he hadn't come over, and said something, I wouldn't have cast my eyes in her direction again. His warning, however, made me even more aware of her. Hyper-aware.I had to scope her out, to see if she was still looking at me.

She wasn't. Most of the time.

I'd glance over and find Versace eyeballing me. Every now and then, when he wasn't looking, she'd smile. At me. I'd turn away. And the stupid game would start over again.

Versace came back to the bar.

The Princess had told him I was still hitting on her. I assured him this wasn't the case. Unfortunately, I also found it all quite amusing. I couldn't help but smile when denying his accusations. He reached over the bar and tried to hit me. I stepped back. He got angrier, shoutier and funnier.

Eddie, the manager, came over. He tried to calm Versace down. An animated conversation was had in Cantonese. The specifics were lost on me. Versace returned to his table and the company of his pet piranha, insecure in the knowledge that such a misunderstanding would never happen again. I was given another section of the bar to cover and that was that.

Until the end of the night.

Most people had left by 4:30am. I was collecting glasses. Wiping tables. Looking forward to closing the bar, having a quick drink and getting home. Someone walked behind me and said goodbye. It was baby-talk. Bye-bye. I turned out of instinct and curiosity. And there she was. Smiling.

The Princess.

Versace stood a few steps behind her. It was all he needed. He lunged and grabbed me by the shirt. I fell onto a table while he attempted to swat me with his tiny hands. Cursing at me in Cantonese. Something! Something-something! The doormen had to separate us. I was shaken but not stirred. Versace was positively livid. Atilla The Honey looked on like a proud mother as he made a final, futile attempt to get a piece of me. That's when he accidentally clipped The Bouncer.

Enough was enough.

The Bouncer picked Versace up like a sack of potatoes and threw him onto the street. This was followed by more yelling and a valiant effort to breach the entrance. Versace was knocked off his feet, onto his ass, again. The Princess helped him to his feet and the unhappy couple walked off, down the street. He gesticulated madly. She had her arms folded across her chest, head down, cultivating the mother of all pouts. She'd trip over that lip if she wasn't careful.

That was the end of that, I thought.

Problem was, when people were humiliated or embarrassed in such a manner, they lost Face. And Versace had misplaced tons of it. Not only did he fail to defend the honour of his partner, he got his arse kicked in the process.

It was all my fault.

Face was responsible for 95% of the problems, frustrations and inefficiencies people encountered on a daily basis.

It would rear it's head again, a few nights later.

Three scrawny thugs walked into Mecca. The American, employing his own special, hybrid brand of racism, called them Gookfellas. He even gave them wiseguy names. Charlie In-The-Trees Chan. Jimmy Zipperhead Wong. Tommy Love-You-Long-Time Lau. I reminded him that, technically speaking, gooks were Vietnamese, as were the bigoted terms of endearment he had bestowed upon them. Riceguys might be a more appropriate, discriminatory and illiberal pun for Chinese gangsters. He was amazed I could think of political incorrectness at a time like this. I was amazed he didn't recognise the irony dripping from my bicultural tones and that, at the end of the 20th century, people still said such things with part-time impunity.

Two of the villains stood by the door. The other approached the bar.

Mecca was not the kind of place where bouncers came to your rescue. There weren't any. My faithful friends and colleagues were too transfixed by what was taking place to do anything useful, like go and get help.

The Enforcer stopped a meter from the bar. He looked at me, menacingly. In much the same way as Versace had tried to intimidate me, yet with more conviction. There was nothing to laugh at here. He raised his right index finger and drew it across his throat. He lifted a leg and drew that same finger across his ankle. He made the same cutting motion across the other. He held my gaze for five seconds. Then turned and left with his two goons. I didn't know what to do.

I stood there and had an anxiety attack.

Later, I went to Mecca and told Eddie what happened. He said not to worry. He'd take care of it. Tomorrow.

This was fine, except I still had to get home that night.

Three staff accompanied me in a taxi. They walked me to the apartment. I crawled into bed and clung to AJ all night. I pretended to be asleep when she got up in the morning. Even if I could credibly explain the turn of events, it wouldn't help to have both of us looking over our shoulders for the rest of our lives. I just had to believe that when Eddie said he'd take care of it he would. Somehow. He'd been around a long time. He used to be a cop.

Eddie would know what to do.

He was sitting at the bar with The Israeli, The Tunisian and The American when I arrived for my shift. They all made you're-dead motions across their necks with their fingers. Hilarious. It was so funny I threw up.

Eddie smiled and put his hand on my shoulder.

Many triad societies were operating, with degrees of efficiency, throughout Hong Kong. As few as twelve, as many as fifty, depending on who you put your faith in. 14K was the most famous. They were a territory-wide group with up to 20 factions. Then there was Sun Yee On, who were particularly strong in a part of town known as Tuen Mun. Wo Shing Wo had the inner-city areas of Mong Kok, Tsim Sha Tsui, Yau Ma Tei and Fan Ling. Wo Hop To was big on The Island and parts of Sham Shui Po. Wo On Lok took care of the other parts of Sham Shui Po, while exercising some influence in Singapore and England.

Versace was a loan-shark from out of town.

He hardly ever came into the city. His patch of turf was somewhere out in Fan Ling. That night, however, he'd decided to bring his girl into Lan Kwai Fong. To impress her. I couldn't quite get my head around that. I mean if I wanted to impress a girl Lan Kwai Fong was about the last place I'd take her. Anyway, whatever his intentions, I'd ruined any chance of achieving them. Even though it was the doorman who roughed him up, it was all my fault.

One way or the other, I would pay.

Eddie had called a few friends who were still in the police force. Then he rang a few of his acquaintances who were also there to serve and protect, although not in a government approved way. To make my problem go away, they said, I would have give this guy some Face. About $5000 worth of Face. If not, I would be taken out to the wastelands of the New Territories, my Achilles tendons would be severed and I would left there to die.

Eddie had taken the initiative to settle the matter. I didn't even have to worry about paying him back. The company would take care of it. We didn't get medical or dental, but they protected employees in other ways.

In this life, and the next.

Outside each bar was a small shrine, dedicated to a deity of preference. Incense burned. Prayers and small offerings were made each night. We all needed someone to watch over us.

Sometimes, of course, even the Gods can't make it on their own. Particularly in a city with the self-defining morality of a multinational corporation, based on the bottom line.

A Buddhist temple, on the eastern end of The Island, was being demolished. A house of trade or a car park would soon stand in its place. It was one of the few genuine antiques remaining in the territory. AJ and I thought we should take in a little more of the surrounding culture, before it disappeared.

We got there not a moment too soon.

With no windows and the roof already gone, the temple was a mere shell of a moral compass. An unsteady symbol of society's spiritual decay.

A small congregation of worshippers had assembled and began to pray, *en masse*. Things quickly went off-mantra and downhill from there.

Contractors intervened. They made a whip of chords and attempted to cleanse the temple, tearing down the remaining vestiges of virtue. A women threw a glass in the direction of the desecrators. Another, in what police later described as a suicide bid, tried to bite her tongue off. She had to be restrained. Others claimed they'd rather die than leave the hallowed ground. Given its state of disrepair, this was not entirely out of the question. In fact, you didn't need the patience of Job to see that if they'd waited a few weeks, nature would have finished the job for them.

That's me in the corner, that's me in the spot-light, losing my religion.

I was low on faith and lacking self-belief when I went to work that night. The crosses I was having to bear were beginning to weigh upon me. The incident with Versace and ensuing death treats. The long hours for short returns. The lack of progress along the career path.

If I wanted to be a barman I could've stayed in Perth.

AJ was still up when I got home at 2:30 in the morning. She'd just got back from a party and was quite excited, for me. Considering I wasn't at the party and my life was currently shit, I figured it was just the Kool Aid talking.

Conversations that night had followed standard introductory lines. What do you do? How long have you been here? How long are you staying? No, no the party, how long are you staying in Hong Kong. Where do you live? Do you have a boyfriend? Are you married? This invariably led to in-depth discussions about local supermarkets, frequent-flyer programs and mobile phone roaming services. She fell in with a bunch of Brits and was expecting them to go on about how much they missed The Pubs, Marks & Spencer underwear and Marmite. This type of thing never failed to amuse. All three were quite easy to find in Hong Kong.

The conversation turned, instead, to advertising.

In a blinding flash of genius AJ had the foresight to tell them her boyfriend was in advertising. A copywriter. This is even more amazing when you consider, at that point, I didn't really know what a copywriter was. Yet, within ten minutes, AJ had sold me in and facilitated an interview at The Agency.

Tell your boyfriend to bring his book in on Monday, a Creative Director at The Agency had said.

You'd think I'd be quite chuffed with this news. In my cynical, deflated state of mind, however, it just confirmed another of my failings.

I was so useless my girlfriend had to get my job interviews for me.

AJ sensed as much. I could show some enthusiasm, she said. Express a little gratitude. I apologised. I was tired. It was great news. She was amazing. I loved her madly. I didn't know what to say. She said I should let my actions do the talking. I rose to the challenge, with her encouragement.

I couldn't even manage that on my own anymore.

Sunday was spent getting my book together. I'd learned, from Lovitz, that books were the *prima materia* of copywriters and art directors. It was a collection of your work. Your portfolio. Your book. There was just one problem.

I didn't have a book.

I didn't have a lot of time to put one together either. So I did what anyone else would've done. What AJ had probably done the night before.

I faked it.

There were some old Australian magazines lying around the apartment. Woman's Weekly. New Idea. Woman's Day. They were full of ads. It wasn't feasible that I would've done any good ones. Although it was conceivable that I could've had a hand in some bad ones. The pedestrian, retail ones. I wasn't after a senior position. I was going in at entry level. Most people just wanted to know if I had done something. Anything. Experience, good or bad. The nationality of the Creative Director also played in my favour. He was British. The chances of him seeing these ads, or knowing anyone who had done them, was slim. I could pad the presentation with that freelance work I did for Alitalia and IBM too. It was nothing exceptional but at least it accredited me some local experience.

Potential. I also remembered some ads I'd voiced and jingles I'd heard during my radio stints in Perth. So I typed those out as scripts.

All that, plus my carefully doctored CV, which failed to mention that I'd failed English in high school, made for a reasonably compelling platform on which to launch a career in advertising.

Didn't it?

Judgement day came. The reckoning was upon me. I sat in reception of The Agency, waiting for The Man.

The lobby was bigger than our apartment.

The Man looked like Mulder from The X-files. Except gravity was conspiring against him. Pulling him down. I shook his hand. He lead me through large open-plan office. It was staffed with local, creative types. I could tell they were creative because they all wore ironic t-shirts and had spent money on haircuts to make it look like they didn't spend money on haircuts. Superhero figurines sat on every shelf and partition.

Mulder's office was separate from all this. It had a door and everything. He wasn't just in advertising, as he'd modestly lead AJ to believe. A mere Creative Director. He was the Executive Creative Director.

The Agency was a big deal, in 52 countries.

Any hope I might have harboured on arrival was immediately crushed. He told me The Agency wasn't really hiring at the moment. He just liked to see who was in town. High turnover rates meant he never knew when a position might come up. My CV didn't seem to interest him either. He took a cursory glance at my book. I sat there expecting someone to burst into the room and cry Fraud! at any moment. I wasn't fooling anyone.

Was I?

Mulder closed the book. He reminded me he wasn't really hiring and thanked me for coming in anyway. Some of the radio was nice. Maybe he'd see me in Lan Kwai Fong. I hoped not. Those red pantaloons could ruin any credibility I might've briefly enjoyed. He walked me to reception, probably just to make sure I left the building and people didn't think the rube in the suit actually worked there.

I stepped into the elevator. And fell 33 floors to the ground.

AJ came by the bar on her way home from work. Her howd-it-go smile faded when she saw my don't-ask face.

Don't worry. Something will come up.

I almost believed her. Her optimism was infectious. She could make you feel that way. Those eyes. The turn of the lips. The way she put her hand on yours when she spoke. Those eyes.

I'd like to say it was an overdose of confidence that inspired the two-day bender that followed. I was still under its influence when the phone rang Wednesday afternoon. I answered it sounding like Orson Welles. Like I'd drunk a bottle of scotch, smoked a box of cigars and eaten a packet of fishfingers. Maybe I had.

Can I speak with Richard please?

This is he.

Did I wake you?

No, I lied. Then proceeded to cough up a lung.

It was The Man. Mulder. Christ, what did he want?

It would be great if I could drop by The Agency, this afternoon.

I showered, brushed my teeth twice and was there by four. He met me in reception and took me on a tour of the office. He showed me around The Agency. He introduced me to people. It hadn't actually twigged that my life was about to change. I was still in a daze and suffering from last night's touch of evil. My bowels could go at any second.

Richard this is Alice Kok. Alice this is Richard.

Hi Richard. I'm The Bitch.

The Bitch, in addition to having a candid sense of self-appraisal, was dressed in a bright pink Chanel suit. Should I call her Alice, Ms Kok or The Bitch? I decided not to say anything. I just smiled and gave a nod that suggested I was party to an obtuse in-joke.

In a massive office on the other side of the building lay the kingdom of a woman who shared The Bitch's predilection for Chanel. Bright yellow with black trim. What kind of place had uniforms like this? The Empress Dowager sat behind a desk the size of *Pont Neuf*. She lifted her head from a pile of paperwork and looked at me. Then reached into a drawer in the desk. She pulled out a small, gift-wrapped parcel and handed it across the desk.

Happy Birthday.

I looked to Mulder for clues. He smiled. I took a few reluctant steps toward her and accepted the gift. She returned to her work. Mulder motioned to the door and we left. You'll get used to it, he said as we walked. I stared uneasily at the package in my hand, and doubted him.

I guess you've figured I'm going to offer you a job, he added matter-of-factly.

I hadn't.

The penny didn't drop until he presented me with a letter of employment. I didn't have to answer him then. I could think about it and let him know before the week was out.

Do you have a work permit?

I responded, proudly, that I did. The red tape was not taking this one away from me. He said The Agency would get me one if I needed it. There weren't a lot of local English copywriters. Agencies found it relatively easy to secure visas for them.

I floated down in the elevator, let out a little whoop and did a victory dance in the mirrored walls.

Richard Tong. Copywriter.

My starting salary was $8,000 a month. Twice what I was making at Mecca. The only person happier than me was AJ. We rejoiced in each other every night for a week.

Christmas had come early too.

This would be our first Yuletide away from home. AJ's parents were coming to spend it with us. That was one of the other great things about AJ.

Her family.

I'd been adopted into it. Our two weeks with them were a warm respite, at a time when the city could be remarkably cold.

Hong Kong, and its commercial catacombs of shopping malls, decked the malls and buildings with Joyeux Noel like no other. The town was lit up like a Christmas tree. Yet it didn't really feel like Christmas. It was cold. Hailing from the southern hemisphere, this time of year was traditionally bathed in sun and soaked in sweat.

Hong Kong was cold in other ways too.

Beneath the decorations and piped-in carols it felt kind of empty. There just wasn't much of anything going on. Quite a feat in a city of six million. Perhaps to most of the population it was just another holiday. A chance to indulge. An opportunity to exploit. It didn't really matter, or blight the occasion.

The only blemish on this season of goodwill would come from within our insulated walls.

Daemons mother had asked AJ's mother to deliver a culinary care-package to her son. Comfort food. Twelve kilograms of vacuum-packed steaks, rib roasts and sausages. It wasn't an usual request. Many people received consumable conferment. The same food was available here. It just wasn't the same as it was at home. It was more expensive too. It didn't affect us that much. AJ leant more toward vegetables, chicken and fish than lean beef. This meant I did too, by default. Besides, being on war rations for such a long time, unable to afford food of any kind, I'd kind of weened myself off choice cuts.

Daemon's mother hadn't even purchased the goods. She'd faxed AJ's mum a list of what to buy and from where. This, needless to say, flew in the face of favour-asking conventions. It was one thing to be a mule. Expecting someone else to finance the covert operation, however, was out of order. In the interests of bilateral trade relations AJ's mum had made no mention of this. And, as a result, our communal freezer was up to its fluorocarbons in cut-price prime beef.

Not for long.

According to my misunderstanding, our refrigerator was run like a co-operative. You took something out, you put something back. Prestige items, like ice cream and bacon, were shared. Question before you consume, this was the unwritten rule.

Do you mind if I have this? Would you like some of that?

Daemon broke with protocol and declared himself Chairman Of The Meat Board. His most hostile of takeovers was based on a simple belief. His mother had invented the idea of food parcels and instigated this delivery. Therefore, he had control of the assets. And a good percentage of them were relocated to his bosses house, in preparation for a Boxing Day barbecue.

Did you guys want to come?

I think we've got something on. Thanks for asking.

I left the matter there, publicly. Internally, it burned. AJ was browned off too. She didn't even eat meat. Daemon had broken with more than the time honoured rules of cohabitation. He'd crossed that line in the sirloin.

This would be our Vietnam.

Some might think it's stupid to lock horns and fall out over a side of meat. To them I say wars have been fought over far less.

It's only meat.

What's so *only* about that?

My last shifts at Mecca were over Christmas and New Year's Eve. The bar served as base-camp for our final assaults on The Goat. AJ and her parents dropped by from time to time. Sometimes just AJ. Sometimes just her parents. Sometimes AJ looking for her parents. It was madness on the gin-soaked streets of Lan Kwai Fong. Almost impossible to move. It could take half an hour to walk to a bar only 75 meters away. Each step fraught with peril. Half my colleagues decided to join the celebrations. The rest of us had to cover for them. We closed at 4am. I had neither the energy nor inclination for celebration. A quick farewell drink was followed by a royal burning of my pantaloons. I wouldn't be needing those again. We said how much we'd miss each other and that we'd stay in touch.

We believed each other's lies.

I could fake sincerity pretty well when I had to. Perfect for a career in advertising.

In other news... a man won $57 million in the lottery.

THERE WAS OVER ONE HUNDRED PEOPLE in The Agency. Only a handful had English as a first language. I was one of them. That, and my English Copywriter status, meant many considered me an expert when it came to the language and formal grammar.

I knew better. I just couldn't tell anyone.

English was the official business language for many. Most of my colleagues spoke it well. Some better than me. All with better fluency than I spoke Cantonese. That was sure to change after '97, when English would probably suffer the same fate as Latin. For the time being, however, many were still interested in it and using it correctly. In addition to providing concepts and copy for advertisements, I was expected to check presentations. Make changes. Corrections. People would ask questions.

Is that because you conjugated the second past participle of the subjective feminine tense?

Er, yes. I mean no.

Because the copular verb needs a clause as its semantic object?

Not really.

Because the present perfect tense has nothing to do with the order of events and just emphasises the completion of the action, linking the subject and the predicate?

No.

Why?

Because it sounds good.

I wished I'd paid more attention during English classes at school. For the first time since arriving in Hong Kong, maybe even the first time in my life, I was beginning to feel a little out of my element.

I hardly spoke to anyone for the first three months. Considering I was in advertising, a communication based career, this could've been considered ironic. Of course I spoke to people *about* work. I had the occasional beer with Mulder *after* work. I just never really conversed with any of my colleagues *at* work. Or *outside* work. Socially. I was scared. Not of them.

I was scared of getting found out.

I'm sure a lot of local people had similar fears. They just didn't hide them behind a cloak of silence. To avoid embarrassment they'd say they understood something when they didn't. They'd shake their head when approving things, instead of nodding. Apparently this was because nodding your head makes you look foolish and submissive. Not as foolish as shaking your head in a negative fashion when you're trying to be positive, but try explaining that to people.

It would often result in over-explanations of the simplest things.

I'd see someone shaking their head and couldn't believe they didn't understand what I was telling them. So I'd take them through it again. Louder and in a more patronising tone. They'd look at me and wonder why I was repeating myself, so loudly and in such a patronising manner. They'd interrupt and tell me to move on. They weren't stupid. I was not, as the saying went, playing a piano to a cow.

Baldrick was my first real friend.

A diminutive Chinese art director, he bore an uncanny resemblance to Blackadder's servant and sidekick. He appeared at my desk one day and asked me out to lunch. This was surprising for a number of reasons.

No one ever really spoke to me, voluntarily. And I hardly ever went out for lunch.

It wasn't lunch time either.

What Baldrick lacked in stature he made up for with personality. He spoke like a rascally Scouser. Unlike Yorrick, he'd been educated in Great Britain. This might also have explained why he wanted to go and get a few beers in the middle of the day.

Finally, someone that spoke my language.

We grabbed a six pack from the 7-11 and sat by the harbour. Over tepid cans of Carlsberg, Baldrick told me how he had earned his reputation as Liverpool's Greatest Shoplifter™.

Like anyone skilled in the Klepto Arts, he took pride is his ability to liberate anything. Food. Beverages. Undergarments. Accessories. Miscellaneous electronics. It was a game that became a business that became a cottage industry. People would nominate an item and he would accept the challenge. The greater the risk the bigger the reward. His speciality, where he established himself in the premier league of thievery, was raw poultry. Chickens. Free range. Any size. He had a nice line in suitcases too. During the festive season he could even see you sorted for a Christmas tree. Pine or plastic.. And a turkey, of course.

Something for the weekend, Sir?

His trick was one of confidence. You just had to walk out of there like you walked in there with it.

Like you walked in to Tesco's with a 20 pound bird?

Exactly.

Balders had been a bit of a rogue during his college days. Not always by design. Sometimes it was simply by default. Like the time he got into a fight. Or, rather, the time he got thrown into a fight.

The lads were mixing it up one Friday night. Baldrick was walking by and stopped to watch the rumpus, as people do. Someone thought he might like a closer look. They picked him up and threw him into the fray. When the police arrived they found him at the bottom of the pile and declared him responsible for the incident. They took him to the station. When asked for his name he said Choi. They asked him how to spell it. C-h-o-y. It sounded the same as far as the rozzers were concerned. A Choi is a Choy is a Tsui by any other name. Whenever he was caught in the act, or implicated in crimes, he'd invoke a different spelling. By utilizing combinations of English and Chinese phonetics he had half a dozen *nom de plumes* at his disposal. That, with the occasional fake address, meant he never got done for the same thing twice. Everything was a first offence. He reckoned there was probably still outstanding warrants for one or two of him.

I told him about my meat fiasco and how it had soured things on the domestic front. We were having issues almost every day. Petty disputes over money. Who owed who for what. Daemon's brother had stayed with us for months and we felt he owed us rent. Labels of ownership were appearing on things in the refrigerator. We weren't being overly hostile to each other. We just weren't talking to each other.

You gotta get a place of your own, he said.

Daemon had arrived at the same conclusion. He'd had enough. Of us, his dodgy employer and Hong Kong. He was going back to Perth. He wasn't going to call the landlord and break the lease. He wasn't going to pay the last two months rent. He'd just let the landlord keep the deposit. It was his name on the lease and his money. He could do what he wanted.

AJ couldn't afford to pick it up even if she wanted too. And my journey to financial independence was still in its infancy. We wanted to put some distance between us and this chapter in our lives.

We found a unit at the eastern end of The Island.

We'd soon learn that you can't bury the past. You can leave it, but you can't leave it behind. History had proven what Herodotus knew to be true.

It doesn't matter where you live, human happiness never remains long in the same place.

Solon himself could have warned me and I wouldn't have listened. Things were looking up. 27 floors up.

You could almost see the future from there.

2. YEAR OF THE MONKEY

AJ HAD LONG, SLENDER LEGS and, as has been observed before, she wore them well. The Family Planning Association did not share this view. They were of the opinion that women who sported skirts that short were inviting harassment.

The way our sex life had been lately, AJ was starting to wonder if I needed an invitation. She was not the sort of person who needed to be asked twice. She was right, up to a point.

The point of ejaculation.

I had become preoccupied with work. I'd discovered I quite liked doing ads and stuff. I wasn't too bad at it either. Like a lot of things. I wasn't brilliant. I was okay. I could get the job done. Quickly, quietly and effectively. One my first campaigns had won a few awards. That garnered me a pay raise. I went from $6,000 to $12,000. Overnight. They moved me from the odds 'n sods crèche, for new arrivals, to a permanent place in the Creative Department. I had my own accounts. They even gave me an art director of my very own.

Ana.

She was as cute as a button and not much bigger. I'd walk past her desk every morning. *Jo sahn, gweilo!* More often than not she'd have a drink on stand-by. A juice, soy-milk or some herbal concoction in a brown paper bag. With the confidence that comes from familiarity I attempted to open the lines of communication. I reached for the bag. What's that you've got there, Ana? She tried to stop me. I peaked within.

Carlsberg.

Probably the best beer in the world, according to their latest ad campaign. Ana had just taken the scab off one for breakfast. Fantastic. She begged me not to tell anyone.

I love it! she said.

It reminded her of her father. He was a shift worker. He'd come home as she was going to school. That time of day was not the morning for him. It was the end of the shift. He'd have a beer. She'd share one with him. It was the only time they had together. Now that he was gone it was how she kept his memory alive.

Some mornings I just have to have beer, she confessed.

I knew where she was coming from. It was a place about 180 degrees from where the rest of our alcohol intolerant colleagues resided. She was worried they'd think badly of her. I assured her I wouldn't tell anyone. Her secret was safe with me. Maybe she'd have to do me a favour one day. Forget she saw something of mine that others might not understand.

She belched in agreement. And went back to directing art.

I'd almost come to terms with the belching. Almost. It was just something everyone seemed to do. At their desk. After a meal. On the train. During meetings. With some aggressive lobbying they could've made it an Olympic event. That and spitting on the sidewalk, in the Supermarket or on the bus. No place was too sacred for the bushman's curse. No person too old. Pensioners always seemed to hock one when foreigners walked past. I'd been told this was because a gweilo was a white ghost. The old folks would clear their throats to ensure the spirit had not lodged there.

Superstition was a powerful force. The Three Fs ruled.

Fate, fortune and feng shui.

The ancient art of furniture arranging, feng shui is a theory calibrated to improve a person's luck. It isn't just about money. There are many different types of luck that can be improved. Boss Luck. Friendship Luck. Husband Luck. It can be used to modify your Star Luck. Fine tune your Plum Blossom Fortune. Clear up a stupid spot in your house. Endow you with Car Luck.

There was a building across the harbour. One of its edges pointed directly into the office of a colleague. It made him deathly ill. The Empress Dowager repainted her Saab a nasty shade of yellow because the feng shui man said it would be a luckier colour. Others placed fish tanks in the centre of their rooms. Mirrors on walls. Faced their bed in a certain direction. The Bank of China building was designed to maximise its own feng shui, while adversely affecting that of the nearby Hongkong Bank building. It would drive a spiritual knife through the heart of the Governor's mansion while it did it too.

Baldrick didn't believe in it but he wasn't taking any chances. He always made sure he flushed the toilet with the lid down. This would stop his money from flowing away.

In other news... 400 people marched upon the Government to protest the bad feng shui a new repository was bringing to their village... Eight teenage students, one as young as 12, beat a classmate to death.

WHEN WE WEREN'T WORKING we'd pass time playing pool in the bar on the 35th floor. If it was before 11:30 we'd take turns freaking Ana out. She was afraid of circles. Rings and other round things. Grapes. Shirts with polka-dots. Balloons, on their own or in deathly clusters. Just viewing a case of soft drink from above would make her anxious. If I scrunched the fingers on one hand together, and pointed the tips at her, she'd totally wig out.

We could devote entire afternoons to burning issues and the things that mattered because they didn't matter.

What would you do with Hong Kong's $70 billion budget surplus?

Buy four and a half billion Happy Meals from McDonald's. Fireworks, 24 hours a day for 18 consecutive days. Give seven million Japanese girls round-trip business class tickets to Hong Kong. Send everyone in Hong Kong to Japan. Buy 30,000 buses. Get 77 million hours of psychological counselling and give everyone 12 hours each. We could make 200 movies, with or without subtitles.

I am damn unsatisfied to be killed in this way.

A normal person would not steal pituitaries.

Take my advice, or I'll spank you without pants.

I will remove your manhoods and leave them for your aunts to eat.

Masturbate in hell!

I have been scared shitless too much lately.

Beware! Your bones are going to be disconnected.

The bullets inside are very hot. Why do I feel the cold?

Yah-hah, evil spider woman! I have captured you by the short rabbits!

Greetings, large black person. Let us team up and inflict the pain of our karate feets on some ass of the giant lizard person.

Movies aside, Hong Kong seemed to be a well-balanced, multicultural city. East meets West, they said. Yet it was still quite segregated. I could enter a different country simply by walking from one cubicle to another. Crossing the street, or the harbour. There were pockets of Europeans. Microcosms of India, Thailand and Japan. Taiwanese strongholds. Hakka communities. Many people seemed to have little sense of their collective culture or shared history. A lot like me, in a way. Abandoned and adopted. Re-educated. No idea of the past, no vision of the future. The present was all that mattered. It was a city of The Now.

Maybe that's why I liked it.

There was a handful of ancient temples and historical buildings but very little evidence of what used to be. For many intents and purposes Hong Kong felt like it was squeezed out of a tube fifty years ago. Sometimes it seemed like only five minutes ago and the people here before were still getting used to it.

Baldrick, Ana and I were on our way into town, to present some work to

The Bank. We had an idea for a game-changing credit card promotion that couldn't wait. Lives were at stake. Debt made the world go round. People could die. We had a couple of Suits in tow. Account Managers. The *yin* to our Creative Department's *yang*, responsible for client relations, developing briefs, paying taxi fares and carrying thing.

Creative make the ads. Suits make the arrangements.

Central was a zoo. Literally. Hordes of farmers were taking hundreds of ducks and dozens of pigs for a walk through the streets. It was good to see people bringing their animals into the city every now and then. They didn't get out half as much as they should.

Farmers were protesting the Government's decision to implement licensing controls. They weren't too happy about the implications of the '87 Waste Disposal Bill either. Originally they'd planned to just take ducks and geese. They wanted to showcase the quality of their produce. Let people know what they'd be missing out on if farmers went out of business. Then the pig farmers thought they should be allowed to put the quality of their animals on display. Pigs would be a symbol of strength and solidarity.

Pork talks, bullshit walks.

We decided to go out for a drink after the meeting. I wanted to visit the Walled City, in Kowloon. It was another cultural landmark marked for death.

The Walled City was kind of like Vatican City, only different. It was a place within a place. It had its own rules and institutions. People went there religiously but it was about as far from holy ground as you could get. They said it wasn't part of the 99-year lease Britain signed when they got Hong Kong. It was like a separate state in the middle of the city, like East Berlin. The Mainland didn't police it. Neither did the British, really. It just slid into disrepute A flea-infested hotbed of crime, corruption and vice. Home to the legendary cage-men. The Government was in the process of trying to evict them from the from the 6x3 enclosures they inhabited on the roofs of the buildings. 10,000 prostitutes, drug dealers, illegal doctors, dentists and bookies were being moved on as well.

It was no place for foreigners or the feint of heart.

We entered a karaoke bar not far from the perimeter. Someone was murdering Unchained Melody. It was almost amusing, in an unbearable kind of way. A group of men across the room didn't agree. They heckled. When it didn't stop they went over to the stage and beat six octaves of crap out of their unrighteous brother. We took our cue and left. For Ana and the Suits, the night ended there.

Baldrick and I went to Red Lips.

It was a hostess bar that someone had tucked down the trousers of a dank, Tsim Sha Tsui alley in the late 60s. The decor, music and women hadn't changed since the Vietnam War.

The ancient muse who sat with us knew every city in Australia, intimately. Yet she'd never been to any of them. They'd all been to her. She'd learnt their history, orally. Another had a thing for Shakespeare. This mistress' eyes were nothing like the sun, but she could recite a dozen sonnets.

Shall I compare thee to a summers day?
Thy glass will show thee how thy beauties wear.

Between beverages Baldrick invited me to his wedding. It was a bit of a surprise. He'd never mentioned a fiancé before.

The *feng shui* man had told her that this particular day would be a lucky one for her to be married. She queued for weeks to secure the slot at the Registry.

Who would dare to argue with that kind of dedication?

Enclosed with the invitation was a gift certificate for twelve sponge cakes. Each with a different mock-cream centre. It was a part of the tradition. Everyone got them. 300 people. A dozen cakes each.

The Registry was thick with brides and grooms. There was a service every fifteen minutes. Happy couples were cranked out hand over fist. Baldrick and his wife were nuptialed in six and half minutes, and sent on their wedded way. The next couple was hustled in before the ink on the certificate was even dry.

The banquet was held at a local restaurant. AJ and I lined up to have our photo taken with Mr and Mrs Baldrick. Being foreigners, and unknown to the family, we were sent to the back of the queue.

We surrendered a small red envelope, stuffed with money, to the newlyweds. No one gave anything as soulless as gifts. You gave something practical. Money. People didn't need or have the space to clutter homes with toasters and salad platters. Feeding 300 strangers wasn't cheap either. Money was such a sensible way to show how much you cared. AJ and I, according to Ana, cared $200 less than we should have. Not enough to cover the ten, fun-sized courses that followed.

Crispy pig skin. Scallops. Sea cucumber. Garoupa. Chicken. Slices of abalone. Shark fin soup. Something with mushrooms. Rice. Noodles.

There was a brief slide-carousel presentation of shots the bride and groom had taken two months before, in their wedding outfits. This was followed by a hastily edited video detailing the evolution of their relationship. Games were played. The obligatory beer drinking contest. Do You Recognise Your Spouse's Knee? The bride changed her gown three times during the course of the evening. At the end of it all a bowl of oranges was placed on each table. Everyone stood up and clapped as the bride and groom left. Ana, freaked out by the golden orbs before her, blazed a trail for the exit that left even Mr and Mrs Baldrick in her dust.

It was a million miles from any wedding I've ever been too. And a far cry from the one I returned to a week later.

I'd been asked to officiate at Blutarsky's big day.

The prodigal son was going home.

My plane arrived just after dawn. I'd been drinking since Singapore and tripped over a bag in the immigration hall. A woman screamed as I toppled back into her.

The floor, as they say, was mine.

Kurtis appeared in my bedroom window as I unpacked. He'd been out all night and was lit up like no one's business. A whole day of activities had been planned. Starting at the beach. He figured I probably hadn't seen a decent strip of water in a while. It would be a good way to ease back into the local culture. Then we'd make our way down the coast, to Fremantle, for a Counter Lunch. Another landmark on the cultural plain. An Australian tradition that comprised sitting in the pub, ordering a steak sandwich and drinking fifteen litres of beer. It was possible to drink fifteen litres of beer without ordering a steak sandwich but then you weren't having a Counter Lunch. You were just on the piss.

The last time Kurt and I were on the piss was just over a year ago.

It was part of my farewell tour. I'd had more swan songs than Dame Nellie Melba and Liza Minelli combined. A dozen of us went to Rottnest for the penultimate show.

Rotto.

A small, relatively undeveloped island off the West Australian coast, girt by baleful reefs and turquoise waters. Like those pictures you see of Greece, Tahiti and Mauritius. Rotto used to be a penal colony. It some ways it still was. Students flocked there to celebrate after examinations. Families vacationed there in the summer. Cars were *verboten*. People got around on bicycles or walked. It was the great escape and a good excuse. The Rottnest Charter decreed that whatever happened there had to stay there. It didn't count and it couldn't be used against you in any kangaroo court.

We arrived on the morning ferry and checked in to Bungalow H, opposite a white strip of beach. We sat on the balcony and waited for three o'clock to roll around. That was when we were going to drop the acid Kurtis had packed in his bag. No one knew why it had to be three. It must have been calibrated against something. No one knew what. The conviction with which it was said was religious. To suggest any other time was heresy.

Is it 3 yet?

No.

It will be soon.

So just wait then.

You didn't fuck with three o'clock. The filters would come off at three and not a second earlier. We cooled our jets with a few joints in the kitchen. People would call upon us, drop in for a beer, and find us sitting around the kitchen table.

What're you guys doing?

Waiting.

What for?

Three o'clock.

When the moment arrived, tabs of acid were passed around in a clockwise direction. Everyone placed the small microdot of cardboard, laced with LSD, in their mouth. It was like an oral Mexican Wave. Then we just sat there, waiting. Looking from one to another.

Waiting.

Kurt winked at me. I winked at him. Blutarsky blinked. Chuck Norris winked at the mirror. Beers were refreshed and we returned to the balcony. People always said don't let life pass you by. They'd probably never been blotted.

Sometimes, watching life pass you by is half the fun.

The sun made a brief movement across the sky, heading West. Like me it had left The East far behind. A giant man lumbered by and cast a long, hulking shadow across the yard. He limped onto the balcony. He'd heard we were going tripping. He was wondering if he could come along.

Sorry. You should've got here at three.

He knew it was too much to hope for, even though it was only a few minutes past three. These things had to start on time, or not at all. He looked at us, individually. Then as a group. Pouted like a kid. A massive kid who'd just found out all his crayons were broken. Then turned and hobbled off, beautifully backlit by the sun.

I began inspecting parts of the balcony. Then corners of the yard. Eventually I strayed out onto the path.

Be careful out there, Melon.

People walked by. I tried not to look at them but they were all so interesting. Bicycles. Incoming. Right at me. My feet had grown into the bitumen. All I could do was stand there and face them. Bicycles. Dozens of them. It was a stampede. I looked helplessly over to the balcony. Would someone attempt a rescue?

You should be able to handle a few bicycles, Melon. That's all they have in your part of the world, isn't it?

I braced myself as the first bike came by on my left. I swayed right. Then another and another on my left. I pivoted on my hips then swung, gracefully, and swayed left. There was gentle applause from the balcony. I was a natural. I could do it all afternoon. Another and another. More. And then nothing.

Just the breeze.

Kurtis took a few fragile steps onto the killing field. He got halfway and froze. Looking down the path there was nothing but bicycles, as far as his dilated pupils could see. I tried to reassure him. I told him not to make any sudden movements.

Let your instincts guide you.

Five. Six. Eight. Ten bikes blurred past. It was intense. Invigorating. Liberating. The two of us, bending and vacillating, in and out of bipedal slipstreams.

And then it was all over.

The sun was setting across the bay, illuminating the water. Chuck Norris, Alby Mangles, Blutarsky, Curly, Kurt and I made a dash across thirty feet of white powder. Shirts were removed in one seamless, synchronised and fluid movement. We waded into the water.

Ohhhh wowwwwww.

I could feel the current on my legs. I dove under. Tiny bubbles raced across my skin. Down the length of my body.

Amaaaz-ing.

I was a dolphin, breaking the surface of the water. Together, we became a leaping, cresting, frolicking, hallucinating pod. Until I got an earache. We returned to the bungalow in a heightened state of awareness. Diethylamide up to the gills. Vibrant. Lucid. Tiny little orgasms firing behind our eyeballs.

We went to the pub but, after five minutes, it proved too difficult. Attempting to relate to others. Staving off paranoia. Even walking through the crowd took a superhuman effort.

Back to Bungalow H.

The H that marked the door had been augmented by scarlet letters. E-L-L. Welcome to HELL. It appeared to have been written in tomato sauce. The ketchup had run, rendering it a bloody warning. It was surreal and evil. An empty tin of baked beans sat on the kitchen table, mocking us all.

Kurtis and I found refuge in a tree.

We took a bottle of port to keep us safe. We stayed up there for hours. Days. Weeks. Until I was cast out and fell through the night, like an almighty drop-bear. I landed flat on my back, nearly impaled on a metal stake that anchored the rubbish bin to the ground. I lay there, playing possum, too scared to move. Maybe I couldn't. The balcony was silent.

Is he dead? someone whispered.

I opened my eyes. Fifteen feet above, amongst the branches, Kurtis was looking down upon me.

Is that you, God?

A smile creased his lips. Wow, he said from upon high. That was close.

And He was casting out a demon, and it was mute; when the demon had gone out, the mute man spoke; and the crowds were amazed.

Here we were, together again. At the front of The Sail And Anchor, in Fremantle. Freo. Where the Swan River meets the Indian Ocean. Where the convicts which colonised West Australia were first interned 170 years before. Before they realised Rotto could be an Alcatraz of the southern hemisphere.

According to a jingle for the local Ford dealership, Freo had busy streets and Fisherman's Harbour, where they're dressing the fleet. What the jingle didn't say was that the pubs didn't open until 11:30. And those streets are really only busy on weekends. The fleet got dressed early too, discreetly. It left a few dollars on the mantle and went out fishing under the cover of darkness. Between the two of us, and our combined 47 years of local insight, you'd think Kurt and I would've known this before arriving in Freo at 10 o'clock on Thursday morning. There was little we could do. Our only option was to find an unoccupied children's playground, sit down and smoke dope.

I was slowly revolving on the roundabout when Kurt had what Oprah Winfrey would call A Lightbulb Moment.

Prison tour.

Olde Fremantle Towne was also blessed with ye olde gaol. A legacy from the earliest days of settlement. Up until 1991 it was a maximum security prison. Now it was a tourist attraction. We spent the next few hours spinning-out in solitary confinement. Cell Block H. Until we grew weary. And hungry.

Cue lunch. Steak sandwiches and fifteen litres of beer.

We had to meet Blutarsky in the city, to get fitted with suits for the wedding. We caught the train and were standing out the front of Tony Barlow Menswear by late afternoon. Waiting for Bluto.

Blutarsky.

A calorie-unconscious advocate of the McDonald's diet waved from across the mall. The decidedly larger than life Blutarsky was lumbering toward us. I recognised his face but he was wearing someone else's body. I'd been warned about this. Still, nothing could've prepared me for a change of this magnitude. Culture shock is not what happens when you go to unfamiliar places. It's what you get when you return to the ones you know. The ones you used to know.

I'd been charged with reading congratulatory telegrams at the reception. They were really just faxes and hastily scribbled notes dictated over the phone. No one sent telegrams anymore.

Good evening, Caucasians.

As an opening gambit I thought that was pretty good. Unfortunately it sailed over the heads of those before me, and made its way to the back of the hall in silence. Unacknowledged. Ignored. Orphaned. For a few terrifying seconds I was trapped in a humourless vacuum. All I could hear was a barely audible snort from Kurt, who loved lead balloons.

This was a tough crowd. And I'd player Kai Tak Arrivals.

The room was divided into two groups. The bride's side, and not the bride's side. There'd been a debacle at the stag party the week before.

Did you hear the one about the groom, the stripper and the bride that comes home early?

Poor Bluto had been caught with his trousers down. Little did he know, half a world away, he had a kindred spirit in Captain Underpants.

Good evening, Caucasians.

I arrived back in Hong Kong just as the Rugby Sevens was kicking off. This was basically a beer festival masquerading as an international sporting event. AJ and I had scored tickets and were weathering the expatriates at the southern end of the ground.

Captain Underpants, for it was he, arrived and took up a nearby position with his crew. He had a new friend in tow. A young, naive Chinese girl. He was greeted with traditional jeering and demands for beer. His special friend must have been terrified.

Way-hey! Mate, how'd it go last night, mate?

Mate, ever tried to push a marshmallow in a parking meter?

This self-deprecating appraisal of what must have been a less-than spectacular sexual performance was met with guffaws of approval. It was declared the most whimsical jape of the season. Whenever the good Captain returned from the washroom, or it was his turn to buy drinks in the lull between games, someone would inevitably launch into The Marshmallow Chorus.

Marshmallow, marshmallow, maaarsh-mallowwwww!

Almost as big on the boozing calendar was the annual Dragon Boat Festival. AJ and I spent that afternoon observing the races from a large yacht, with a collection of advertising's elder statesmen. Listening to war stories, eating chicken and drinking some of the finest chardonnays known to mankind.

I made the mistake of sitting with my ankles exposed to the sun.

By the time I got home they'd swollen to twice their normal size. I'd suffered third-degree burns. I couldn't walk for days. The skin blistered and peeled. I lost four epidermal layers. My life was now bookended by corium traumas and integumentary violations. Top to bottom. The rug matched the curtains, and the collar complemented the cuffs. I made a mental note to never go skeet shooting, for fear of shooting myself in the clay pigeons.

The Governor of the colony was also shedding his skin. He hung up his four-feathered hat. A ridiculous helmet he wore on ceremonial occasions. It looked as if a chicken had perched on his head. And he wondered why Mainland politicians didn't take him seriously. I don't think anyone really missed him, or his *chapeau de cock*, despite the emotional send-off they both received. Beijing would get used to someone else's tongue being firmly down the back of its trousers.

Wouldn't they?

Rudderless, for a week, the colony somehow maintained its course and ploughed on toward 1997. Anxiously awaiting the arrival of Patten.

How exciting, I thought. Old Blood And Guts himself. George S. Did they have him exhumed? He always said he'd be back. Had America's Fightingest General™ been cloned?

Battle is the most magnificent competition in which a human being can indulge.

No one was going to send an American to do an Englishman's job. To steady the wheel for the duration of its occupation.

Gimme ten days. I'll start a war with those God damn Reds and make it look like their fault.

Chris Patten arrived in a flurry of pomp and circumstance. A British MP, he was said to be the architect of Major's recent victory in Britain. Hong Kong was his reward. He brought his wife and two daughters with him. One became an overnight sensation and favourite of the tabloids, due to her buxom figure and penchant for miniskirts.

The Director of Family Planning was not amused.

Wrestling the spotlight from the fruit of his loins, and exhibiting some of his namesake's fighting spirit, the new Governor embarked on a campaign of his own. His sole purpose seemed to be annoying the Mainland administration at every available opportunity.

I had been given a mandate too.

Steal a coveted beer account from the agency down the street. Baldrick and Ana were conscripted in to help. The pitch would be hotly contended.

The Empress Dowager usually made opening remarks at these things. I was charged with bringing her to the conference room once The Client arrived. She was wearing another in a long hemline of Chanel ensembles. The gold earrings would not have been out of place among the curls of butter at the Holiday Inn breakfast buffet. She reached into the bottom draw of her desk and handed me another gift. She kept a ready supply of gratuity there. Things clients had bestowed upon her. Promotional items from media companies and suppliers. She rarely opened any of them because she figured it was all just ill-conceived crap. Maybe a lot of it was. I still managed to glean a Bulgari watch and a Waterman pen from her over the years. Sometimes I'd just walk in and see what happened. I think she figured people only came to her on special occasions.

Happy birthday.

It's not my birthday.

Why are you here? Leaving? Saying goodbye?

The pitch. The Client is here.

The Empress welcomed them all and handed proceedings over to The Suits like an unwanted gift. She was asleep before the first acetates were finished. Her head precariously balanced at that point where it would either jerk forward or drop back, and snap her into consciousness. Suddenly, she stood up and walked across the room. I thought she was going to make an announcement. She turned the air-con down instead. Then returned to her seat. Fifteen minutes later, she went through the same process. Sleep. Sudden consciousness. Air-con adjustment. Sleep. Halfway through my presentation of the print ads, she interrupted.

It's just like mini movie!

What was? Her life? The dream she was having before we interrupted with the pitch?

The Client invited us to join them for lunch. Things must have been going well. Either that or they were looking forward to a matinee from The Empress. If they were she didn't disappoint. She had a habit of missing the start of conversations. And then just wading in regardless.

Forrest Gump?

I'd heard Coppola had a similar experience when he gave Marcos a private viewing of Apocalypse Now. Imelda would interrupt every time an actor appeared.

Is that Brando?

The Empress Dowager had a similar Forrest Gump fixation, not to mention a Marcosian love of footwear. At irregular intervals she'd lean across the table and Gump someone. This would've been fine if anyone had been discussing the movie, or cinema in general.

Forrest Gump?

There'd be a brief pause while we all looked sideways and then returned to the original topic of conversation. Trying to pretend it didn't happen. By the third outburst I decided to see what would happen if I played along.

Forrest Gump?

Yes, brilliant. Have you seen it?

Seen what?

Forrest Gump.

She looked at me like I was the crazy one. Maybe I was. Maybe we all were. The Client must have been. They gave us their business. I got a promotion and a pay raise.

Richard Tong. Senior Writer. $30,000 a month.

Lovitz came to work at The Agency. On Fridays he'd organise for a small group of the creative community to meet at an Indian restaurant. It became known as the Fuck Friday Club. The FFC. A riff on the FCC. Foreign Correspondents Club. We'd spill beer and spend the afternoon disparaging each other. I quickly became John Oates to his Darryl Hall. Andrew Ridgeley to his George Michael. Luke to his Obi Wan. Bill to his Ted.

AJ made a friend of his wife.

In the wake of a particularly gruelling meeting of the FFC I was summoned to The Big Office. The one in the corner with the sweeping harbour views. It was occupied by the CEO. I'd been told he'd liked the campaign I'd written for the Tobacco Council. Full-page advertisements defending cigarette manufacturers and their right to advertise. I'd weaved a warning about the perils of government sponsored fascism in there while I was about it. The usual arguments. Maybe he wanted to talk about that.

Maybe it was social.

He'd met AJ a few times. I knew he thought she was distractingly attractive and I liked the way his wife enunciated her vowels. Maybe he wanted to get us all together. Dinner. A Bryan Adams concert. Nude Twister.

As I approached his office he called out to his secretary. Is that Richard, er, Richard whatever-his-name-is back yet?

He was gazing out the window. Eating peanuts from a jar. Scanning the buildings. As if my surname might be written on one of them. He could never remember it. I went in. Coughed, like you do at the doctors, to let him know I'd arrived. You wanted to seem me?

Hey! How're you doing?

Good. Yeah, good. How's things with you?

Me? Hell. I'd be fine. If these damn 'gators weren't snapping at my ass.

Ah, yes. Those 'gators. Damn them.

I had no idea what he was talking about. He must've have sensed my confusion.

Fuckin' haemorrhoids.

Oh.

So what are you and your lady friend doin' Saturday night?

He always referred to AJ as my lady friend. He couldn't remember her name either.

In other news... Governor Patten expunged the old guard from the Legislative and Executive councils. This was part of his evil plan to enfranchise all Hong Kong people with the right to elect their rulers. It displeased a great many people in Beijing. And their Canton-dwelling toadies. Someone suggested the move could potentially bankrupt Hong Kong, presumably in the hope that if money was brought into the equation people might actually care about something as insignificant as the future. Patten doubted the decision to give a few people the right to vote would jeopardise the city's $236 billion in reserves. China threatened to abandon or overturn any and all parliamentary changes, once it gained control of the territory in 1997.

AJ THOUGHT SHE COULD SMELL SOMETHING BURNING. And it wasn't my desire or passion for her. I opened the front door of the apartment. Plumes of smoke hung from the ceiling. I smashed the glass on the fire alarm and investigated the stair well.

A 185 year-old woman was burning something in a bucket. Paper money, or some other kind of offering. She smiled and waved.

What was she doing? What was she thinking?

The security guard arrived. Looked at me as if I was the one causing the problem. I pointed at the woman and her bucket of fire, expecting him to go and punish her. He just shrugged. Turned and walked away.

The alarm stopped.

Our neighbours turned out to see what was going on. People came from floors above and below. All of them shaking their heads, talking amongst themselves. Mocking the stupid *gweilo* on the 27th floor, no doubt. They were clearly more comfortable with the potential for disaster right there on their doorstep than I was.

In other news... 110 millimetres of rain fall in an hour... Four died when half a mountain slid into their living room... A 12 year-old boy was swept into a

*storm drain and never seen again... 150 tonnes of mud buries a policeman...
Lighting strikes a man, twice.*

WHEN A TYPHOON BLEW IN we had two options. Go to the pub and
hope for a lock-in. Stay home and listen to the neighbours play mahjong, for
18 hours. Daytime television, now that I wasn't on it, had nothing to offer.
Baywatch was only broadcast on Saturday nights. The video library was a
wasteland. Panic-buying meant only Dolph Lundgren and Shannon Tweed
movies remained on the shelves. The supermarket and 7-11 were no better.
It was like the shops would never be open again. Ever. Every bottle of water,
every beer and packet of chips and bread, all the instant noodles, rice and toilet
paper would be gone.

I had a few episodes of The Simpsons on video that we'd only seen about
23 times. And a couple of last year's football finals. We'd just have to grit our
teeth. Do the best we could. Invoke a bit of the Dunkirk spirit. Dig in and suffer
though the mahjong marathon. Try to maintain our sanity and dignity, amid the
nonstop slapping, rattling and rumbling of tiles.

27D was perpendicular to our apartment.

We shared a right-angle. We could see into each other's living room when
the curtains weren't drawn. They also played mahjong when there wasn't a
storm. Public holidays. Alternate weekends. Twice a month they'd partake in their
preferred leisure activity somewhere else and annoy someone else's neighbours.
Their apartment would be empty, except for a little Shih Tzu. He'd put on his
big-boy pants and race up and down the length of the windows. Yapping at us.

AJ was a tolerant woman. There were times, however, when little Fei-fei
drove her barking mad.

I came home one afternoon and found her leaning out the window. The
neighbours had decamped and were airing the apartment. AJ had seized
the window of opportunity. She was trying to coax the dog onto the ledge.
Attempting to orchestrate a tragedy. She'd even gone to the pet store and
bought a selection of treats, to assist with Fei-fei's suicide.

*In other news... China threatened to cancel contracts negotiated prior to July
1997, if Patten refused to withdraw his plans for electoral reforms... The
racing season was postponed when horses in the Jockey Club stables were
struck down by a mystery virus... Gang members lobbed grenades at police
from the 27th floor of their Tuen Wan hideout.*

SARAH INVITED AJ to the Natalie Cole concert. This completed their trifecta of pedestrian musical experiences. It didn't really worry me that I wasn't invited. Although I did suggest that if she was going to take a ride in our ex-flatmate's Pink Cadillac, as it were, I should be allowed to ride shotgun.

At least someone is interested in showing me a good time, she replied.

Maybe I was taking AJ a little for granted. Maybe I needed to remind her how much I loved her on a more regular basis. Present her with a token of my affections.

I bought us a new bed.

This was probably not the most romantic of gestures. Still, it wasn't as self-serving as power tools or a bowling ball with a liquid centre. The carnal subtext would compliment the wanton practicality.

Wouldn't it?

The bed, technically speaking, wasn't new. It belonged to a friend of Mulder's. We could comfort ourselves with the knowledge that she was of above-average personal hygiene and rarely saw any action, at home. Compared to the stained relic we'd inherited with the apartment, this was daisy-fresh. I had to collect it on Saturday afternoon.

I called Hang, The Moving Expert.

Hang know how it go-go! All you lift is phone! Best rates!

We loaded the king-size mattress and the base into his van. He seemed like a nice guy. When he asked after his money I gave it to him. I wanted him to think I was a nice guy too. I helped him carry the mattress through the lobby even though, contractually, the only thing I had to lift was the phone. At first it didn't appear as if it would fit in the elevator, but The Moving Expert delivered. A masterful combination of kicking, bending, squashing and squeezing won the day.

AJ greeted us on 27th floor. She'd dismantled the old workbench and figured Hang could dispose of it. I made throwing gestures in the direction of the window. He thought this was an excellent idea. It took me five minutes to explain I was only joking about tossing it from on high. He wanted $200 to take it away. I thought that was a little steep. Best rates, anyone?

Hang moving expert, not removing expert, he reminded me.

We took it down in the elevator. I was going to put all the pieces by his van,while we went back with the king-sized base. He took them over to the carpark and dumped our somnambular remnants on the pavement. Next to the Do Not Be Placing Refuse Here sign.

Hang know how it go-go.

The base of the bed wouldn't fit in the elevator. It was a remarkably solid piece of craftsmanship, nowhere near as malleable as the mattress. It was two inches too big, with the wheels off, as the actress said to the bishop. Hang looked at me, smiled and walked out.

The moving expert would be all over this. Any minute. We'd have this baby upstairs and AJ and I would be rolling around in each other's precepts. Any minute now. As soon as Hang gets back.

I waited fifteen minutes.

Hang never returned. I went out to the street. His van was gone.

Hang, Vanishing Expert. Hang know when to go-go.

Disappointed, hurt and confused, I left the base in the lobby and went to see if AJ liked the idea of sleeping on a mattress on the floor as much as I did.

She didn't.

She wasn't mad keen on helping me carry it up 27 flights either but what other option did we have? The clock was against us too. We had a dinner date at 1930 hours. We returned to base-camp with heavy hearts and tried to keep our sense of humour. For twelve storeys it was hilarious. The next nine weren't so funny. By the time we got to 21 our situation comedy had become an expletive-laden drama and war of attrition.

Would it end in Shakespearian tragedy?

We dragged it into the bedroom at 1943 hours, exhausted. We collapsed onto the naked bed. Dirty. Sweaty. Angry. I looked at AJ in a dirty, sweaty, angry way and we made dirty, sweaty, angry love. By 1958 we were bathing in post-coital affection. And somehow still managed to make it to the restaurant just forty minutes the other side of fashionably late. We didn't even try to explain or apologise.

We had climbed our Everest and, unknown to me crossed our Rubicon.

In other news... the Hang Seng Index collapsed, wiping billions from the market... Hong Kong's porcine stocks were decimated when Foot & Mouth Disease killed 30,000 pigs and left a further 120,000 infected... Prince Charles and Lady Diana officially announced their separation.

NEW ADDITIONS TO THE AGENCY had a special honour bestowed upon them. Come December they would be responsible for organising the Christmas Party. How difficult could it be?

Venue. Booze. Music.

That formula might've held true in the male-dominated drinking culture I hailed from. Not in the female-dominated food culture I was immersed in.

Alcohol was not high on the agenda for the majority of my colleagues. There were much more important things. Ridiculous things like dining, entertainment, games and the lucky draw. I should've figured something was up when the Core Organising Committee of Our Party for Office Personnel (COCOPOP) held its first meeting in a conference room. There was a perfectly good bar upstairs.

What was the point of being on a steering committee if you couldn't drink and drive?

Popular convention dictated that the lucky draw would be the highlight of the evening. COCOPOP's chief responsibility was to ensure clients, suppliers and vendors sent us prizes. Airline tickets. Holiday packages. Televisions. Karaoke machines. Stereos. Video cameras. Microwave ovens. Rice cookers. Restaurant vouchers. What we didn't want was book vouchers. Sunglasses. Bottles of shampoo. Condoms.

Fuck that shit.

The rules were simple. Everyone had to win something. Preferably something good. I seemed to be the only one concerned that this kind of removed the luck component from the lucky draw. Ensuring no one left empty-handed wasn't going to be easy either. The Agency had grown to almost 200 staff. Someone was going to have to make do with a record voucher and a feminine hygiene product.

What games will we play?

How about Let's Get Drunk? It's fun and people can play it on their own, or in teams.

Not silly enough.

You've obviously never seen me drunk.

According to the rest of COCOPOP I wasn't taking the fun part of the evening seriously enough. People needed games. They didn't particularly like them but it was easier than trying to talk to each other. The ritual humiliation that came at someone else's expense was a critical equalizer.

How about a Beer Drinking Competition?

Not silly enough.

You've obviously never seen me drunk.

Maybe get boys to dress as girls?

But I do that every weekend.

And with that I was excused from the Games Subcommittee. They made me responsible for locating the venue and finding budget entertainment.

Do we want a band, or a DJ?

It needs to be funnier than that.

If we all get drunk and start dancing it will be hilarious.

Should be something crazy.

I can get pretty crazy after a few drinks.

It was the last Friday in December when The Agency converged upon a restaurant in the middle of Hong Kong Park. I'd appointed myself MC for the evening and decided to open proceedings with the famous Rodney Rude *fuckin' nothing* joke.

So I walked into Mulder's office the other day, I said. I found him just standing there with his hand on his hips. Thrusting his pelvis in and out. In and out. Clenching his buttocks as he pushed back and forth. In and out. So I said, Hey Mulder! What are you doing? And he looked at me, as he thrust his hips backwards and forwards, and he said... *fuckin' nothing.*

I guess you kind of had to be there but trust me when I tell you it went down a storm.

I found out later most people didn't really get it. They just thought it was funny because I'd said *fuck* in front of The Empress Dowager. And it looked like I was having sex with a ghost.

The all-you-can-eat buffet didn't endear itself to many either. Mainly because I had an office of Homer Simpsons to feed. They took the all-you-can-eat thing personally. As a challenge.

I had to pull the plug on the Mexican band and give them their mariaching orders. Not because everyone figured out the Mexicans were actually Filipinos in disguise. It's just that once the food ran out the only thing anyone wanted to hear was their name being called in the lucky draw.

I still had one sure-fire piece of entertainment to unleash but it could wait until the Christians had been fed to the lions.

Most were happy with their Lucky Draw Luck. Even the ones that didn't win a 36" colour television, a microwave or a laser disc player (with karaoke microphone!). Only the Finance Director felt undervalued. She was of the opinion that a box of ribbed condoms were beneath her, even after I went to great lengths to explain how they were ribbed *for her pleasure*. She asked if I had anything else.

The bottle of strawberry douche didn't blow her skirt up either.

The Empress ended up telling her PA to go back to the office and get something from her drawer. She even padded the mystery gift with a bonus $1000, just in case. No one seemed to think it was odd for the Finance Director, the third-highest money earner at The Agency, to be complaining about the value of their prize, or that her dissatisfaction was pandered to in such a manner. I guess they felt she needed to be given some Face, or she might start cooking the books.

Not without that microwave oven she wasn't.

It was time to deploy my secret weapon. The scud missile in our own private war on Christmas. A double-barrelled, biological weapon of mass distraction.

Clare had been a regular visitor to Mecca. As patron and performer. She was a fire-eating belly-dancer, or a belly-dancing fire-eater. Either way, the sighs of disappointment, which fell around the halting of the Lucky Draw, went up in flames of hysteria as Clare shimmied, shaked and baked.

Baldrick tried to claim her as his prize in the lucky draw.

I was going to catch up with her after the show, but The Agency demanded an encore. Then she had to go home and pack, for a trip to Cambodia. She was starting a new chapter in her life. I should come visit some day.

I gave her a card and told her to send me the details.

Months later, there was a picture of her in the paper. A passport photo, alongside two others. Her boyfriend and his brother. They'd been kidnapped by the Khmer Rouge. Held for ransom. Executed.

People came in and out of your life all the time in Hong Kong. More travelled through it than to it. It was a stopover. A fly-by. A two-year contract. Folks were ferried in and then, pfft, they were gone. Just like that. Making friends was a kind of pointless, futile exercise. No one would be around when you needed them.

Who knew what Fate had in store for any of us?

Despite leaving the lucky draw empty-handed, fortune still managed to smile upon our little corner of the island.

AJ's mum sent us tickets to join them in Bali, with the rest of their extended family. I'd never been to Indonesia. For someone my age, from Perth, this was unusual in the extreme. Bali was the destination of choice for young Sandgropers. In much the same way people from Queensland were Banana Benders and Victorians were Gum Suckers, West Australians were known as Sandgropers. In entomology, the Sandgroper is an indigenous slug found rolling in the dirt on the Perth side of the rabbit-proof fence. Little is known of the Sandgropers preferred holiday destinations, or if they behave like complete yobbos when they get there. Their upright namesakes, however, were all over Bali like a rash. Like a sexually transmitted disease with bad personal hygiene and ill-considered tattoos. Bali was cheap. Cheaper than flying from Perth to Sydney or anywhere else in Australia. It was only a few hours away. In the 80s the island bordered on ubiquity and was already drifting into cliché. A hairy band of Australian communists had written a novelty single about it, and enjoyed eleven weeks in the charts.

I've Been To Bali Too.

Getting out of Hong Kong at that time of year wasn't easy. Like Hebrews out of Egypt, a large percentage of the population fled the colony at Christmas. Buying a Business Class fare was often the only way to guarantee a seat on your preferred flight. Something AJ's mum had gone generous lengths to secure.

I always seemed to bring out the best in other people's parents. If things didn't work out in advertising I could make a career out of being adopted.

My hangover and I boarded the plane, with AJ. I was not in great shape nor looking forward to the flight. Nonetheless, the excitement of spending another Christmas in a place that wasn't Western Australia soon caught up with me. As did the outstanding beverage service afforded to those in the pointy end. My mid-flight anxiety attack almost went by unnoticed. I blamed it on the cumulonimbus clouds and the turbulence that seemed to live in them. I wasn't afraid of flying.

Was I?

We arrived in Denpasar in the early evening, a little worse for wear. I was sweating bullets. The humidity didn't help. I crawled through immigration. The heat seemed to be affecting everyone. They all moved sooooo slooooow. In Customs. In Arrivals. In traffic. In life.

I became a product of my environment, again.

The main road of Kuta looked just like it did on 60 Minutes. Jeeps navigated narrow, poorly paved roads. Locals were taking ridiculous looking tourists for a ride on and off the streets. Herding them through poorly lit souvenir stores and surf shops. Singlets, shorts, sarongs, sandals and thongs. Weaving Bo Derek braids in their hair. And on the girls too. It was like the bogan population of a rural town had been magically transported to an exotic bargain basement.

I acquired a fetish for starry shirts.

Blue shirts with big white stars. White shirts with little blue stars. Blue shirts with small yellow stars and crescent moons. A bright red shirt with thick, blue vertical stripes and white stars, like the Confederate flag. I bought one for Kurtis too. The Duke Of Haphazard.

AJ's parents had rented bungali off Legian Beach. A safe but not inconvenient distance from Kutamundra. The two huts were self contained, with a landscaped pool and garden between them. At the end of the driveway a breezy bar served chilled beer until about one or two in the morning.

Each day would begin at the breakfast table, between 9 and 10 am. Bacon sandwiches. Fruit. There would be tactical deliberations. What would be the least-difficult thing to do today? Walk on the beach. Drive up to the volcano. Go to the other side of the island. Lunch. Come 5pm we'd meet at the pool for cocktails and work out where we were going to eat dinner. Nights ended with half a dozen beers in the bar, a swim in the pool and pointless, meandering conversations under the ceiling fans until one or all of us fell asleep. Not necessarily in that order. This is about as good as it gets. And, for us, AJ and I, it was about as good as it had got for some time.

So close and yet so far away.

I became friends with the manager of the pub. Manni. He invited me to his village, to see the cockfighting. Probably not the most PC of things to be doing but, when in Gunung Agung, you do as the Agungians do.

AJ and I piled into Manni's topless military vehicle. It was in good shape for something that had managed to survive The Big One. He drove. And drove. And drove. AJ began to get worried. I could tell by the way she whispered things like What the fuck have you gotten us into? Where the fuck are we going and when will we fucking get there? With no beverage service to take the edge of her nerves I did the only thing I could.

I smiled and shrugged my shoulders.

It's not like he was going to drive us up into the mountains and kill us for a couple of hundred bucks and a few pieces of jewellery.

Was he?

Manni turned off the road less travelled and drove to a small collection of half-finished, erector-set houses. He proudly showed us his wife and newborn son. Slices of mango, parcels of sticky rice and a curious citrus drink were offered for our enjoyment. Then he led across the compound and showed us his cock ring, as I assumed the poultry battlefield was called.

Fifty-four men crowded around a three-by-three concrete slab. Manni shouted something in Bahasa. They all turned and flashed big, toothless smiles.

Money was thrown around like confetti which, considering there was three hundred million Rupiahs to the Dollar, is all it was really good for.

On one side of the slab a young boy held a rusty looking rooster. It had impressive legs, for a chicken. They were made all the more impressive by three chrome talons attached to its right drumstick.

On the other side of the slab stood an old man with a large, black, oily cock in hand. He had fitted his out with a Krueger Bloodsports Kit too.

Would the experience of age triumph over the boldness of youth?

Both carried their champions before them, ready to rumble. They began proceedings by bumping the beaks of their birds together, to ruffle their feathers and get them in a fighting mood. Once satisfied they were of sufficiently foul mind-set, they were dropped into the ring.

The two birds stood there, sizing each other up. Eventually, Rusty approached its opponent.

Oooh!

Rusty raised his bionic leg and brought it down across his enemy's breast. Ahhhh!

Black Mamba spread his clipped wings, attempting some futile defensive manoeuvre. Then fell over, fricasseed. Not dead, yet, but leaking enough sauce to suggest he would soon be up to his giblets in giblets.

Oh.

Not really what I, or the assembled crowd, was expecting from this gladiatorial contest. Where was the action-packed spectacle Hollywood had promised me?

No thrills. One spill.

Many of the villagers shared my disappointment. They turned their backs on the ring in disgust. Angry at themselves and life. I asked Manni if we should head back to Legian. It was quite a drive and there were cocktails waiting by the pool. My good friend seemed surprised and amused by the request.

You want me to drive you back?

No, Manni, we want to stay and live in the mountains with you. Forever. Build a new world, here, in the shell of the old.

We wanna be free to do what we wanna do. We wanna be free to ride our machines without being hassled by The Man! And we wanna get loaded. And we wanna have a good time.

Negotiations were swift. They included but were not limited to the cost of fuel, time, refreshments and cultural attractions. We barrelled down the mountain in silence, plucked and gutted. We'd got our fingers burnt and, now, our faces and forearms were fried under the equatorial sun. That night there was a sting in the sheets which no lotion could soothe.

Christmas in a Hindu state is an indifferent occasion. And lunch at the bungali was a lukewarm affair. *Nasi lemak*, or *le muck* as it's known in France, with all the trimmings. *Ayam betutu, ikan bakar, nasi goreng, jukut urab* and *gado gado*. AJ's grandfather thought he'd muck things up further and ducked out to buy some champagne. He returned with two bottle of rice wine instead. 90% proof. This stuff could vivisect your viscera, and gut you in ways no fish nor fighting foul would ever endure.

New Year's Eve was spent at Double Six, an outdoor nightclub on Legian Beach. As the countdown drew near, gallons of soap suds were pumped onto the dance floor. Bubbles filled the air. Slippery, foamy people watusied in and out of our personal space. They were high on *arak*, a popular local drink and form of non-vintage methanol. I was still recovering from Grandpa's Grange and had neither the stomach nor the mind-set for it. I couldn't help but think how much better it might have gone if we'd all dropped tabs of Lysergide around three o'clock.

AJ and I took a long, silent walk along the beach. Alone, together. So close yet so far away.

All was quiet on New Year's Day.

We farewelled family and were back on the tarmac in Denpasar by mid-afternoon, fortifying our faith in flying with Business Class bubbles.

More champagne, Sir?

As newspapers were dispensed passengers became audibly distressed. Uneasy whispering filled the cabin. I asked the Cathay hostess for a copy of the South China Morning Post. She said she'd try to find me one but all the dailies had been taken.

Nineteen people had died in Lan Kwai Fong on New Year's Eve.

Trampled to death. The inclined streets of the neighbourhood were packed to capacity, sluiced with spilled drinks and celebratory sprays of champagne. At the top of the hill, as '92 rolled into '93, a person fell. Others began to trip and tumble into those below them. It was a disastrous domino effect, all the way to the bottle-necked intersection. Irresistible forces met immovable objects and those who toppled were macerated by the mullered masses behind them.

Nineteen.

Most of them were teenagers, one as young as fifteen. The life crushed out of them. Right where AJ and her parents had stood the year before. Where we would've been if we hadn't been to Bali too.

Baldrick was on the perimeter when the first wave washed down. He fell to the side. He grabbed his wife and pulled her into a doorway. All they could do was stand there, together, and watch the mortal mudslide suffocate the crowd.

3. YEAR OF THE COCK

PATTEN WAS ADMITTED TO HOSPITAL. He had to have a couple of arteries widened. Angioplasty. Stress related. Trying to pass his electoral reform bill. It was giving Beijing a coronary too.

As I walk through the valley of death I fear no one, for I am the meanest motherfucker in the valley.

My heart skipped a few beats when The Agency intern arrived. Niña. A comely Filipino-American. I was charged with introducing her to the heady world of advertising. She introduced me to A Thousand Years Of Solitude. Eva Luna. The magic-realism oeuvre. She gave me a first taste of dried mangoes too. I'd never been tempted by them before but, in her cosmopolitan hands, they held an appetising appeal and were hard to refuse.

We spent a lot of time together, during office hours. Talking. Drinking in the bar upstairs. Flirting, I guess. In a relatively harmless, high-school way. We became friends, with a thin possibility of more.

She made a mixed tape for me.

It was a TDK C-90 of sonic subterfuge. Can't Help Falling In Love. Looking Thru' Patient Eyes. Waiting. Throb. The Body That Love You. Your Love Has Got A Handle On My Mind. Be My Baby. Maybe I was reading too much into it but, in the list of songs on the cover, wherever *love* appeared in a title she'd drawn a little heart.

I can feel your body pressed against my body,
Wrap yourself around me.

Niña was an exciting prospect. Rich, honey skin. Almond eyes. Fleshy lips. She whispered to herself in French when she was reading or thinking aloud. Of course nothing would or ever could happen between us.

Could it?

She was a colleague's niece. And I was in love with AJ.

Wasn't I?

Boom boom boom until noon noon noon.

The cornucopia of cultures that percolated through life was never more apparent than when pitching new business. There was I, an Australasian working for a British guy in a Chinese agency owned by Americans presenting to Japanese clients for a Korean softdrink account. Or was it Korean clients and a Japanese soft drink?

Advertising. 15% commission. 85% confusion.

They walked into the conference room. Introductions were made and business cards were exchanged. Fluids were discussed. Or was it business discussed and fluids were exchanged. Judging by the way our MD fawned over the client the latter was certainly on the cards. We told them about some of our other accounts and what we knew about the beverage market. There were some barriers they would have to overcome to win the hearts and minds of Chinese consumers. And we knew how to do it.

Over to Creative.

I opened with some shtick about bringing the product alive. We'd decided to employ the services of a gimmick to personify this point. And when I say *we* I mean me. I'd like to say it was all Niña's idea. I wish I could. It was supposed to be a metaphor that visualised what our advertising would do for their product. Maybe it could help surmount the language barrier while it was there. It might even help lighten the mood of proceedings.

I'd attended funerals with more zip in them.

Someone had given me a dancing Coca-Cola can. One of those soda cans that bend and twist in the middle, dancing to a jingle, activated by a clap of your hands. I'd taken the Coke label off and replaced it with The Client's brand. It looked pretty good. I'd even put little sunglasses on it, which I'd taken off a dancing sunflower, to make it look cooler.

This was going to work on so many levels.

I put the can on the table. I clapped. Once. Twice. Thrice. Nothing. I lifted the can, turned it over and switched it on. Then clapped again.

Ta-da.

It shimmied with reckless abandon, like a coked-up can of *arak* on New Year's Eve. In the spirit of the occasion I clapped and danced along, like AJ's grandad.

Way-hey.

With the exception of the can-canning can, and its muffled monophonic jingle, the room was deathly still. Not a grunt of acknowledgement. Not a smile of recognition. Not an ounce of support from my colleagues either, as the shadow of a large lead balloon moved across a sea of constipated faces.

Oh the humanity.

The cellophane cylinder crinkled with embarrassment. It boogied self-consciously on the boredroom table.

I turned it off and tried to move on, launching into a presentation of the storyboards. I waded deeper into the dark nether-regions of Pitch Hell.

This is page

88

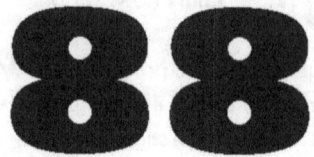

It's quite auspicious, you know.

I used to think it was just a number. Two fat ladies, clickety-click. Now I knew it was a special number. Here, it's auspiciously set in 88-point Gill Sans UltraBold.

People in advertising, and clients, like to know that type of thing.

With each TV concept a little more of my life was sucked away. With every print ad I became smaller and less visible. I was never so glad to hand proceedings over to our Media Department. If anyone could make my work look exciting it was them. Media presentations were the stuff of legend. Tedia was the message. They could turn a man to stone with just one acetate.

It's just like a mini-movie, enthused The Empress Dowager in summation. Any questions?

All eyes deferred to the quiet Japanese man in the corner. His was the only opinion that mattered and there he sat, in quiet contemplation.

Or was it a cryogenic coma?

The Empress Dowager adjusted the air-con, perhaps in an attempt to defrost him. As far as pregnant pauses went, this was in danger of being weeks overdue.

Did you say you could save us 15% on our media?

Across town, Patten was also singing for his supper and tap dancing before an unreceptive audience.

Do not fear failure.

Remarkably, he too met with success. And managed to gazette his electoral reform bill.

Perpetual peace is a futile dream.

It went down as well as my novelty soda can with Mainland officials. The move effectively destroying any chances of Sino-British talks in the future.

AJ was given a glimpse of what lay ahead for her too. Mrs Lovitz had put her in touch with a fortune teller. She thought I should go too.

Just for fun.

I'd never been to a psychic. I didn't put much faith in these things. Experience had led me to believe that when shit happened you would never see it coming. It was hard to trust anyone, let alone a woman called Kushla. Her name suggested an Indian mystic or a romantic, gypsy-like figure. She looked like the slutty one from The Golden Girls and sounded like Mrs Doubtfire. I went out of curiosity and a desire to please AJ.

Helloooo there!

I sat there, cynically, subjected to another examination. Detached from the experience. Scrutinized as if I were someone else. Observed myself and my life as if I were another.

According to my palms I had creative hands. Of course they would say that, wouldn't they? They were so self-serving. I had a good eye too. I noticed stuff and could see through things.

Things like this? Could I leap tall buildings with a single bound too?

Kushla told me to stop interrupting. I was supposed to be a good listener. Receptive. Open to new ideas. I had an appetite for life and sought new experiences. My opposable thumb was strong, like my mind. I was analytical. Stubborn. Yet I had low self-esteem. I was a loner. Untrusting. A long, dark cloud hung over me. I wanted to get away. Escape. I needed my own space.

Granted, witchcraft was not my area of expertise. It seemed to me, however, most Girl Guides could look at anyone's hand, say things like that, and earn a Soothsaying Merit Badge.

She put the tarot cards on the table and dealt me a hand.

Big changes were coming. I had a steady relationship. This was good for the time being but things would be different fourteen months from now. Work. Career. Lots of travel. There was a third party, who was like me but not like me. I had to be careful. Be more cautious in my personal life. I was curious and could be easily tempted. Led down a dark path. Travel. A lot of work to do. More responsibility. I would forget something important. Lose it. There would be more money too. Rapid changes. A good seven year stretch. It would be different. There would be change. In me and around me. Remote, distant places. Something to do with photography. Film. Seven years and then a break. I would surprise myself and others. There was a woman in my office. Bonnie? She has problems with her leg.

$800. Cash please.

AJ's reading was similar, she said. It focused more on the past and there was a lot of talk about me. And travel. She shrugged it off and refused to elaborate.

Wherever you go, go with all your heart.

Yea verily, forsooth, as it had been foretold in The Prophecy, AJ and I took off on a spontaneous adventure.

Destination: Krungthep Mahanakhon Amon Rattanakosin Mahinthara Ayutthaya Mahadilokphop Noppharat Ratchathani Burirom Udomratchaniwet Mahasathan Amon Piman Awatan Sathit Sakkathatthiya Witsanukam Prasit.

Translation: City of Angels, Great City of Immortals, Magnificent City of the Nine Gems, Seat of the King, City of Royal Palaces, Home of the Gods Incarnate, Erected by Visvakarman and Indra's Behest.

AKA: Bangkok.

It was the first time we'd been on a holiday, together. Alone. Gone to a place where we didn't really know anyone and knew even less about the culture. Urban legend had it the streets were paved with prostitutes. There were sex shows on every corner. Women with magical vaginas. Drugs were dropped in your drinks and you woke up in hotel rooms without your kidneys.

Captain Underpants had taken a girl back to his room and found out she was a he. I had all that and more in mind. Mixed emotions with uncertain horizons.

And then the plane hit turbulence.

The bluebird of anxiety was no longer a visitor. It had taken up residence. It was nesting. Breeding. I maintained a vice-like grip on the armrests for the remainder of the flight. As if such precautions would stop us from streaking across the sky in a fiery ball of twisted metal, or cushion the impact of terminal velocity upon my bones.

Once you have tasted flight you will walk the earth with your eyes turned skywards, for there you have been and there you will long to return.

I should've been more worried about the slapdash, hit-and-miss journey from the airport to the hotel in Chinatown. Yes, we'd travelled from Hong Kong to Thailand... and were staying in Chinatown.

The King was there to greet us.

A life-size facsimile of His Royal Highness was standing at the lobby entrance, in all his majesty. He was everywhere. Omnipresent. On buildings and billboards. In shopping malls. Each portrait drawn in a different style, depending on where the artists drew their influence. There was Versace King, Miyake King, Armani King, Van Gogh King and even Warhol King. These observations, of course, were made with the utmost respect. One does not mess with the King Of Thailand, or his Queen. Both were much loved. They were treated like royalty. Things would not end well for those who dissed the monarch.

We hailed a tuk-tuk. The ride-on lawnmower that masqueraded as public transport. One of thousands that gave intravascular coagulation to Bangkok's palpitating heart.

Patpong was remarkably well lit for a seedy side. It was nothing like legend had led me to believe. As a red light district it made an excellent night market. Fake designer bags and t-shirts. Sunglasses. Toys. Lighters that looked like guns or penises. Penis guns. Water pistol penises. Pirate CDs, cassettes and video tapes. Wooden *objets d'art*. Bongs. Bongs that looked like penises. Tacky silver jewellery set with green and blue stones. A cut-price cavalcade of tourism and consumerism, where doobry and doodah met genitalia.

Misogynism waited in the wings.

Dancing girls. Show girls. Massage girls. The performing seals of sexuality. Girls seeking penises. Girls with penises. Doobry and doodah with genitalia.

The spruikers were pushy, but polite. Respectable, yet comical, in their pink shirts and ties. They thrust laminated menus under my nose.

Beverages and snacks?

Sex acts and show times. A litany of the lewd and lurid. Curiosity, and the good folk at Superpussy, would not be denied.

For a few hundred Baht there was no point arguing with either.

Inside, an attractive group of she-men thrust their manginas in our general direction. Janet Jackson blared. Black Cat. At the end of their routine they passed the hat, soliciting donations for their next operation.

Two Hobbit women took the stage. 35 going on 55, and long gone from The Shire. They pulled things from their reproductive organs like magician's conjuring rabbits from a hat. Items that had no right to be there were drawn out with flair, finesse and extreme prejudice. Razor blades. Raw eggs. Rabbits. Bouquets of flowers.

They're for you, Doctor.

The transsexuals returned, grooving to U2. Even Better Than The Real Thing. One of them even looked like Bono. A dance troupe joined in. Most of the girls were too young to be up that late, on a school night. Head down and arse up, they should've been hitting the books. Not inserting tubes into their superpussies and blowing darts at balloons.

New Sensations, sang INXS.

It was hard not to feel a little sad for all involved. Ourselves included. Were the women being exploited, or was it our base instincts, deviant curiosity and appetite for life that was being preyed upon? Looking across the streets and bars you couldn't help but think it was the constraints of the West being squeezed, manipulated, fleeced and enslaved by the unfettered East. And they went at it like there was no tomorrow.

Maybe, for a lot of them, there wasn't.

In the morning we went in search of a floating market. The Concierge was helpful and courteous. I thought he was going to come with us, just to make sure we got there. Taking a look at some of the names on the map it might not have been a bad idea.

Borommaratchachonnani. Somdejphramthamineeong.

A fast lesson in futility followed, as the city conspired against us. For twenty minutes we sat in the cab out the front of the hotel, attempting to enter the traffic. The next hour was spent driving around the block.

Welcome to Bangkok.

This was why Sarah had told AJ it could take half an hour to arrive at work in the morning. And three hours to get home at night.

Seeing the potential for comedy in our situation, my body decided to make an ironic commentary on the constipated carriageways of Siam city.

Now playing: Revenge of the breakfast buffet.

I asked the driver to take us back to the hotel. It was only 450 meters away. At our current rate of progress, however, that could've taken anything from half an hour to half a day. The cramps that had been gently pinging away inside dialled themselves up to eleven. I apologised to AJ, opened the door and sprinted to the hotel. The rest of the day was spent suffering one sudden and hideous movement after another. Only after 8:30 did I feel stable enough to continue our uncharted journey.

We found a strip of bars in another part of town.

We entered a club packed with young and glamorous Thais. A lone European sat on the opposite side of the bar, entertaining a couple of painted ladies. Or were they entertaining him? From time to time we made incidental eye contact. There were moments when I could feel his gaze upon me. I'd casually glance across the top of my glass and there he was, eyeballing me. It was going to be Versace all over again. I knew it. He stood and walked toward me. Slowly. He narrowed his eyes and smiled confidently.

Déjà vu.

In the middle of The 80s, after flunking out of school, I travelled to the far north of Australia. It was my first attempt at running away from the past. The great escape. Kunaratha was about as far from Perth as I could get without leaving the state. It was the first official stop on my circumnavigation of the country. I thought I'd work there for a few months, earn some money and move on. To Darwin. Then Queensland.

It was as close to a plan as I'd ever made.

A year later I was still there, managing the Kunaratha Roadhouse, its restaurant and drive-thru liquor store. Most people visited one or all of these at some point. Regularly. Someone even drove through the drive-thru liquor store one night. Literally. The culprit got so drunk on the debris police found him asleep at the wheel in the morning.

I got to know most everyone. Most everyone got to know me, and my mullet. I was the Patrick Swayze of the Kunaratha Roadhouse.

Socially, I aligned with the rurally hip, diamond exploration crews when they were in town. The hardworking, hard-drinking builders and labourers where my mates when they weren't.

I also found companionship and pleasure in some well turned curves.

She looked like Cleopatra. The one in Asterix And Cleopatra. Cartoon sexy. She had that black bob of hair, a sharp nose and ruled the Ord River in much the same way Egypt's Queen reigned over the Nile. Transforming triple pillars of the world into a strumpet's fool, as The Bard would say.

Lisa was my first real lesson in the vagaries of women.

She was English and worked at the Commonwealth Bank. She played tennis every other Tuesday night and would come to the Roadhouse, bathed in sweat, with her tennis partners. Straight-set victories were toasted and formidable back-hands admired. They'd sit there long after everyone else had gone and wait for Patrick Swayze to ask them to leave.

I began to frequent the bank more than necessary. Just to see her. I re-arranged my schedule at work. I joined the tennis club, as a sociopathetic member. I began playing on Tuesday nights. Hoping she'd notice me. Invite me to join her coterie.

Fie, wrangling queen!
Whom everything becomes, to chide, to laugh,
To weep; whose every passion fully strives
To make itself, in thee, fair and admired!

After a month of unnecessary deposits and withdrawals she waved at me, from across the bank. She asked if I was going to tennis that week. I said probably. She said she hoped to see me there.

I've been wanting to play with you for a while.

This was ten years before anyone had heard of Mr Johnson, or Sexy Tennis School. I was only eighteen. I thought she was talking about tennis. It wasn't the first time my naiveté would end with a rude awakening.

It wouldn't be the last.

Mixed Doubles was part of the Tuesday night program. I manoeuvred into her general vicinity and tram-line of sight when it was time to pair up.

Game on.

My serve. She was on the net in her tennis skirt and bobby socks. Bent and braced for a volley, revealing well-tanned thighs and buttocks, girded by narrow black loins. I didn't know much about the by-laws of the Ord River Sports Club but I was pretty sure this wasn't regulation attire.

Advantage server. Match-point.

On the back of a heated victory I asked her out for dinner. We could eat crayfish, drink Black Russians and revel in the luxury of the Kunaratha Club Dining Room on Saturday night. It was quite the place to be, with a stringent dress code. Classy. No singlets, thongs or dirty dancing. People would speak in hushed, gossipy tones as we walked by their laminex tables and chairs.

There goes Lisa and her latest lapdog.

I drove her home and kissed her on the cheek. She tasted like sultry nectar. I said goodnight and pushed her out the door. Chivalry and Swayze, I told myself, was alive and well and living in The Kimberleys.

Two days later she called, in tears. She didn't understand. I took her out for dinner, licked her on the cheek, threw her from the vehicle and drove off. Why didn't I come in for coffee or tea or something? How come I didn't make a move on her? Did I know I was the only guy in town who hadn't tried to open an account with her at the bank?

I told her I was nervous. I didn't know what to do. What if she wasn't interested? No one wanted to make a deposit more than me. What if I wasn't trading in the right currency? She insisted I go to her house, immediately. It was time to square the ledger.

Let's do it after the high Roman fashion.

Lisa, for want of a better phrase, was quick to put baby in the corner. The Pretty In Pink soundtrack played on her American-sized stereo. If You Leave, Orchestral Manoeuvres In The Dark. Bring On The Dancing Horses, Echo And The Bunnymen. Please Let Me Get What I Want, The Smiths. Do Wot You Do, INXS.

We were joined at the hip for a month. Sultry nectar at night, bittersweet mornings. She'd usher me out under cover of darkness, before her housemates awoke. Looking for a lie-in one Sunday, I made the mistake of telling her how happy she made me. How lucky I was.

How much I loved her.

She said she had to go to church, with her parents.

She stopped returning my calls. She was busy at the bank. When I went to her home she was on her way out. She switched to playing tennis on Thursdays. Sometimes I'd get a call, just before closing time. She'd ask me stop by after work. Late.

For her own person,
It beggar'd all description; she did lie
In her pavilion, cloth of gold of tissue,
O'er picturing that Venus where we see
The fancy outwork nature.

One quiet Wednesday I was preparing to close the bar. I'd just received the call of the wild and was deciding whether I would accept the invitation to a private audience with Her Royal Highness. We both knew I would but I wanted to pretend I had some semblance of pride and choice in the matter.

Two regulars had been on a marathon Bundy binge. They were getting a little abusive, toward me and each other. It was sure to end in tears, or worse. Their propensity for violence was as legendary as the amount of booze they drank. Bundaberg Rum. There's a fight in every bottle, as they say. They'd done two between them. Triple over-proof.

Way-hey.

I overheard one suggest they should go and beat up the Telecom workers in the corner, rather than hit each other. I wasn't sure what to do. It was another of those moments where I found myself stalled within myself, observing a moment from above. Very un-Swayze. Part of me didn't think two guys would simply walk over and lay some chin-music on eight strangers. Part of me wanted to see what happened if they did.

I didn't have long to wait.

One of them got things going by picking up a heavy jarrah bar stool and tossing it across the room, at the unsuspecting government employees. I watched in a state of disbelief, for thirty seconds, as the destruction raged.

I rounded the counter and asked the barmaid to call the police.

She didn't. She was having an affair with one of the navvies. I guess you could say she was a builder's labourer, learning the tricks of the trade. A ganger banger, in the old parlance. Legend had it there was a dragon tattooed beside the entrance to her vagina.

I arrived at the melee and made a bootless attempt to calm things down. A couple of the besieged had made it out the door as the Wrecking Balls grew weary. They stopped almost as inexplicably as they started, and went back to the bar. The Dragon's Keep served them a drink. I dusted off what was left of Telecom, helped them up and out to the carpark's safe harbours.

The police arrived as I was explaining to our resident deconstructionists why they would have to leave and why they would find themselves banned from the bar for quite a while. My boss had recounted many chapters from the establishment's glorious history of insurrection. The penalties for those who wrote a page in it were well documented, resolute and firm.

The Dynamic Duo surrendered to The Law without further incident. They were taken away to contemplate their crimes.

I didn't make it to Cleopatra's house that night, or any other. My trusty barmaid confessed that watching men fight aroused her. She invited me to slay the dragon. She insisted I take her in the big fridge, out back, so to speak.

Police rang the next morning and invited me down to the station. They took me to an interrogation room. Two officers were waiting. I recognised them. They'd backed a wagon up to the storeroom a month ago. I'd loaded it with cases of beer, a donation from my employer to the annual Peelers Picnic. Now they sat opposite me. They'd heard there was some trouble at the bar last night and I'd done nothing about it. If one of the victims hadn't managed to get out and alert them I'd probably still be there, with my friends, drinking with the perps. Senior Sergeant O'Reilly picked up a phone book and dropped it on the table for dramatic effect. He wasn't going to hit me with it.

Was he?

Kunaratha's finest reckoned that I reckoned I was pretty hot shit. That I could come up from the big smoke with my long hair and fancy' clothes, my smartarse mouth and slick dancefloor moves and do whatever the fuck I want.

Constable Roy Baker was just getting started.

You think you can just roll into town, he said. The rules don't apply to you, do they? You think you can cruise in, play tennis and take our Lisa. Well you can't. You've got another thing coming and you'd better pull your head in or we'll send you so far south so fast your head will spin. Do you understand?

I did. It was Roadhouse, Dirty Dancing and Footloose rolled into one.

They weren't concerned about the fight in the bar and the grievous bodily harm inflicted upon Government employees. It was my frolicking on Cleopatra's barge that went against the law. I'd upset the delicate social balance and, more importantly, a suitor-in-blue. Wednesday Nite Smackdown was just a convenient cover under which to let me know I'd fucked up royally.

The Builders Labourers Federation felt the same way. They held me responsible for their lifetime ban.

I was having a drink with one of their fellow Trade Union members shortly after the event. Lawrence. Larry. Lazza. Laz. Or Lazarus, depending on how you felt about the whole brevity thing. He'd been working with them on a site that week. He'd overheard them say they were going to fucking get fucking Richard. Despite the fact that it was them that started the fight, and it was my boss who banned them, it was all my fault.

I'd seen what they were capable of when they were angry. I'd also heard The Instigator's wife had pulled a gun on Dragon's Keep when she found out about the affair she was having with her husband. Idle threats did not run in their family. What if he found out about Little Jackie Paper and Puff The Magic Dragon frolicking in the autumn mist of Honah Lee's big fridge? I did what I figured Patrick Swayze and Kevin Bacon would do.

I took a holiday and flew south for the winter of discontent.

After a few days sitting on the beach amongst friends, good friends who didn't punch or kick or shoot other people, I concluded I needed Kunaratha like I needed a hole in the head.

I met Isabelle. I needed her. I needed to go back to school. I needed to put the top-end to stern and fetch me a new horizon.

I thought I had.

Yet there it was, bearing down. There he was, under full sail, on an Eastern ocean of deviancy.

Lazarus?

Richard?

He spent three months of the year in Thailand, during the monsoons. The off-season. He had a house down the coast. He hardly ever came to Bangkok. He'd never been in that bar.

What were the chances?

I thought he was The Instigator. I told him, when he started walking over, I thought he'd been biding his time for a decade and was finally going to deliver on his promise to fucking get fucking Richard.

That was highly unlikely, he said. The Instigator had become crocodile food not long after I'd left.

The Builders Labourers Federation had been banned from almost every pub in town. They did most of their drinking at the river, beside the abattoir. One night, someone bet The Instigator he couldn't swim to the opposite bank. It was 200 meters across, maybe 300. He won the wager. Not knowing when to hold 'em, when to fold 'em, when to walk away and when to run, he went again. Double or nothing? He waded out and never came back.

That was probably my fault too.

Laz introduced us to Ninoy and A. That was the second girl's name. A. It was short for Angchawadechasilparongsongkram, or something like that. Thais are very generous with consonants and vowels when it comes to proper nouns. A was as judicious as an abbreviation could get. When I introduced them to AJ they thought that was hilarious. I told them it was short for Ajiengsatapattapornajasai. We had few drinks together, toasting women of letters and their singular beauty.

The bar pulsed with singular, slender, sightly twenty-somethings. And the night took on a physical dimension. It became a contact sport of sorts. They didn't squeeze by, they slid across. They didn't tap you gently on the back, to let you know they were coming through. They ran hands along the length of your shoulders, or across your chest, trading smiles as they went. Some would hold you by the waist for the duration of their passing. It was like being trapped in Woody Allen's Orgasmatron.

The middle-aged woman behind the bar said something to the man next to her. They both looked at AJ. Others gathered. They inspected her and smiled. Others touched her long, brown, voluminous hair. A and Pinoy translated what they could hear above the music.

AJ was some kind of deity. No, wait. Not a goddess. A supermodel. They thought she was Cindy Crawford. And if she was Cindy Crawford then I guess that made me Richard Gere. There was probably even a gerbil down in Patpong with my name on it.

We revelled in AJ's newfound celebrity.

After half a dozen bottles of beer, nature called and a visit to the executive washroom was in order. An elderly female attendant greeted me with a smile. Her eyes pointed me to a saucer on the table that stood at her station. It seemed in Bangkok one didn't spend a penny. You parted with a Baht. I dropped my gratuity, nodded to her and stood at the urinal.

I'd only just begun to strain the spuds when her hands came down upon my shoulders. She began to massage them. It shocked the bejezus out of me and induced a wild slash across the stainless steel. She laughed and continued to knead me. I got to grips with the task at hand and, overcoming some initial stagefright, soon became accustomed to the custom. So much so I began to wonder how I'd managed on my own for all these years. Unfortunately, her hands-on approach didn't end there. As I prepared to make my finishing flourishes the attendant joined in the dance. She reached around and gave a healthy shake to the unemployed. Then towelled me off and tucked me back into my pants.

Déjà vu.

It jolted me back to the last time a stranger touched me in the bathing suit area, unbidden and unsought. This wasn't as debasing, humiliating and mortifying, nor such a biblical betrayal of trust. I guess I'd unwittingly asked for this particular third-party experience. I'd even paid for it in advance. And I was drunk. Nonetheless, it cast a pall over the remainder of the evening. I didn't talk to anyone about it then, and I couldn't talk to AJ about it now.

Is something wrong?

Just a bit of a stomach cramp. I'll get over it.

In the morning I had to call a photographer. An art director at The Agency was getting married. She'd asked me to deliver a wedding invitation to her long-lost lensman.

Our hangovers met in the lobby.

I asked him what it was like to work in Thailand. He told me it was tough at first but, once he learned the language, a world of opportunities opened. Thai crews were great. Skilled, committed and famously patient. They had a great sense of humour. More often than not, he said, all they wanted to know was how much fun were they going to have and would there be enough to eat. It could be difficult for foreigners to establish a business. Thais were open and amiable, socially, yet they were fiercely patriotic and protected local industries. He had an advantage, he said.

He had a Thai wife.

She enabled him to assimilate and be accepted quicker. To integrate. With her help the studio was up and running and prospering in no time.

Six months later, he got up to leave a nightclub and ran into a bullet. He was shot in the head. Dead. No one knew why. Some say his wife was having an affair with an official. And they thought it would be better if he was out of the way.

Not far from the hotel, hordes of teenagers were armed with buckets, water pistols and aqua-canons. They were soaking all and sundry who wandered their way. There were drive-by drenchings from the trays of trucks. Waterbabes were everywhere, loaded with weapons of mass saturation. Some clung to motorcycles and launched balloons. Others soaked the unsuspecting with hoses.

The Songkran Festival was the evolution of an ancient celebration.

Once upon a time people would simply bless each other and sprinkle holy H_2O about. Over time, fun-loving Thais had turned it into a week-long waterfest. Moist with anticipation, AJ and I continued our quest. Due South, by South-west.

Pattaya.

We travelled at night in the belief traffic would be less intense and, hence, reduce the time it took to get there. The theory proved correct. What we hadn't calculated was the license this would give our driver. He packed the worst parts of our journey thus far into the car and rocketed down the coast. We bounced, swerved and careened along the pot-holed expressway for three hours.

I am the Nightrider. I'm a fuel injected suicide machine. I am the rocker, I am the roller, I am the out-of-controller!

We arrived, shaken and stirred, at the hotel in time for Happy Hour. Just as the Filipino band was launching into Guantanamera. I'd be lying if I said it didn't make the trip worthwhile. Few things are as guaranteed to soothe the soul of weary travellers than a half-assed rendering of this classic tune. One can only imagine the restorative powers of a fully armed, operational and in-tune iteration of Guantanamera.

Guan would probably come in guan's pants.

AJ insisted we go to the health club in the morning. She thought they could see to some of the manifesting tensions. Not wanting to compound them, nor willing to discuss why I would be unwilling to have someone invade my space, again, I gingerly conceded to her whims.

In order to overcome my fears, perhaps I needed to confront them. That being the case, two hands would be better than one.

Wouldn't they?

The Double Siamese Massage suggested an experience that would involve two pairs of hands, or two sets of Siamese Twins. The spa split the difference and put forward sisters. Twins. They probed, prodded and ploughed the length and breadth of my reluctant real estate with professional proficiency. Whispering and giggling amongst themselves in the vernacular. No doubt they were deciding who would get the short end of the stick, so to speak.

Captain Underpants had regaled us all with his Happy Ending joke a number of times. I'm pretty sure it was one of those urban legends but, according to him, it had happened to a friend of his on an end-of-season football trip to Thailand.

Mid-massage, the therapist became aware of his erection. You want wank? she inquired politely. Woody thought about it a while and, after about 1.3 seconds, responded as if there was more in it for her than him.

Oh, all right then.

The woman left the room. Woody lay there, hands behind his head, anticipating the pleasures to come. The girl did not return immediately. Woody figured she must have gone to wash her hands. And brush her teeth. Slip into something more comfortable. Time wore on. Maybe the special oil was on the top shelf and she needed help to get it down. Maybe she had to go upstairs and fetch the in-house expert for these type of services. Just as his interest was beginning to flag, the masseuse stuck her head back through the curtain.

You finish wank?

There was no question of happy endings in the dusky basement of this four-star establishment. They weren't those kind of twins and I wasn't that kind of guy.

Was I?

Affairs concluded with a flurry of activity all the same. I'd been pummelled, pounded and tenderised like a Kobe cow for the best part of two hours. It was time to see how supple I had become. My legs were drawn behind my head. My spine was clicked and cracked. They pushed my head between my knees and I kissed my ass goodbye.

AJ was waiting by the pool. How do you feel? she asked.

Invincible, I replied.

We took a walk along the coast. It was like a scene from Omaha Beach. Germans as far as the eye could see. Buried in the sand. Hiding in the dunes. Cameras for carbines, they shot from lay-lows on the ramparts. Jack-booted in long white socks and sandals they marched into bars, laying waste to smörgåsbords, schnitzels and steins. Specials were etched on chalkboards in Deutsch. Ranks of overweight Germans walking hand-in-hand with petite Thai girls. Red-raw Germans being basted in oil by young Thai boys.

Close your eyes with holy dread,
For he on honey-dew hath fed
And drunk the milk of Paradise.

We retreated to our balcony, firing cocktail fuelled barbs across the pool at our fellow tourists. AJ and I were united in mockery, slipping in and out of consciousness on the opium bed. Spooning in the sunset.

Pattaya after dark was not that different to Pattaya by day. People were just a little better dressed and emboldened by the cloak of shadows. The Germans swapped shorts for slacks and ill-fitting polo shirts. A few of the local boys swapped resort uniforms for miniskirts and sequined boob-tubes. There was something for everyone on the streets and in the bars. It was a twisted, fucked-up Xanadu where Kublai Khan a not-so-stately pleasure dome did decree.

A savage place! As holy and enchanted...
And from this chasm, with ceaseless turmoil seething
As if this earth in fast thick pants were breathing.

Back at The Agency, Bonnie was sitting in reception with a plaster cast on her left leg.

Psychics: 1

Sceptics: 0

I spent the morning apologising to a stream of secretaries and account executives. Each had dropped by to pick up the gift I was supposed to have bought for them. Someone should have warned me of this. The Bring Back Something For Everyone Rule. It should've been printed in The Agency handbook. Still, at least it meant, on some small level, I was on the verge of being accepted.

I was becoming one of Them.

Baldrick came to laugh at me. He just stood there, smirking. Shaking his head with theatrical disappointment. Disillusionment. Like he'd caught me trying on women's underwear. Or rummaging through The Empress Dowager's drawers.

What? I asked defensively.

We saw you-hoo!

Where? I haven't been anywhere. Well, nowhere here.

We saw you at karaoke.

I wasn't at karaoke. I was-

My worst fears had been realized. I'd been recognized. Caught on film. Or, rather, on video. Karaoke video.

Baldrick, Ana and a few others in the Creative Department had been to

a karaoke lounge, celebrating someone's birthday. Feeling sentimental, Ana put in a request for an old song. My Hong Kong. They shrieked when they saw me sitting on the bus with my motley crew of tourists. They howled as I ran around the Cultural Centre like an idiot. They wept as I pined for the Teutonic tour guide on Victoria Peak. And they watched it again. Again. And again. Wherever I went in The Agency, for the next two weeks, that melody would follow me. Like a character in a sitcom I had my own theme tune.

My Hong Kong.

In other news... 17 Vietnamese refugees went on trial for murdering an inmate at Whitehead Detention Centre. The victim was stabbed more than 80 times... A seven meter shark kills two men in separate attacks at Hong Kong beaches.

SWIMMING WAS FRAUGHT WITH INHERENT DANGER. Oil slicks, like the one encountered at The Frog And Toad, were common. The shipping lanes were among the busiest in the world. Bilges were pumped. Hulls leaked. Cargo was dropped. Latrines were flushed. Raw sewage sluiced. Emerging from the shallows of Repulse Bay, Shek O, Tong Fuk or Chung Hom Kok and you'd often find a thin film of something on your submersibles. Adding a shark to the list of aquatic threats raised almost as many questions as it did eyebrows.

How had it managed to survive?

The Government established a Shark Prevention Committee. It was empowered to think of new and interesting ways to net the toxic avenger. And create the public-funded illusion that it actually cared.

Legendary shark molester, Vic Hislop, was imported from Australia. Mostly for comic relief. Like a thick, thalassic Crocodile Dundee he bobbed around the bays in a media-fueled junk for two weeks, issuing unintentionally hilarious missives from his floating HQ. By the end of his tour he'd landed nothing more than a bout of dysentery.

It's shit, Bob.

I know it's shit. But what did they do to it?

Vic slipped quietly out of town. The poisoned predator slipped across the border and snatched two more swimmers in Shenzhen.

I swam laps in the public pool at lunch times. Partly to avoid the awkwardness of meals. Partly to counter the consumption of cigarettes that came with creative enterprise. Baldrick began to accompany me. It was only a short walk from the office. We'd chuck a few laps, throw down a few beers and smoke darts while discussing the merits of Agency ad campaigns. Word got around and we were soon joined by others from the office. The awkwardness of meals, that I'd been trying to avoid, was replaced by the self-consciousness of changerooms. Instead of watching colleagues eat I now had to see them struggle with Lycra.

Fanny was a Mammazonian secretary and administration officer. Big head. Big eyes. Big mouth. Big teeth. Big boobs. Big bum. Big thighs on long, powerful legs. Her arms looked small in proportion. She galumphed around the corridors, wreaking havoc. A corporate T-rex. Baldrick said the only place to hide from her was in plain sight. Stand perfectly still, directly in front of her, in the twilight zone between her eyes. This was her blind spot.

Fanny was known affectionately, in Cantonese, as Big Cunt. Probably not the most pleasant nickname in any language but, in the vernacular, it was quite special. It worked on many levels and was open to numerous interpretations.

This I would learn, first-hand.

I pushed off the wall at the end of lap seven and ploughed straight into Fanny. Right up her gusset. I was up to my elbows in Fanny and had to be surgically removed. The only person in The Agency, maybe even the world, who'd been more intimate with her was The Weasel. The Account Manager that had Tyrannosaurus Sex with her in a taxi after the Christmas party.

Big Cunt was a moniker that transcended the physical.

When someone was fired or laid-off or they resigned, she'd immediately get on the phone and in their face. Telling them how many days holiday they owed the company, or how much money they wouldn't be getting. She was the kind of person who took delight in letting others know she knew they were out of work or out of pocket. She delighted in compounding the frustrations that came with office procedures. She held them over you in her small arms, flesh-flecked gnashers grinning wide.

Like a Jurassic dominatrix, her primary objective was to fuck you up.

I had a chair that was slightly different to others. It was not standard-issue. Lovitz had convinced the Office Manager that writers were prone to bad backs and required additional lumbar support. A bigger, wider chair with more wheels was needed. A greater variety of elevation and reclining options. Comfy Chairs were a coveted item. They aroused envy, jealousy, anger and despair in all who encountered them.

How come *you* got a Comfy Chair?

My Comfy Chair fell into disrepair. I suspected sabotage. Corporate espionage. A disgruntled co-worker. Baldrick or Ana were my chief suspects.

The back had fallen off and, almost before it had hit the floor, there was Fanny. In my office. Flashing that Mesozoic Carly Simon smile and plaster-cast teeth.

Your chair is broken.

I know.

You want it replaced?

No. This nouveau Ottoman is fine. I like to fall on the floor every time I sit down. Of course I want it replaced.

Things had not been the same between us since The Pool Incident. She pivoted on her fuck-off heels and stomped out, like I was the one who got all doctor-patient in the taxi and hadn't called her in the morning.

When I returned from a meeting in the afternoon, it was there.

My new chair.

It was a chair of low esteem. A small chair. An Ikea chair. A cheap chair. A mere shell of a chair. It certainly wasn't my chair. I called Fanny. I told her there had been some mistake. This chair was not like my chair. My chair was different. This chair-

It's a chair.

I know. My chair was ergonomic. I have a bad back and I can't sit in chairs like this. They're too small. You know, my legs are long and I need to sit a bit higher.

That's all we have.

Can we get another one?

We need permission from Office Manager, Finance Director and your Department Head.

Let's get it then.

It's not in this year's budget.

Really? The *feng shui* man didn't foresee this? Of course it's not in this year's budget. It's a chair. Show a little initiative, will you?

She hung up which, I guess, was a means to an end. Not the most original way to solve a problem, but effective. My relationship with Fanny, like her Cretaceous cousins and The Comfy Chair, was beyond repair. It was extinct. To remind her of this I disassembled the remaining fossilised pieces and left them on the floor of her office, like an administrative archeological dig.

By doing this, of course, I had committed one of the classic blunders.

Never get involved in a land war in Asia.

Fanny would become my Vietnam. The Comfy Chair, an intra-office Tet Offensive that would echo throughout the occupation.

I'd like an employee review form, Fanny.

No one in your team is up for review. Why do you want a form?

I want to recommend them for a pay raise.

No one in your team is due for a raise.

I know. They've been doing some nice stuff. Working hard. I think I can get them one. I need a form so I can take my proposal to management.

Who?

It doesn't matter *who*. It's none of your business *who*. I don't have to explain who to you. Just put your hand in that fucking draw and get me a fucking form.

No.

This sort of thing would happen at least once a month, every month, for years. I'd made another of the classic blunders.

Never go against a Chinese woman when protocol is on the line.

Lovitz was embarking on a crusade of his own. Making a push for global domination. The first phase was on the Australian Front. AJ and I thought he was being was really selfish, putting himself and his family and his career before us. We'd miss him and his wife. A lot. We hadn't made many of our own friends. They all seemed to be incubated by someone else and we'd just end up getting them too. Like a virus. AJ had Sarah. I had Baldrick. We had Lovitz and his wife, The Duchess.

He offered me the keys to his Nissan 280ZX. The Fair Lady, as it was known in Cantonese. Probably because Big Cunt was already taken. Whatever colour it used to be, The Fair Lady was now banana yellow. No doubt this was done at the *feng shui* man's behest. The interior had been refurbished with red vinyl. It was one of the most hideous things I'd ever seen. So, naturally, I had to have it. Lovitz was practically giving it away. The first six months of parking was going to cost more than the vehicle. Besides, his leaving had paved the way for my next promotion and pay raise.

Richard Tong. Group Head. $45,000 a month.

This now meant, in theory, there were more people in The Agency who had to pretend to listen to me than those who didn't.

One of my first responsibilities was the important matter of Lovitz's farewell party.

Baldrick, Mulder and a few surviving members of the Fuck Friday Club went on a tour of Wan Chai bars. They weren't really strip clubs and they weren't really brothels. They were a semi-hygienic hybrid. Young Filipinas and Thais, clad in colourful leotards straight out of Jane Fonda's Workout, danced on small stages against a backdrop of mirrors. The look was about fetching as a nun's habit and harder to pull off than a Sister's wimple. Only Jamie Lee

Curtis had ever really managed to do it with a degree of sexuality, in Perfect. Decorous dancing was a feature of their regime too. Occasionally they'd gyrate against a pole with porn-star gratification. For $300 they'd come and talk to you in pidgin English. This was guaranteed to be fifteen of the most tedious minutes of your life. Fork out between $2,000 and $4,000, depending on the time of night or how recently the US Navy had been through town, and you could go beyond the velvet curtain. For the price of a beer you could just sit there and be a bloke. And look. And try not to look like you're looking. Despite the suspicions, fears and accusations of significant others, there was always more of the latter going on in these human petting zoos.

Wan Chai was really nothing to get excited about.

I got drunk and tumbled out of Country Club 88, or Club Hawaii or The Firehouse or Club Whatever, quite early. In the morning.

Planes weren't the only modes of transport that had begun to cause me grief. Taxis, busses, trains and lifts were all modes of tranxiety. Shouldn't it have started slowing down by now? I'd ask myself, or anyone unfortunate enough to be plummeting to their death with me in a hellevator. I'd brace myself and bend my knees in anticipation of impact. This would prevent my limbs from telescoping through my body. Sometimes I'd recite a passage of high-school German, out loud, for the benefit of my fellow passengers. To distract us all from the impending doom.

In other news... at least seven women were raped and three killed by a man in Tuen Mun. One victim lay dead in a stairwell for hours. 43 neighbours stepped over her before someone called the police... A woman killed and dismembered her lover's wife with a cleaver, then doused the limbs in alcohol and set them on fire... Suspected of having an affair with a Mainland woman, a man was killed and cooked by his 57 year-old wife.

ALL THREE LIFTS were out of order. As much as I disliked elevators I hated stairs more. I gave serious consideration to camping out in the lobby until repairs were made, except the floor was covered by a thin sheet of water. If I wanted to sleep, and I did, I had to climb.

A small stream cascaded down the stairs as I ascended Tai Koo's K2.

It dawned on me, somewhere between the 13th and 14th floors, that perhaps a fire had recently been extinguished. The air had been burnt. It was smokey and damp. One of the old pyromaniacs in our building had probably let her offerings get out of hand. Maybe management would listen to me know, before those superstitious firebugs were the ruin of us all.

My interior monologue became audible muttering as I continued to make my way up the north face of Mount Unpleasant.

I should've slept in the car. That's what I should've done. I could've just tipped the seat back. Why didn't you think of that? It would've been nice in there. No broken elevators. No waterfalls. It's got a radio. I could've played music and everything. I'd be asleep by now.

The nineteenth floor was inches-deep in water. The walls were carbon-dated. I left the stairwell and found a burnt-out flat. I walked around, inspecting the damage. Looking for things. Clues. Stuff. Whatever. I didn't know what I was looking for.

Who does?

I lit a cigarette. Surveyed the scene. Kicked over some wet, charred furniture and continued on my way. I would submit my preliminary report to Management in the morning.

I fell into bed, barbecue flavoured, and kissed AJ on the forehead. She said something about me smoking too much and rolled over.

Most nights I fell asleep in front of the television.

I'd wake at three or four in the morning and find AJ had gone to bed, alone, not wanting to wake me. I'd kid myself this was because I just looked peaceful and too darn cute to disturb. Truth be told, I could be a grumpy bastard if woken in the middle of a sleep cycle. Many times she'd witnessed the terror evinced if I awoke to find someone standing above me. Even the most gentle hand on my shoulder, unannounced, could induce a startling, near-violent response.

It wasn't her fault.

It was just one of things I didn't really feel like going into, if you want to know the truth.

One night I was roused by the sound of crying. Nothing hysterical. She wasn't sobbing or anything. It was just some shallow, shaky breathing. Only a few tears. Of course there's nothing *just* or *only* about that to a woman, or anyone with a beating heart. Guy Logic, however, is calibrated against a sliding scale.

I asked what was wrong.

She accused me of having an affair and preferring to sleep on the couch than with her. This wasn't true but I could see how she might arrive at that conclusion. Sleeping on the sofa, three or four nights a week, might lead the jury in that direction. Maybe she was right. Maybe I was having an affair. With myself. With work and my selfish pursuits. The cooling of our jets could be presented, circumstantially, as Exhibit B. The further our journey had gone the less active we become. It didn't mean I was any less in love.

Did it?

Few relationships maintain the ferocity that accompanies those initial explorations and discoveries. The exhilarations of The New. The comfort of strangers. As time marches on we find other attractions in each other's funhouses. There was no less intensity in those acts of passion, there was just less frequency. They were more spontaneous. Clumsier. Fumbling, fast and fierce. Precipitous peaks and protracted troughs. It was just the way it was, for everyone.

Wasn't it?

Some might say leaving the special Pamela Anderson issue of Playboy lying around didn't help. I didn't think she'd mind. We'd laughed at CJ Parker every time she bobbed up on Baywatch. It had lead to many discussions on the evolution of popular culture, and how far the revolutionary concept of using women in swimsuits to attract primetime viewers had come since Charlie's Angels. I thought AJ might be curious to see how Pam stacked up, in the flesh. Girls in the office could be more breast obsessed than boys. Some wore theirs as a badge of honour. Best Boobs In The Agency was a coveted, keenly contested title. Ana had told me. Such things were deliberated, openly, with puerile glee. This, of course, was one of the most stupendous examples of Guy Logic ever. It was probably not the first time I had misjudged AJ's interests either. Still, it was a minor error. A storm in a D-cup. It would blow over.

Wouldn't it?

Don't you worry, it's gonna be alright,
I'm always ready, I won't let you out of my sight.

The physical side of a relationship was important to AJ. I might not have had a need for intimacy and to feel loved but she did.

Pandas put out more often than me, she quipped.

Oh.

I was a little surprised by her attitude. We'd known each other, intimately, for years. And yet I didn't know this. Do we ever really know anyone and what lurks beneath the surface? Magazines and sitcoms had led me to believe a woman's hierarchy of needs was codified differently.

I thought trust and commitment was most important.

Yes, she tacitly agreed. A commitment to sex. Trust me.

What about listening?

Listening goes hand in hand with sex. Try getting some if you don't.

Sense of humour?

A prerequisite to having sex with most men.

I was sorry I'd made her feel that way. I didn't know she wanted to have sex with most men. Or that she equated sex with love. In my observation it was more of a substitute for love than an expression of it. A tender act of violence. A primal urge. Love and sex often intersect but it's hard to quantify or qualify one by the other. The absence of sex is not an absence of love. Sometimes it's more about what you don't do than what you do. We'd gone beyond carnal ticks, crosses and tallies.

Hadn't we?

If love was about trust, then I guess it's fair to say I had trust issues.

It wasn't her fault.

Betrayal is often the price of confidence. And I'd paid it. An unexpected, unsolicited act in my formative years had framed my views. They'd been corrupted at a critical stage in my development. It was an experience that would subconsciously govern my attitudes, skew behaviours and accompany me through life.

If you want to know the truth, if you really want to hear about *it*, the first thing you'll probably want to know is where *it* was, what happened, and all that other David Copperfield kind of crap, as Holden Caufield called it.

If you want to know the truth.

I was making plans for my first sexual encounter. I went to The Clinic to make sure there was nothing wrong with me. I didn't know you had to have sex to catch a sexually transmitted disease. I'd been told they could be picked up from toilet seats. AIDS was rife in the 80s, the scourge of underpants everywhere. People could get it from kissing, they said. Or just touching someone, down there. The unknown known was not going to cock-block me. I was going to prove how clean I was.

First-mover advantage, Kurt called it.

The waiting room, and its attendant horrors, had me feeling dirty on arrival. Guilt by association in a public petri dish. Any relief I might have felt, when The Doctor called my alias, was short-lived.

I confided in him. Confessed my private agenda. The virgin purpose of my visit. He grinned, I thought, sympathetically. My naïvety. He took blood. He asked me to remove my clothes, behind the screen. I disrobed. I waited. Awkward. He stood before me. Sensed my trepidation. Placed a stethoscope on my breast. Auscalation. Cough. Turn. Cough. Face me please. Let's see. He studied, grinned and sensed my dread. He grabbed me with his glove. Cough, he said. Again. A frown. He pointed to the bench. Lie down.

I had no gown.

Recumbent. Prostrated. I waited. Exposed. He tapped my chest. Two fingers. Percussive investigation, I guess. My body, not too shoddy, he said He probed my abdomen. Palpated organs. Then took the exploration south. I shut my mouth.

Hernia scars, there they are. A curiosity, under scrutiny. One each side, his fingers glide. Effaced, now traced. I'm red in the face. A bridge too far. He's overreaching. Breaching. Boundaries transgressed. Nervousness becomes uneasiness. Anxiousness. Is this what I should expect? Humiliation. Mortification. I closed my eyes. No escape. A kind of rape. Quiet violence. Suffer in silence. Palms on pelvis. Caressed. Pressed. Glands, in his hands. Lifted. Shifted. Shafted. First-mover. Disadvantaged. He breathed. Squeezed. Pleased himself. Misappropriation. Mocking his Hippocratic Oath with a slick hypocritical simper. Traction. Reaction. His self-satisfaction. Unnecessary protraction. I was fifteen going on sixteen, I had a lot to learn. Totally unprepared. Timid, shy and scared. Peeled, pinioned and compressed. Wretchedness. I wrung my eyes, gritted my teeth. Screamed in my chest. How much further would he take these tests?

Physician, heal thyself.

Fear. A tear. I wept. He stopped. Stepped away. Enough for today. Cold. Clinical. Detached. Undone. I dressed, cloaked in shame. Will I have to see him again? Dismissed with a smile. Come back in a while. Or call. We'll give you the result.

It wasn't AJ's fault.

I hadn't told her. I hadn't told anyone. It was my cross to bear. I bottled the indignity and cellared it for decades. The stigma of debasement. Oak-aged, wood matured. It's not the sort of thing you uncork and pour on a first date at The Sunflower. If not then, when? The more you know a person the less you want to talk about it. You don't want them to pity you and you don't want them to patronize you. Even if it helps them understand you they'll never understand. And they'll try to make you feel good about it.

Everything happens for a reason.

Really? It must be a hell of a fuckin' reason. An absolute beauty. Tell me, what justifies the molestation of a minor?

It's awkward for everyone. It changes the way they see you. Damages their view, the way it's distorted yours.

You're not the person I thought you were.

Neither am I.

Green screens, sliding doors. A fork in the road. I turned away, from everyone and everything. All that might've been, that could've should've would've been, died then and there. I withdrew, socially and academically. Disengaged. Departed. I hid it and hid from it. I observed my own life from dark shadows. I left as soon as I was able. Went as far as I could without leaving the country. I got into the Performing Arts so I could become someone else for a living. I fled to The East, part romantic notion part self-preservation. An attempt to elude the past on the other side of the earth. To lose myself in the maddening crowd and start again. I dove into advertising. I manipulated the truth and inhabited lies for a living. Repackaged and rebranded myself. Same shit, different wrapper.

It wasn't AJ's fault.

I was passive when it came to intimate affairs. That's how they were first defined for me. My notions and associations had been adulterated. Doctored. Innocence taken, not shared. Manifested in abashment, ignominy and discomfiture. Relationships were random encounters. Vehicles of convenience, taken or missed with indifference. Desire was a streetcar. And I was Kowlaski and DuBois.

I have always depended on the kindness of strangers.

It's easier to engage people you don't know. You don't have to worry about their feelings. You're the centre of the universe and self-gratification is the sun. Things change once you get to know them. Once you start to care. Familiarity doesn't breed contempt. It begets contretemps. What if she isn't in the mood? Will it upset her? Anger her? Make her think you didn't consider her feelings? Were you being selfish? Violating her personal space? My yen to please was greater than the need for pleasure. Where to start, how to play a part? Let her take the lead and make the first move. Wait for an invitation. Just in case. Wouldn't want to arrive unannounced. It was Guy Logic in reverse. Inverted. Perverted. A bastardised Madonna-whore complex.

Like a virgin, touched for the very first time.

This wasn't what I had in mind, back then, as I packed my bags in preparation of my maiden voyage. I should've been holed up in a comely cabin, not having my barnacles scraped and bilge pumped by the midshipman. A splintered crate of psychological freight was piped aboard instead, to be hauled across the oceans for eternity. A dead man's chest aboard The Flying Dutchman. There would be no yo-ho-ho and bottle of rum for me. Ever.

Ne'er turn your back on the sea.

AJ and I had embarked on many a salacious sortie and regular amatory razzias. We'd pushed the boat out and rode her undulating waves home. Deplaning upon her shores, at times, could create anxiety. Moments of awkwardness and indecision. *Don't just do something, lie there.* It could be the silent terror. Echoes of the past creep up on you, like the stalker who watches you sleep. Or the silhouette standing over you when you awake. The unannounced hand on your shoulder. A stranger in your comfort zone. *Déjà vu.* The flashback. *Déjà you.* It wasn't something you talked about with people you loved. Or with people you wanted to love you. If you want to know the truth. It was information divulged on a need-to-know basis. And nobody needed to know.

Did they?

I wasn't the type to make excuses. I didn't owe anyone an explanation or an apology.

Did I?

It wouldn't have made any difference.

Would it?

You're not the person I thought you were.

Neither am I.

Her birthday was approaching. I browsed the racks at Intimate Apparel and Woman's Privates in search of lingerie, for her. Ladies regarded men inspecting their undergarments with suspicion. Especially if they were still wearing them. Here, attendants giggled and whispered in tongues as you contemplated racks of underclothes. Small things amuse small minds. If they didn't take it seriously, why should I?

New Arrivals. Bio-ceramic Health Panties.

To the naked eye there seemed little to distinguish them from regular health panties. Or panties in general. How little I knew about knickers.

Treated with the highest quality flavour, the pleasant flavour will accentuate your decency. They are specially processed to expedite metabolism in the dermal structure. The anti-sperm material is contained, restricting dissolution of air-repellent materials from sweat or skin and remove bad odour. They have prominence on the fibre surface which depresses the cell in chiropractic practice.

Hard to believe they were only made from 100% cotton.

Typhoon Dot crashed the party and placed us all under house arrest. Cruel and unusual sentences were metered out in the form of Dolph Lundgren movies. The Punisher. Universal Soldier. Red Scorpion. A repeat of the previous year's Miss Hong Kong Beauty Pageant broke the monotony. AJ reminded me The Alphabet Babes were in there, somewhere. Miss A, B, C, D and E. We wondered who looked most capable of performing gratuitous sex acts. She stood and opened her robe. Revealed her bio-ceramics. Did they accentuate her decency? What did they do for her dermal structure?

Expedite me.

I didn't want to be the kind of person that had to be asked twice. She'd made her point. I pandered to it and drove it home.

What was so hard about that?

I couldn't explain it to her. I didn't understand it myself.

Betrayal is the price of trust.

My tax bill arrived. It was my first. They'd forgotten about me the year before. I'd earned so little I wasn't worth assessing. They'd let me fall through the fiscal cracks. Worthless in their eyes too. At first I thought there'd been some kind of mistake. I asked The Agency's Finance Director to look at it. She said it seemed about right, although she could've still been pissed-off about the Lucky Draw. It wasn't unusual for the Government to hit you for two years on your first bill, and demand you pony up a percentage for the year ahead. Provisional Tax it was called. Probably because it meant you couldn't buy any provisions once you paid it. Two and a half year's tax in one hit.

I hadn't saved a cent.

I had to take out a tax loan. It took a year to pay off. By then I had another bill to deal with. So I took out another loan. And the cycle of debt began.

Money's too tight to mention. Repeat ad infinitum.

The Empress Dowager was not alone in looking for ways to reap financial rewards and curry favour with the powers that be. She made sure she took us with her. By her command, and royal decree, The Agency was charged with producing propaganda in support of Beijing's bid for the 2000 Olympics. We placed ads in the paper.

Beijing 2000!

We knocked up leaflets and other distributable paraphernalia. We excavated, blocked and mounted a Terracotta Warrior. Then sent it to Switzerland. A timely reminder for the IOC.

Beijing 2000!

Apart from a few people out by the Kazakhstan border, there wasn't anyone who cared less about The Olympics than I. Yet it was hard not to identify and commune with the red faces in Beijing, as jubilation turned to disappointment, when they realised Australia had won.

Sydney 2000!

I'd barely settled into my ergonomically superior chair when The Empress arrived to congratulate me and my fellow countrymen on our victory.

Well done. It was a good fight, she said, shaking my hand violently.

Had I been successfully integrated, or begrudgingly accepted? I was my own Myth Of Sisyphus. Pushing that boulder of approbation up the hill. And, still I had such a long way to go. Coleman had nailed it. I was a necessary evil. Not Chinese, not *gweilo*. A writer. The expensive writer. Something to sabotage at every opportunity. I'd be invited to attend, but never welcome. Often ignored. People were polite in a way that let me know what they really thought. I was there because someone said I could be. If I tried to fit in I'd be laughed at. If I didn't, I'd be laughed about. Whenever I was feeling good, when I least expected it, something would happen. And, just like that, I'd be reminded of what I knew all along.

I didn't belong.

It's what made a part of me want to leave. And a big part of me want to stay. To outlast. To out-stare. To achieve, despite the chances of success.

Lovitz offered me a job in Australia. A way out. And I declined. I wasn't done, yet. I had something left to achieve. I just didn't know what it was. This was no time to retreat.

I attacked a women in the 7-11.

I assaulted her with a hot dog. Like Michael Douglas in Falling Down, only with pork products.

I was in a good mood. I'd just been to the petrol station. I got a tank of gas, two complimentary boxes of tissues and a free bottle of water. I stopped by the 7-11 to celebrate. With a hotdog. For some it was Dom Pérignon. Moët & Chandon. A Rolex. *A crown for every achievement.* For me it was hotdogs. They were my Whammy Burger.

I zapped it and unwrapped it.

The ketchup bottle was empty but I knew where the reserves were kept. I'd seen her put half a dozen bottles beneath the tucker-fucker a few days before. She knew I knew. She knew what I was looking for. She'd sold me the hot dog. I was holding an empty ketchup bottle. What else would I have wanted? She ignored me and hid behind the language barrier.

Don't just do something. Stand there. Outlast, out-stare.

The events of the next ten minutes gave a lightning performance in the theatre of my mind. A flashback from the future. I could see what was about to happen but was unable to avoid it. I was sucked slowly, steadily toward it.

These were the droids I was looking for.

I picked up the empty bottle. I looked at it and looked at her. I smiled. I held up the bottle and gave it a shake. I placed it on the stainless steel counter.

She blanked me.

I held up the hotdog and the empty bottle. I pointed to the cabinet beneath the microwave. She gave me The Look. Apathetic. Unsympathetic to the cause, to the core.

Desperate to avoid an incident, I sought out a mediator.

Every Kwik-E-Mart has one. The guy who's ready and willing to give his twenty-cents worth. And there he was, my knight in shining Armani. I asked him to ask the lady, in Cantonese, to get some ketchup. Tell her it's in the cupboard under the microwave.

He did. She shook her head.

Tell her it's there. Under the microwave.

He did. She shook her head.

I said it was.

She shook her head.

I saw her put six bottles in there yesterday.

She gazed out the window.

Fearing union reprisals, my confrere at the counter went out in solidarity. He surrendered his neutrality and turned away.

I took a deep breath, swallowed my pride and, hotdog in hand, moved toward the door. There was ketchup and mustard in the fridge at home.

Forget it, Jake. It's Chinatown.

I had a change of heart at the door. What I had at home didn't mater. This was in a convenience store. And I deserved a little convenience. If she wasn't going to even try and provide some, she had to accept the consequences.

I threw the hotdog at her.

Not too hard but it was no underarm girl-throw either. It bounced off her shoulder. The sausage separated from the bun.

I was gone before it hit the floor.

When the doorbell rang, two hours later, I thought it was AJ. She often forgot her keys when she went to the gym. I opened the door and was greeted by two cops instead. Great. I was going to be arrested for assaulting a woman with a wiener.

Mr Lee?

Er, no.

When will he be back?

I don't know. I don't know Mr Lee.

Mr Lee is living here?

Mr Lee is not.

This was Mr Lee's last known address. They wanted to speak with him. He'd been selling other people's televisions. They apologised for interrupting.

No problem, I replied. Sorry about the hot dog thing.

What hot dog thing?

Never mind.

In other news... property speculation became Hong Kong's number one leisure activity when real estate deals topped $53 billion for the month... 28 property agents from rival companies assaulted each other with meat cleavers and clubs... Mainland bandits engaged in a fire-fight with police on Nathan Road. Eight people were injured. Two of the robbers were shot dead as they tried to escape, in a taxi... Colourful triad boss, Andalay Chan, was shot dead in Macau... Fire in a Shenzhen toy factory killed 87.

I WAS STANDING AT OUR WINDOW, wondering what had happened to Fei-fei. I looked out, across the expressway, at the harbour. Two cars had stopped in the left lane below. A minor collision. The other lanes began to fill, as cars and trucks slowed down. The approaching motorcycle had no idea what was waiting for him around the bend. By the time he did he had no time to react.

Look out! I shouted pointlessly.

He'd never hear me with that helmet on, from 27 flights above. Even if he could he was going too fast to do anything about it. All he could do, when he finally saw his fate screaming toward him and 100kph, was lay the bike over and slide toward it.

Unofficial Urban Street Luge Champion of Tai Koo Shing.

The manoeuvre slowed him down, a little. It wasn't enough. The bike shattered upon impact with a car. His helmet flew as he hit the rear bumper and slid under the vehicle. I was on the phone to police as people got out of their cars. A man walked over to the helmet. I was giving my details when I realised it wasn't the helmet that had drawn his attention. It was its contents.

The rider had been decapitated.

Whacked right out of his skull man. He ain't never comin' back. You better send a Meat Truck. Charlie's copped a saucepan in the throat.

The sun stopped shining on the Chairman of China Light And Power shortly after. Our regular service was not affected. Still, a period of darkness settled over our corner of the Island.

It was a shadow from which AJ and I would never emerge.

I've seen fire and I've seen rain.

I've seen sunny days that I thought would never end...

But I always thought that I'd see you again.

We were on our way to see James Taylor. Live! In concert! AJ knew her way around that part of town. I didn't. We waited at the intersection, with 157 others. There was a break in the traffic. As good as being given a green light. A girl beside me took three quick steps onto the road. And disappeared.

The life got knocked out of her at 120kph.

In that brief moment of collision I saw a final breath leave her lungs. The soul vacated the body. Her legs went out from under her. The slap of her head on the bonnet obscured by the shriek of rubber tearing on bitumen. The car's windscreen cracked as it collected and ejected her. The lifeless body sailed on its final, pathetic arc through the air ,and flopped onto the road like a sack of axe handles.

The blood drained from AJ's face. A silent scream hung in her mouth. Her hands reached to catch it. I threw an arm around her and spirited her to a small park. I sat her down. And tried to hold her together.

She fell to bits.

Sweet dreams and flying machines in pieces on the ground.

When are we going to leave?

Everyone had asked us that question. More than once. And the answer had always been the same.

One day. Soon. I don't know.

I'd never really had a plan, for anything. I didn't think AJ had much of one either, except to maybe get married one day. Another of those things we never discussed, like kids. Everyone just assumed we would, one day.

When are we going to leave?

I'd never been asked by AJ. The way she said it didn't sound like a question. It was a request. A plea.

When are we going to leave?

I got promoted. Richard Tong. Associate Creative Director. $60,000.

Who'd want to leave?

In other news... Boris Yeltsin stormed into Russian parliament with tanks and guns blazing... Mandela and De Klerk shared the Nobel Peace Prize for giving black South Africans the right to vote... Anson Chan became Chief Secretary. The first non-expatriate to do so... Terrorists tried to bring down the Twin Towers of New York's World Trade Centre.

A CONSTRUCTION LIFT on the building site opposite the office plunged seventeen floors. Twelve died. Photographers swarmed into The Agency's reception to get a better view of the carnage. They took photos from the boardroom.

The *feng shui* was bad on our block.

Anyone who occupied the corner desk would leave within a year. My theory was based more on the power of suggestion than the flow of *chi*. Whoever sat there had a view of the airport. Departures. They'd see planes taking off, day after day. Every five minutes. The message being delivered was *take off.* I only ever seemed to see incoming flights.

Arrivals.

One afternoon I looked up as a plane hit the tarmac late and kept right on going. Straight off the runway, into the drink. Police boats swarmed. Helicopters hovered.

For a while my fortunes were arriving in slightly better shape.

In addition to a pay raise and the promise of a healthy end-of-year bonus, I won a $600 hair treatment in the Christmas party Lucky Draw. Fate was indeed smiling upon me. Although happiness, as has been said before, never stays long in the one place. When I offered the voucher to AJ she insisted I redeem it. The *feng shui* man had said it was important to get a trim before Chinese New Year.

Shorter was better when it came to Hair Luck.

A communication breakdown at the salon resulted in shear tragedy. A fatal blow to my follicles. The mullet was massacred. Cut down in its prime. I looked up from the pages of Hello! Magazine as the last of my heroic locks shuffled off their mortal coil.

How like a winter hath thy absence been
From thee, the pleasure of the fleeting year!
What freezings have I felt, what dark days seen!
What old December's bareness everywhere!

The decapitation made my head eleven kilos lighter. It took days to adjust to the sudden loss in weight. I flicked my head getting out of the pool, expecting to send a thick swathe of saturated mane into a majestic arc, and gave myself whiplash.

Gone, flitted away,
Taken the stars from the night and the sun
From the day!
Gone, and a cloud in my heart.

Sarah didn't recognise me when we arrived at her apartment for Christmas lunch. She thought I was someone else. I put it down to wishful thinking. We gifted her a thoughtfully selected, hand-painted ceramic vase.

She gave me a jar of nuts.

I met a photographer. You could see her work in the weekend edition of The Paper. She was responsible, amongst other things, for the social pages.

We interrogated, in depth, a list of the local glitterati. We ranked them in order of hideousness and took our findings to the court of public opinion.

Votes were tallied over lunch.

The Snapper claimed to have invented #3. She'd noticed her at a few functions, yet no one knew who she was. A lone satellite, orbiting celestial bodies. Out of boredom The Snapper conducted an experiment, to see if she could turn a nobody into a somebody. It was a Pygmalic quest that involved nothing more than taking #3's picture and placing it in the paper. Every week. Captions were punctuated with adjectives like enchanting, delightful, charming and radiating. Nothing succeeds like excess.

It was a pleasant day and perhaps the most normal Christmas we'd had for years. Remarkable for how unremarkable it was.

It was the last I would share with AJ.

Was I a post-modern Samson, and AJ my my my Delilah? Was a man without a mullet half a man, or not even a man at all?

The game was afoot and, not for the first time in my life, the best man for the job was a woman.

Sarah had bought an apartment in Sydney. AJ was welcome to stay there anytime, for as long as she wanted. Recent observations suggested it would be sooner rather than later. If it hadn't been determined already.

You can tell when a place is starting to grate on someone. There are signs. Like when AJ came home from the local supermarket and told me how good she was at kneeing little kids in the head. She'd grown weary of them charging blindly around the aisles, unchecked, like it was a playground. There was barely room for a trolley to get by. She'd give them a complimentary lesson in retail etiquette. A short sharp jab from her patella into whatever *les enfants terribles* were leading with at the time. Forehead. Chin. Shoulder.

Clean-up in aisle seven!

The expiration date on the city was rapidly approaching for AJ. She knew if she left it to me we'd never get off this island. She accepted Sarah's offer and went to Sydney. For a holiday. In search of opportunity. For us.

She went to check things out.

4. YEAR OF THE DOG

MANY COLLEAGUES LIVED WITH THEIR PARENTS. At least until they were married, and sometimes after.

Ana didn't.

She had an apartment in Kennedy Town. At the base of The Stairway To Hell. We'd practically been neighbours. Hard to believe, in a city of more than six million, we hadn't bumped into each other before.

She knew I was at a loose end while AJ was away and invited me over, for dinner. I assumed it was an office thing. Baldrick and a few others from The Agency would be there.

Wouldn't they?

I arrived with bottles of wine and cans of beer. The six-pack, with its circular tops clustered together in plastic rings, caused a brief moment of panic. We worked through it and managed to get them into the fridge without the need for further psychological counselling.

It was a bohemian pad, in a Canto way. There were bits of fabric draped over second-hand furniture and lampshades. Clean, white walls were punctuated by Doisneau prints and Alain Delon one-sheets. A book of Herb Ritts nudes was on the coffee table. Griffin And Sabine. The Sandman. A large plush pig lounged about. The room was lit by candles. This was a more romantic setting, compared to other Agency piss-ups. The Algonquin Round Table was only set for two.

I felt a little uncomfortable.

If Ana noticed it didn't seem to worry her. She handed me a beer. I watched her cook a variety of small dishes. Shrimp. Fresh, green vegetables. *Choi-sum. Bok-choi. Do-mui.* Fish. Pork. Rice. Soup. We ate and drank, Japanese style. On the floor.

Plates were cleared, the table pushed away and we lounged back against the sofa. Sade's silky tones floated through the room, suggesting all manner of languid activities. Kiss Of Life. Cherish The Day. Feel No Pain. No Ordinary Love. Ana had got turned on to these tunes after hearing the latter in a movie.

You know, the one where the stupid bartender from Cheers lets that old man fuck Bruce Willis wife for a million dollars.

I wasn't sure if Indecent Proposal was originally pitched to the studio that way, but it could have been how it was promoted here.

Not content with the level at which she was messing with my mind, Ana decided to open a small, lacquered *boîte Chinoise*. She pulled out a bag of electric puha and rolled a Camberwell Carrot. We gave the mighty Mezz a friendly nudge and got carpet bombed. A dozen games of Jenga were played. Ana allowed me to win all but two of them. She made hot chocolate and asked me if I wanted S'mores.

The S'mores the s'merrier, I replied.

This was found to be hilarious. We rolled about the floor, laughing, until our lips stuck to our teeth. We sucked on iceblocks and marvelled at their hidden properties.

Ana wanted to know if I'd seen Betty Blue.

Not recently. Does she live around here?

Alain Delon, fried on the frodis, smirked from the wall above. I guess he'd seen it too and knew where this narrative was heading.

The film opened with a fairly passionate display of horizontal folk dancing. I didn't need Freud to read me the subtitles. A miasmatic fugue of liquor, lula and angst-ridden French fornication closed in around us.

37°2 le matin.

Ana woke me at two in the morning. I groggily apologised for falling asleep and said I should probably go home.

If you have to, *gweilo*, you have to. But you don't have to.

I do, I said. It's been great. Thanks.

Next time you bring a toothbrush.

There comes a moment when the silence between two people can have the purity of a diamond

AJ returned. She enjoyed being back in Australia. She thought it would be easy to get a job there, with all the experience she had. Lovitz was running an agency in Sydney so, you know, it would be easy for me to find work too. She asked what I'd been doing. I said I'd been out to dinner a couple of times, with people from work. Which was true.

Wasn't it?

I never was much for fucking around, I never got much out of it. I know everybody else does it but it's no fun if you just do it like everybody else.

Baldrick and I were in Central. We left a client meeting and stepped onto the street. Some serious shit was going down. Police were everywhere. Bulletproof vests. Helmets. Most of The Landmark and entrances to the MTR lay sealed behind police lines.

Van Cleef And Arpels had been held up.

Big Spender, apparently, on another big spending-spree. The Peelers had been alerted before the gang could make their getaway. Streets and subterranean labyrinths had become a battlefield. Bandits opened fire with automatic weapons. A woman was killed. Four others were injured.

This type of thing was happening with alarming frequency. Was it one gang, or every gang getting a piece of the action before '97?

As the Handover drew nearer anxieties climbed higher. It had been five years since student protests in Tiananmen Square were crushed by the People's Liberation Army.

The wound had not healed.

I went to the June 4 candlelight vigil in Victoria Park with 49,999 others. It was encouraging to see so many people take a few hours to think about something other than themselves. Tiananmen and what happened there wasn't so far away anymore.

It was getting closer every day.

Why are you here? My city is in chaos because of you!

Not to be outdone by AJ and her fact-finding mission, I boarded a flight for The Land Of Opportunity.

San Francisco.

Ed was living there. We'd been to school together. Now we were going to New York, with a few dudes from his agency. Flying, unfortunately, had become one of my least favourite things to do. And my first long-haul across the Pacific was a traumatic, ten hours of turbulence. Cabin attendants were genuinely concerned for my emotional state and mental health. I arrived in The Bay Area in a very fragile condition.

I had jet-lag and Ed's punishing schedule of activities to contend with.

Art galleries. Microbreweries. Alcatraz. Pacific Heights. Haight Ashbury. Chinatown. No, really. Chinatown. In case I was feeling homesick. We drove up to Portland for an REM gig.

It's the end of the world as we know it.

I even squeezed a couple of interviews with ad agencies. Not bad for three and half days. I was hoping my in-flight anxiety would be as equally somnolent by the time we boarded the midnight horror to New York. Sadly, my irrational fears were compounded, with interest. Ed noticed. The way I clutched my manbag was a bit of a giveaway. Swilling dirty brown booze before we'd even left California's borders made it all too obvious.

Wash one of these Rohypnols down with it, dude.

I didn't remember changing planes in Chicago. By all accounts it was a relatively smooth transition. I did whatever I was told, like a well trained Labrador. When my faculties returned the first thing I saw was Manhattan Island. We were crossing the bridge and there it was. The Apple, stretching and yawning. Morning. New York, putting its feet on the floor. Just like Grace Jones said it would be.

We checked into The Paramount.

Ethan Hawke was milling about, on his own. He looked like he needed a shower. I offered to buy him a sandwich.

The Whiskey Bar beckoned.

It was hard to believe there could be this many good looking people in the world, let alone in one bar. In every bar and restaurant. On the streets and in the museums.

I would've traded them all for a hotdog.

They were on every corner. The *ne plus ultra* of hotdogs. The alpha dog. A simple three-biter. Soft, warm buns. Ketchup and condiments within easy reach. I'd buy one, walk a block and by the time I got to the next intersection, I was ready for another.

It was the best of times, it was the worst of times. It was the age of wisdom, it was the age of foolishness. The epoch of belief and the epoch of incredulity.

You could be anonymous on the streets, among the never-ending pageant of freaks. The city had a visual presence as imposing and impactful as Hong Kong, but on a bigger scale. Like a giant, living, breathing thing it was moody, passionate, dramatic, vain, proud and indulgent. Seven deadly sins and heavenly virtues rolled into one. It resonated in the head and heart.

It got under my skin.

We hired tuxedos and went to the annual adfest. Gongs were won. In no time at all I found myself ploughing through award-winning lines of cocaine. We crashed parties in penthouses and presided over proceedings in the kitchens. The masses were entertained. Drinks were mixed. Snacks were made. Australian accents were kicked into overdrive, amplifying our celebrity. Coke and booze annihilated any sense of propriety or reserve.

Two days later I awoke in my hotel room, heavy with the mephitic odours of spiritual putrefaction, hostage to the chronic paranoia, guilt and depression that inevitably result from such dizzy highs.

It was the season of Light, it was the season of Darkness. It was the spring of hope, it was the winter of despair.

The cumulative effects of wide-eyed tourism, sleep depravation and chemical imbalances on my swing-set of emotions and doubts were taxing. I'd get on the phone and tell AJ how much fun I was having. Then tell her how lonely I was. How much I missed her and wished she was with me. I'd flick mindlessly through channels at four in the morning. Infomercials, evangelists, hard-core cable porn. My companions were gym Nazis and God-botherers, chicks with doobries and doodahs.

Ed retreated to San Francisco.

I bunkered down, too depressed and brittle to make the interviews organised on my behalf. The phone would ring and ring. A dozen times in two hours. I never picked up the call. I was too tired, scared and heavy to answer. Housekeeping had been trying to get into my room but I wouldn't let them. They sent someone from hotel security to check. He couldn't get beyond the latch on the door. He was about to kick it in when I regained consciousness and warned him away, or Ethan Hawke would be the least of their problems. I'd had about as much of New York as my mind and body could take.

I took two Rohypnol. And flew home.

Home.

A scary thought. Yet that's what Hong Kong was starting to feel like. I was looking forward to seeing all the miserable faces at Kai Tak arrivals. Running the gauntlet to the taxi rank, looking like I knew what I was doing. Like I lived there. I'd speak to the driver in Cantonese to prove it.

Tai Koo Shing, m'goi.

Mostly I was looking forward to arriving safely. Escaping the sub-sonic cylinder of death. Seeing something and someone familiar.

In other news... a number plates inscribed HK1997 sells for $4.8 million... Patten's equally maligned and anticipated electoral reforms survive Legislative Council, by one vote. 29 to 28. Two counsellors, not wanting to participate in the democratic process, abstained.

IN MY ABSENCE from The Agency there had been a coup. A night of long knives. The Empress Dowager had been unceremoniously ousted. We'd all queried her sanity from time to time. Agency principals must have asked themselves a similar question. They'd arrived the day after I'd departed for New York. They came not to praise The Empress but to bury her. I guess we all had it coming and never knew whose hand would be on the hilt.

Et tu, Brute?

I was asleep on the couch when AJ returned from the gym. I pulled her close and held on tight. So happy, relieved, contented and conflicted I almost cried. We were *in flagrante* in seconds, much to Fei-fei's disgust. The dog acted like she'd never seen animals going at it before. Maybe she hadn't. This would be more educational than anything on the recently launched Discovery Channel. And her subscription was free.

You should go away more often, said AJ.

It was a throwaway comment, exhaled in the heat of the moment. I took it personally. I took it literally. I flew to Los Angeles.

I had beer commercials to shoot and long-haul hysteria to hone.

OJ Simpson was all anyone there wanted to talk about. Everyone said he did it and everyone knew he'd get away with it.

I went to The Comedy Store in search of laughs. They gave me a table by the stage. A request for something further back was denied. Full house. No one wants to sit this close. I offered to stand up at the back and was told, without a hint of irony, that was not possible.

You have to sit down for stand-up comedy.

When the first act came on I new why they'd placed me front and centre. The comedian kicked things off by asking me to call him a nigger. Like 99% of the audience that night, he was black. Call me a nigger, he said.

An enigma?

A nigger. Call me a nigger.

I couldn't. I wouldn't.

He continued to demand that I did. Three times. Call me a nigger. This, apparently, was comedy. I sat there, waiting to die. Everyone else thought it was hilarious. Eventually, when it became obvious I wasn't going to be part of the show, he stopped and looked me in the eye.

You damn right you not be calling me a nigger.

The house erupted in laughter. He continued with his act. A litany of OJ jokes. More comedians followed. They all worked the room with variations on the same black humour. I left. Mirthless. Scared shitless. Incredulous at how racially charged LA was. I didn't get that sense of The Great Divide in New York. Probably because I'd been too obsessed with myself. LA, however, was a constant reminder of how black was black and white was white and never the twain would meet.

New York, like Hong Kong, was a concentrated, organic being. You could see her moods changing and prepare for them.

LA was a sprawling mass of Hockney. It teetered on a giant banana lounge, loafing half-naked beside the pool. Tip the world on its side, said Frank Lloyd Wright, and everything loose would land in Los Angeles. It could change. Just like that. Without warning.

On the second day of the shoot, our feature model's ample bosom spilled from her dress. It's hard not to look when things like that happen. Regardless of how professional you're trying to be.

This was my first real encounter with augmented breasts.

They were like nothing I'd ever seen, or imagined. The laws of physics did not to apply to them. They were impervious to gravity. Judging by the welts that dominated the area beneath her nipples, they were freshly minted too. She seemed a good humoured, uninhibited, self-effacing sort. I got talking to her between takes, at the Craft Services table, over a low-fat, gluten-free, sugarless Mesopotamian donut and litre of diet soda. Ariel confessed to being a good church-going Christian, trying to keep it real and stay true to herself. I asked her what God might think of her surgical enhancements and how they sat with her keep-it-real ethos. She replied as earnestly as only a 23 year-old starlet can.

God had empowered and blessed her. He would want her to, like, totally do whatever it took to fulfil her dream.

The director, producer and I took both of her to dinner. A flash Beverly Hills eatery. Robert Duvall was sitting next to us with Rob Reiner.

Duvall.

The Consigliere. Tom Hagen. Lieutenant Colonel Kilgore. Bull Meecham. Frank Burns. Right there. Next to me. This was about as cool as seating arrangements were ever likely to get. Unless Christopher Walken joined us.

I went to the washroom and was standing by the urinal when he came in. Lucky Ned Pepper. We acknowledged each other with a nod, as latrine etiquette dictates in such situations.

How're you doing? he asked.

G'day. How's it 'garn?

I allowed him a brief moment of silence, while he got things underway, then told him how great he was in The Godfather. Tender Mercies. Mac Sledge. What was that song? Hard To Face Reality? The way he sang it. Cool. The Great Santini.

Glad you liked them.

Apocalypse Now is my favourite film. *It smells like... victory.*

Not in here, but thank you. Where you from?

Hong Kong.

Hong Kong? Shit, you don't look Chinese.

I told him I was from Australia. I was living in Hong Kong, working for an American advertising agency. We were shooting a commercial in LA, for a German Beer.

He thought that was hilarious. He wished me luck, washed his hands, and left before I could tell him about Colors.

Two cops. Two gangs. One hell of a war.

He was in the room when I first met AJ. Corporal Bob Hodges. He was there at the beginning of my one great love. When my Crips first tangled with AJ's Bloods.

Would he be there at the end?

Returning to Hong Kong, I misappropriated a cue from the Consigliere and decided AJ and I should get away from the heat at home. Take a time-out from the emotional turf war between. Have a sit down with the Five Families of our feelings and see if we could broker a peace. We didn't have a home on Lake Tahoe to escape to. I opted for a youth hostel instead. It was a three-hour walk from The Frog And Toad.

This was another spectacularly ill-judged leap of Guy Logic.

We took a ferry to Cheung Chau. A sampan spirited us to The Toad. We decided to stop by for a few drinks. Experience the place unencumbered by douchebags. In a lightweight backpack I carried toothbrushes, deodorant, a change of bio-ceramic underwear, a lighter, Bob Dylan's biography and a Swiss Army knife. Overnight essentials, capable of dealing with any situation.

What could go wrong?

It got dark. AJ suggested we make a move before it got too late. Of course, by then, I was confident of being able to find the hostel quicker and easier than anyone. We set off an hour later, down a very leaden path, without a torch. Just as I was telling AJ not to worry, assuring her we'd be there in no time at all, I stepped off the way. And disappeared into dank air.

I rolled twenty meters down a steep decline. It didn't scare me half as much as it did AJ. All she could hear, for twenty-three seconds, was moaning. When I made it back to the path she was in tears. I wasn't far off them myself. I decided it would be best if we walked back to The Toad and slept on their tables, under the stars.

It was closed and shrouded in darkness. Black and silent. Neither of us had the courage to wake anyone, or venture onto the property uninvited.

We can camp on the beach, sweetpea. Build a fire. It will be romantic. We can tell each other horror stories.

She said that wouldn't be necessary. She was already in one.

And it was about to get worse.

A pack of feral dogs began to follow us, as we walked the path through the rice paddies. They must have sensed our fear, or been in a predatory mood. We picked up the pace. They kept on our heels. We ran. They ran after us. They chased us to the beach and across the sand. We scrambled up a large, dome-shaped rock by the water. It was too steep and smooth for The Hounds Of Bastardville to get any purchase.

We sat in silence and reflected on our situation.

The dogs gave up. Some lay down and slept. Others skulked off to snigger at us from deep in the gloom. Mosquitoes arrived. Thousands of them. I sprayed the rock with Rexona, to mark our turf and ward off our assailants. It only seemed to inflame the insects. They attacked with renewed enthusiasm. I was sure I could hear dogs rolling around with laughter at the aerosol on the hill. It was going to be a long, quiet and Spartan night on the bedrock.

We sit here stranded,
Though we're all doin' our best,
To deny it.

When the sun peeked over the horizon it was obvious why the dogs had disappeared. The tide had come in. The rock was surrounded by water. We had to strip to our underwear, under the gaze of local fisher-folk, and wade ashore. I carried the clothes and the backpack above my head. The silence that followed was so uncomfortable it made the rock look like a pillow. Eventually a sampan arrived and, by noon, we were back in our small, silent apartment. Now even smaller, with extra silence.

The honeymoon was over.

Not even two hours with INXS could resurrect AJ's flagging spirits. They'd abandoned their mullets too, and were all the poorer for it.

AJ folded and fell onto the couch.

She was leaving. She was going to Sydney. A date had been set. There was so little in Hong Kong for her anymore. Just me. And she wasn't even sure about that anymore. The jig was up. The game was over. She'd made up her mind, she said. Although I was sure Sarah would have helped her with that too. First-mover advantage. Lawyers know a thing or two about that.

I wasn't ready to go, yet. I had to stay, I told her. Just a while longer. A few months. There were some things at work I wanted to finish. We went along with that and hoped it would be true. Even though we knew it might not be. Dylan knew the truth. He always did.

Let's call it a day,
Go our own different ways,
Before we decay.

I started looking for somewhere to live. AJ started packing. We both prepared for the inevitable in our own way. Some nights I'd hear her crying in the kitchen. She'd just be standing there, looking at a cup or a plate. A photo on the fridge door. I had no idea my inability to commit would be so devastating. For her, at first, but my turn would come. Eventually. Inevitably. I sewed the seeds and would reap the bitter harvest. Perhaps the most distressing aspect of those weeks was the cold detachment from which I observed them. I knew what was beating her up and I knew there was something I could do about it, to make it stop. I just wouldn't let me do it.

Oh well, whatever, never mind.

Kurt Cobain took a shotgun to his head and permanently relocated, rather than go on living with Courtney Love.

Oh well, whatever, never mind.

I watched our life get separated into piles. His and Hers. Staying and Going. Like it was someone else's stuff.

She had to go. Didn't she? She was miserable. Wasn't she? It didn't have anything to do with me. Did it? It was Hong Kong. Wasn't it?

My immediate objective was to minimise the pain. Get her packed up. Quickly. Cleanly. She seemed so sure of what she wanted.

Didn't she?

Maybe I had to find out if I wanted it too. Maybe it was time to find out what we both meant to each other. Did I think life would be better without her? No. I didn't even want it to be. I just wanted it to be different, for a while. I didn't know how long. Maybe I was hoping geography, or someone else, would make a decision for me. Dissolve at least one of those insoluble tensions that Kierkegaard had me sandwiched between.

All I knew for certain was I didn't want to stay on the 27th floor, alone with the memories. With Fei-fei reminding me every weekend of the mistake I had made. I didn't want to live on my own elsewhere either. A man is never in good company when he's by himself. And I couldn't take on a long-term lease. It wasn't that I had a growing fear of commitment. I just needed a place I could pack up and leave in a few months. If I had to.

Baldrick had a friend of a friend who was looking to share an apartment, in the Mid-levels. An air-hostess. She'd hardly ever be there. Maybe she could help me over my fear of flying too.

We met, in a bar.

She was an attractive Filipina. She had another attractive Filipina with her. They both flew for The Airline, and we were instantly cleared for take-off. I could see my airborne anxieties disappearing over the horizon.

Pull on the strap until the vest fits snugly. You can inflate the vest by pulling down firmly on the red tabs. Or it may be orally inflated by blowing into the inflation tubes as demonstrated by your in-flight crew.

They liked the idea of having a guy around the house. It would be would be good for the social dynamic. I wasn't sure what a social dynamic was, whether it came with the apartment or cost extra. I just thought, if I had to share an apartment, two pulchritudinous women with professional predilections for servility was a nice option. I didn't tell them I might only be there for a month or two. That sort of thing could sour negotiations and upset the social dynamic. The latter must have been as important as it was powerful. I didn't even have one and I was already worried about it.

Whatever it was, I'm sure we could accommodate it.

The apartment was all class. 2,500 square feet of Mid-level luxury. Wide-bodied, with three bedrooms. Liz wold be up the pointy end, in First. Florence would take Business and I'd be in Economy, hoping for an upgrade at The Airline's discretion. The living area was large, like an airport lounge. The kitchen verged on industrial. There was even a separate room for a maid. All for $45,000 a month, including parking for The Fair Lady.

Please ensure your seat backs and tray tables are in their full upright and stowed positions, your seat belts are securely fastened and all your carry-on items are securely stowed.

I might've been losing a girlfriend, but I was gaining a balcony and sweeping harbour views.

In other news... a China Airlines jet crashed, killing 160... Five people died when a retaining wall collapsed in Kennedy Town... A man was fatally speared in the chest by a metal pipe that fell off the awning of a fruit shop, selling durian, during a storm.

SHE WENT OUT IN STYLE. A final night at The Ritz. We escaped the insoluble tensions and truth of our future in a hot tub of affection. We found cold comfort in each other's embrace. We spread ourselves thin on fine cotton sheets and found passionate peace, languishing on a melancholy mattress of Moirai. We packed and parted with a promise of more to come. It was a break, not a break-up.

Wasn't it?

Truth is, it fractured my life. In breaking from AJ, I broke from myself, again. And fell into the void that churned in her wake.

A PART

I fought with my twin, that enemy within,
Til both of us fell by the way. Bob Dylan

YOU DON'T GO TO WORK. You don't call in sick. You stay in bed until 3pm. Not sleeping, just lying. Avoiding. You get up. Unpack boxes. All two of them. That's it. Three years of your life, compressed into a couple of cardboard boxes and a crappy suitcase. You sit on the couch and stare at the space where a TV should be. You moved in a week ahead of the girls. An advance party. A sortie, of sorts.

It's not going well.

Flatmate #1 arrives. She has more shoes than Imelda Marcos. It takes professionals half a day to put the essentials in place.

Liz brings sad tidings with her too.

Florence, your other hostess with mostess, will not be arriving. She's lodged a new flightplan and departed on an alternate runway. The will be no opportunity to go with the Flo'.

But who's going to help me with my jet-lag?

Liz tells you not to worry. She's found a replacement. A comely, noisy, Chinese substitute.

Daisy

It's a phonetic bastardization of her Chinese name. Da-ji. Many Western males would consider her to be a classic China Doll. A surrogate Suzie Wong. Slim. 5'6 or 5'7 in the nude. Slightly less when bending over in heels. Long black hair. Slits for eyes. Pert breasts. She speaks English in short, clipped sentences and probably goes off like an Exocet missile.

Daisy is Liz's new best friend forever. For two weeks.

Cracks in their relationship soon appear. You would've noticed them earlier if you hadn't been staring into your own, ever-widening chasm of disrepair. Set adrift from the responsibilities of a relationship, however, you dived into work and immersed yourself in bars. AJ was extending her hands across the water, pulling you toward The Fatal Shore. Her daily calls were a sober reminder of the life she left behind and what the future could still hold. Between the campaigns, hangovers and AJ's tears, it took a while to notice the change in the social dynamic of 6D.

Liz and Daisy are rarely seen together. One enters, the other leaves. They don't speak to each other. They communicate through you.

You ask Daisy what's going on. She confesses to accidentally stealing Liz's boyfriend.

Accidentally?

Daisy didn't know The Guy was Liz's boyfriend until it was too late. Neither did The Guy, apparently.

I guess we were all living under one delusion or another.

Liz's imaginary relationship came to end when she returned home from a flight, at three in the morning, and found Daisy giving The Guy a hand with his carry-on baggage.

Oh. One of those accidents.

It gets a little more complicated, admits Daisy, with mischief in her eyes. They were on a junk the week before. She was on the upper deck, flirting, with anyone and everyone. Liz was working below-decks. Piping The Guy aboard. Blowing the bosun's whistle. It was only after their carry-on confrontation that The Guy revealed all. It seemed he thought he could switch carriers, earn points on two loyalty programs and help himself to the in-flight service. Have the chicken and the fish, as it were.

Oh. One of those accidents.

I might be losing a girlfriend but I'm gaining a balcony, sweeping harbour views and built-in sociopaths.

Daisy thinks Liz isn't as pissed about The Guy as she is embarrassed. The prospect of people knowing she blew him in the brig would ruin the refined, elegant and urbane image she is attempting to cultivate. She comes home to find you and Daisy on the couch. Talking. Smoking. That's all. It's enough to steam her cookies. She knows, with a high degree of certainty, you've been told about her rollicking adventures with the able seaman. You raise your eyebrows comically, and smile phlegmatically, just to be sure.

Rumours bruit. Liz tells people Daisy is spreading herself about the apartment and sleeping with you.

Isabelle calls.

She wasn't the first but she was the first one that mattered. She was your first *girlfriend* girlfriend. You broke up with her to date AJ. She didn't take it too well. She showed you the error of your ways. She dated a couple of your friends and a few people you couldn't stand. A pretty effective strategy for anyone in the revenge caper.

Izzy wants to know how you are.

You tell her you're going great. She can tell you're lying. She always could. She says she has a new job. She's moving to Sydney.

You'll be there in a month or two, you say Maybe you'll be able to catch up then. It's been a while.

She sews the small talk with seeds of curiosity. AJ has been seen in Sydney. Is everything okay?

You tell her everything is fine. You sound like you're trying to convince yourself more than her.

You go back to work. To the bars. Filling the hole in your life. Feeding the hole within. AJ's long distance yearning is churning the void. Mind games are being played at home and abroad. Subdivided houses. Erratic views. Tenants. Tenets. Beauty is as mysterious as it is terrible, said Dostoevsky. It's unlikely he was talking about flight attendants or flatmates when he said it, but God and the devil are fighting there all the same. The battlefield is the heart of man.

Liz says Daisy wants a live-in domestic helper. An amah. A maid. You don't. Someone to come in a few days a week will be fine.

She agrees.

Daisy says Liz really wants a live-in helper. You tell her you know, but a part-time one will be fine.

She agrees.

They both think a full-time helper is unnecessary, yet they both tell you how much the other wants a permanent *au pair.* For two people that aren't speaking it's amazing how conversant they are with each other's thoughts. It's Yojimbo and Sanjuro on the sixth floor. A Fistful Of Domestic Helpers. The Good, The Bad And The Amah. Both ends being played against your middle.

Enter Maria.

For $5000 a month the 23 year-old Filipino gets to clean, cook, wash clothes and do your grocery shopping. On Saturdays, as a special treat, she can give The Fair Lady a wax. You'll even get her some driving lessons, so she can get a licence and take you to work, or pick you up from the airport.

Liz says Maria needs a uniform. A maid's uniform. Unless it's one of those French ones, you don't think it's necessary. Neither does Daisy. This is not a nursing home. Liz claims Maria would prefer to wear one. You think it's a bit of a colonial idea, more at home on a plantation than in a Mid-levels apartment.

Frankly, my dear, I don't give a damn.

Phone calls from Sydney are frequent. AJ sounds weak. You try to sound strong. Encouraging. Don't worry. You'll be there soon. Everything will be fine. She has a job, in advertising. Something you always thought she'd be good at. By all accounts she is. It was good of Lovitz to make it happen for her.

Home. I'll go home. And I'll think of some way to get him back. After all... *tomorrow is another day.*

A week before you're due to arrive in Sydney, a week before you're going to get on that plane and make everything right, it all changes. You can hear it in her voice. It's got spirit. Confidence.

Things will be different when you get here.

Different? How? What's changed? What will be different?

Just, you know, things.

Who is he? you ask.

Who?

The guy you're seeing.

I'm not seeing anyone. I've just been thinking, that's all. And I want you to know things will be different when you get here.

How different?

Just, you know, different.

Things are different now. Do you still want me to come down?

That's up to you.

Whoa.

Now it's your turn to feel weak and vulnerable. Days pass, slowly. Imagination eats you up. Insecurity moves in.

Things are going to be different.

In preparation for the flight, and life in general, you visit the doctor. He gives you a bag of Valium.

Things are going to be different.

Twelve year-old Sai-ming goes missing. He wanders away from his mother in a mall and somehow makes his way to the border. He has no ID card. He doesn't appear to understand what is going on. He doesn't speak Cantonese. He urinates on the floor. He throws food. Immigration officials think he's from China. They deliver him to their Mainland counterparts and he is released onto the streets of Shenzhen. Sai-ming isn't from China. Sai-ming is autistic.

DAISY'S SISTER is returning from London. She says you'll like her. You don't know why but you believe her. You've seen the pictures. You offer her the use of your bedroom. She can stay there while you're in Sydney, if she wants.

Who's been sleeping in my bed?

You take the long walk out across the Kai Tak tarmac, on the way to your apocalypse. You are Willard, going up the Nang River to terminate Kurtz's command, with extreme prejudice. What if you get there and find out you're also Kurtz?

Never get out of the boat. Unless you're going all the way.

The doors slide back and there she is. There it is. The smile you'd hoped for. How different could things be? The hug is warm. Reassuring. Comforting. So far so good. She drives through the quiet Sydney morning, in Sarah's car. We'd go for coffee, AJ says, but she has to get the vehicle back soon. Sarah needs it.

Sarah?

Yes.

When did she get here?

A week or so ago.

Oh.

You arrive at Sarah's place. Together, alone.

And you may find yourself, in another part of the world.

It's been raining. The air around the Botanic Garden smells fresh, clean and sad. Standing on the pavement you look up at Sir Walter Davidson's 1923 homestead. Grimwade House. It's an impressive, intimidating example of Federation architecture. Sarah obviously has a thing for colonial living. She bought the first floor. Straight from one British outpost into another.

You climb a polished flight of stairs and stand in the limbo of the lobby, wondering where to put you bag.

You can stay in my room.

Oh.

Is that okay?

Yes, of course. It's just, last time you said, you know, things were going to be different.

They will be.

They already are. You can feel it. They way she said it and smiled. Like she knows something you don't. She probably does. There's certainly something else there, in the bedroom. You can't see it but there's no mistaking it. Right there. Beckoning.

The future.

It's fifteen minutes from now. Fifteen days. Fifteen weeks. Months. It could be fifteen years. It's that big. You can't ignore it. There's no denying it.

Where did it come from and who was responsible?

Did you bring it down, like excess baggage, or did Sarah give AJ a hand carrying it up? It's taking deep breaths. It's growing. It's filling the room and pushing you out door. Out of the house and out of her life.

You may ask yourself, well, how did I get here?

There's voices in the kitchen. Whispering. AJ and Sarah. She's leaving tomorrow. She'll leave us to it. You wonder what she means by that. By *it*. What is *it* and why are we being left to *it*?

Things will be different.

You should make love to AJ, right now. Have sex. Fuck her, or whatever the young folks are calling it these days. Fill the void. Seal it forever. Put your flag in the ground. Claim it for king and country. Maybe that would change things.

Inspire a rude awakening, or demand a foreclosure. People need endings and sex seals relationships, one way or the other. Maybe that's all she wants. An ending. If religion is the opiate of the masses, sex is the opera. The theatre.

This could be our final act.

You lie down next to her that night and listen to her breathing. You want to hold her. Give her an ending worth remembering. You're too scared to touch her. You don't want to infringe. Impinge. You might fail the test.

Things are going to be different. She said so.

The vows that we kept are broken and swept,

'Neath the bed where we slept.

AJ works all week. You don't really see her. She's busy, she says. She gets home from the office late. And slips into bed.

You're a stranger in your own backyard.

You meet Lovitz. Go to the pub. Have a few beers. He asks how things are. How things are between you and AJ. You tell him you're not sure. They're probably not that great. You force a wry smile and tell him you're just waiting to find out who the guy is that she's been seeing.

Oh, they're not really seeing each other. They've just been out a few times. I don't think it's anything serious. He said he's waiting to see what you do. To see what happens.

He?

She didn't tell you?

He?

It's not supposed to be He. It's supposed to be She. He is supposed to be Sarah, talking her out of things. Telling her she deserves better. You'd prepared for that scenario and were almost willing to accept it. You'd put her off men for a while. There is no contingency plan for He. Christ. It's only been six weeks.

And you may tell yourself, this is not my beautiful wife.

You can't even talk to her about it, or demand an explanation. You head straight for the moral high ground and map out a claim. Prepare to dig in. Even though you knew this would happen. You allowed it to happen. You made it happen.

You just didn't think what it would feel like when it did.

It empties you, like the last day of a summer holiday. When you walk off the beach for the last time and know you can't go back tomorrow.

You get Lovitz to call AJ and tell her you're staying at his place.

It's a long night on the couch, chain-smoking cigarettes. Drinking whiskey. You hate scotch. Now you hate it with a passion. And punish it.

The sun rises.

You go for a walk and sit in the park. You're not really there. You're in Perth, at AJ's front door. You're swimming in her pool. You're climbing the spiral staircase to her room. You're picking her up from the airport. You're in Bali. You're walking toward her. You're lost in those eyes and warmed by the smile.

You're delusional. You're fucked and you know it.

You stand out the front of Lovitz's agency. Now it's AJ's agency too. And His agency. He's waiting, with her, to see what you do. To see what happens.

What are you going to do?

You walk the longest mile. The hard yards to the agency door. You stand in the foyer. The receptionist is looking at you, pitying you. She knows what's going on. They all do. They always do.

She's in a meeting.

Lovitz does his best to distract you, lunch and dinner, but AJ is everywhere and nowhere. You sleep on his couch, again. She's been here. Her fragrance is upon the leather.

Was He here too?

In the morning you change your flight. You call AJ and tell her you're leaving. Tomorrow. She's not really surprised. She'll take you to the airport in the morning. She wants to have dinner.

The last supper.

Dinner is quiet and strangely calm. Dead calm. She's sorry she didn't spend more time with you.

You say you're sorry too.

We all remember the moment love arrived. It's something we want to believe in. One clear moment of connection. Romantic. Singular. A mental Polaroid, on the fridge of life. Like AJ in a light blue t-shirt. Hair in a ponytail. Head slightly cocked to the right. There's a few freckles splashed across her cheeks and small, sunburnt nose. She's embarrassed. Self-conscious. Eyes deep and sad above a reluctant smile. That's your moment. When you knew.

You may ask yourself, am I right? Am I wrong?

Who remembers the moment of disconnection? When love breaks down and no one admits it. To each other or to themselves. When you know it's over. There'll be no more furtive, playful glances or kisses in the dark. Sharp breaths. Silky thighs. Silhouettes at the window. No more escalators or elevators. No more Baywatch on Saturday nights. No more Oops! before plates and glasses hit the floor. You've lost something. You've given it away and you can't have it back.

And you may tell yourself, my God, what have I done?
You're standing on the damp footpath. Waiting for her to bring the car around. It arrives and brings the chill of the wind with it. You look at your watch.
8:17am.
That's your moment. When you know.
Black day, in the coldness of winter.
She looks scared. Not of you, but for you. She knows. Your heart knows. Even the radio knows. Crowded House drives it home.
It's hard to let go, of all that we know, as I walk away from you.
She accompanies you to the gate. Immigration. You turn to her but can't find the words. Any of them. You stand there, gurning. She looks at you, helpless. She moves to console, to hug and embrace. You walk away.
Departures.

A gunman takes a woman hostage after a failed robbery. He attempts to flee in a taxi. Police open fire on the vehicle. Both are killed.

YOU'RE CATATONIC for the duration of the trip. Half a dozen Valium can do that to a man, when washed down with a duty-free litre of Olde Regret.
You drift through the apartment. There could be four or five people at the dining room table. You're not paying attention.
There's a suitcase on the floor by your bed. Clothes are folded neatly on the mattress. Singlets. A camisole. Bicycle shorts. French knickers. Tiny briefs.
Hi.
The voice is soft and warm. English. It comes out of nowhere and startles you. A sonic hand on the shoulder. You turn, too quickly. Fall over the suitcase. Drop your handcarry. Small fingers reach out for you, to steady you.
Ooh. Careful.
Little feet on the floor. Thin legs. Smooth arms. A soft smile. Sorry about the mess, she says. Daisy said you'd be back tomorrow. I was moving my stuff out. Chuck it on the suitcase if it's in the way. I'll pick it up it after dinner.
You cast uncertain eyes across the bed and back to her, not really comprehending the situation, befuddled by the bouquet of her charms. She scoots across and collects a pile of her smalls.
Maybe I'll take these with me now. Wouldn't want you putting them on by mistake. Thanks for letting me use your room. Hope I didn't leave too many stains on the mattress.

The offhand remarks go over your head. She narrows her eyes and makes another attempt to penetrate the haar in your head.

Richard?

Yes. Sorry. Hi. I'm, er, a bit, you know.

I'm Daisy's sister. Seizure.

Seizure? you query, unsure if you've heard correctly or it's just one of those lateral names Cantonese choose for themselves. Like Mucus or Wagina. Bile. Methyl. Creamy. Seizure doesn't sound so odd these days.

Yes, Seizure. As in the one you're having now. Xi-shi, she lambastes playfully. Look at my mouth. Xi-shi. Sounds like Zee-sher, or See-shur. Xi-shi. Call me Xi or Xi-xi, if that's easy-er. Or Seizure. I've been called worse things. Most people prefer to know a person's name before they get into their bed but with you I had to make an exception.

Sorry. Yes, you reply, confused by the dryness of her wit and full wetness of her lips. Daisy said you'd be here.

Rough trip was it? Are you hungry?

I'm fine, thanks. Maybe.

I'll put something on a plate for you, for later. If you want it. And, you know, you can put my things anywhere.

She leaves you there, stranded. Marooned. Beclouded behind the vallum and berm of impedimenta. You shower. You sleep, surprisingly easily. The slumber of the dead. Embalmed in scented sheets. A whisper of Xi remains in the valley of lost anima.

The next day, work is all questions. You have neither the capacity nor inclination to answer them. You hide behind a mountain of briefs, stepping carefully between the claymores and dodging barrages of salaried bullets.

A note is left for you at home. It's an invitation to join the sisters for dinner. A drink. You leave them to it. People like to be left to *it*. Whatever *it* is.

A pattern begins.

You hide in your office during the day. Take refuge in your room at night. Incommunicado. Your thoughts are clouded. Infiltrated. Her fragrance hangs in the hallways and corners. On your pillow. Chanel. Allure.

Xi. Xi-shi.

Liz is hardly ever home. You wouldn't notice if she was. You're preoccupied. You're organising your CD collection, *a la* John Cusack. Rob Gordon. High Fidelity. Autobiographical order. You start with Talking Heads. Stop Making Sense. And progress from there. You wonder how you got from Blonde On Blonde to Doolittle in twelve moves. If anyone wants to find anything they'll need to be you, or require a doctorate in Melonology.

If they want to hear Love Will Tear Us Apart they'll have to know it comes after The Clash but before Hunters & Collectors. Right next door to Simple Minds, Elvis Costello and Hank Williams. That completed, you begin work on your next trick.

Convincing the world you don't exist.

The goal is to become a myth. An echo. An irrational quantity. An Area 51 of the atman. The unknown pneuma. Keep everyone and everything at a distance, away from your self-absorbing misery, lest they dilute it or corrupt it.

Xi finds a way in. By osmosis. Low concentration to high intensity. Assimilation. She's beside you. Inside you. All around you.

Allure.

You call her from work, a week before she's due to leave. You apologise for being a bit withdrawn. Preoccupied. Unavailable. Anti-social.

You can add rude to that list, she says.

Would she allow you to make it up to her. Dinner? A movie?

She's standing out front of the cinema. It's the first time you've really seen her. Really looked at her. Straight, shoulder-length hair. High cheek bones. Sad, almond eyes. Honey skin. Petite frame. A little bit China Chow. A little bit Betty Rubble.

Hi.

She smells clean. Fresh. Labile. The fragrance ignites her. Allure. Fomentation. Provocation. Discombobulation.

Heavenly Creatures, Casper or Dead Man Walking?

It doesn't matter what's on the screen. Xi is the feature presentation, projecting herself through the dark. She rests on your chair. An arm. A shoulder. A spark leaps across the space between.

The end. Closing credits. A new beginning.

You take her to The Peak and walk halfway around Mount Olympus. Hong Kong pulses below. You ask her what she's studying in London.

She's almost finished her degree. A few units and a thesis to go. Quantum Physics. Don't laugh! she obtests.

Sorry. You didn't think people actually did that. You thought it was one of those joke subjects. Something people said. Well, it's hardly quantum physics. It 'ain't rocket science. It's not brain surgery. What do physicists, rocket scientists and brain surgeons say when something is simple and straightforward? Sorry. You thought it was funny. And the way she said it. You didn't mean to be rude. Sorry.

It's okay, she laughs. Advertising.

What?

Advertising. Come on, we say, it's not advertising.

She's smart, she smells great and she's funny. She was raised in Hong Kong and went to school in Sydney. She's the opposite of you. Born in Australia and getting an education in Hong Kong. She wants to know what you've learned.

Nothing, apparently.

Maybe it's your teacher, she suggests.

Xi gets you talking, about the year gone by. Recent months. The last two hours. She was waiting for you to take her hand. To hold it, during the film. You apologise, without thinking if it's the type of thing you're supposed to apologise for. You were nervous. You are nervous. You've never been good at that kind of thing. .

What kind of thing is that?

This kind of thing.

What kind of thing is this?

You never know if girls are interested. What if they're not? It can be embarrassing, or upsetting.

It can be interesting, she counters. It can be exciting. Surprising,

Like quantum physics.

Yes, like quantum physics, smartarse. Like chemistry. And biology. Don't worry, she reassures you. Relax. I could tell. That's why I tried to help. Didn't you feel me leaning against you. Into you.

Oh.

Well?

You're looking out over the city. Over the harbour. Over the miles. Wondering if you still have a girlfriend in Sydney. Even though you know don't. You're in Hong Kong, in denial. Great, only anger, depression and acceptance to go. You can feel Xi studying you. Inching closer. Resting on the rail. Against you, again.

What are you thinking? she asks.

Nothing really. What're you thinking? asks Richard, aged twelve.

I'm wondering if you're going to kiss me. What do you think about that?

I think I need to go to the toilet.

You take a few steps to the right and hide behind a bush. You go about your business. She laughs, like she can't believe it. You apologise. You're nervous. You've been bursting to go for ages.

She's amazed, at you candour and your priorities.

You walk away. It's time to go, except you haven't told her. She doesn't follow. She stands there. Staring at you. Delicate hands on slender hips. Taught lips. Her smile slips.

I tell you I'm waiting for you to kiss me. You go to the toilet and then you walk away?

Sorry. I wanted it to be spontaneous. I wanted to wait until, I don't know, later. On the way back. So it didn't seem like I was doing it because you told me too. I wanted you to think it was my idea and I did it because I wanted to.

Do you?

You walk to her, slowly. Cautiously. You lean in and kiss her, on the cheek. You pull back, to see what happens. She squints. She steps toward you. Raises her chin and offers her lips. You accept them. She closes her eyes. Yours are wide open. She takes your hands.

She takes you home.

You open the door and usher her in. A gentleman to the end. You thank her for a nice evening. You kiss her on the cheek and go to your room.

You hear her speaking to Daisy, in Cantonese. Someone is laughing. At who? At what? You try to finish a book. Perfume. Grenouille is having an olfactory orgy. There's a knock at the door. You get out of bed.

Hi.

You're standing before her, in your underwear. You don't feel exposed. Your inhibitions have fallen away. She doesn't seem to notice or care. She's in an oversized t-shirt. An airbrushed kitten is cleaning its paws.

Daisy wants to know if you have any cigarette, she says.

You give her a pack.

Do you have menthol?

Dunhill Lights is the best you can do.

She looks at the pack for a moment. She says thanks. Goodnight. She pivots sharply and almost skips away. You close the door. Return to Grenouille, fornicating with his fragrances.

There's another knock at the door.

Do you have a light?

Of course you do. Although there's probably a box of matches in the kitchen. You're pretty sure there's a lighter on the coffee table, in the living room, too. Daisy keeps a drawer of them. She slips them into her purse every night she goes out. Trophies.

I know that, she says. I want to know if you have one.

Xi walks to your side of the bed. You pass her the lighter from the side table. You tell her she can keep it and return to the pages of your book.

She flounces out. And pulls the door tight.

Oh well. Whatever. Never mind.

The door flies wide. Xi steps in and leaps onto the bed. She punches you on the arm, like a girl. She slaps at your chest and curses you in Cantonese. She draws a fist back to clock you again. You grab her wrist and laugh at the hostility in her eyes.

She throws a leg over you.

Her t-shirt climbs her thighs, over naked hips. She wants to know what the fuck is wrong with you. She kisses you. Angry. Like the answer is deep within.

She peels her shirt.

You've never seen skin like this. That colour. The same colour, all over. Like a New Age liquid. She smiles. She knows. She holds you with her eyes and lowers herself onto you. Venus descending. Searching your face. Piercing. Guiding. Sustaining her first-mover advantage. Apart and together, again, until you capitulate. She throws her head back in victory.

Iniquity.

You close your eyes and observe the moment from high above. She moves off the bed, onto the floor and out the door. Steps recede down the hall, into the night.

You return late from work or whatever. You pass her. Hallways. Corridors. On the couch. In the kitchen. The room she shares with her sister. She appears, in the door. Bare feet on wood floor. She makes her way up the bed in the dark. She kisses you. The sensual stranger shores herself against you. Drains you. Abandons you. Ne'er a word is spoken.

You wouldn't know what to say anyway.

She, as Charles Aznavour sang, is the beauty and the beast, the famine and the feast. She draws the life out of you and, for a few moments, you live. Then die. Another little death. She retreats without a word. To count the dead.

Bury the corpse. Fill the hole. Feed the hole.

You take her to dinner. To the airport. She's going back to London. Back to school. Back to her own confederacy of facers. Her holiday fling has been flung. The sun has set on her summer romance.

If that was your idea of romance, Richard, no wonder you have problems with women.

What was it then?

Fucking for fun and distraction. Sexual attraction.

Only sex?

What's so only about that? said Altenberg.

Then I guess I should thank you.

There was something in it for me too.

You got a ride to the airport.

Win-win.

Xi?

Richard.

Why do people think sex is the answer to everything?

Sometimes it is.

Oh.

Take care.

Study hard. Make us proud.

Try not to be too grumpy. I'll be back soon.

Oh, good. Something to look forward to.

She's the mirror of my dreams, the smile reflected in a stream but she may not be what she seems. Aznavour might not have been thinking about Xi when he wrote it but he knew her all the same.

You hate to see her go but happily watch her leave.

It will create space. Deepen the void you drift in. You have no need for an anchor and don't want to be another's mooring. You kiss her cheek. She walks away. She turns and smiles. She disappears.

Departures.

Sai-ming, the missing autistic boy, is sighted, across the border. His parents move into a Shenzhen hotel. They search. They sit by the phone. They wait.

DAISY BRINGS THE GUY HOME, regularly. She parades him through the living room, while Liz is watching the financial news.

A dog of that house shall move me to stand,

I will take the wall of any man or maid of Montague's.

Reconciliation between the halves of our house seems unlikely. Particularly when Liz starts telling people you've slept with both sisters. A half truth that doesn't really worry you or Daisy. It annoys the hell out of The Guy. You tell him not to worry. It wasn't like it was at the same time.

Letters arrive from London.

Daisy hands them to you. Woo! My sister's writing to you! Someone made an impression! Richard and Xi-xi sitting in a tree. K-I-S-S-I-N-G! The candid, brutal confessions are charged with insight, intelligence and intimacy. She may be the song that summer sings, or the chill that autumn brings. She could be a hundred different things. She confides in you. Confesses. Thoughts and feelings. She commits. Too much, too soon. She's the love that cannot hope to last, she comes from shadows of the past. You tell Daisy you think her sister is making decisions based on what she thinks you want, not what she wants for herself. The letters stop shortly after.

For the second time in as many months you adopt the scorched earth policy. Take a flame-thrower to the sweep and burn the whole thing down.

My my my pariah.

You come home late. In darkness. You switch on the television and walk to the couch. Crash position. Brace. Brace.

It's gone.

You walk around the living room, looking for it. Like someone might have mislaid it. An eight-foot sofa. You open cupboards, like it might have been packed away. You slam doors. Turn lights on and off. You try to wake up an explanation.

Liz does not come out from behind door number three.

Daisy is back twenty minutes later. She tells you Liz has moved out and taken the couch with her. Our couch. Your sofa.

Didn't she tell you? She found someone else move in.

You call Liz in the morning. She should've told you she was moving out. She had no right to take off with the couch. She can't just pack up and leave with whatever she wants. She has responsibilities. Commitments. A deposit. She apologises. She didn't want to trouble you. She didn't think it was a big deal. You don't want her apology. It was a big sofa. It's a big deal. You can't watch television on her apology. You can't read the paper, take an afternoon nap, spill beer or masturbate on her apology.

You can keep the deposit, she says. Buy a new sofa to masturbate on.

Oh. Well, okay then. Who's this mystery replacement? you ask, expecting to see another trolley dolly in you domestic aisle.

Gina is from Brisbane, Queensland. A Banana Bender. She weighs just south of 250 pounds of pineapples. Within a week she installs a separate phone line and cable box in her room and is never seen again. Sometimes you see her on the way out the door in the morning, or when Food-by-Fone make a delivery at night. You're not around that much yourself. She could walk naked through the living room, five times a day, and you wouldn't know.

A last minute trip to India is cancelled at the last minute. Pneumonic Plague. You're not sure if this means there's been an outbreak of pneumonia and other respiratory infections, or an alarming increase in the number of acronyms and other devices students use to remember things.

Roy G Biv. Please Excuse My Dear Aunt Sally. O Be A Fine Girl Kiss Me.

You send yourself to Coventry. Self-imposed exile. You're determined not to be a person of consequence, vacillating between work and bed. You just want to get by unnoticed. The unknown known. You'll feel more comfortable with yourself if you act like somebody else. You make it through a long-weekend without speaking to anyone for three days. When you finally do talk the sound of your own voice scares the bejezus out of you. You wander blindly toward an unknown destination, swinging between guilt and rage. Filling the hole. Feeding the hole. Churning in the monsoonal chaos of alcohol and drugs. It's a lock-in. Turn off, tune up, drop out.

I didn't wanna be with any people I know,
But god knows I didn't wanna be alone.

You start in a bar at one end of town and drink yourself home, kicking that tin down Heartbreak Alley. You forget who you are and you don't care. You're comfortably numb. Neurologically, psychologically, pathologically. The human Nerf ball. Dull. Blunt. Spent. A damp squib, bouncing off walls. Unenthused, uninspired, unaroused. Even the inherent charm and appeal of masturbation is lost, no longer sex with someone you love and trust.

Baldrick walks in to your office. He's worried about your health. You look tired. Stressed. Under the pump. People are complaining about your attitude. The petulant, splenetic behaviour.

You want massage?

It's a sweet gesture. You don't want to hurt his feelings. You thank him for thinking of you but he can keep his hands to himself.

Not me, dickhead. Sauna.

They punctuate passages of the retail narrative. One-stop sweat shops of the empiric, heuristic kind. Different strokes for different blokes. Windsor Sauna. Sunning Kok Sauna Steam. Sauna Lotto. Big Spender Sauna & Bath. Lucky Sauna & Massage. Crystal Spa & Sauna. Sunny Paradise. King's Sauna. Bangkok Turkish Steam Bath. Five Star Sauna. Hong Ling Steam Bath. Yu Kok Massage Sauna. Big Boss Sauna. The ostentatious, lavish sounding Sauna de Palais. You've never given them much thought, or entertained the notion. In your current mind-set, however, disappearing into the darkness for a couple of hours is not without appeal. The silence. The anonymity. Alone, together. The comfort of strangers. Just to see if you're capable of feeling something, anything, might be worth the promotional price of admission.

Everyone in the supply chain of this unique business model seems to be removed from the experience. This is not unusual in the service industry. Sometimes you just have to go through the emotions. The officious meat-greeter in reception. The sentry on the shagpile in the faux-oak surrounds of the changeroom. Aging orientals, lounging naked in plunge pools and jacuzzis. The teenager fitting you with baggy boxers, a world too wide for your shrunken shank, draping you in a plush robe. No one makes eye contact. We're all keen to avoid each other's dirty secrets. You're passed down the production line. Ushered into a waiting room, a passé purgatory, furnished with banks of armchairs stolen from Grandma's house. There are lace doilies on the armrests. Financial figures and racing results are broadcast on large televisions. Pensioners sit on ottomans, absentmindedly dispensing foot massages. You find an inconspicuous space against a distant wall. A woman in a cheap twin-set presents Chinese tea. From a wooden box on the sidetable, you fire a menthol. Blow smoke at the ceiling.

Ready for massage?

She leads you through a dimly lit warren of chambers. She guides you through a portal of frosted glass and leaves you standing beside the massage table. You listen to muzak and try to identify the musky aromas. The familiar, mephitic odours of moral and spiritual putrefaction.

In Xanadu did Kublai Kahn a stately pleasure dome decree.

A woman enters. There's not enough light to determine what she might look like or how old she may be. What does it matter anyway? It's a short, slim silhouette in canary-yellow tracksuit pants and polo shirt. She lays towels across the altar, where the gods of osteopathy and onanism shall receive their sacrifice. She assists with the removal of your ceremonial vestiges and points you to your final resting place. Face down. Head in the hole upon the bowsprit, at the cutwater of her pleasure-craft. She goes to work on your shoulders and executes the usual effleurages across your back. Like a magician removing a tablecloth, without disturbing the crockery, she deftly whips your boxers away. Buttocks are kneaded, thighs navigated and occupational hazards brushed aside with professional courtesy.

Time-out. Intermission.

She proffers a pillow. She raises a towel, a temporary screen to protect false modesty. She's seen it all before, no doubt, and probably half a dozen times today. Still, to everything, turn turn turn. A time to every purpose under heaven. Time to flip the discs and play Side-B.

The second act commences.

It's game of two halves. Parts are plied, positions assigned. Batter up. Bottom of the ninth. The pitcher is on the mound. Designated hitter at the plate. Merkle's Boner. She rounds second base and slides into third.

You shut your mouth. And close your eyes.

Your memory is not yours to command. The past comes unbidden. Humiliation. Mortification. Palms press. Caress. Gland in hand. Professional misconduct. Traction, reaction. Her self-satisfaction. You were fifteen going on sixteen, you had a lot to learn. Unprepared. Timid, shy and scared. Peeled and compressed. Distressed. That silent scream in your chest. The woeful ballad of shallow breaths. You leave your body and look down upon yourself. The curtain falls. The last scene of all, a strange recurring history and second adolescence. Oblivious.

She steps away, enough for today. Cold, clinical and detached. Undone. Deaf and dumb. She helps you into your robe, cloaks you in shame. Will I have to see her again? Dismissed with a smile. Come back in a while.

Massage okay? asks the locker-room attendant.

You have no idea how to answer a question like that, after an experience like that. You feel drained. Wrung out. Light-headed.

I was trying so hard to cleanse myself, I was turning into somebody else.

Gina is away for the weekend. Daisy decides to host a party. The idea doesn't thrill but it will give you a chance to workshop some nihilistic brooding you've been working on.

You position yourself on the balcony.

Daisy's friends were supposed to arrive from 8pm. At 10:30 there's still only a handful of them to turn your back on. One hour later, seventy people are crammed into the living room. The Guy comes over. He says something about the quality of the women inside. You survey the crowd and ask who the one in the tiny white dress is.

She's Oriental.

I see she's Oriental. Who is she and who's she here with?

Not Oriental, he corrects you. A rental. A hooker. She came with the fat guy. He's getting married next weekend. His friends bought her for him. A going-away gift cum wedding present

By 2am you've had enough of everyone. You call the police and pretend to be a neighbour. You complain about the noise. The Peelers arrive soon after and shut the party down.

That night, despair arrives like Genghis Kahn in your head and heart. It lays waste to the civilisations there.

The parents of missing Sai-ming maintain their vigil in a Shenzhen hotel.
Bogus sightings, crank calls and ransom notes cannot dim their hope. They
sit behind a birthday cake, illuminated by candles. Their room is carpeted
with photos of street children, sent to them with demands for money.
YOU DECIDE TO SELL THE FAIR LADY. You're going to trade up. Alpha Romeo. At only $15,000 it's a steal. It was probably stolen. The second-

hand market for cars lies over the border. For an Alpha, with one or two careful owners and a reputation for breaking down that even boat owners think is excessive, you can almost name your price. All you have to do is find someone stupid enough to buy The Big Banana.

Fair Lady seeks companion. $10,000. ONO.

Mr Chan calls. He wants a test-drive. He arrives at 8pm sharp, with Amy. A beauty queen from pageants past. You asked Daisy to hang around, in case anyone feels the need to speak Cantonese. And to even the teams. With the right outfit she could pass as a Motor Show Miss. You ask her to plump her plumage and drape provocatively over the chassis.

Does *she* come with the car?

Mr Chan goes for a spin. Daisy, reluctantly, rides shotgun. You stand on the sidewalk with Amy. She was a Miss Hong Kong finalist. A couple of years ago. You tell her you thought she looked familiar. You'd seen her pictures. She smiles and giggles. She was one of the Alphabet Banditas.

Mr Chan returns, eyes permanently on high-beam. He's satisfied with the performance of The Fair Lady. He looks luridly at Daisy when he says it. She is not so ebullient. You suspect this has little to do with fuel consumption and power-to-weight ratios.

You lead them all upstairs to sort out the paperwork.

Mr Chan thinks $5,000 would be a fair price.

You say maybe $8,000.

Maybe six?

How about seven-five?

Let's round it down to seven.

Amy claps and giggles. Daisy exhales, relieved. She buttons her blouse. Show's over. The need for optional extras has passed. Mr Chan signs a few pieces of paper and counts out the cash. Do I look familiar? he asks, peeling off the banknotes.

Not really but, you know, I'm not very good with faces.

I'm quite famous.

Really?

Chinese all look same, eh?

No. I just, you know, never learned to read.

I'm the Acid Bath Killer!

He does a Leo Getz gesture. Joe Pesci, Lethal Weapon. Hands up. Ta-da. You look at Daisy for a reaction. Confirmation. She nods her head in the affirmative, like I don't know half of it.

A Cathay Pacific hostess was found in a bath of acid. Dissolving. Bizarre love triangle gone wrong. Mr Chan was found guilty of murder. They said he forced his girlfriend to help chop the corpse into pieces and dispose of them. He went to jail for a few years. Then convinced his girlfriend to confess to the crime. Miscarriage of justice. Mr Chan was released. Now she's doing porridge in his place.

He's sitting in your living room, buying your car.

Prior to this revelation you hadn't considered Amy to be the sharpest knife in the draw. She wasn't too bright. Now she stood blindly in the shadow of a psychopath, under a giggling cloud of dimness. Doped and duped into positions *delicto*, she now cruised with a killer.

What would her next headline be?

Mr Chan takes the keys to his new car. Maybe we can all go out for dinner, to celebrate, he enthuses.

Oh, sure. Great.

You shake hands with The Acid Bath Killer and wish Amy luck. Daisy locks the door after them, puts on the latch, nails up some boards and makes a barricade out of furniture. She sits on the sofa and gives serious consideration to moving apartments. You sit beside her and light up a smoke.

Holy fuck.

You don't know what holy fuck is, she asserts. Holy fuck is getting hit on by the Acid Bath Killer while he test-drives your car.

You're not sure if things like this are factored into the equation that sees Hong Kong declared Stress Capital of The World™, but they probably should be. You tell Daisy if she's feeling a bit on-edge you know a place that might be able to help her take a load off.

She says she has a Guy of her own for that.

To celebrate your sale of the century, and make sure you're nowhere to be found when the Acid Bath Killer returns for your flatmate, you take the Alpha for a victory lap of The Island.

Shek O sits out on the eastern tip. It's an old fishing village that is gradually being converted into an enclave for wealthy families, bohemian expatriates and over-rated seafood restaurants. Its greatest assets are the two beaches that buttress it and the golf course that lines the approach.

During the Battle Of Hong Kong, in WWII, the Japanese did not endear themselves to local inhabitants. Many basic human rights and tenets of the Geneva Convention were violated. Shek O, consequently, is haunted by many ghosts of Christmas past.

An abandoned building has been left empty, to afford the spirits a place to call home.

The road to this quaint, seaside hamlet hugs the base of The Dragon's Back. A minor mountain range of moderate peaks and troughs. One lane in, one lane out, with some exciting twists and turns. Illegal road-racers love it. Their passion, unfortunately, can sometimes collide with the demands of public transport. Bus drivers, also known to suffer from White Line Fever, barrel around the cliff-faces playing beat-the-clock between depots.

Baldrick lives out here. His wife is having a few colleagues over for a barbecue. You've been asked to support him. Talk him through the finer points of barbecuing. Chinese have no natural affinity with such things.

Sam is in the kitchen.

She has a great Joan Chen vibe about her. The Twin Peaks Joan Chen, not The Last Emperor Joan Chen. Compelling. Beguiling. Mesmerising. She disarms you. Charms you. Animates, attracts and elevates you. This shouldn't be happening. You're supposed to be wallowing in self-pity, moody and bitter. Not bathing in ethereal wiles, like a gangling schoolboy.

Conversation bounces from her work at a television station to music, film, your work and hotels in Europe. Stanford University. Restaurants. Her decision to return for The Handover because, although she's a Hong Kong girl, she was raised in the US. She thought it was an appropriate time to return to her roots. She thinks you can probably relate to that because you're half Chinese. You agree. Although you've never really thought of it like that before. She's causing you to rethink a few things.

Oh to be a cherry in that mouth.

She weaves a path from a dream she had to the fate of Sai-ming, her passion for volleyball and the beach, as if its all part of the answer to one question. *Mai oui!* French phrases salt the dialectic. *Merde! Tout le monde sur le balcon.* How bourgeois. The kitchen orbits around her. Others come and go, like comets, but her gravitational pull has you by the core. Building the requisite escape velocity is beyond your means.

Time passes all too swift. She has to leave.

I'd love to pick this up again, she says. Maybe you could do some freelance work for us, if you're interested. The money's not great but the benefits are good. Can I have your phone number?

You can have anything you want.

She bids *adieu* with a peck on each cheek. *À la mode française.*

Some sheets of copy arrive mid-week.

Can you take a look at it?

Sure.

What kind of money do you want?

For this, for you, nothing.

I wouldn't want to take advantage of you.

You wouldn't be the first.

Pardon?

Nothing. It's okay. It's no big deal.

Hey, what you're doing this weekend?

Probably nothing, you say a little too quickly.

She invites you to a housewarming party. Bring a friend, if you're nervous about being there on your own.

You explain your predicament to Daisy. You want to go but don't want to look like a dickhead. On your own. In a house full of strangers.

You'll look like a bigger dickhead if you don't go, sh says. She'll drag you there herself, if she has to.

You spend Saturday trying to find an appropriate housewarming gift. Something personal but not too intimate. Tasteful but not typical. You don't want to put all your street-cred in one basket. You settle on a copy of O The Places You'll Go, by Dr Seuss, and a set of burnished steel candle holders.

You arrive late. It wasn't deliberate. You were having an anxiety attack. It took Daisy an hour to talk you off the balcony.

Sam opens the door.

Daisy blasts across the room, to a familiar face, before you even get a chance to introduce her. You're left standing there, drifting self-consciously in the social vacuum. Like a fourteen year old kid, waiting for his date to come down the stairs, while over-protective parents give him the once-over.

Sam drags you across the threshold. She notices the gifts you're carrying, which now feel awkward and stupid. Can she can take them off your cack-hands?

Yes. They're, um, for you. A housewarming present. Presents.

That's so nice. *Merci.* Thank you. She turns to her guests and exuberantly admonishes them. Hey! How come none of you guys brought me presents?

The room swallows you. She devours the attention. You shrink under the scrutiny. She laughs and apologises, enjoying your abashment. So are you, in an outré way. She sits by the window and unwraps the gifts.

Dr Seuss, she observes, momentarily confused. I love Dr Seuss!

This is the best one, you assure her. The theme is more universal than Grinch. It's deeper, with a greater spectrum of characters, than Sneeches. Not as one dimensional as The Sleep Book.

Better than Green Eggs And Ham?

I figured you'd already have that, Sam-I-Am.

Doesn't everyone?

It's bigger in scope and scale than Eggs. What it lacks in French Absurdest pataphysicality and gastronomy it makes up for with levity.

Appraisal of the Seuss oeuvre complete, she turns her hands to the candle holders. They meet with a less cerebral, more physical approbation. Or maybe she's bored and wants to get back to her party. She jumps up, throws her arms around you and pulls her slender frame to yours. Thanks. So sweet. The move garners the attention of a few guests.

Daisy raises an approving eyebrow.

You spend the afternoon bouncing between strangers. Taking extended bathroom breaks. Retreating to Daisy when silences become too uncomfortable or the toilet is occupied. After a few hours, your flatmate declares an intention to leave.

Okay. Just give me a minute to say goodbye.

Don't be crazy! she admonishes. You can't go!

You can't stay here on your own, like a hanger-on. You'll run out of things to talk about. There's a million stupid reasons to leave and one truly great reason to remain.

Naturally, you leave.

A 200 pound woman, Fei Fa (Fat Flower), cruises the streets of Tai Po. She preys on taxi drivers, running up substantial amounts on the meter and claiming to have no money. She offers to perform sexual favours in exchange for the fare. When drivers decline she insists on having sex anyway, for free. One driver claims to have been raped.

SAM PHONES. She asks you to do her a favour. A friend has organised a charity ball. A group of them are going. She doesn't have a date. Would you accompany her?

Are you her first choice, or last resort?

You arrive at her apartment early. Neneh Cherry blares behind the solid oak of the door. Buffalo Stance.

Who's looking good today? Who's looking good in every way?

It takes a couple of hits on the doorbell to get her attention. She answers wearing an embarrassed smile and a damp towel. She's just got out of the shower. She apologises for not being ready. You apologise for coming early. She says don't worry. It's more common than you think with guys your age. *Pas de problème.* There's a bottle of wine in the fridge. Pour her one too. She'll only be a minute.

You do as instructed, sit on the arm of the sofa and scan the room. Candles are burning on a sideboard, in your holders. Through a thin slip of doorway Sam stands before a mirror, naked. She steps into a backless, midnight-purple gown. She reminds you of Ali MacGraw in The Getaway. Those shoulders. She turns and offers an ephemeral flash of delicate breast as she zips the dress. She lifts her eyes and nails you. Busted. Caught in the act. She smiles. *Excusez-moi.* Those lips.

Je ne serai pas une minute.

The doorbell chimes. Couples arrive. You're probably not the person they were expecting. Sam sweeps through the room. A force of nature. She carries all before her.

We hurtle through the night.

There is dinner. Entertainment. Dancing. The galah at the gala. Hundreds of people that you don't know and probably never will, if fate is kind. You end up in Lan Kwai Fong. Club 97. Return of the prodigal son. The American, the Englishman, the Israeli and Eddie are as surprised as you to see you with someone of Sam's calibre. Drinking and dancing with Sam.

I'll give you love baby not romance,
I'll make a move nothing left to chance.

A dude emerges from the crowd and takes her to a corner. They talk. It's animated. Intimate. You can hear the sound of a heart breaking. Yours. You try to drown it with a couple of furious drinks. Is she really going out with him? Is she really going to take him home? She waves from across the dance floor.

Huh, sukka? Smokin.' Not cokin.' Get funky.

You exit, stage left. Grab a taxi and go to your cave. You crawl in and hibernate for the weekend. You're a bear with a headache and it lasts all week. Until she calls on Thursday and asks you out for lunch. *Déjeuner, Samedi.*

You meet at the Peak Cafe on Saturday.

It's unseasonably hot and humid. She thanks you for a great night, last weekend. She had a good time at the ball. Why didn't you say goodnight? One minute you were there and then, pfft, you were gone.

She seemed a little busy at the time. Preoccupied.

Oh, that. Drama.

You didn't know she had a boyfriend. She said she didn't really, that night. She'd sort of been seeing a guy, that dude, but didn't want to take him to the gala. Too cool for school. He wouldn't have been any fun. That's why she asked you.

Oh.

He came up to her. He was angry. *Jaloux.* You just got up and left. You didn't say *ciao, adios* or *au revoir.* Not even a *merci, grazie, gracias* or a goodnight kiss. So she went home with him. *Voulez-vous coucheer avec moi, ce soi?* He's not really her type but she's never had a Chinese boyfriend before. With '97 coming and all, well, she'd thought she'd follow this one through. See what happens. Does that make sense?

Sort of, you lie. Not really.

She's taken dating to a sociopolitical level. Conducting an ethnological experiment. It's an elite form of racism. She wanted to try a Chinese boyfriend. To see what that was like.

What am I? you wonder. A ham sandwich?

Ham on rye maybe. A hybrid. Mélangé.

Still, if she wants her investigation to be statistically relevant, she should at least put you under the microscope. Has she considered all the variables? 9 out of 10 anthropologists recommend blowjobs as an important control when it comes to validating this type of research. *Le sexe oral.* Shouldn't she collect some qualitative and quantitative data? Weigh up the pros and cons? Do some SWOT analysis?

Maybe she already has.

She wants to visit her eight month-old nephew. Take Junior for a walk. Go to the park. *Promenade.* His parents are away.

They live On Old Peak Road.

It's a large block of apartments, right behind Sarah's. We liberate the infant from the amah and walk down to the park.

What if Sarah sees you with Sam and child? Word would spread to Sydney. Would that contradict the bed's-too-big-without-you routine you've been phoning in, three times a week? That wouldn't be good. Although it might not be too bad either. If she, and everyone else, saw you with Sam.

That would show them.

You wind your way through the park together. Instant family. People look you over and pass judgement. What's she doing with him? Wow, that's one really chic-looking amah you have there. Turns out there's a zoo in the park. Monkeys, parrots, flamingos, lions and a puma. A black leopard. A cougar. And a galah. Sam is straining under the weight of the child on her hip. You offer to take that millstone off her for a while.

That would be great. Thanks.

You reach across to relieve her burden. Your hand brushes her breast and pushes haphazardly against the nipple. Your eyes meet hers, briefly, then dart away. Embarrassed. Sorry.

Don't worry. *Peu vilain garçon.* Junior's been tweaking me all afternoon. I should've worn a bra.

A nursing bra, you say too quickly. And wish you hadn't. Now you feel like a right tit.

It's getting late. She has a dinner to attend and we still have a long way to go. There are hills to climb and children to repatriate. Outfits to be chosen. Engagements to be attended. Moments to be seized. Demons to conquered.

To each their own Iwo Jima.

The amah airlifts the infant to safety when you return, red-faced, from your assault on Mount Suribachi. Hill 262. Perspiring at the basin, in the bathroom, you splash water on your lineaments. Sam enters. She stands beside you and pulls at her tanktop. Sweaty. She runs a handtowel across her neck and dabs at her chest. *Décolletage.* Blood rushes around your body. She smiles at you. Busted, again.

Iced coffee, tea or me?

Sam holds court on a large white couch, her pavilion, cloth-of-gold of tissue. You kowtow at her feet, on the ottoman. She exhales heavily and runs a hand over the sofa, like a gameshow hostess that's about to give it away. I love this couch. *Un fauteuil moelleux.* It's soooo soft. The down is amaaaazing. *Douillet.* She sounds like she dropped a tab of non-vintage lysergic French acid. Vat $C_{20} H_{26} N_{2O}$. She motions you over. Feel it, she beseeches the Sneetch.

She's right. It's a sublime, mellow dream. Deep. Supple. *Souple.* Firm. Welcoming. Couch heaven. You could stay here forever.

You apologise for leaving early and not saying goodbye the other night. You misunderstood what was going on. She apologises for the confusion. She takes you by the hand, leans in and brings her face to yours. She kisses you and you melt, lilting against the sofa. She throws a leg over and straddles you. Pinning you to the feathered barge and burnished throne. She takes your head in her hands and kisses you again. Long. Probing. The litmus test.

Interrupted.

A key in the lock and a sister in the door. Sam climbs off, casually. Nothing to see here. She makes the introductions. You make excuses.

She sees you out.

Don't wait for things to happen, she whispers. *Carpe diem.* She kisses you on the cheek. Smiles, like a nurse comforts a crash victim. She tells you to call her sometime.

You don't.

You still feel like you have a girlfriend in Sydney. Even though you know you don't. These encounters are an exam. A trial. Invitations arrive but you decline. You fail to show. You don't go. You blame work and, like a self-fulfilling prophecy, lose yourself in it.

The Agency sends you to Kuala Lumpur.

The campaign for a luxury resort needs to be presented. An Account Manager travels with you. Creative make the ads, Suits make the arrangements. You arrive on the morning of the meeting in a state of disrepair. The city also seems to be a work in progress. The labourers have downed tools and walked off the site halfway through the job. They're not in any hurry to get back on top of it either. The Suit says it's not too bad. It used to be worse. She's looking forward to trying the local food. It's great. They have many types of durian too.

Great. Just what you need. 57 varieties of mustard gas.

The Marketing Manager of The Resort meets you in the lobby. She's an attractive, mature woman. Malaysian-Chinese. Sharp, intelligent, bedroom eyes. She takes you to meet The Board.

We sit for an hour, waiting for her boss. He eventually makes an appearance, with a besuited phalanx of female attendants. The Sultan Of Schwing. We present our work. He glances at half a dozen layouts. Grunts and leaves.

That went well, says The Client, breaking the post-Sultan silence. Other agencies were dismissed before they finished their presentation.

To celebrate she takes you and your colleague to dinner. No doubt the restaurant was all the rage in 1987. These days it specialised in overpricing and undercooking. After a couple of bottles of obnoxious wine your colleague surrenders and returns to the hotel. The Client has other plans for you. She insists on a nightcap in a local bar. A dimly lit affair within walking distance of the restaurant. After a couple of drinks, and a compilation CD of supermarket jazz, you declare the war on taste over.

The world's smallest taxi drops you back to the hotel.

Is that Petronas Towers? They look uneven. Do they look uneven to you? They look uneven. I thought they'd be bigger. They don't look very tall, do they? How tall are they?

She asks what room you're in.

7-11.

Open all night, she jokes. Same floor as me. Just across the hall.

She holds onto the door and invites you to join her for one last drink. The hotel left complimentary champagne in her room. It's tempting but you have an early flight. She promises to get you to the airport on time.

You know where to find me, if you change your mind.

You call AJ and leave a message on her answering machine, at three in the morning. You get Interflora to deliver a dozen roses. You send a fax.

Just in case.

just in case we both got lost
and discounted the cost
just in case the world is small
and you fall
just in case we lied
don't say I never tried
just in case you change your mind
and love is blind
and deaf
just in case he starts to shout
and the lights go out
just in case there's no one home
and you're all alone
just in case
you can never tell
just in case we chewed it up
and spat it out
just in case we fucked things up
and they don't work out
just in case it still feels wrong
it's not too late
just in case
you never know

KELLY PHONES. His wife is friends with AJ. You haven't seen them since you fell into the hole. Since AJ left. It makes you realise how much of your life, and social life, revolved around her.

Why don't we grab a couple of beers?

You meet in Lan Kwai Fong. He's been climbing the corporate tree and swinging from it's lofty branches. He's pulling heavy freight, financially speaking. Truckloads. Motherlodes. He lives on Mount Olympus now.

How're things are going with AJ? Spoken to her lately?

No, you reply. And jokingly add how you're just waiting for her to tell you she's getting married.

So you heard about that?

Oh.

You didn't know?

I do now.

A spectre hangs over the remainder of the evening. After a few polite bourbons, Kelly excuses himself. Sorry for, well, you know.

I do now.

You kick that tin down heartbreak alley. Filling the hole. Feeding the hole. You go home when there's nowhere left to go.

Hi there. Sorry it has taken me so long to write. I hope life is treating you well. The main reason for this letter, other than to say hello, is to give you some news that I am not sure how you'll take. There is no easy way to tell you this so I am going to be straight with you. I am engaged. I know you will not be happy and I don't expect you to be, in fact I am sure you will be hurt and upset and I am sorry if I have made you feel this way. All I can tell you is that I am very happy and blah, blah, blah... I wanted to tell you this myself, and I hope you haven't heard from anyone else. I want you to go on and do something for yourself and really be happy as I don't think you have been for quite some time. Take some risks if need be. Most importantly, I want you to be happy and blah, bah, blah...

IT'S LIKE READING SOMEONE ELSE'S MAIL. You feel bad for that guy and give him a moment of silence. Kelly's *faux pas* was an emotional airbag, prolonging the moment of impact. Slowing it down. Cushioning the inevitable. The trajectory, however, is irreversible. The missive has a velocity bordering on terminal. The trauma is deep. An artery is severed. You're flatlining.

The ghost of Christmas past.

Lost in the crowd at California, Lan Kwai Fong, she walks by on short but shapely legs. Slender hips. Her long black hair is permed, still enjoying the 80s. Balders notices you noticing her. He sails over. The Liverpuddlian icebreaker.

He pilots you in.

Her name is Mandy. She speaks in deep, throaty Chinglish tones. Like a raunchy news anchor. Corporate sexy. She's an insurance rep. A few gin fizzes see a change in her policies. They soften the crisp edge of her voice and loosen the buttons on her blouse.

Smokey eyes ask the question.

Balders suggests all may not be what it seems. The deep voice. The scar where an Adam's Apple might have been. High cheek bones. Firm hands. He thinks Mandy used to be a man. He starts singing Aerosmith. Dude Looks Like A Lady. Hands up whose seen The Crying Game?

You walk her home.

The building is in the middle of a Wet Market. A haggling hive of harvested activity during the day. At night it's hollow stalls, empty boxes and cane baskets. The air is cut with the corpses of rotting fruit, lettuce and cabbage. She leads you up three flights into a small flat. Buttons are tugged. Skins are quickly shed. Bodies explored with urgent, ungainly ardour. She pulls you to the bedroom. Pushes you to the bed.

No boom-boom tonight.

Oh.

I falling off the roof.

Oh. I hope-

It's holy week. Red dot special for you.

Oh. *Oh.* Whoa.

She puts you on the stand and worships at the alter. Carnal karaoke. A pitch-perfect rendition of an unfamiliar tune, despite some confusion when she gets to the bridge.

Tell me when you come.

Hmm?

Tell me when you come.

I think you'll know.

What?

I think you'll know. When I come.

You tell me before.

Oh, sure. Yeah.

You hold up your end of the bargain, just. Issue a late, quaking warning. Back arched, toes curled. *Coitus interruptus* with Canto-pop. She sings ballads and lulls you to sleep with a Faye Wong medley. It is the deep, unencumbered and eternal sleep of the damned.

Bury the corpse. Fill the hole. Feed the hole.

You call The Agency in the morning. Sick-leave. An away day. You'll work from home. Mandy has policies to sell. Targets to meet. KPIs. She leaves you to lounge in her louvre.

By mid-afternoon you're exploring the shelves and drawers. There are recent photos of her and girlfriends. Office gatherings. Old black and whites of her mother, or grandmother. Nothing between now and *then.* Nothing of her as a child or teenager.

She returns at 7:30, take-out in hand. Dinner is served in the Styrofoam containers. Fried rice. Hainan chicken. Vegetables.

You inquire after her family.

She never knew her father. Her mother lives in the New Territories. She has a brother but she only sees him once or twice a year. He tried to kill her with scissors, once. You can still see the scar on her throat.

Boys will be boys, you remark.

What?

Nothing. It's an old saying. About kids.

What does it mean?

I don't know. Just that boys do that kind of thing.

You tell her you'd like to stay the night but have to be at The Agency in the morning. She says you should stay. The factory is no longer closed. The battle station is fully armed and operational. It's a tantalizing proposition but you have duties of another kind to perform. The office Christmas Party is tomorrow night. You thank her for the hospitality. You'll catch up with her on the weekend.

You spend the day replaying the encounter in the theatre of your mind.

Before the first act of The Agency's festive foolishness is complete, you leave. You won the Lucky Draw the night before and want to claim your prize. Chance your arm again. You jump into a cab and charge up Hamburger Hill to the Gate Of Heavenly Peace.

The lights are out. Nobody's home.

You return to your room, consumed with thoughts of Mandy and her feline charms. The purr in her voice. The kitten that got the cream. The cat that must be scratched. The hostages that must be released.

Gina, armed to the teeth with take-away, walks past your open door. It's probably the closest she's been to a sexual experience this year. Maybe her whole life.

You sit in front of the television and watch a dozen episodes of The Simpsons. You drink half a dozen beers and smoke a packet of cigarettes. You fall asleep on the couch and endure twisted dreams within dreams.

You take Mandy to lunch in Stanley. A beachside balcony. You tell her the story of last night's quest for glory. The stab in the dark. She leans back in her chair. Runs her hands through her hair. And drills you with her eyes.

Check please.

You bundle her into the Alpha and peel out of the parking lot. Driven to distraction. A moving violation. You throw the car on the curb and fly up three flights. There will be no navel gazing this afternoon. The Bastille must be stormed. Checkpoint Charlie crossed. The Iron Curtain drawn. The Great Wall surmounted. It will be long, it will be hard there will be no withdrawal.

It's over in seconds.

Like a Chinese thumb puzzle she cuffs you. With every move her grip tightens. A libidinous lock-in. The only way out is forward, through the middle.

Post-coital analysis is just as swift and no less confounding.

To satiate your curiosity, and sweep The Agency pool, you ask if the goods have been repackaged. Hardware reconfigured. Software upgraded. Your contumelious accusations and anatomical incorrectness is met neither with a slap in the face or a kick in the guts. The calumniation of her chromosomes is neither confirmed not denied. She laughs. Diabolically. Demonically.

Dick Dastardly.

Is it your stupidity, naiveté or absurdity that she finds so amusing? Sniggering, snickering or in stitches? With you or at you? Not that it matters. Natures niche, or turn of the surgeons hand, she's all woman now.

Isn't she?

At the end of a mad, crazy sexual Spring Break at Disney World, riding the Crush 'n Gusher, she sends you flowers. It's a big bouquet in the classic Cantonese fashion. Lilies and sunflowers, sequestered in purple teal, swathed in lilac chiffon and chintz. A small Garfield is stapled to the card. He seems just as surprised to find himself in your office on a Monday morning.

You've never received flowers before.

It's a sweet, albeit, unsettling gesture. You're not sure what to make of them or the signals they send to The Agency worker bees. Your room becomes a hive of inquiry. A space oddity. The den of impiety.

Pollination. Anthers, stigmas and stamens. Fertilization.

Secret admirer? asks an unfamiliar voice.

Not really.

Birthday?

No, just, you know, from a friend.

Boyfriend?

No.

Are you sure?

Yes. Don't believe everything you hear.

She must like you very much.

The Garfield tell you that, or something else?

She steps through the door, reputation preceding her.

Tucson.

Stay the hell out of Tucson, said Woody Guthrie.

She's a rich man's bitch, that what she is, and nothin' else but.

As dry, empty and inscrutable as the Arizona dessert she studied in, Tucson is the current squeeze and honey-cycle of Moneybags, The Agency's resident brat. A millionaire in the making, marking time in marketing until the family business can't be run into the ground without him. He's probably only doing her to annoy them too.

What's Tucson doing here?

She prowls the desktop perimeter and takes the foliage between her fingers. She issues a languid, patronising smile. A curl of the lip. She strokes the stem. Floral sex. Pollination.

The Queen is in season.

She perches the firm curve of her fruit on the table. Pin-striped slacks. Open-necked blouse. A small pearl, suspended by a silver chain, rests against unblemished skin. Shallow cleavage.

Busy? she asks. What're you working on?

Sanitary napkins, you reply, unable to think of a lie more impressive and less embarrassing. You're distracted by the size of her head.

It's huge.

She's a female Melonhead. Her proportions put her at a disadvantage. At least your frame goes some way to disguising the enormity of your Medulla Oblongata. This Princess' petite five-foot-five brings hers into sharp relief. Her crowning glory, a thick mane of black hair, exacerbates the dimensions. She probably thinks you're staring dreamily into her eyes. You're wondering how such a delicate neck can support such a load, and which way you'd run if it toppled in your direction.

It's strange we've never spoken or had a common account, she ruminates. I've been here a year now.

Happy Anniversary. Hope you like the flowers. I wasn't sure what to get. Still, nothing says hello-stranger like lilac.

Maybe you can buy me drinks to celebrate.

I'm not sure your boyfriend would be party to that.

It's not his party. We don't have to invite him.

Oh.

What's your portable number?

Portable?

Mobile phone. Your mobile number.

You don't have one. You're one of the few people in The Agency, and on the Island for that matter, who doesn't have the latest in telecommunications.

You'd should get one, she instructs.

I don't really know much about them.

Get one like mine. Come on, she says, standing.

What, now?

Orange is my client. I'll get you a discount. Let's go.

You feel like you're playing hooky. Skiving off from school in the middle of the afternoon. It's very exciting. Maybe we'll stop in the lane on the way back and have a smoke.

She takes you to the nearby telecom shop and sets you up with an Ericsson GH337. The chunky candy bar with the B&O earpiece. You walk back to the office, together. Stopping for a smoke by the water feature. You ride the elevator in silence and part company in reception. She'll call you soon. See you later.

The future's bright. The future is Orange.

Your lines of communication remain silent for days. It's your dirty little secret. So secret you're wondering if the number is active or the phone is defective. You adjust the settings. Call your home number to test it. Daisy answers. You hang up. You call back and breath heavily. She curses you in Cantonese. When it finally rings, on Thursday night, the shrill electronic tones scare you half to death. The tidings they bear almost finish the job.

Let's meet for a drink. 7:30. *Le Jardin.* A bar in Lan Kwai Fong.

The Garden.

Pollination. Anther, stigma and stamen. Fertilization.

The Queen is in season.

Her questions are as unexpected as they are direct. Does being mixed make you feel different? Do you know who your parents are? Which parts of you are most Chinese? The conversation turns to Mandy. She-beast, as your part-time lover is known affectionately around the office. Thanks, Baldrick.

Did She-beast used to be man?

You laugh out loud. You don't know. Everything appears to be in the right place and good working order.

She probes a little deeper. What's She-beast like, down there?

I'm not really one to kiss and tell. Besides, I don't really have a lot to compare it too.

Maybe you should do some research.

A focus group?

She makes a call and you're soon ensconced in The Ritz. Vodka Bar. Tucson plus two. Moscow Mules kick the sensibilities out of her friends and the conversation into the gutter. The preoccupation with anatomical plugs and sockets, batteries and adapters, borders on unhealthy. Inebriated, beyond comprehension, you help shepherd the confrère corpses into a cab.

Alone on the sidewalk you ask if Tucson wants to go for coffee, or get something to eat.

Okay.

Coffee? you ask, unsure if this is really happening.

Great.

Public or private?

What?

We could go public, to Post 97. Or we could go private, to, um, my place. You know. And have coffee there. In private.

Private.

You hold the door. She slides by. She can hear your heart pounding. She tells you to relax. Just two colleagues, having coffee, right? The way she looks at you, as she says it, suggests she's probably expecting you to pour it over her body and lick it off.

You go through the machinations of caffeine production, to keep it all above board. She waits on the couch and switches on the television. Punches through the channels. MTV. No. A movie. Christopher Reeve and Jane Seymour. Somewhere In Time. No. An exclusive behind-the-scenes look at a Christian Slater film. No.

You got porno? she asks matter-of-factly, like it's milk and sugar. Like we're all engaged in an ongoing brown study into the nether regions of anatomy and it would be rude not to ask. There are thirteen year-old boys less pensive about other people's particulars.

You offer to order some adult pay-per-view, if that would help. And ask how she likes her coffee. Regular, or decaf?

Regular is too weak, she replies. I like it black. And strong. Up all night.

You're not sure if we're talking about coffee or porn, or both.

You sit next to her on the sofa and, despite Nescafe's best intentions, fall asleep watching Superman fall in love with Solitaire. Somewhere In Time. The caffeine must have supercharged the vodka shots and sent them rocketing to your brain.

Beyond fantasy, beyond obsession, beyond time.

The movie is beyond fucking belief. It doesn't have enough explosions or side-boob to keep you conscious.

Come back to me.

You awaken to find Tucson's giant head weighing heavy upon your lap. Upon a cushion. Upon an Irish toothache. Too scared to move you sit there and consider the paradoxes of time travel, choice and hedonism. The blood rushing through your body must be roaring in her ears. She stirs and slowly pushes herself vertical. She shakes out the cobwebs in her head and shambles her hair. She looks through her fringe at you, then walks to your room. She slips out of her skirt, unbuttons her blouse, unhooks her bra and places them on a hanger. It's done with such accidie and nonchalance she could be sleep-walking. She collects her tresses and loosely bundles them atop Mount Rushmore. She brings a hand down to caresses the small potbelly that is taking shape there. She frowns at it. And, from across the universe, asks what you're doing.

Watching.

You going to watch all night?

You walk to her with a mild sense of purpose. You put hands on her hips and pull her toward you.

You got a toothbrush?

Her priorities at this juncture are a little surprising. You're all in favour of good oral hygiene, it's just the Cantonese wield a peculiar brand of bluntness. It takes some getting used to. Like the way everyone tells you how fat you are when you come back from a holiday. She doesn't understand why you're laughing and you don't bother explaining. You show her to the bathroom and squeeze some paste onto a brush from a Cathay Pacific toiletry kit, a memento of air hostesses gone by. She rinses her mouth. Splashes water on her face. She turns and returns the favour, watching with keen interest as you polish your pegs. Each one, twice. Inside and out. She reaches around and releases the buckle on your jeans. Slides a hand beneath the band on your boxers and squeezes where it pleases, like she's appraising the firmness of low-hanging fruit. Feeding her Freudian fixation. Is that a grunt of approval, dissatisfaction or concern? She leaves you standing, stranded on the plains of Abraham. A lone sentry against the Marquis de Montcalm, befallen by a musket-ball beneath the ribs.

You advance upon her position in the bedroom.

Colgate tingles on her tongue as she prepares you for battle. Rousing the troops with stirring choruses and by thy victorious hand, 'til it is time to bear the breathless maid away and join the horrid war. She retreats down the linen embankment, rests upon her laurels and presents herself for plunder.

Cry havoc and let slip the dog of war.

There's nothing tender in the ensuing minutes. It's a feeding frenzy. An all-consuming casserole of carnage. You carve at her loins. She devours you.

The art of our necessities is strange, and can make vile things precious.

You're lost in the madness of Lear. Edgar unbound. Tom O'Bedlam. The ghost of Cordelia whispers in your ear.

Let it out.

Pardon?

Let it out, she repeats.

Let what out?

Let it out!

The cat? You mean the cat? Let the cat out? We don't have a cat. Do we?

Let it out!

What is she talking about? If you knew what *it* was you'd gladly let it out. You'd insist it leave. Issue it with marching orders. Immediately. Whatever it is, it has to go.

Let it out. You're so quiet. Let it out!

Your silent abstraction had been a vein of amusement for AJ. And Xi. A curiosity for Mandy. Borne out of that quiet, clinical assault on your innocence, no doubt. It wasn't the sort of thing you made a song and dance about. You suffered in silence and, consequently, congressed in dumbness. Mute. Rarely daring to even breath. It's a source of discontent for Tucson. You make a feeble attempt to satisfy her sonic desires.

Oh. Yes.

You're no Ron Jeremy. You're not even Mr Johnson. It makes your performance in Sexy Tennis School positively Oscar worthy. What is she going to ask you to do next, spank her?

This is more work than work.

She pouts. A full-curl, bottom lip moue. You promise to do better, try harder and give the neighbours a good scare next time.

There is no next time, she warns like a menopausal Jedi Master. An oversexed Yoda. There is only now. There is no try. Do. Let go of your anger. Let it out!

She flips you in frustration and finishes you. Ferociously. You barely have the strength to light a cigarette.

Different from She-beast, yes? she asks proudly.

The next two weeks present boundless opportunities to compare and contrasts the two. Quantitative and qualitative research. Focus groups. SWOT analysis. Opportunity cost.

She-beast is the unassuming enigma. The Mandy of a thousand faces. Low maintenance adolescence. Easy come, easy go. She lifts you up and lays you down, gently.

Tucson is the cold warrior. A house of hard stares. Freydis Eriksdottir. Half-woman half-machine. She aggravates you with her clinical apathy. She keeps you at a distance. Heightens the tension. Revels in the collision.

Bury the corpse. Fill the hole. Feed the hole.

It's like someone cleaved Xi-shi in two and you're trying to glue her back together, with bodily fluids.

The gods are just, and of our pleasant vices make instruments to plague us.

A farewell dinner is held for an esteemed colleague. You don't even know her name. The Agency has gathered at Classic Passion Restaurant. King of Lobsters! You're seated across the Lazy Susan from Tucson and Moneybags. Bizarre triangle. Uncomfortable points of convergence. Unsettled eye-contact. Unconvincing conversations.

At evenings end you stand roadside with Mulder, Baldrick and Ana. Karaoke bound.

A squad of hoodlums, wielding knives, metal pipes and wooden poles charge into the restaurant.

Five men, dining on lobsters, are chopped and bludgeoned to death by a large group of assailants in a busy North Point restaurant. There are no witnesses. Police, from the station less than a kilometre away, take twenty minutes to arrive at the scene.

IN A COSY CORNER of California Red Karaoke Box, a small selection of the advertising community is assaulted by a brutal rendition of Rhinestone Cowboy. The sheer gusto and punk bravado of your performance pummelling it beyond recognition.

The night continues to unravel from there.

Girls become tired and emotional. The cause of their despair hidden beneath a booze-riddled veil of Cantonese. Moneybags makes a concerted effort to reassert and ingratiate himself with Tucson. It's a shameless display of fawning and sycophantasy. She's probably having half of it. You, on the other hand, are having none of it. You leave them to it.

Time shall unfold what plighted cunning hides,
Who cover faults, at last shame them derides.

Daisy is curled on the couch, working her way through a bottle of bourbon and a packet of Marlboro. You keep her company and pitch tales of woo. Part of you hoping they'll work their way back to Xi-shi, in the old dart of Blighty, and part of you hoping they don't. Daisy understands the politics of sex and the currency of physicality. More trope than trollop, she's the harlot with a heart of gold. Once Upon A Time In The West. Rio Grande. El Dorado. Trading Places. You could trust her with almost anything, except a man. Always the opportunist, forever the predator, there is no boundary that cannot be breached or broached. She acts on impulses and heeds her wanton mores. Tonight she's half a mind to exercise her conjugal options and fulfil the prophecy of Liz. In the carcinogenic haze of smoke and dirty brown liquor the notion is not without appeal.

The wolf shall dwell with the lamb and the leopard shall lie with the goat.

The doorbell rings at 4am. Tucson has found her way to you. She sails by and makes straight for the bedroom. Daisy sings hello. Tucson continues on her way. You raise you hands in self-defence.

What's a guy to do?

Daisy passes comment on Tucson's dominant feature. She makes an inflating gesture around her head. You respond in kind, with a similar ballooning, gesture at the front of your trousers.

You wake in an empty bed, Tucson slinking away in the early hours. Daisy is banging on the door. She wants you to go Christmas shopping.

Ho, ho, ho.

On Central's corridors of consumerism she infects you with the festive spirit. You corner the market in Polaroid cameras. All for one and one for all. Tucson. Mandy. Baldrick, Ana and Mulder. Daisy, Maria and Gina.

You find yourself in Ferragamo, augmenting Daisy's wish list. An old man holds a handbag out before him. An offering. A young woman, on all-fours, crawls toward him from across the floor. She pleads for the purse. The shop assistant wears the expression of someone who sees this type of shit every day. Maybe she does. You can't help but think how much better the shopping montage in Pretty Woman would've been had it included a scene like this. Another nubile treasure-seeker skips across to her Master Of The Universe. He gives theatrical consideration to her whispered plea before assenting to the request. She claps like a schoolgirl who just found out she's going to Disneyland.

Maybe she is.

You observe the misogynistic, chauvinistic, sexist display in stunned silence. Daisy laughs. She used to know an old guy like that. He had half a dozen mistresses, housed away, ranked and filed in order of preference and pedigree. Some people have pets, she says. They take them for a walk. Men like this have women and take them shopping.

Every dog has their day, you suppose. Yet it's hard to imagine a household pooch or family moggy treated with the contempt of these penthouse pets.

Sir, you are no gentleman.

And you, Miss, are no lady.

Your next port of call in the quest for stocking-stuffers is paved with gold.

One of many local jewellery stores that encrust the street, loaded with gilded figurines, taels, chunky bracelets and polished necklaces. Watches, pearls and pieces of jade.

It's clear Daisy has the interests of her sister, and sisters from other misters, when she suggests you should buy tokens of affection for your mistresses. Xi. Mandy. Tucson. The triple pillars that will, no doubt, see you transformed into a strumpet's fool.

You're not sure, you tell her. You feel like they're wearing the pants and you're the one crawling across the floor. Would it send the wrong signal?

Any signal better than no signal, she says. Besides, it's Christmas. Gold, frankincense and myrrh. You got to give if you want to receive.

You get thin, 18-carat bracelets for them. And, warming to the spirit of the season, a mid-priced Breitling for yourself. There was a time when that would've represented two month's salary. Now you're not even thinking twice about it. You can see why shopping is the preferred pursuit of the lonely, loveless and unloved. It brings you to someone's attention. Focus, flattery, flirting and fawning. The excitement of something and someone new. It fills a void and satisfies a desire, in the comfort of strangers. Hong Kong had made it an Olympic sport and you've made it through the open try-outs.

With this timely purchase you've also consigned The Lucky Watch to history. Another piece of the past is purged.

And you may find yourself in another part of the world.

Your father bought it for you, reluctantly, on your thirteenth birthday. A Seiko Sports 100. The Tag Heuer of its time. Omega and Rolex for grown-ups. Timex, Citizen and Seiko for kids. The Sports 100 was orological cool. Digital across the top, traditional hands below. Your name and number engraved on the back. You replaced the standard issue stainless steel wristband with a white Velcro action strap. The kind surfers wore to stop their watch being ripped from their wrist by pounding waves.

It looked fantastic.

Until you emerged from the water and realized it had been torn asunder. The unbreakable strap had failed to uphold its promise.

I knew you were too young for a watch like that.

It's what my father said, as he posted reward notices in kiosks and asked beach-goers to keep an eye out for it. Like it might just be lolling about in the surf. We ran into an old acquaintance jogging along the seashore, and he got a spray too.

Bloody Richard has lost his bloody watch. I knew he was too bloody young for a bloody watch like that.

Two months later a package arrived in the mail. The Lucky Watch was inside. It had been found by the guy running along the beach. About a kilometre from where you'd lost it. He'd sat down to catch his breath and seen it glistening, where the waves lap at the sand. He picked it up, put it in his pocket and jogged on. It was only when he got home and discovered the name on the back that he recalled the conversation.

It had spent nine weeks underwater, travelled 1,000 meters up the coast and was found, in perfect working order, by a friend of the family.

What were the chances?

From that day forth you stopped wearing it in the water. You'd wrap it in a t-shirt or the corner of your towel. Until, years later, you forgot it was there. You raced out of the water and picked up your towel. Gave it a flick, to shake out the sand, and sent it hurtling through space and time.

I knew you were too young for a watch like that.

That night you went to a party. Drowned your sorrows in The Stranger's kitchen. You got to talking. He said drop round any time. Bring a few beers. Shoot some pool. Watch the footy.

A week later the phone rang. The caller wanted to know if you'd recently lost a watch at the beach. He gave his address and said come and get it. You bought a slab of beer, a gesture of thanks, and drove over.

He answered the door.

It was The Stranger from the party. This was the party house. You'd been drinking in his kitchen a week ago. He was surprised to see you. He was expecting some idiot who'd lost a watch at the beach.

The Stranger was also surprised to learn you weren't just the guy from the party, dropping round for a few beers, to shoot some pool and watch the footy. You were the idiot who'd lost his watch at the beach.

What were the chances?

And you may ask yourself, well, how did I get here?

Mandy arrives just as Daisy and The Guy are leaving for the airport. They're going to Phuket. Gina has returned to Queensland and won't be back until mid-January. Maria flew to The Philippines yesterday.

You two lovers will have the place to yourself, Daisy sings, then leans in to confide her approval of Mandy. She's much nicer than the other one, she whispers. She's got a normal size head too.

It's a ringing endorsement.

It's the kiss of death for Mandy.

Peer approval can work in mysterious ways. When you're in a negative space you're not interested in doing what is right. You want to prove everyone wrong. Armed with the jawbone of an ass, like a Samson torn between Delilahs, stripped of dignity and blinded with self-loathing, you'll bring the walls of the temple down to prove a point.

Oh well. Whatever. Nevermind.

A mulatto, my libido, yeah.

You step into a conference room at The Agency. Surprise! Tucson and Moneybags are suffering a moment together. She sits, looking up with apathetic eyes. He stands against the table, looking down on her, arms crossed. Intense. An ultimatum. A deadline missed. Aggravated. Agitated. Infuriated. You know how he feels.

It's something else you share.

She comes to you when the life forces are weak. Late at night. Three in the morning. Or on her way to work. If you phone in sick she comes over for lunch and puts the devil into hell.

She enlivens a languid Saturday afternoon. Blocks your hat and knocks the dust off your sombrero. Her phone rings. She takes the call in hand and the bishop in the belfry. It's Moneybags. She'll meet him on the corner in fifteen minutes. No, make that half an hour. The look in her eyes is evil. She hangs up. You rip her guts down. Tucson for lunch. Mandy for dinner. Insoluble truths. Again.

Fucking Kierkegaard.

It's a big night before Christmas, with strangers in Wan Chai. Burying the corpse. Filling the hole. Feeding the hole. The bars are as easy to like as they are to hate. Freedom. Anonymity. Intimacy. The comfort of strangers. Anything goes, for a price. You can be anyone you want. The girls are a blank page onto which you can write any story. You can lose yourself. Separate yourself from yourself. Disguise yourself so well that even you don't know who you are.

You leave Country Club 88 around 4am. The Mama-san helps you into a cab. She offers to send one of the lonely hearts club band home with you, to help you up the stairs. She can hum a tune and sing you to sleep.

Does she know The Marshmallow Song?

You belt out a solo instead and wake at 10am. Billy Shears. Shave and shower. You're expected at Mulder's house, on Mount Olympus, for lunch. You sit on the sofa, waiting for Baldrick and his wife to pick you up.

A cigarette fuels the fog of time. Outside, rains fall on the balcony. Grey. Another black day in the coldness of winter. You think about last Christmas. What you were doing and who you were doing it with. What are they doing now? You open a beer for the Ghost of Christmas Past. And toast the ghost of Christmas Present.

Sai-ming has not returned for Christmas. His parents leave gifts beneath the tree, and a candle in the window, hoping he'll find his way back, soon.

WITH THE PREVIOUS NIGHT'S EXCESS still coursing through your body, three beers feel like six. You put on your favourite Yuletide tune. Baby Please Come Home. U2. A Very Special Christmas. Proceeds from the album raise money for the Special Olympics. You love the equine events the most. They way they move, despite their handicap, with such grace, elegance and strength. It's hard to believe those horses are retarded.

I remember when you were here, and all the fun we had that year.

By the end of the first verse your face is leaking. And it's not like Christmas at all. You weren't expecting tears but, like an uninvited guest, you welcome them anyway. Rewind. Replay. Repeat. Increase volume for maximum impact and self-indulgence and self-destruction. Tears for a paradise lost. For forgetting. For accepting. You haven't cried like this since the end of Thelma & Louise.

You're a part of me, I'm a part of you,
Wherever we may travel, whatever we may do.

Next on the holiday season playlist, Apocalypso. Mental As Anything. Followed by the patron saint of tuneful misery, Ian Curtis. Love Will Tear Us Apart. Joy Division. Paul Kelly. How To Make Gracy. Then David Bowie and Freddie Mercury bring it home, amplifying the misery. Under Pressure.

This is our last dance, this is ourselves.

These are great tears. Much better than the ones you had when Mork wasn't allow to marry Mindy and when Isaac went blind on The Love Boat. They commiserate. Validate. Alleviate. You can fall in love with tears like this. You welcome them, arms wide. Beer in one hand, cigarette in the other. You tilt your head back and surrender to them. Crucify yourself upon them. Instant martyr, just add Bono.

I remember when you were here, and all the fun we had that year.

Baldrick and his wife deliver you to Mulder's house. You're introduced to his girlfriend and a few other couples. The flotsam and jetsam of Christmas orphans that abound at this time of year. Couples. You make do with a couple of champagne toasts. A couple of beers and a couple of glasses of wine. Double-fisting. You go out on the balcony for a smoke. You look inside, through the window. There's everyone, together, with their other half. You shed a couple of tears. Desire and regret. Disappointment and disgust. Joy and amazement too. You're surprised you're capable of feeling all these things and nothing. Zero. Nero, on the balcony, fiddling with your emotions while Rome is burning.

Mulder materialises behind you.

Hey.

You turn. Surprise! Polaroid. The camera clicks, whirs and spits out a picture. Mulder takes a good look at your face and see you smile looks out of place. Sorry. Are you okay?

You're fine. You're the one that's sorry, for putting on such a stupid display. You're sorry he had to see it. Not the kind of Kodak moment you had in mind when you bought the camera for him.

Lunch is almost ready. You can come to the table in, when, you know, a minute or two. When you're ready.

There is fine wine and good humour. Fine wine and crap music. Cheap wine and pudding. Amusing anecdotes. Dessert wine. One guest trips on a rug. He spills his tankard of port on someone's girlfriend and the carpet.

Balders helps you up. He offers you a ride home.

You thank Mulder for making it a very special Christmas. Another altruistic initiative for the handicapped. You apologise for the incident on the balcony and that accident with the port. There are a couple of handshakes and awkward air-cheek kisses.

Against his better judgement, Balders drops you in Lan Kwai Fong.

You return to past glories. The gang from Mecca. Take a look at me now. You attempt to sit on a bar stool and balance a bourbon. You call Tucson and try to string together a conversation. She's whispering. You ask her to speak up. She can't. She's probably with Moneybags, underneath his million-dollar mistletoe. She can't speak now. She'll call you later. She hangs up.

O Mistress mine, where are you roaming?

You phone again, desperate for conversation. Whining for company. She tells you to go home. Don't ring again. The red flag to your bull. You won't be told what to do. You dial again. The phone is off. It goes through to voicemail. You start to leave some kind of message but quickly lose the thread of your thoughts and fade away into the digital ether.

O Mistress mine, where are you roaming?

O stay and hear, your true love's coming.

You mumble as you walk the empty streets, fumbling with cigarettes. Telling the bitumen she'll be there when you get home. She will. Or, she'll call. She'll tell you she's on her way. You'll fall asleep on the couch. The doorbell will ring and there she'll be.

Trip no further, pretty sweeting;

Journeys end in lovers meeting.

You wake on the couch in the morning. Boxing Day. Three Missed Calls.

One number. Hers. A voicemail. 2:17. She's at your door. You go and open it, hoping she'll still be there. Waiting. Eight hours later.

Merry Christmas fuckhead.

You go to bed. Depression. Paranoia. Guilt. Pizza.

You call Mandy. She invites you over. You spend a few days in her bed. The nurse. The handmaiden tends to your self-inflicted wounds. You take her out for lunch. Repulse Bay. The Verandah. You can see the disappointment in her eyes. You're a junkie in withdrawal. Your phone rings. Tucson. The addict's *idée fixe*. The ice in her veins, your crack cocaine. She wants to see you now. At your place. The hit you've been craving. A chance to ride the dragon. You dispose of Mandy, a spent syringe of sensuality.

Mother told me, yes she told me, that I'd me girls like you...

Surrender, surrender, but don't give yourself away.

Tucson's waiting, smoking at the gates when you arrive. She goes to the balcony. You follow in her vapour trail. She leans against the rail. Braced against the balustrade. You take her from behind. Mainlining her elixir. She smokes. In the kitchen window of a neighbouring tower a Filipino maid washes vegetables. Tucson takes a deep breath, exhales. Let it out. She kills the cigarette and evicts you. Ejects you from her opium den. Like a drunk at closing time, you don't have to go home but you can't stay here. She kisses you on the forehead and walks to the washroom.

Some of them want to use you,

Some of them want to get used by you.

Vegetable Woman looks up, gourd in hand. She sees you standing there, pants around your ankles. Your failings exposed for all the world to see. You light a smoke and exhale a shaky, rattling plume.

Is that emphysema, or the sound of your soul leaving your body?

Tucson is going to spend New Year with family and friends. Whatever. You don't believe her. She tells you not to call. Makes you promise. You say you're staying home. New Year. The worst night of the year. Every year. Celebrating what? She'll come over tomorrow. Sure, whatever. She hugs you. Kisses you. She tastes nice. Clean. Oral hygiene. That won't last the night.

You call Mandy.

You're sick. Maybe it was the prawns. She offers to come over. You tell her not to worry. She's arranged a night with her friends, she should go. It's New Year. She says she'll come by later and usher it with you. You tell her not to bother.

Out with the old, in with the new.

Just like that, like an impulse purchase, like the lucky watch, Mandy is consigned to history. Another piece of the past is purged.

You call Mulder and thank him for Christmas lunch. Apologise for The Incident. He says forget about it. You wish you could. All of it. Everything. He asks if you want to join him for dinner. His father is in town. His girlfriend and a couple of others are going to a restaurant, in Lan Kwai Fong. You should join them.

No. It's okay. Thanks.

Come on, he insists. You can't stay home.

You can, but he coaxes you out anyway. You give a passing wave to '94 and a brief nod of recognition to '95, barrelling out of the restaurant at about 2am. Sticking with the spontaneous spirit of the evening, and throwing caution to the wind, you let them drag you into a rave.

Doof-doof.

It only takes three revolutions of the mirror ball before you see her. Tucson. In a corner with Moneybags. You exit, stage right. And retreat deep into the cave.

Some of them want to abuse you,
Some of them want to be abused.

She arrives on your doorstep, true to her word, in the shadows of New Year's Day. Out of guilt, need or boredom? She jumps before you can ask, wraps her arms around your neck and clings to your trunk.

Happy New Year!

It's an uncharacteristic and impulsive display of emotion, or a calculated one executed with inspired sincerity. Whatever. It works. You're happy she's come and decided to stay a while. She asks what you did last night. You mention dinner and leave out the bit about the rave. You ask what she did. She mentions the rave party and leaves out the bit about Moneybags. Let's call it a draw.

It's guilt edged, glamorous and sleek by design,
You know it's jealous by nature, false and unkind.

For three days the two of you wander the cultural desert. Sitting around. Lying around. Lunches. Dinners. Movies. Babe. *That'll do pig.* Twelve Monkeys. *There's no right, there's no wrong, there's only popular opinion. I am insane. And you are my insanity.* Heat. *Don't let yourself get attached to anything you are not willing to walk out on in 30 seconds flat.* For three nights she's almost human.

It's hard and restrained, and it's totally cool,
It touches and it teases, as you stumble in the debris.

You're not doing everything wrong. You're making headway in other areas. Your responsibilities at The Agency have grown to incorporate one chapter of a globe-straddling shampoo franchise.

The new year starts with another trip to Kuala Lumpur.

Your emergency kit is now packed with double-doses of Diazepam. The simple prospect of being airborne sends you into the crash position. Any hint of turbulence has you rummaging in your manbag for salvation. You descend from outer space and arrive in the early evening. After half a dozen drinks in the lobby you return to your room. TV. Shower. TV. Guest Services Directory. In-room dining. Massage.

You open the door.

A tall, overweight woman offers a contractual smile. Her eyes are dull from the hours spent on the organic assembly line. Remnants of a discount perm haunt her head. A one-piece, floor-to-ceiling uniform struggles to contain her generous portions. Thirty going-on forty-five. You welcome her to your room, like Kublai Khan decreeing a stately pleasure dome. If Kublai Khan had been wearing a white robe atop Calvin Klein boxers. Where you lead she follows. You turn at the bed, in anticipation of instructions and permission to remove your gown.

In the five steps it's taken to get here from the door, she's slipped out of her dress and left it in a pool on the floor.

She stands there in an elaborate and ridiculous ensemble of black lingerie. Not the sort of thing you find on display at Intimate Apparel and Womens Privates. Although new age, bio-ceramic technologies were probably invented with this in mind. A lace camisole, over a bra, struggles to restrain her ample bosom. The heavy freight of her feminine mystique is clad in a double-gusset of bicycle shorts beneath industrial steel suspenders.

Take off robe, lie on bed, she commands, hauling undergarments over her head. Pendulous breasts, unsupported and devoid of a Cooper's Ligament, drop off her chest. You stare in abject horror. Afraid to watch yet unable to look away. You like special, body massage?

This appears to be a rhetorical question.

She's unpacked her assets and is rubbing oil over the scarred, unforgiving terrain of her flesh. You don't want to offend her, yet, you feel the need to tell her there's been a terrible miscommunication back at head office.

No sex. Just massage, she reminds you.

No sex. Absolutely, you agree with her.

$100 extra.

You are so far out of your element only the Hubbell Telescope can see you now. There are probably people, somewhere in the universe, who like the idea of naked women writhing over them like some slippery necromantic shadow. As a concept, maybe it has its merits. The reality is completely alien. Even you, with your sliding morality and sexual decrepitude, are not prepared for a journey like this.

You give her $100 and tell her to put her clothes on.

You don't want? It's okay. I can do for you.

You're sure she can. It's just not what you had in mind. You'll take care of that yourself, later, so to speak. Much later. If this experience hasn't rendered you impotent for life.

You still going to give me $100?

$200, just to go. Now.

There are bruises on her pulpy thighs. Abrasions on her buttocks and breasts. You ask what happened.

Some men get rough, but the money is good.

Some of them want to abuse you,

Some of them want to be abused.

You're equal parts embarrassed and amazed. Stuff like this is happening in hotels all over the world, no questions asked. It's ordered up like pizza. Does that make her a hooker? Would engaging with her mean you had been unfaithful? Do body massages count? Are they worth $100?

Like everyone else in Malaysia that night you go to sleep pondering these questions. Unaware the Vice Premier is apparently out there, somewhere, sodomising his driver.

Some of them want to use you,

Some of them want to get used by you.

You endure a day of shampoo banter and inquiry. A year in the life of a brand. Advertising. Promotions. Sales figures. Forty-three commercials. Fourteen countries. One sandwich, two muffins, three Diazepams. Cosmeceuticals. Strategies. Initiatives. New products. Packaging. Hair porn. Signature shots. Demonstrations. Proclamations. It's enough to make you look forward to getting on the plane.

Back to Hong Kong.

All roads lead to Tucson and that enormous mane of hair. Atop that gigantic head. Atop that outrageous body.

She welcomes you back. The pleasure dome. A rigorous hosing. She presents you a Polaroid. Provocative posing.

Next time you go, take this. And I will go with you.

It's a nice sentiment, regardless of how sincere. It's a nice shot too. Semi-nude, in silhouette. It raises an eyebrow and a question.

If that's her, who was the photographer?

Time shall unfold what plighted cunning hides:

Who cover faults, at last shame them derides.

Daisy bought a cat to keep her company, in your absence. Chairman

Meow. Just what you need. Another feline in your life. Still, you have a haircare summit in Kobe to look forward to.

Japan.

Finally. Land of the rising sun and submissive daughter. The stuff of legend. Weirdness awaits on streets paved with geishas. Nothing can ruin that for you.

Can it?

An earthquake in Kobe kills more than 5000.

Stupid earthquake.

5. YEAR OF THE PIG

YOU MAY HAVE TO BEND OVER and let the client fuck you, Albert, but that doesn't mean the rest of us have to take it in the ass.

A pleasant way to start the day, every day. Aggressive. On the offensive. It's not business, it's personal. It's getting you down. It's not their fault. You're dragging yourself down.

Tucson drags you further.

She takes you away for your birthday. To Macau. A quaint Portuguese fishing colony with a nice line in gambling and prostitution. The ideal romantic getaway.

You meet at the ferry terminal. Queue for five minutes to collect the tickets. She tries to pay by credit card. They wont let her. Credit card payment is for phone booking only. She steps to the side, takes out her mobile and dials. The phone behind the cashier rings. She books two tickets, reads her credit card digits down the line and rejoins the queue. She approaches the window. Gives her details and collects the tickets.

Sometimes you need a system to beat the system.

You board the ferry. She falls asleep on your shoulder, just like a real girlfriend. One hour later you're in another country and, apparently, in another time. Somewhere in time. Beyond fantasy. Beyond obsession. Beyond fucking belief.

Come back to me.

Macau is how you imagined Hong Kong to look in the 70s. If Hong Kong had been a Portuguese colony instead of British drug distribution centre.

A taxi takes you from one island, across a bridge to another island, across another bridge to a smaller, less developed island. Considering how undeveloped Macau appears to be, this is really saying something. Or is it just because Hong Kong is so overdeveloped?

You check-in and attempt to get the party started. She blocks your moves. Almost pushes you away.

Not now.

It's holy week. She's fallen off the roof. It didn't seem to worry her before but today is another day. Another place, another time. There'll be no red dot special for you either. She wants to take a nap before dinner.

You go to the bar and order a beer.

Happy Birthday fuckhead.

The attendant gives you a recommendation for dinner. You make a booking and continue with your celebrations, in the salubrious lobby bar of the hotel at the end of the world. You watch the changing of the guard for entertainment.

The day-hookers clock-off. The night-hookers clock-on.

Tucson is awake when you return to the room. Things are looking up. She asks where you've been.

At a party, with all my friends.

She apologises. She was tired. She'll make it up to you later. Right now she's hungry for less carnal comestibles.

You take her to a beachside restaurant. Eat average food off each other's plates and get staggeringly drunk on each other's cocktails. Her head begins to take on planetary proportions. It develops its own gravitational pull. By the time you get back to the hotel, you somehow manage to reach escape velocity and chart a course for The Forbidden Planet.

Hopes of a successful re-entry are scuppered almost as soon as you slingshot past the moon.

Tucson blasts into the bathroom and sends the contents of her stomach into orbit around the bowl. You hold her hair back while she hugs the porcelain and goes supernova. Over and over. You run a bath. Ease her into it. Zero gravitas. Her neck struggles to support its load and hangs on her chest. You put the loofah under her chin to stop her from drowning. Leaning back against the basin, you strike a match and light a cigarette. You stare into the flame and look forward to the year ahead. It burns down toward your fingers. The pain from the heat is comforting. It means you're still alive. You snuff it out. A candle without a wish or a hope.

Happy Birthday fuckhead.

You're both nursing hangovers in the morning. A walk around the ruins of the old fort does nothing for your enthusiasm. Egg tarts, coffee and cigarettes fill the gaps. You even talk to each other from time to time. She apologises for not making it much of a celebration. You tell her not to worry, there'll be other birthdays.

Yes, she agrees, with all the enthusiastic conviction of an oncologist who's read the report. You begin to suspect this weekend retreat may have been conceived as a farewell tour and parting gift.

Returning on the afternoon ferry, she holds your hand and rests her boulder on your shoulder. Her phone rings. She heeds the call. Long silences and one-syllable answers mean it must be Moneybags. You raise your eyebrow when she terminates the call and wonder if that's all she just ended.

She can't come home with you, she says quietly. She has something to do. She'll come by later.

Sure, whatever. Nevermind.

It's 5:37 when the doorbell rings and there she is. Ridiculously happy to see you. Loaded with affection. She steps in, takes you by the hands and gives you the soft, lingering, full press of her lips. And that's when you know for sure.

It's over.

This is the Cosa Nostra kiss-off. You're about to get whacked.

Her eyes are glassy. She runs a coy finger along the buttons of your shirt. The one with the small yellow stars and crescent moons.

Your happy shirt.

If she doesn't want to see you anymore, you explain, that's okay. Just don't go back to him. Anyone but him.

The Marquis de Sade, who knew a thing or two about abusive relationships, said that a lover, if he be of good faith and sincere, would prefer to see his mistress dead than unfaithful.

This is not too wide of the marque.

You'd never wish death upon anyone. There are times, however, when it wouldn't hurt for them to suffer some biological misfortune. Something they could share, in good faith, with their partner in treachery. A sincere bout of syphilis or gonorrhea, or something else that feels like a part of you has died. Amoebic dysentery perhaps.

She pulls you close. She has to give him one last chance, she says. He's learnt his lesson.

And there it is.

Bang.

The smoking gun. The silver bullet. The exit wound.

It was a charade. An exercise. Another sociopolitical experiment. Revenge served cold, calibrated and calculated.

You'd heard the rumours. Baldrick told you. Moneybags had two-timed Tucson with someone in the office. She wanted to give him a taste of betrayal. Find out what it feels like when your other half cheats with a colleague. When you have to see a walking, talking reminder of their infidelity at work. All day, every day. That day. Flowers in the attic. She phoned it in. First-mover advantage. She chose the person that would irk him the most. The mulatto. The gweilo. The tourist. The guy from the karaoke video. She had to get back at him and rub his nose in it. Make him sing for his supper and beg for her to come back. To give him a chance.

Some of them want to use you,
Some of them want to get used by you.

You take her massive head between your hands. A kiss before dying. You push her against the wall. She smiles. You tear her out of her clothes and nail her to the wall. She laughs. Let it out. She cackles. Two birds with one stone. You set her on the dining table and heap just desserts upon her. The last supper. The final chapter. They all lived happily never after.

The end.

You leave her drawn and quartered on the table. You sit on the couch and light a smoke. She dresses. She says she's sorry. Of course she is. She's sorry. She's so fucking sorry. Not as sorry as you are. Not as sorry and sad as your life.

Time shall unfold what plighted cunning hides,
Who cover faults, at last shame them derides.

She stops by the gift store in your bedroom on the way out, and souvenirs a t-shirt. Live Bait, NYC. Her favourite. She can wear it to bed.

That's nice.

He can stick his hands up it and try to pull it over her head. He might need some help with the buttons. They can be tricky. It'll be the closest he's been to manual labour in his life. Someone else usually does those things for him.

Don't forget to handwash it.

She brushes her teeth. Kisses you on the forehead, patronizingly, and disappears out the door.

The cat jumps up on the table and purrs with satisfaction.

You recount the long weekend to Daisy. She's empathetic but not surprised. She reminds you of Aesop's fable. The dog with the bone. That's what happen when you get greedy. You end up with nothing. It's probably a mixed blessing, she says, sounding like your mother. A blessing in disguise.

It's a pretty fucking good disguise if it is.

You could hide anything behind that head.

Forget it, Jake. It's Chinatown.

You pass Tucson in the corridors of The Agency. She smiles, quietly, like you never happened. Moneybags sits opposite you at meetings and grins. The idiot grin. Like he just won the lottery.

Maybe he did.

You hide behind your work and pour bile on your colleagues. Baldrick is leaving for another job and you didn't know about it. At home you're a ghost.

The cat shadows your every move. It sits there, judging you. Reminding you. Mocking you.

Meow.

Sai-ming's parents celebrate his birthday. Presents. A cake. They wait. And wait... In Singapore, a 28 year-old loses $1.4 billion on the futures market and brings down Barings, Britain's oldest merchant bank.

YOU RETURN TO THE HIGH SEAS. Ana and a few of The Agency irregulars have organised a junk, in Sai Kung. Most of our crew sit in the stern, jockeying for position at the mahjong table. You take a position at the bow with Mulder, Ana and a couple of art directors. The water is calm. Like the still waters of your soul. Currents of torment rip beneath.

A six-foot snake glides between nescient swimmers. The call of nature hangs quietly on gentle breezes, competing with the ever-present slap of ivory tiles.

Ana says she heard about Tucson. She can't imagine you with her. She didn't think she was your type.

That's funny, neither did she. You were on the rebound, you tell her. Any offer was a good offer. Some offers are too good to be rued.

The sun sets.

Ana suggests we buy seafood from the market by the pier, then take it back to somebody's place to cook. Her flat is too small. Your apartment has a balcony. We could go there.

Couldn't we?

Someone wants to know what else can they do there.

Sit on the balcony. Eat seafood. Drink. Smoke some of Ana's pot and see what happens, you suggest.

Do you have any games?

Games? Like mahjong?

We've been playing that all day. Cards? You have Sega? Playstation? How about karaoke?

Sure. Whatever.

Two buckets of prawns, half a dozen crayfish and a pot of mussels later, you have six half-pissed people on your balcony. Maybe you should've eaten something. No on can understand why you don't eat seafood. A deck of cards is produced and the inebriates move into the living room. Y

ou stay outside with Ana. She rolls a Camberwell Carrot.

Mazel Tav.

You raise a glass in her direction.

Gon bui.

She corrects your misappropriation of the term. *Gon bui* is unlucky. It means drink until the glass is dry. Cantonese don't like dry things. Water, in *feng shui* terms, is symbolic of money. Ergo, dry things are poor.

That explains why I've had such bad luck with women.

Because they are dry?

Now that you mention it, yes, but no, I meant I've been doing it wrong all this time.

If they are dry you are definitely doing it wrong.

Toasting, I mean. I've been *gon bui*-ing all these years. No wonder I'm cursed. The Frane Selak of the Orient.

Yum sing is the lucky way to do it. *Yum sing.* Drink to win.

Well *yum sing*, then.

Yum sing.

Ana looks like she stepped straight out of Pulp Fiction. A mini Mia Wallace. Black bob. White collared shirt, open at the neck.

Girl, you'll be a woman soon. Soon, you'll need a man.

Everyone decamps to a karaoke bar. Ana stays to swing from the last bottle of wine with you. She throws a bag of Alaskan Thunderfuck in your direction. Roll us a trainwreck, Schnazzleberry, she says and goes in search of new tunes. She's tired of Radiohead. It's been on repeat for the last hour.

I wish I was special, you're so fucking special.

You've got the Purple Urkel Jumbo Shrimp wrapped and ready to blaze. Ana hasn't returned. It's been quiet in there for quite some time.

Too quiet.

She's sitting on the floor. In front of the bookshelf loaded with CDs. A pile of possibilities rest beside her. She takes one from the shelf, looks at the cover and reads the back. It goes on the pile or is returned it to the shelf. Repeat. You lie on the bed and set fire to the Sheherazade Skunk. She draws upon it for inspiration and settles on Massive Attack. Unfinished Sympathy.

You're the book that I have opened, and now I've got to know much more.

In the fugue of Grand Funk Goza your hands touch hers. Fingers entwine. You shotgun the blunt.

The curiousness of your potential kiss, has got my mind and body aching.

Lips meet. Eyes close. Passion burns. Hands fumble. Bodies tumble.

Like a soul without a mind, in a body without a heart,

I'm missing every part.

You don't know who starts to feel weird first but the anatomical inquisition loses its urgency. Kisses falter. Eyes open.

Whoa.

Ana is a bridge too far and too far gone. She turns and curls her figure into the cradle of your frame. Trip-hop *berceuse*.

Unfinished Sympathy.

A note sits beside the bed when you wake. See you tomorrow. Ana. She's drawn a little smiley face next to her name.

You spend all morning worrying about how you'll react when you see her. Should you go to her? What if she comes to you, or you meet in the hallway by accident? Has she told anyone? Newcomb's Paradox. The Prisoner's Dilemma. The Swedish Drill. You work up the courage to walk by her desk. Catch her eye, accidentally-on-purpose. You search her face for clues.

Hi.

How're you doing?

Good.

Great.

Busy?

Yeah.

You?

Busy?

Yes.

Yeah, busy.

Okay.

Good.

See you later.

Yeah. Bye.

See you.

Yeah. See you.

Bye.

That went well. It's like it never happened. You're getting good at this. Getting by unnoticed. Not being a person of consequence. Convincing the world you don't exist. Becoming a myth. An echo. The known unknown.

It was just a taste. Sometimes that's all you need. A taste. Sometimes you need more, much more. Not with Ana. She's too sweet.

Just a taste will do.

Your first soupçon of Nippon is rescheduled and relocated from the ruins of Kobe to Tokyo. Until someone drops a can of Sarin Gas in the subway. Eight people die and thousands are poisoned. Mounting paranoia tells you this is all part of a grand, international conspiracy to keep you out of Japan.

You board a plane to Borneo instead.

The Client thought it would be good for you to experience the charms of The Resort. To give you a feel for the place. A deeper understanding of the culture. Always better to speak from an informed position than ignorance.

It's a bit of a boondoggle, but then so is life.

She sends her driver to pick you up from the airport. Miss June is not able to meet you this evening, he says. She'll meet you at the office tomorrow.

Miss June. He makes it sound like you have a date with a Playmate. Miss Conception. Miss Understanding. Miss June.

He drops you at the Hyatt. You check in and check out the pub across the street. There's a bevy of hostesses in the corner. You recognise one of them, from your flight. You try your luck.

Yum sing.

You lose.

Gon bui.

You get a table in the hotel restaurant and order an excuse for a steak. You wash it down with a bottle of wine. A woman approaches. She's noticed you're alone. She wants to know if you'd like to join her and her husband when you finish eating. She walks away. Nice rump. Too bad she's married.

Jenny and Steve are from Australia. They're here on holiday. He wants to know where you're from because you sound a little Australian.

Your mum had a little Australian in her, you tell him. Which means you've got a little Australian in you too.

Would you like some more? quips Jenny, arching an eyebrow.

You perambulate through a brief, PG-13 history of your life and try to sound worldly. Jenny, it turns out, is not actually Steve's wife. They work together. Qantas. Cabin crew. They just pretend to be married to stop people getting the wrong idea.

The wrong idea about what?

Jenny orders another round of drinks for you and Steve. She has to go to the room and make a call. She asks what you're doing tomorrow night. You're not sure. Maybe dinner with your client. Maybe not. You and Steve should swap room numbers, she says. Whoever gets in first can leave a message for the other.

Alrighty then.

You have a couple more drinks. With Jenny gone, however, the social dynamic of the table has changed. You admit to being tired. You have to be up early tomorrow. You excuse yourself and leave Steve to his own devices.

You take a shower, turn on the TV and light a smoke. Not all at the same time. The phone rings. Jenny sounds nervous. Embarrassed. I don't normally do things like this, she says, but we're only here for a while.

Don't worry about it.

She's going to ask if you want a night-cap. In the bar. In her room. In your room. You know it. She umms and errs and apologises. Laughs nervously. She wants to ask you something.

No problem. Ask away.

Are you gay? Steve really likes you. He wants to know if you'd be interested in whatever whatever whatever.

You're not listening. You're stunned. You're sorry to disappoint Steve but it's kind of funny in a way 'because you were just about to phone her and see if she wanted to come over for a drink, or something.

Oh no, I couldn't do that to Steve.

She couldn't do that to Steve? She wouldn't be doing anything to Steve. That's the point. Neither of us will be doing anything to Steve. We can not do anything to Steve together.

That's sweet but I don't really do that kind of thing.

Do it for Steve. Let him live vicariously through you.

I don't think so.

If you change you mind you know where to find me.

You sneak out of the hotel in the morning. You walk down eight flights of stairs to avoid bumping into them in the lift and skirt the lobby. You even hide behind a pot plant while the doorman hails you a cab.

Miss June greets you with a double air-kiss. It's a little too familiar and too early in the morning for that kind of thing. She smells of talcum powder. You could use a puff or two yourself. The humidity is off the charts.

She takes you on an inspection tour The Resort. It's half-finished, or half-started, depending on how you view these things. You look at the plans for the bungalows. She talks about the type of guests they hope to attract. There's the obligatory golf course. She stops at the driving range. You admire her form as she belts through half a bucket of balls. This could be how the sequel to Sexy Tennis School begins.

Sexy Tennis School 2: Sexy Golf School.

She drives you through a local village. Talks you through local customs and crafts. Points out a few landmarks on the cultural plain. Then drops you back at the hotel. Freshen up, she says. She'll meet you in the bar at 7:30.

You get there early. Miss June is fashionably late. She arrives with a friend who scowls at you as introductions are made. Miss Anthropic.

It's okay, you tell her. I hate me too.

The cabin attendants are back in their corner. A constant distraction and flight of fancy. The Client says she'll set you up with one of them if you'd rather be over there. You apologize and tell her not to worry. You tried that already. You recount your tale of unrequited love from the evening before. *Gon bui.* Jenny and Steve. The Honeymooners.

Finish your drink, she says. She's got a reservation at the Shangri-la. Maybe you'll have better luck there.

Miss June proves herself to be a gracious host. Miss Congeniality. She's perceptive and gameful with a licentious sense of humour. Munificent too. She's given her driver the night off.

Her munificence doesn't stop there.

She drops Miss Anthropic home. They exchange a few boisterous words in Malaysian or Bornean or whatever. A short detour and then you're back on the road again. On the road again. Going places you've never been, seeing' things you may never see again and you just can't wait to get on the road again.

It's not her love of country music and Willie Nelson that is surprising. You'd just picked her to be more into Johnny Cash or Hank Williams.

My lips could tell a lie, but my heart would know.

She takes her mobile from her handbag and dials a number. She tells her daughter she'll be home late. Later.

Her daughter? Later? On a school night?

Miss Conception pulls up at the entrance of the hotel like she own it. Maybe she does. She tosses the keys to the doorman, hooks herself into your arm and steers you across the lobby. She waves at the night manager, ushers you into the elevator and pushes the button confidently.

Eighth floor, right?

You've done your homework.

I made the booking, she confirms.

Oh.

808. Lucky number, for some.

It wasn't last night.

It will be tonight.

The game is afoot. She takes you to the threshold and stands there, waiting. Waiting. Waiting for you to remember that you have the key.

Oh.

You unlock the door. She whacks you in the stomach with the back of her hand as she slides by. You follow. The door closes firmly. She says she's not normally this forward but if she waited for you we'd still be thinking about it at the launch party. She kisses you. Hard. Steps back. Hooks her index finger into the top of your jeans and drags you to the bed.

It's a shame Steve and Jenny aren't here to see how not-gay you are.

She tells you not to worry. She'll make sure you're up in time for your morning flight. You have no reason to doubt her. Sleep doesn't appear to be on her agenda.

Bury the corpse. Fill the hole. Feed the hole.

Miss Appropriate is good to her word, paying more than lip service to the cultivation of client-agency relations. She drives your from Thunderdome to the aerodrome at dawn's crack. She looks forward to seeing the campaign and welcoming you back. The golf course will probably be finished by then. You can play a round with her.

200 people watch as a young hairdresser is mauled by a shark, pulled from the shallows and dies on the beach... A woman loses an arm and a leg in a separate shark attack. She dies in hospital a day later. Officials decline to enlist the services of Vic Hislop, after local environmental groups label him nothing but a vigilante on a killing spree. A spokesman for Hislop denounces the accusation and reminds critics that the only thing he caught last time was dysentery and the only thing wounded was his pride. A vigilante on a diarrhoea spree would be more appropriate.

THE AIR-CON IS ON THE FRITZ. You call The Landlord. He says to go ahead and get it repaired or replaced. Whatever you think is best. Send him the invoice and he'll reimburse you later. You do and he does. This type of trust, honour, probity and sincerity is unheralded in the annals of rental agreements. If he isn't hung, drawn and quartered by the land pirates, they should have him bronzed. Cousin Dougal probably knows a guy who could get him a deal.

Equally admirable and no less worthy of recognition are the bronze curves of Vikki. She speaks three languages, only two of which are verbal.

You meet at the Rugby Sevens, in the Southern Stand. The scoring end of the ground. She's the rose among the thorns of beer-soaked expatriates, and looks as lost as you feel in the sea of inebriety. A siren on the rocks, her save-me smile is the seductive song that lures you to your doom. Part Filipino, part Jalapeño.

And though she be little, she be fierce.

New Zealand win the tournament but you leave with the prize.

Dinner at a Thai restaurant leads to dancing at JJ's, The Grand Hyatt's infamous nightclub and nocturnal wet market. Vikki seems to know almost everyone there, including the staff. She gets all her drinks for free. If you were thinking straight you'd probably wonder why and how she enjoys such celebrity. Your interests at this juncture, however, lie in other areas.

If music be the food of love, play on.

You throw yourself into another intensely physical, ultimately soulless relationship. For weeks.

Mother told me, yes she told me, I'd me girls like you...

Surrender, surrender, but don't give yourself away.

She works as an Administration Assistant at a large Tsim Sha Tsui hotel. Her hours are unusual and irregular. She is often at work for days at a time, pulling double and triple shifts. She can't be reached by phone. You begin to suspect her of being an in-house masseuse, or more. Room service. The girl has skills and a cavalier approach to living. She delivers experiences so intense they can alter your political views. Maybe she lives a dual life.

Don't we all?

Vikki makes the mistake of uttering five of the scariest words in the lexicon of post-coital colloquy.

Baby, when we get married...

Such delusions are not to be treated lightly. You begin a rehabilitation program, of sorts. Re-education. Reorientation. Preferably somewhere there isn't a bedroom, bathroom, broom closet or automobile nearby for her to manoeuvre in and change your mind half a dozen ways.

Men, as observed by Joyce, are governed by straight lines of intellect. Women by dangerous curves of emotion. You think it through and figure it's best to deep-six her in a Tsim Sha Tsui cafe. Somewhere not too far from her work, while she's on a break. Strategically, this is sound. Hopefully the curves of her emotion will be easier to contain in a public space. The need to return to the hotel in twenty minutes will stop it from dragging it out unnecessarily.

If she has any idea she's about to get hit by a bus she doesn't show it. The smile is as broad and captivating as the afternoon we met.

I have to tell you something. It's not you. I'm not ready for the kind of commitment you're looking for. Actually, it is you, Vikki. You're too full-on. You scare me. Some of the things you say.

She takes it well.

By that you mean she doesn't appear to be taking it at all. She says she'll just stop doing and saying things you don't like.

You tell her that's not the point. She makes you uneasy. You don't feel comfortable. You want to move on. Meet other people.

She offers to bring other people over to the apartment for you to meet. To get comfortable with. She was going to give you one of her girlfriends for Christmas but she can arrange it this weekend. Just the three of us. It was going to be a surprise.

It certainly would've been. And now she's made you feel bad for ruining it.

You're quick to remind yourself that at least one third of that fantasy hinges on a delusional, sociopathic hoyden of Pleasure Island. You feel like Homer Simpson, caught between the insoluble truths of Lisa's recital and a monster truck rally.

Oh cruel fate! Why do you mock me!

Advantage Vikki. She grins at her infallible ingenuity. She moves in to the net, to smash your feeble return across the court. You astonish her and yourself, and a couple at the adjacent table, with a backhander down the line.

That' a generous offer, Vikki. A guy would be crazy to turn it down. But it wouldn't feel right.

It would feel pretty good, Reechard.

I'm sure it would but, after, it wouldn't change the way I feel now. I'm sorry Vikki. That's just the way it is. Maybe I'll see you around but I can't see you for a while.

You don't even give her the right of reply. You just walk off. Leave her there, like the last kid waiting to get picked in the softball team.

And that's that.

Until your phone rings at 10pm. She's decided to deploy that other weapon in the woman's biological arsenal. Tears. She can't accept what you said. She's going to kill herself. Jump out the window. Cut herself in the bath.

It's not fair.

Neither is this phone call. Your Filipino Jalapeño has just turned Hellapeño. Mulder had warned you about this type of thing. He woke up one morning with an ex-girlfriend sitting on the end of his bed with a knife. She was threatening to kill him and herself.

What can you do?

You go to her flat, primarily to make sure she hasn't written a note that incriminates you. If she's going to kill herself there's no need for her to ruin your life as well. She thanks you for coming. She understands but doesn't want to be alone tonight. Just tonight.

Maybe she thinks she can work her charms on you once more and engineer a reversal of fortune, or maybe she really just doesn't want to be alone, tonight

Maybe she's too tired and emotional to go to JJ's. You give her the benefit of the doubt and agree to stay over. Tonight, but that's it. Tomorrow she'll have to get on with her life because you have to get on with yours.

Okay Reechard.

She makes no attempt to seduce you. Maybe everything is going to be alright. Still, you don't allow yourself to fall asleep. Just in case she changes her mind and tries to kill herself. Or chop your dick off.

Taiwan's President accepts an invitation, and a visa, to visit the United States. China responds with missile tests in The Straight.

YOU ADD ZOLOFT to your regimen of prescription drugs. The next few weeks will be a trial. You have to film the same shampoo commercial nine times. For nine countries. On the upside that means nine different shampoo girls to scrutinize, cast and get into Wardrobe for a fitting.

Day One passes without incident. You meet The Director. The Producer. The Crew. They're all on the ball and those that aren't seem to know where the ball is, or that there should be a ball around here somewhere. You just wish they'd pick their feet up a little when they go in search of the ball.

Day Two brings fresh challenges. New faces. Talent. The girls. Japan, Korea, Thailand, Philippines and Indonesia are as advertised. Hong Kong and China aren't really working for you. You're not even sure it's the same girls from the casting tape. It's possible their agent pulled the old switcheroo. It's happened before. You can probably substitute Malaysia or Singapore for those two markets anyway. Keep the Thai girl in reserve as a last minute Hail Mary, just in case, and hope no one notices the difference. All shampoo girls look the same.

We roll film on Day Three. The same scene, nine times. Each requires approval. The Hair Police crawl out of the woodwork. Corporate goon squads. The Gestoppo. Everyone's an expert. Allies are thin on the ground.

Nazarate is even thinner. And taller.

Nazarate. Naz. Or Na-na, depending on how you are with the brevity thing. Nazi, if you feel like invading her Poland and seeing Warsaw. You vaguely remember her from a Hair Summit. She's poised and fluid in her movements, with expressive hands. On a sliding scale of distractions, with Korea being a nine and Singapore being a three, Nazarate is a sinewy seven. Maybe an eight by the time you get to the bar.

Mother told me, yes she told me, I'd meet girls like you.

Day Four pans out and dollies much like Day Three. You shoot through two sequences, nine times. Or is that nine sequences two times? Nazarate says there's a good restaurant nearby the hotel. It would be nice to try it one night. Whatever. You try to read a magazine but end up running over the same paragraph seventeen times. You're up and down all afternoon, looking through lenses. Finding excuses for Korea to do a retake from a different angle. Every angle. Her geography and topography are extraordinary. Can we get a close-up? Closer. Closer. Any closer and you'll trip on those lips. Then drown in the deep, dark pools of her eyes. At the end of the day, cast and crew and colleagues meet downstairs for dinner. You order Room Service and nod-out to the warm, familiar glow of television.

Nazarate starts Day Five expressing her concern for your health. She didn't see you at dinner. She hopes you're okay. It's important to eat healthy when you're on a shoot. You need to keep you energy up. People depend on you. Tonight she'll make sure you have a good meal. She'll feed you. No excuses. She'll make a booking at that restaurant.

Let's see how it goes today.

Truth is you could use a decent meal. The caterers put the muck in *nasi lemak*. The recurring buffet of *roti canai, murtabak ayam* and *ikan kurau* is wearing thin. You can't live on bread, salty crackers and Coke forever.

Can you?

Truth is you don't mind being mothered, and Nazarate seems keen to adopt. Why break the habit of a lifetime?

Adopted. Abused. Abandoned. Repeat, ad infinitum. Ad nauseum. As it was in the beginning so shall it be until the end. Amen.

The last shot is wrapped by 8:30. Nazarate is waiting in the lobby shortly after. She wears a svelte, full-length maroon dress. Cut deep in front and slit high on the thigh. She turns and burns like a flame. Long hair swept across a shoulder.

Dinner is three courses of Mediterranean mediocrity, sluiced down with a weird white. Funky cold retsina. Nazarate makes it seem almost palatable and enhances the appetite appeal. She takes a couple of sips, licks her lips and you know that she is with it. She's a spiritual mélange, of Hindu descent, who admits to flirting with Christianity. She preaches with her hands and her body sings in chorus. She leans forward to make a point. A small breast slips free and makes another. She pretends not to notice until she's sure you have and, oh, winsomely re-adjusts. Did you want some dessert?

Coffee, tea, or Nazarate?

You call for the check. She insists on going Dutch.

You hardly ate anything, she says.

And you didn't drink much.

I drank enough, she admits with a smile.

Funky cold Medina.

You hold the door open as she leaves the restaurant and usher her into a waiting taxi. You're such a gentleman, she says as she glides across the seat, exposing a fluid fricandeau of caramel thigh. It remains that way for the duration of the journey. You'd like to plane your hand along it but that's probably not the type of thing a gentlemen would do.

You walk her to her room. Kiss her on the cheek and walk away. You take about three steps and hear what sounds like a whimper. You stop and listen.

There's that mewl again.

Her chin is down, wide mouth at full pout. She looks at you through the fringe of her hair. Why didn't you give me a proper kiss? she wants to know.

You weren't sure if that would be appropriate. Business and pleasure. The Geneva Convention. Church and state. And all that.

Her eyes suggest she believes more in the United Nations charter. Harmonizing actions. Friendly relations. Cooperation. The right to an education. This is neutral territory. We come in peace. And all that.

You move toward her, take her cheek in the palm of your hand and press your lips to hers. She drifts away, drawing you with her, against the door.

It peels open.

A sultry dip and shimmy of her shoulder sees the dress spill to a puddle at her feet. She lifts your shirt, unbuckles your belt and flirts with Christianity.

Sweet Jesus.

Go bathe, she purls. And leads you to the washroom.

She subjects you to some kind of solicitous cleansing ritual, in preparation for the feast. You're soon in a right lather. She elevates you to a state of *jhatka* and you're *satvic* as hell by the time you arrive at her alter, ready for sacrifice. The goat is swiftly, deftly slaughtered. Toes curled and stomach cramped, the heavens are called from the sky.

Bury the corpse. Fill the hole. Feed the hole.

She levitates from the bed, drifts to the desktop in the corner and beckons from the blotter. She opens a drawer and invites you to take down a letter. Opening remarks are made, a spirited salutation, swathed in the silk of her legs. She leans against the wall and recites her tantric mantra. In the mirror we're both one with Vishnu. All arms and legs braced against the furniture and walls. Pages of The Kamasutra are recreated across the canvas of the room until you have nothing left to give.

You collapse at her side and pray for a cigarette.

Day Six begins on uncertain legs. You sidle from Nazarate's shrine of the fallen warrior, boots in hand, stealing across the courtyard by the dawn's early light. A blind turn into a corridor brings you sharply into focus for The Cameraman. He's on his way to breakfast with a shit-eating grin on his face.

Undress rehearsal, was it? he quips. Can I get you something from the buffet, or did you have breakfast in bed already?

By the time you get to the set, cast and crew are involved in a game of Chinese Whispers. Rumour has it you were helping one of the models with her dialogue last night. Running through her lines until the wee hours. Speculation is rife. The Producer asks what you're doing for dinner. You tell her you'll probably just have a swim. Get to bed early.

Bit tired are you? Don't stay up too late.

You loll in the shallow end on a raft of duty-free liquor and an air-mattress of meds. Nazarate arrives, unannounced. Uninvited. The sea-nymph glides through the water to intercept you. A veritable Varuna-in-wading she pilots your through celestial seas in search of safe harbour. Any port in a storm.

Hell is empty and all the devils are here.

When the tempest subsides you find yourself cast upon the dimly lit cotton shores of your room. Was it just an aquatic reverie? A wet dream?

Misery acquaints a man with strange bedfellows.

You kill a cigarette. See swimsuits strewn upon the floor. A willowy figure silhouetted in the bathroom door. Hair turbanned in a towel. Nothing more.

'Tis some visitor, tapping at my chamber door,
Only this and nothing more.

You're awake, she says happily. I thought you might've fallen asleep. Had enough, or do you want some more?

Then, methought, the air grew denser,
Perfumed from an unseen censer.

The high priestess slips through the darkness and engages the pagan member of the congregation. Christ the redeemer. For her own person, it beggars all description. Twisting and turning, converting. Stand up for Jesus. She leads you into temptation, delivering you unto evil. He is risen. He is risen indeed. She commands you to sin against her. Do it after the high Roman fashion and make death proud to take us. For hers is the kingdom, the power and the glory. Forever and always. Amen.

And his eyes have all the seeming of a demon's that is dreaming,
And the lamp-light o'er him streaming throws his shadow on the floor;
And my soul from out that shadow that lies floating on the floor
Shall be lifted, nevermore!

Day Seven. Or is it Eight? The Director asks if you enjoyed yourself in the pool last night. He hadn't seen a show like that since he took the family to Sea World in '87.

Nazarate, the Loch Ness Sex Monster, turns from succubus to octopus.

She hangs off you all day. She brings coffee without asking if you want it. She lights cigarettes and passes them to you between set-ups. She folds your newspaper when you get up and talk to The Cameraman. She hands it back on your return. She stands behind you and massages your shoulders while you're talking to The Producer. She makes suggestions, interjections and voices her approval. She brings you plates of fruit. Bananas from Na-na. She's crossed the line with her cloying.

Her public displays of affection are an annoying affectation.

After lunch, as luck would have it, The Director is laid low with a chronic bout of gastro. That will teach him to make smartarse comments. He'll see more of the khazi than the shoot for the rest of the day and be better off in his room, back at the hotel.

You have take the reins for the remainder of the production.

Nature works in mysterious ways. And so does Nazarate. She mistakenly assumes this puts her in the driver's seat too, riding shotgun. Before she can go off half-cocked, however, The Producer reminds her she only has responsibility for one country. Indonesia. The de facto director must drive a rag of nine colts before him and can do without the distraction.

The mantle of responsibility and breathing room are a welcome reprieve from the suffocating yolk of Oedipal doting. You immerse yourself in the task and the talent pool. There's a great performance in Korea and you're determined to get it out of her.

When the day is wrapped, clients, cast, crew and attendant agency reps are dismissed. You remain with The Cameraman, The Producer and The Hairdresser to work through a shot-list and call-sheet for tomorrow. It's the last day of the shoot and we're behind schedule. The prognosis for our fibreless leader is not positive. You'll probably have to bring this baby home.

It's not as daunting as what is waiting for you at the hotel.

Nazarate arrives at your door with a bowl of soup. To keep your strength and spirits up. Such eleemosynary gestures are hard to refute, even when you know there's a hidden cost to be extracted at a time posterior. She sets the bowl on the table and disappears into the bathroom.

Finish your soup, she exhorts. I will give you a massage.

With ghosts of massages past haunting your memory, and a flashback to the future manifesting in the steam of the consommé, it's difficult to savour the flavours of the victuals and concomitant prospects. Still, it has been a long day. And such open-handed gestures, as has been mentioned before, are hard to refute. There is a tightness in your shoulders and a Korean knurling in your core. You wash down two Howard Blues with the dregs of the soup and resign yourself to a hollow fate.

Nazarate returns in a robe. You aren't yourself, she says.

Who am I? you wonder aloud, asking more of yourself than her.

The Director, she replies. Behind the camera all day. Not a moment to rest. A massage will help relieve the stress and pressure of the shoot.

Ah yes, the stress of the shoot. So demanding. All this sitting around and sexual convocation has really taken its toll. I could hardly make sheep's eyes at the talent by the end of it all.

You lie face-down on the bed. She mounts you. Her telling hands hold a deep conversation with the timbre of your timber. A thick fog cascades across the dark moors of your mind.

Tumbling. Turning. Rolling.

She spreads oil on your chest, positions herself above and abases. *Rectus abdominus. Linea alba. Obliquus externus.* She glides. Long and slow. Communing with your conflicted core until neither of you can take it anymore. Reconciliation. Repent. Join the Eucharist. She takes the holy Host and gleefully accepts the hotly prized Christian Fellowship Award.

Nurse Shakti concludes her duties with warm towels and a bedside bathing. She says she'll let you sleep, pulls up the sheets and disappears into the ether.

The End Of Days begins, as expected, with The Director *in absentia.* You've half a mind to send Nazarate and her healing hands to nurse him back to health. It'll make that trip to Sea World seem like a visit to the dentist.

You assume your position behind the monitor and put people through their paces. Shower scenes. The swimsuit competition of our beauty pageant. The water heater, by default or design, is barely generating enough degrees to keep the goosebumps at bay. To protect their modesty you clear all nonessentials from the set. The girls show their appreciation at the end of each take.

It's good to be The King.

Shooting finishes late but no one really cares. It's over. We can all go back to our miserable lives. Except for you and The Director. You'll spend the next week in an editing suite, cutting the same 30-second commercial nine times.

The wrap party is a riotous affair.

You sit with cast and crew in the middle of The Boom-boom Room. At one end, a catwalk extends from behind velvet curtains. Hey Big Spender boom-booms across the room. A tall transvestite, dressed as Liza Minelli from Cabaret, steps into the spotlight. She raises a plucked eyebrow to the ceiling and brings a riding crop down across her fishnetted thigh.

Bah dah da-dah dah dah!

She walks toward you and, through the subtle art of mime, suggests she doesn't pop her cork for every guy in town. She invites you to spend a little time with her. At this point, it's fair to say, she pretty much knows all there is to know about the crying game.

Mother told me, yes she told me, I'd meet girls like you.

You manage to avoid Nazarate for most of the night, until she corners you by the toilet. She's probably been waiting there. Anyone drinking that amount of beer would have the break the seal eventually.

You curse your Chinese bladder.

She tells you she's going back to Indonesia tomorrow. You feign disappointment. Like you just crashed out of the Olympics. She wants you to go back to the hotel, now, for a swim. A lap of honour. Gee, you'd really like to but you promised The Hairdresser and Make-up you'd go out with them. You'll drop by her room on the way back. She says you can't. Two of the models were supposed to leave tonight but missed their flight when the shoot ran-over. They're staying in her room.

Which two?

It doesn't matter.

Yes it does.

She punches you on the arm, in mock frustration at your cantrip and goak.

No really, it does.

She says she can wait in your room.

You aren't sure that's a good idea. Best she calls you at three. You'll make sure you're back by then. She can drop by. Bring a friend with her, if she likes.

You're back at the hotel with The Hairdresser and Make-up shortly after midnight. Worried the courtyard might be under surveillance, you hug the dark corners until safely behind doors.

The phone rings.

You let it be, make a meal of a mazzie and knockout the lights. There's a rap on your door at two, three and four. Then no more.

Take thy beak from out my heart, and take thy form from off my door!

Quoth the Raven, Nevermore.

The next five days are spent Han Solo, diving into edit suites and crawling out of swimming pools. No interruptions. No problems. No Nazarate. You present the commercials to The Client and there are handshakes all-round. After the obligatory dinner you end up at a refuge centre for battered businessmen. Three of them, sitting beside you, smoke cigars and wonder whether they'll ask Anita and Ruby to dinner tomorrow night. That way they won't have to fork out for hookers as well.

Returning to the hotel, The Concierge greets you and wants to know if you had a good evening. You tell him it was okay. You're leaving tomorrow. He leans in and asks if you'd like a girl tonight. You must be lonely. He motions toward a couple of nylon nubiles at the other end of the lobby. If you take them both he can get you a good deal. Two for the price of one. They've just finished in one room and are on their way back to the bar. He can probably get the call-out fee waived. You laugh, perhaps a little too loud, and thank him for thinking of you. Not tonight. Thanks anyway.

A late night snack, Sir? You can't sleep on an empty stomach!

Thanks but I had congee for breakfast. I couldn't possible have another man's porridge for dinner.

The children of the night afford you a smile as you walk by. One of them has, or had, a cleft palette. A hair lip. The scar is pronounced. Hers eyes suggest she might even be retarded.

We are such stuff as dreams are made on,
And our little life is rounded with a sleep.

A taxi spirits your from Kai Tak to your Mid-levels favela. The driver wakes you in the carpark. You're still floating on whatever it is you took and the glasses of Shiraz that made the trip with them. You wouldn't have noticed the small man in the corner of the elevator if he hadn't pushed the stop button and brought the carriage to a halt. Between floors. Between two worlds.

He pulls a knife.

You smirk. This might not actually be happening. Or is it? He demands money. The prospect of physical harm doesn't register.

Through the darkness of futures past, the magician longs to see,
One chants out between two worlds, fire walk with me.

He's tiny, like the midget in the Red Room. Twin Peaks. He looks more worried than you'll ever be. You're just annoyed at the inconvenience of it all. You open your wallet and give him a fistful of Malaysian Ringgit and Hong Kong Dollars. You reach into your pocket and hand over another $7:60 in change. He stuffs it into his grubby jeans then makes a playful jab at you with his knife, to remind you who's in charge. He pushes and pulls at the button, to set the lift in motion. Nothing happens. You look at him. He looks at you.

Now what?

He goes to work on the button again. We're going nowhere. His anxiety climbs north. You move to engage the intercom. He makes that same pathetic stabbing motion with the knife. You raise your hands in surrender.

I'll get help. Okay? *M-ho mun tai.* No problem.

He looks like he wants to believe you and is surprised at your rudimentary Cantonese. *M-ho mun tai.* No problem. He reluctantly allows your hand to touch the panel and call for help.

It's slow in coming. You're in there for almost an hour.

You sit on the floor, while the unluckiest mugger in the long and sad history of mugging stands beside you, worried you'll sneak off without him.

The elevator lurches into motion.

He waves his knife about and holds a hand over the pocket where your money now resides. *Sau sang.* No tell, he whispers. *Sau sang.* It sounds more like he's asking for a favour than a command upon which your life may hang. He gives you a last look and conceals the weapon beneath his John Lennon t-shirt.

Imagine.

Two policemen, four firemen, a couple of nerdy engineer types and the security guys from the building are there. Your new friend mutters something in Cantonese and points at you. You're not worried about his hollow threats. You just don't want to spend the next three hours pressing charges, making statements and signing forms. It's only a grand. You just want this Cleesian farce to be over.

You want to go to bed.

You apologise to those assembled and tell them you accidentally leant against the stop button. *M-ho esee-ah.* Sorry. *M-ho esee-ah.* The tribal elders roll their eyes and condemn you to a lifetime of stupidity. The bandit remains schtum. *Chee-sin gweilo,* he says as he disappears into the night.

There's a letter on the dining room table.

Your beloved landlord has died. Pneumonia. His wife has mailed you a copy of the death certificate to let you know. She's also furnished you with details of a new bank account for the transfer of rent deposits.

A burglar breaks in to an apartment and makes off with money, jewellery, bankbooks and credit cards. He leaves a ransom note for the title deeds to the apartment, including his pager number, so the owners to contact him. Police trace the number and arrest him... Three gunmen hijack a Macau jetfoil and escape with millions... Sai-ming's parents are told their son is lost, never to return. If he hasn't been abducted, and taken to work in a factory, he probably curled up and died with thousands of homeless others. They refuse to accept he is gone. They know he is out there, somewhere, trying to make it home. He just can't find his way.

YOU'RE REVISITING SOME DYLAN with Chairman Meow. Desire. Hard Rain. The cat is not a big fan of the latter's live recording. You're not so keen on it either. You just haven't listened to it for a long time and feel obliged to justify its purchase.

Where you been?

No place special.

Hi, she says. Like she's never been away. Like nothing's happened, to either of you, in the months between.

Xi-shi.

The days of future past pass quietly. Exchanges are as polite as they are brief. No mention of what went before. No talk of what might come to pass. Just furtive glances in moments of weakness.

You look different.

Well, I guess.

Daisy invites The Guy over. The Guy brings a friend for Xi-xi. CC, as he calls her, unable or too lazy to get his mouth around the phonetics. CC. Like she's a document to be copied, circulated and distributed. A dosage to be administered. A liquor. The Guy wants to set her up with his friend. Get a sister for his Bro. He's always looking for new and tiresome ways to annoy you. It's a hobby of his. As predictable as the jibes about your shirts.

Your star fetish is over, consigned to history like the well-worn apparel of your past. Your shirts are nitid, not knitted. Shiny silver. Sheeny blue. Burnished white. Nylon/cotton blends. Rayon. 5% Kevlar. You even found a glow-weave bodyshirt in Swank. A suit of psycho-sartorial armoire, to counter your less-than sparkling personality and combat your unsunny disposition.

You gonna stay?

If you want me too, yes.

You're working late. A jingle for the crunchy coconut drink proving more elusive than first thought. The phone rings. It's Xi-shi. She's drunk. Just a little. She's shouting to be heard above ambient noise in a Tsim Sha Tsui bar. She's sorry to interrupt. You say it's okay. You're glad she called. She wants you to join them. Her and her sister. The Guy and a few of his friends. For a drink.

Are you lookin' for somethin' easy to catch?

I said I got no money.

He said that ain't necessary.

You want to see her. Talk to her. The thought of her being objectified by The Guy and The Bro pisses you off. If there's any objectification to be done around here it's going to be done properly and done by you.

What drives me to you is what drives me insane

She stumbles past a couple of chairs toward you. Denim jeans. White t-shirt. Jet-black, Jennifer Aniston fuck-me hair. She hugs you. Allure rises from beneath the stench of cigarettes and wine. She kisses you on the cheek. Fuel to the ire you've lit under The Guy and his Bro.

Thank you, she whispers in your ear.

I haven't done anything, yet.

You came.

On a low wall outside you sit beside her and light a smoke. You tell her you've been wanting to talk since she got back. She looks and listens. You plough on, umming and erring about what happened. You felt she was making decisions for you, rather than herself. Her dashboard confessions scared you. Maybe you should've told her how you felt. It wasn't fair to let her sister pass on the information. You're sorry.

She looks at you, silently. Straightfaced. Eyes at half-mast. Maybe she's not going to let you off that easily. Perhaps she thinks you're not finished and wants to see where this is going.

You tell her you feel the two of you have unfinished business and you want to try again.

She smiles. She didn't mean to scare you. She wasn't trying to crowd you or pressure you. She was confiding in you. She thought you'd understand.

You apologise and start to repeat your excuses.

Let her finish, she says. She feels the same way. The two of you are not done. She realised how much she missed you when she saw you sitting there, listening to that horrible music with that stupid cat.

Great.

But things will be different.

Oh, great. Again.

She wants to know what's so funny.

Nothing. You'll explain later. It's just a spot of *déjà vu.*

Groundhog Day.

Ned Ryerson?

Bing!

This time, she says, you'll have to tell her more. Not keep everything to yourself. She doesn't want to pry but you should feel you can talk to her, like she feels she can talk to you. Maybe you'd be a little happier and easier to get along with if you realised you weren't alone.

You say you'll try.

She looks deep into you. You look at her hands. Take one in yours. Lean forward and kiss her on the cheek.

Let's go home.

In the taxi she recounts the break-up with her boyfriend. It is a story of abuse, violence and stolen money.

You have more in common than she thinks.

You tell her you had no idea how difficult life would be, post AJ. How abandoned you felt. How confusing it was. You were supposed to be miserable but then she came along and made you feel needed. You recall the Tucson Files. How you knew what was going on and how it would end. How you probably wanted to get fucked over, again, to prove that what happened with AJ wasn't your fault. You post-rationalise Mandy and how you burnt that bridge for no other reason than it felt good to put the shoe on someone else's foot. You tell her it's good to see her. You've missed her.

Let's find out how much.

Things are different. There's giving and getting. Taking and receiving. There's two of you, banishing the elephant in the room. Fucking for more than fun and distraction. She is liberating. Generous and involving. Anger gives way to passion. Forgiving leads to forgetting. Bitterness is swallowed by bliss.

Things are different.

You take walks and go out to dinner, just like a real couple. You complain about work. She listens and, sometimes, offers advice. She's smart. Smarter than you. You have the occasional argument. The money you spend on clothes, and the type of clothes you buy with your money. Movies. Her appalling taste in music.

Things are different.

There's an invitation to a celebration. Blowback from the AJ years. You arrive at the restaurant, hand in Xi's hand. A series of tables link Little Australia to Little Britain and Little America. The populations of these continents are vastly unfamiliar to you. Twenty sets of eyes give Xi the once-over and quickly pass judgement. Some are invigorated by her presence, others are enervated. A few women are intimidated and resentful of the attention she commands. This is partly because she's the only Chinese person there. This is partly because the dress she's wearing is so tight it would split at the seams if she farted. Over the course of the evening three guys make thinly veiled passes at her. One makes a special trip from the other end of the table to garner an introduction. He finds some excuse, during a laugh, to put his hand on hers. He even looks at you while he does it, as if to ask permission. Mind if I have a go, mate? As if that might somehow be okay.

Xi is almost as embarrassed as you are.

Driving home she asks if all your friends are like that. You say not really. They're not really your friends. You don't really have any friends.

You have me, she reminds you.

She knows how grumpy you get. How moody you can be. It doesn't trouble her. She's almost too understanding at times. Too forgiving. She's intelligent and strong. Demanding, physically. Sexually. More of a man than many will ever be. And many times the woman others can never be.

Things are different, for a while.

As weeks roll into months you begin the process of shutting down. Locking her out, little by little. The closer she gets the further away you move. She knows. She tries harder to please. To convince. It only makes it worse. Except when you're together. Alone.

Chemistry rules.

OJ Simpson is found not guilty of murder. LA erupts.... A mainlander tells reporters Sai-ming was taken to a detention centre in Guangdong, beaten and starved to death. Officials deny the boy has died in custody.

IT'S TOO MUCH. Maintaining a constant physical and emotional rapport with Xi-shi. Living with four women and a cat. It's too hard. The apartment is big but you can never be alone. Anywhere. There's always someone, somewhere. Maria. Gina. Daisy. The Guy and his Bro. Xi. The walls are closing in. You need companionship on your own selfish terms, not a constant companion. An intrusion. You want to slow it down. Stop it happening too fast. Put distance between you and her and everyone else.

You decide to break the lease.

No consultation. Action and consequence. You come home from work and convene a meeting. They'll have to find a a place of their own. Except the cat. The Chairman can come with you if no one else wants her.

Xi is surprised. And hurt.

The cat over her?

Gina is pissed-off at the inconvenience of it all. Maria is worried she'll have to find another job or return to the Manila. Daisy, never surprised or troubled by anything, only has one question.

Can I have Maria? I'll swap you the cat for the maid.

Xi comes to your room. She nearly always gives the impression she's looking forward to something. Not tonight.

Why? she asks quietly.

You tell her the apartment is getting too small. She says she'll give you more room. You say that's not it. Don't look so upset. It's not like the two of you are breaking up, even though you probably are. It'll be better. You won't be living in each other's pocket. You'll be able to see each other when you want to, not because you have to. Just like a real couple. You'll be together most nights. You'll just have more space in-between.

It's an amazing, unprecedented, nauseous clutch of clichés and she looks as convinced by them as you are. She, who always seems so happy in a crowd, whose eyes can be so private and so proud. No one's allowed to see them when they cry. She's the love that cannot last, that comes to you from shadows of the past, that you'll remember till the day you die.

It's the first night you haven't slept together, since things were going to be different.

You call the wife of your deceased landlord. She tells you to call her son. He handles these things now. He sounds nice enough. You explain how you want to break the lease. You're calling to give him two month's notice, in accordance with the agreement you had with his benevolent father. After one year he said you could opt out at any time. As long as you gave two months notice. He says there'll be no problem.

Go ahead and move out.

You send him a fax, confirming the date you'll be vacating the flat. You propose a date for his final inspection. The Handover. The keys in return for the deposit. Bring a cheque. Any problems, just call.

M-ho mun-tai. No problem. *M-ho mun-tai.*

You resume normal relations with Xi. Abnormally normal, with added intensity. Maybe she's making the most of what she has while she has it, or is trying to fuck you into changing your mind. Maybe she's fucking you out of her life. It doesn't matter. You take it all, and her, for granted.

I'll take her laughter and her tears, and make them all my souvenirs

You inspect and reject apartments from Quarry Bay to North Point, Fortress Hill, Tin Hau, Causeway Bay and Wan Chai. You're as tired of the Mid-levels as it is of you. You need a new hole-in-the-wall. A secret hide-away where no one can find you.

Not even you.

Eventually you arrive at a Lilliputian four-room apartment in Tin Hau. It's a six-flight walk-up with a view across Victoria Park to the harbour. One and a half bedrooms. The kitchen is cleverly disguised as the living room. The shower and bathroom are cleverly disguised as a toilet. It's perfect. There's even a bar at the base of the stairwell.

The Forever Lounge.

Your new landlady is charming and quite possibly insane. She doesn't even want a security deposit. She gives you the number of a moving company, if you need a hand with that type of thing. Can she get you any furniture? A bed or a couch or a television? You tell her you have everything you need and a few things you don't. You warn her about being so accommodating. If the Landlords Association finds out she treats tenants this way they'll have her crucified.

You're surprised by the number of possessions you've accumulated. There's things you don't even remember buying. Clothes. A lot of music. Books and videos. Fifteen boxes in all. Two suitcases. None of which come close to filling the gap that AJ left.

The movers are not too happy about lugging your crap up six flights. They drop the boxes on the terracotta tiles in your living room. When the last is thrown down, six shirtless men stand in your kitchen. Their leader steps forward. You give him $1,200 and thank him.

M-goi. Dor-jeh. Dor-jeh sai. M-goi.

This, it seems, is not enough. The Jimmy Hoffa of the Canton Teamster Union speaks. *Yum cha!* he says. Drink tea! You think he's asking you to join them for lunch and decline the offer. But Hoffa will not be denied. *Yum cha!* he insists. *Yum cha!* His words are accompanied by a simple hand gesture. The international symbol for money. A thumb rubbing across the tips of two or three fingers. He is not inviting you to drink tea.

He's demanding gratuity.

You open your wallet and pull out $800 in loose bills, intending to count off a few. $200? 300? Hoffa sees you struggling with the concept and generously makes the decision for you. He takes it all.

Dor-jeh! Dor-jeh sai!

The Sisters have found a place on the other side of the park. You can almost see it from your bedroom window.

Xi visits. She can't believe how small it is. It's not the first time you've heard that from a woman, you tell her. Said the bishop to the actress. You tell her the cat likes it. She says there's barely enough room to swing the cat.

It's okay, I assure her. Chairman Meow's not much of a swinger.

That's not what I heard.

She walks across the room and admires the view. She stands on the tips of her toes and leans out the window. Her skirt rises above the milk of her thighs. You move in behind her. Unpack her crates. Relocate her. Manhandle without care. This end up. A one-man Teamster union. Where would you like it, ma-am? Put it there. No, wait. Over there, by the sofa. Take that, Hang The Moving Expert. You know how it go-go. Careful. Don't put your back out. Bend at the knees when lifting.

Chairman Meow is not amused.

You return to the old Mid-levels apartment. Waiting, with Daisy, for the dead landlord's son. The Handover. A final inspection. Keys for deposit. The doorbell rings.

The Albino enters.

He's almost bald. His pink head is pasted with a thin film of platinum hair. Red eyes are framed in thick glasses. He's accompanied by a sister, a cousin or a wife. A tradesman brings up the rear and starts changing locks on the door.

What's he doing? you ask.

Changing the locks.

Why doesn't he wait until we've finished?

Oh, no problem. We can do it now. Everything seems to be okay.

Maybe, you say, but you insist on walking him through the apartment. You want to show him how clean the walls are. You need to point out that you're leaving the two hot water systems that you installed, as act of good faith. You'd like to mention the dining room table you're leaving too. And how about that sofa? Wait 'til you try masturbating on that.

Pardon?

Nothing.

You give him two sets of keys. He says thanks and walks you toward the door, as if to see you out. He's forgotten the small issue of the $90,000 deposit he is supposed to return.

You remind him of his financial obligations.

Cannot give you back your deposit, he says calmly. You have broken the lease. It was a two year contract. He pulls a copy of your lease from his back pocket to underline his point .

Technically speaking, he's right. Except he's forgetting the break-clause we negotiated with his father. We agreed either party could terminate the lease after one year, with two months notice.

You're not breaking the lease at one or two years. You're breaking now, Mr Joshua reminds us.

Are you not going to give us back our deposit?

Yes.

Yes, you're going to give the deposit back or yes, you're not?

Yes, I'm not.

When I asked you to come here to inspect the place, get the keys and return the deposit, you said yes.

Yes.

So you were lying then? You had no intention of returning the deposit? When I called last week, to remind you of this appointment, did you have any intention of giving back the deposit.

You are breaking the lease. You-

Are you saying, after seeing how well we've taken care of this place, after getting two brand new hot water systems, a dining room table and a sofa, you're going to keep the money?

One or two years was the arrangement. Now it is-

Don't keep waving that contract at me. We had an understanding with your father. He was cool. Whatever needed doing he did. Whatever we wanted to do was fine.

My father is not here.

I know.

We cannot ask him.

I know.

He's gone to England.

I know.

He-

Hang on. What did you say?

My father is not here.

I know. Where is he?

My father has gone to England.

Your father is in England?

Yes. We cannot call him.

Are you sure? you ask incredulously. You know his father is not in England. His father, bless his soul, has shuffled off his mortal coil, run down the curtain and joined the choir invisible. The Albino's mother sent you the death certificate.

Your father is in England.

Yes, he replies, confidence waning.

Who are you?

Mr Chan.

No, tell me. Who, the fuck, are you?

I don't understand.

Who the fuck do you think you are coming in here and saying something like that? Your father is not here alright. He's dead.

Oh, he falters. Well, yes. Okay. He went to England. He died. How did you know?

I've got a copy of the death certificate.

How did you get that?

Your mother mailed it to me when he fucking died, you fucking cunt. She asked us to change the account we were paying rent into. Never fucking mind how I got the fucking death certificate. How the fuck do you come in here and lie like that and try to fucking rip us off?

The contract-

Don't give me that contract shit, you fucking weasel. How dare you come in here and cheat us out of our fucking money? Your father was a good man. Whenever we had a problem we'd call him and he'd have it fixed. No problem. And now you come in here and try to fuck us over and you lie and dishonour his legacy and you're the type of person that gives landlords a bad name. If he was here now we'd be having a friendly conversation and he'd be thanking us for taking such good care of this place and for the new water heaters and the fucking table and giving us our fucking money. Instead you're being a sneaky shit and, you know what, we're going to have you fucking arrested. I'm going to call my fucking lawyer and get the police and have you arrested for attempted fraud and perverting the fucking course of justice and fucking embezzlement you fucking fuck.

You have no idea what you're saying but you feel like you're on a fucking roll. The important thing is not that you believe you, but that he believe you.

The guy changing the fucking locks can stop what he's fucking doing and put the original locks back in too.

You tell The Albino you're not leaving the apartment. If you still have six months left on the contract then you'll keep the apartment for six months. He reminds you that you've already moved everything out. You remind him that you don't give a fuck. If he wants to play it this way then you're more than happy to oblige. You'll have two apartments for a while and you'll stay here for as long as his cherished contract states. It will be your summer party house. We'll invite the fucking acid bath killer around and give the bathroom a make-over.

You pull out your mobile phone, call your work number and pretend you're speaking to a lawyer. Ranting into voicemail.

You ask The Albino for his identity card and, bizarrely, he hands it to you. It's all happening too fast for him. He's scared and confused. You read his details to the answering machine and tell it to call the police if you haven't phoned back in half an hour. The Albino is shitting himself. His companions walk out of Daisy's room like they've seen a gangland murder at Classic Passion and want to leave before the police subpoena them as witnesses.

While it's clear you're in control of the situation, there's still the issue of the security deposit and how to get it back. You go with the moment. *Carpe the diem.* You are Travis Bickle. You're through the looking glass. You're Dennis Hopper. You're Tony Montana. You're improvising at 24 frames a second.

Nobody is getting out of here alive.

You push the two women back into Daisy's bedroom. It happens so quickly they don't have time to think. Nobody does. Even Daisy is starting to look worried. She's probably thinking of sneaking off herself. You push her in after them and pull the door shut. It locks from the inside. They could open it and leave if they wanted to but they know what's waiting for them out here if they do. They're probably happy to stay out of the way for a while and let The Albino deal with the fate he has engineered for them all.

You jab your finger at him.

Now you go home, get your fucking cheque book and you come back here. You write us a cash cheque for $90,000 or the fucking police will fucking arrest you and your family for conspiracy, extortion and whatever else we can think of that will ruin your fucking life.

But I live-

I don't care where you fucking live. You get back here in half a fucking hour or you're going to fucking wish you never came here at all.

You point him to the door. The locksmith scurries after him.

Daisy slips out of the bedroom and cowers in the corner. She's wondering what has got into you. Where all this anger and melodramatic bullshit is coming from. You go to the balcony and light a cigarette.

Two drags from your bionic lung decimates it.

What if he calls the police? What if he comes back with some friends? Tough guys? Triads? Albinos always know triads. No, they're usually the head of triad gangs. White Dragons. Isn't that what they call them? Whatever. Nevermind.

A mulatto, an albino, yeah.

After the longest ten minutes in the long and quiet history of prolonged silences, the door opens. And there he is. The Albino, with his albino cheque book in hand.

Found it, did you? Didn't have to go home after all. Had it in the car all along, didn't you. Well open it up, snowball, and write out three cash cheques for $30,000. That's right, three checks. $30,000 each. If they fucking bounce or are cancelled or we have any fucking problems you will have no fucking idea how shit your fucking life will be.

Your can feel your superpowers fading.

He hands the checks to you, hesitantly. Not because he doesn't want to give them to you. He's worried about getting too close. You fold the IOUs and jam them in your back pocket.

Who do you fucking think you are?

You say it like a disappointed parent and storm out the door. Daisy scoots along behind, like a kid worried she'll be left at grandma's.

The lift doors close. You burst into tears.

Daisy waits until we're in a taxi before she tells you that was quite a performance. She'd never seen you so passionate. It was quite scary and sexy at the same time. You apologize. You don't know what came over you. It's just when he said his father was in England you couldn't believe he would lie about something like that.

Actually, he was kind of telling the truth.

What do you mean?

In Chinese, when someone is dead, we say they are not here.

Oh. Okay. But he shouldn't have lied and said his father was in London.

He didn't. He said his father had gone to England. In Chinese, when someone has died, we say they've gone to England. It's a colloquial saying.

Oh.

I don't think his English was very good. He was just using the literal translation of the Chinese.

Oh. Well he should've of said something.

You didn't really give him a chance.

Why didn't you say something.

You locked me in the bedroom with his sister.

Sightings of Sai-ming are unsubstantiated. Not everyone has given up hope, but no one is holding their breath either.

YOU BUY A $60,000 TELEVISION. It's so big it barely fits through the door. The delivery guys, quite rightly, expect a little more for their labours. *Yum cha* of wide-screen proportions. You also have to get a hole knocked in the wall of your hole-in-the-wall. Between the living room and the small bedroom. To stick the back of the TV through. If you don't, the screen will be seven and a half inches from your face when you sit on the couch.

The interior designer in you seizes control and before you know it you're talking to an upholster about building a giant chaise lounge. A 1930s casting couch, in red velvet. A statement piece of furniture. You have no idea what it's trying to say. Between that and the television there's not a lot to say or room to move.

Around the corner forty-three Filipinas are living in an apartment that's only twice the size of yours. 800 square feet. It's a refuge centre for abused women. Housing them there is part of the abuse. In an overload of irony police are called in to arrest ten of the women for assaulting each other.

In Sham Shui Po some have just twenty-one square feet each to live in. There's only one toilet for thirteen residents. Fifteen of them share a kitchen. Imagine the trouble that could erupt should a meat parcel arrive from Australia. Or if someone moves out and takes the sofa with them.

You count your blessings and unpack the last of the boxes. Amongst the CDs, videos and laser discs you find a few cassettes. Mixed tapes. There's a blank one. Unmarked except for the date. A year ago. You drop it into the Walkman and put the headphones in your ears.

Play.

It's Kushla. The Blanche Deveraux and Mrs Doubtfire of the paranormal. She's talking to AJ. You weren't the only thing she left behind. This is her psychic reading. It starts the same way as yours did. She's a good listener. She needs her own space from time to time. She's good with people. In a nice relationship, for now. There will be an explosion of success for him, next year. Lots of travel. Don't analyse it too much. Don't think about it too much. She sees AJ leaving Hong Kong within twelve months. There will be big changes. She'll go to Australia but not for long. She'll get married and move somewhere else. Kids within three or four years.

It's the prophecy of a death foretold .

You carry it up and down six flights, half a dozen times. You buy it drinks at The Forever Lounge.

Kushla saw it coming, for both of you. Or, by saying it, did she make it happen? Did that make it easier for AJ to believe it was the right thing to do? Did the prophecy become a blueprint?

Things are going to be different.

To convince Xi and yourself how much better things are now, you tell her you're going to take her to Perth for Christmas. She can meet your parents. Kurtis. Curly, Bluto and Chuck Norris. Enjoy a counter lunch in Freo. Drop acid on Rotto. 3pm. Don't be late.

How's that for commitment?

Unfortunately you're incapable of directing energy in more than one direction at a time. It goes to work or it goes to someone else. You expend it on her or spend on yourself. The office is your ruling planet. Xi is a minor moon in an irregular orbit. She's only a phone call and a public park away but the time between sightings, and nights spent in the dark shadows, is increasing. You know only too well what happens when women who crave affection are left alone. Yet you work towards it, like you're trying to create an opportunity for estrangement. So you can take the moral high ground and become Martyr-man again. You're looking for a way out and, rather than have a truthful conversation about the state of the nation, you rumble towards the inevitable uncivil war.

You're trying to write a script for bathroom products. Toilets, basins, baths and faucets. Important, world-changing stuff. You say you'll meet her at 9:30. Then ring and tell her you'll be later. 10:30. She calls to say the restaurant is calling last orders. You apologise and tell her to meet you at the bar across the street at 11:30.

You arrive just after midnight.

She's been waiting for hours but she's not angry. She buys you a drink and puts the world of bathroom fittings into perspective. Can I ask you a question? she inquires.

Is that the question, or was there something else?

She called the airline and checked your booking for the trip to Australia. There are no seats reserved in your name.

That's because I haven't booked anything, yet.

Oh.

Hang on a minute. You did what?

You get up, without a word, and walk out. Straight across the park. It takes her a while to realise you haven't gone to the washroom. She catches up with you, mid-park, by the statue of Queen Victoria. A person who was also untroubled by great events yet irritated by trifles.

What's wrong? demands Xi. What are you doing? You can't get up and walk out on someone like that.

What am I doing? What are *you* doing? Checking up on me? What else have you been looking into? You talk about trust and honesty and here you are conducting private investigations.

You walk away and leave her there, slack-jawed. Tears in her eyes. You stomp across the park and mutter your way up six flights. The cat sees you reaching for a Bob Dylan CD and takes refuge under the sofa.

She can take the dark out of night time, and paint the daytime black.

A floral apology arrives at the office. She phones. You screen your calls. At work, at home, on your mobile. After a week in Coventry you call her from purgatory. She sounds relieved. Optimistic. It will be good to see her. This has gone on long enough.

Let's catch up soon.

You return home that night, late. You've left your keys at work. Instead of going back to get them you decide to walk across the park, to her place. It's a good excuse to see her. Maybe you can even stay the night.

Daisy answers the door. She's surprised to see you. Very surprised. Xi isn't there. She's gone to visit a friend who is, er, having trouble with her boyfriend. She just left. She'll get her to call you when she comes back.

You explain you've left your keys at the office and were kind of hoping you could sleep on the couch.

Oh.

She hesitates but grabs you a pillow and throws it on the sofa. You hear a flurry of phone activity, in urgent Cantonese, behind a closed door. You fall asleep waiting for Xi's return.

Waking, just after 8am, you look in Xi's room. She's not there. Daisy says she called just after you went to sleep. She didn't want to wake you. Her friend was quite upset. She stayed the night there.

You go to work, oblivious.

In the evening you meet her at The Forever Lounge. You want to maintain a home-ground advantage. She sits on a stool and lights a cigarette. One for you, one for her. You look at her, accusingly, through a haze of smoke and over the wide lip of a beer. The silent treatment.

She was at a friend's a house, okay? A guy friend.

You laugh. Shake your head. Throw $300 on the counter. You hike the stairs to your ivory tower with grim determination and wonder what music would be appropriate for this situation. The cat looks worried. Not Dylan again, please. The doorbell rings. Song Of Joy in 8-bit digital. She senses danger and scrambles to safety.

Can I come in?

Xi says you can't keep walking away from her like that. She looks at you, like one of those teary-eyed porcelain angels. She only rang her friend at Cathay Pacific to check on the flight because she wanted to know if it was true. She wanted to believe it. She didn't mean to upset you. It's not that she doesn't trust you she just wanted to know. Like kids sometimes sneak into the parent's bedroom and look for Christmas presents.

Can you understand?

Maybe she deserved to be treated this way, maybe she didn't. You didn't talk to her for days and then this guy called. He asked her out. She was lonely and angry with you. She had a few drinks. A lot of drinks. She got drunk. Really drunk. She went back to his place. Daisy called and said you were at the house. She tried to sober up. She threw up and lay on his couch, for a minute. She fell asleep.

You find it all quite ridiculous, so unbelievable, it could be true.

She tells you he kissed her. She said no. She went to sleep on his couch, alone. Nothing happened. She implores you to understand.

Can you?

Maybe you can. You're trying to. You want to. It's stupid enough to be feasible. Except you know her and her appetites. She's a sexual piranha, down to the bone. She'd never stop at a kiss. She likes the attention and needs no encouragement. Maybe she's only like that with you. How would you know? Who is this guy anyway? What's she doing going back to his place after one date and a couple of drinks?

It wasn't the first time I'd seen him.

Oh.

I've been out with him before. With Daisy and her boyfriend.

Oh

He's one of The Guy's friends. The Bro.

Fuck no.

You were at work so much or just sitting at home on your own, not wanting to do anything. So I went out and-

Jesus Christ, Xi.

I know but you weren't here.

It's my fault? you ask, thinking of all the laughs The Guy and his Bro must be having at your expense.

Yes. No. Look, I'm sorry. Can't you understand? I want to make things better. To start again. Can we? I'm sorry. I don't know what else to say.

You look into her and see a reflection of yourself in the black ink of her eyes. Another person churning in the void. Filling the hole in their life. Feeding the hole within. Satiating a highly strung hierarchy of needs.

Déjà you.

She takes your face in her hands and kisses you. Seeking the words you cannot say. The salt from her eyes runs down her cheeks and onto her desperate lips. The two of you go at it again. Six ways to Sunday. Unforgiving. Top and tail. Hammer and nail.

I guess this means we're back, as a couple, she states optimistically.

Why would you think that?

You just slept with me.

More like fucking for fun and distraction, wouldn't you say? It didn't feel like sleeping. You slept at another guy's house last week. Does that mean you're a couple too?

Of course it doesn't. I just told you. I was angry. I was drunk. I wanted some company. I wanted to feel needed.

So did I. Thanks.

You look out the window, across the park. Queen Victoria reigns supreme. She was also of the opinion that, for a man to strike any women was the most brutal act. Far worse than any attempt to shoot a woman, which, wicked as it might be, was at least more comprehensible and more courageous. She would've commended you for your courage in this moment, shooting Xi right through the heart.

Arise, Sir Richard, Baron of Bastardry, Duke of Douchebaggery, 15th Viscount de Wanker and Grand Pontiff of the Brazen Serpent.

She looks at you, so close to tears it makes you feel sick. Thanks, you said. Just like that. As coldly and malicious as that. Thanks. She swedges angrily with her clothes. Haphazardly pulls on her heels and hobbles out the door, a broken woman. You stare at the faded, cracked walls. Burn through two cigarettes. Tell the cat not to judge you. It knows nothing of such matters.

There's a knock on the door.

She's been on the roof, thinking. Crying. She calls you, quite correctly and in every sense of the word, a bastard. A fucking cunt. She hits you on the arm. She pounds at your chest. She flings her arms around you. The kisses are urgent. Her caress is violent. She pushes you into the room. Onto the bed. She pull her dress over her head. She drives you into the mattress and collapses onto your chest.

I guess this means we're back on, again.

No.

She's too stunned to speak. Shot through the heart, again. She dresses and leaves in deafening silence. You've often wondered what that sounded like. Now you know. It makes you ill. Even the cat can't believe what she just witnessed. She can't believe what you just did.

Neither can you.

Merry Christmas fuckhead. Keep on spreading that goodwill and peace to all you encounter.

I remember when you were here, and all the fun we had last year.

The halls of shopping malls are decked with folly. Families aimlessly search the multilevel shores of consumer islands, for days on end. Every now and then feral children are found, half starved, wandering remote corners of Pacific Place, Harbour City and Times Square. Living like primitives. Hunting pigs and lighting signal fires. Like a post-modern Lord Of The Flies only with better air-conditioning, more escalators and food halls.

Maybe there is a beast. Maybe it's only us.

On your maiden visit to Shanghai you find out what happens to some of China's other forgotten children. The ones not fortunate enough to work in the sweat-shops and factories and live in stairwells. When the entire population of Australia is packed into one sprawling city it's inevitable some will fall through the cracks in the pavement.

Ralph wept for the end of innocence, the darkness of man's heart, and the fall through the air of the true, wise friend called Piggy.

It's late afternoon on the expressway. The taxi leans into the chicane of the exit ramp and breaks before piling into the backlog of traffic. At the side of the road lies the body of a child, wrapped in rags. Boy or girl? Six, seven, eight, nine or ten? It's so hard to tell when they're in such an advanced state of decomposition.

Further downtown, there's a riot going on. A small group of 500 has gathered in a back street. They're shouting. Throwing stones and bits of wood at a building. A short, bald man sticks his head through some large wooden doors, yells something and then retreats under a barrage of rubble.

Shanghai, mid-90s, is a big, bold and beautiful building site. New landmarks are being raised on every corner. Architecturally it's quite intimidating. If someone told you fifty percent of all the cranes in the world were here you'd have to believe them.

In the lobby of your cut-rate hotel visibility is down to 27%. Dust from half a dozen constructions swirls through the coffee shop. You wait for the elevator. A man is absorbed by his reflection. He squeezes off a few pimples, right up against the chrome doors. Focussing on a particularly stubborn whitehead, he bears down hard and, just as it blows, the doors slide open.

Bam! Right in the kisser of a woman exiting the lift.

No one reacts as if something terrifying has just occurred. Maybe they didn't see it. Maybe this type of thing happens all the time.

You venture out at night, keen to get an eyeful of the legendary women of

Shanghai. Like all things of great beauty there is an inherent risk. They come with a warning.

Be careful, said Baldrick. They can be sticky. Not difficult-sticky, or moist-sticky. Glue-sticky. They cling to you and can be very hard to shake off.

In the Hard Wok Cafe a group of men gather around a young woman. Her peak-a-boo cheongsam leaves little to the imagination. You're told she's the biggest thing in Chinese porn. She's not that big, anatomically, but is largely famous for her pornographic endeavours. There's no denying her pneumatic appeal. She has the prefabricated, wide-eyed beauty of a Nexus Six android. A replicant. Almost perfect in a biomechanical way.

It's too bad she won't live. But then again, who does?

Her agent asks if you want to meet her. Of course you would. You can tell her about your part in Sexy Tennis School. Swap amusing anecdotes about your respective adventures in porn. Run your idea for the sequel past her. See what she thinks of Sexy Tennis School 2: Sexy Golf School. You ask if she speaks English. Astonished, The Agent reminds you the girl is not built for talking

What are you going to talk about? You don't make conversation. Her mouth will be busy with other things. Ha-ha. $1,000. Can negotiate for overnight.

You pass on the heavily discounted pleasure of her company and move to another bar. You blend right in with all the others who are obviously in China for the first time. Two girls smile at you. One walks by and says hello. She asks if she can buy you a drink.

If Hong Kong is where East meets West, Shanghai is where it greets it.

She's tall. Almost as tall as you and her name is Yue-na. She introduces her friend and you wonder if either are the sticky ones you've been warned about. The Friend has a boyfriend. You buy each other drinks and end up at a disco an hour later.

Yue-na wants to dance.

The floor is heaving. She sweats. You find a corner. A bottle of water. A kiss is a loaded, reckless encounter between two worlds. You ask if she'd like to come back to the hotel and be the second biggest thing in Chinese porn.

Hotel security does not approve of this idea.

The Guard won't let her into the elevator. You offer him money. Cigarettes. He's not interested. You've somehow stumbled upon the only person in China who can't be swayed by the promise of a trip to Marlboro Country. You have no choice but to pile Yue-na into a taxi and take her home. It's one part noble gesture, to make sure she gets there safely. Three parts desperate measure, to see how far you can get in the cab.

As you rummage around the back seat, the city gives way to the suburbs. Suburbs surrender to the soil. Cars become cows. You start to worry. She can tell. She asks if you're scared. You admit that, well, yes, you are. Just a little. She cackles. Relax. She squeezes your hand. Nothing will happen to you with Yue-na. You want to believe her. Still, as you approach an isolated covey of concrete houses somewhere south-east of Nanjing, one thought prevails.

This is it.

This is where you get ambushed. Your life ends here.

She kisses you good-bye and says she'll take you out for lunch tomorrow. You say okay. You'll see her then. She says something to the driver and you're on your way. To your death.

This is where the driver takes you to meet his partners in crime, in a field. They will rob you, beat you and bury you. Your demise will be a footnote on page eight of the South China Morning Post.

Missing expatriate seen leaving club with prostitute.

You make mental notes of any place that resembles civilisation as you drive by. That's where you'll run when the taxi pulls off the road.

As the city draws near you look for buildings with the lights on. Safe-houses. Only when you start to recognise a few of the inner-city structures do you begin to relax.

You alight at the hotel. $750 lighter.

That's probably more than he makes in a week. He gives you his card and tells you to call him if you want go back to see your honey again, or be a tourist. He'll take you. Of course he will. No wonder he didn't kill you. You're worth much more to him alive than dead.

And you may ask yourself, well, how did I get here?

The phone beside the bed rings. 11:30. Yue-na. Good morning. She reminds you of your luncheon appointment. She'll meet you in the lobby. 1pm. This would be awesome, if you could remember what she looks like. Tall and smoking hot is a pretty generic description that can be applied to a healthy percentage of the population.

You wait by the hotel entrance. Conspicuous. You're the first thing people see on arrival. Hopefully she'll recognise you. You begin to panic. What if the rumours are true and all foreigners look the same?

The doors slide open.

A vision enters the hotel. Vidal Sassoon bob. Sunglasses. Short black dress. Long legs, toned and smooth, like points on the imperial draftsman's compass. She floats, three inches off the floor. Even the walls are staring at her as she glides toward you. She waves. She calls your name. You can't believe your luck. She's here for you.

Where's that security guard? He shall pay dearly for last night's vigilance.

She gives you a hug. The twin-fists of her chest push against your rapidly beating heart. Defibrillation. Her killawatt smile punches you square in the middle kingdom.

No chance of a dance, she waltzes you off to lunch.

Shanghai dumplings, steaming in the basket. Almost as succulent and moreish as the morsel at your table. A walk in Yu Yuan Garden. Across Qianteng Bridge. Over to The Bund. You promenade with a cast of thousands. Staring, whispering. They think you're Keanu Reeves, she says.

Of course they do.

A family stops and asks for a picture with you, Keanu. It sets off a chain reaction of photo opportunities. Maybe we do all look the same. A crowd starts to gather, feeding off each other's curiosity. Yue-na politely excuses us and we take a taxi to the hotel. No time for a stroll in her Fuxing Park or to worship at her Jing'an Temple. You have a plane to catch. She gives you her fax number. Let her know next time you're in Shanghai. Bring a present. She will show you more of her beautiful China.

A dozen men and women are executed for murdering seventeen truck drivers. They used prostitutes to lure them to their deaths.

YOU BUMP INTO XI-SHI on your way to work. Colliding as you make a dash for the sliding doors of the MTR's Island Line. The massive diamond on her finger nearly takes your eye out. The wedding band is just as hard to ignore. She just got married to the guy that nothing happened with that night.

The Bro is her beau.

What kind of conspiracy is this? Why does every girl, after breaking up with you, feel compelled to marry an American and peg themselves to the Dollar?

You're not sure what to say. Anybody else would mistake it for rudeness. She knows you better than that. She's surprised and in a hurry too.

Let's get together soon.

You say sure, without thinking what that might come to mean. And continue on your way to Seoul.

Our memory is not ours to command. The past comes unbidden, or not at all.

It's a pre-Christmas mercenary mission. You have to rescue an ailing shampoo franchise, armed only with your wits and a full clip of Zoloft, Paxil, Atavan and Wellbutrin. These days you don't even queue for the bank without one or the other. Or more.

Seoul reminds you of Pittsburgh. Or, rather, how you imagine Pittsburgh. It's like a romantic steel town, where the factories are closing down and a young, rebellious quarterback wants to escape.

Let's get the hell out of this damn town, Darla. Leave all this behind and just start again. On our own.

You see snow for the first time, outside a boardroom window. You excuse yourself from the presentation to call Ana. You have to tell someone. She says you sound like a child. By the time the meeting is over the snow is reduced to slush on the pavement.

Just like your life.

You're given an interpreter for the night. Miss Kim. A short, aging Korean woman. Miss Take. She takes you to some chi-chi bars and a restaurant. There's immaculately dressed shampoo girls at every corner. Your interpreter being the exception that proves the rule. She even has a small bald spot on the top of her head. You catch sight of it in the all-mirrored elevator and wish you'd seen it before she invited herself up for coffee.

Miss Judged.

You watch CNN and order Room Service. Twice. Miss Leading tries to make it easy for you. She sits next to you on the bed and undoes a button on her blouse.

It's not easy to be intimate with a woman sporting a monastic tonsure.

Departing, at the airport, your belt buckle sets off the metal detector. Two soul-destroying women in uniform confront you. They smile and ask you to step to one side. There's not much you wouldn't do for them.

They scan your body with security devices. They pat you down and up and down. Both of them, at the same time. If this doesn't deter the terrorists nothing will. They say something in Korean, laugh a little and send you on your way. Have a safe trip. Thank you for visiting Korea.

No, thank *you*.

Two days later you're lazing on the balmy beaches of Perth, dreaming of a white Christmas in Korea. You've flown south for the summer in an effort to avoid the yuletide humiliations of seasons past.

A few blistering weekends with Kurt will cure you of most things.

An old flame is briefly rekindled over lunch, with Isabelle. After a few bottles of wine the rose tinted glasses that look over the past magnify half-full emotions. You wonder if you're both still in love with each other, or just pining for a post-lunch walk down memory lane. Izzy confesses she's probably more in love with the idea of you than the reality of you. You're reclined to agree. There's not much to love about a twenty-eight year-old bastard with an inability to handle relationships and a rapidly deteriorating, misogynistic view of women. If you could take your mind of her precepts and her parabolas for just a minute you might even tell her.

Kurtis has a few ideas of his own.

To cleanse yourself of impure thoughts you wade into the surf at Cottosloe Beach. The seventh wave breaks on you and dumps you. Churns you. A lungful of brine compliments the bile in your veins. You lose your sense of direction and consider the possibility you may have taken your last breath. A shadow passes through the water. The sea goes dark. You close your eyes and wait for the last picture show.

Peace, at last.

Kurt pulls you, spluttering, from the surf. The hereafter must wait.

You ride a bike back in time, past AJ's old house. The ghost of Christmas past. Aristotle said every action is due to one or other of seven causes. Chance. Nature. Compulsion. Habit. Reasoning. Anger. Appetite.

Do you get extra points for using all seven?

You go see Midnight Oil, live. You pour your soul onto the dance floor. It sticks under your feet like spilled beer and cheap spirits.

How can we dance while our earth is turning?

How can we sleep while the beds are burning?

You get high on life. The idea of you collides with the reality of you. Kurt produces a giant bag of blow and you grind away what's left of you.

Fortune magazine proclaims Hong Kong to be dying, but they won't say of what... Twenty-one die on New Year's Eve when a fire sweeps through a Christmas decorations factory.

ON THE HIGHWAY OF EVOLUTION, somewhere between bus drivers and taxi drivers, sit mini-van drivers. This one has chosen a rainy Saturday afternoon to tailgate you down the freeway. With the memory of Hang, The Moving Expert, still burning in the stairwell of your mind you decide to teach him a lesson.

You squeeze the brake. It's a warning. Back off. He stays on your bumper. You pump the pedal again. And again. He whips out of the lane and accelerates past you. Then swerves in front of you and jams on his brakes.

Contrary to popular opinion, there is nothing fun about travelling sideways at 100kmh.

You regain control of the vehicle and take off after him. Hot pursuit. You return his late-braking favour and position your car across two lanes. Forcing him to pull up. You exit the vehicle and walk toward his van, like the cop in Terminator 2: Judgement Day. He winds down his window and shouts obscenities in Cantonese. Without missing a beat you reach in through the window and turn his engine off. You pull the keys from the ignition and hurl them over the barrier into the harbour. You present the stunned driver a tight-lipped smile and continue your bitter, twisted journey.

Next stop, Japan. Hello Tokyo. Sorry for the delay. Traffic was a bitch.

With a population of almost 125 million, there's a vending machine for every man, woman and child in Japan. Anything you could desire, from drinks and snacks to panties and mobile phones, is dispensed from them. It's the most convenient country in the world. Come 2000, machines will outnumber people, two-to-one.

Tokyo is another of those cities, like New York and Dublin, where everything you've ever read, everything you've ever heard, is true. Everything. Even if it sounds made up, it's not.

Flicking through channels of hotel television you arrive at a panel of middle-aged men and women. They're in heated discussion about something. There's probably a vending machine somewhere that dispenses subtitles and translations but it's not in your lobby.

The camera cuts to a room filled with steam.

A title appears on the screen. Bizarrely, it's in English. This is another thing you soon learn in Japan. English is used for effect, not for relevance or clarity.

Bathroom Cinema.

The fog clears to reveal two cute and quite possibly naked girls. They are immersed, shoulder deep, in a large spa bath. They giggle and converse in the vernacular. You have no idea what they're talking about. You suspect, as they appear to be in a bathroom, it probably has something to do with cinema.

The girl on the left begins to express herself in a very animated manner. She stands, excitedly, to emphasize a point and ends up highlighting two. It's an impressive argument, well presented. Her companion, equally ebullient, joins her in the vertical state. She reaches off-camera and returns with a poster of Jean Reno. At this point, in the country's celebrity dominant advertising culture, The Cleaner can be found on a majority of billboards endorsing cars, whiskey, cigarettes and pain relievers. Often at the same time.

A third woman emerges from the foggy depths.

She wears a large pair of black Gucci sunglasses and nothing else. She talks in authoritarian tones. The ladies in the lake hang on her every word. They're all ears and boobs. She wades in behind one of them and cups her breasts. The aquatic dissertation on the Reno oeuvre continues, now with juggling. Somewhere, someone pushes a button and the spa erupts in bubbles.

Cut to a clip from Leon The Professional.

Back at Bathroom Cinema the hosts are spent. They're sitting on the edge of the spa, wrapped in towels. They have a short discussion about something. The golden age of cinema? Soap on a rope? Who's going to clean the ring off the tub? The blanket of steam returns and we are left with a strange desire to run a bath, or at least take a cold shower.

You flick through the numbers, arriving at what you assume is a news channel. A young, studious female is making a report from outside a building.

Cut to a dark hallway and our intrepid correspondent continues her exposé. She is illuminated by a small light, mounted on the lens of the camera. She motions for us to follow her, on the QT and very hush-hush. She opens a door and enters, quietly, beckoning us to follow.

In the bathroom she crouches in the shower recess and retrieves something from the drain. A mess of short black hairs. She presents them to the camera and waves them around with the same enthusiasm as naked schoolgirls discuss Jean Reno. Like their Cantonese cousins it appears Japanese also feel the need to sound excited whenever they appear on television.

She sneaks into a bedroom. The camera seeks out a figure beneath the covers. The reporter whips them away.

Hey-presto!

A young woman who, up to this point, was sleeping peacefully is now thrust into the limelight wearing only her underwear. Frightened, alone and confused she attempts to cover herself. The reporter makes her closing remarks and throws back to the studio.

A panel of experts nod sagely and discuss the sociopolitical significance of these revelations.

I want a doctor, to take your picture,

So I can look at you from inside as well.

You recount your televisual feast to anyone in the local office who will listen. Their response is summed up by two words.

Mizu shobai.

Loosely translated it means The Water Trade. It's a term that covers pretty much everything, from the geishas of Kyoto to the Korean and Chinese handmaidens that labour in saunas and massage houses off the Ginza.

This, presumably, includes Bathroom Cinema too.

Somewhere near the middle of it all is Roponggi. A small district of less than one square kilometre. Home to a thousand bars, pubs, cabarets and nightclubs. Karaoke, lap dancing and hostesses.

You start the evening in an upmarket, dimly lit hostess bar.

The clientele in local. You've probably contravened half a dozen a protocols just by being there. Ryuichi Sakamoto escorts you to a table by the wall.

You order a bottle of wine.

A beautiful young woman decants it for you. She asks where you're from and what type of work you do. Another urbane *shojo* brings over a leg of parma ham. She carves half a dozen thin slices and delicately places two melon balls beside them. Honeydew and cantaloupe. Helping herself to your Bordeaux, your host enquires as to the health of your girlfriend. If you had one this might be considered an inappropriate line of questioning, considering the nature of the establishment. Then again, in this town, maybe not.

You tell her you don't have a lady in waiting. She is surprised, although not genuinely. Her sincerity is matched by her command of English. The brief encounter ends with the ceremonial presentation of the check. 750 million yen. This is probably something between two or three grand.

You make your way down the street, then turn into an alley at the intersection of Random and Hope.

The orange glow of a small, unmarked doorway captures your imagination. You enter and ascend the poorly illuminated stairs. The gentle doof-doof of bass becoming stronger with each step. It hits you between the ears and drops to your stomach when you enter the strobing midnight blues of the club.

Welcome to WooHoo!

It pulsates. It throbs. Arms are waving, hips are rolling and sweat is peeling. Inhibitions are reeling. This is a social experiment of seismic significance. Cocktails transform you to a semi-solvent state. You're drawn, via osmosis, from the sparse outer-reaches through the semi-permeable social membrane to the concentrated core.

WooHoo!

You're Cheap Trick. You're Live At The Budokan. I Want You To Want Me. The Dream Police. Surrender.

Mother told me, yes she told me, I'd meet girls like you.

Naoko. Kumiko. Sanyo. Kokomo. You don't know.

Whoa-ho!

What time is it? she shouts.

Bed time! you reply optimistically.

Okay. But we can only stay for two hours. Work. 8 o'clock.

WooHoo!

My friend will watch.

Woo, er, Hoo!

Back at the hotel you launch your own episode of Bathroom Cinema. The international edition, with English subtitles. Special guests and a studio panel of one. You turn on, tune in and space out. Take a break from scheduled programming. It's a stunning expose. You close your eyes. Throw to the next segment and wait for the inevitable break in transmission.

A bushfire in Pat Sing Leng Country Park traps 48 children on a hike. Three students and two teachers die. A two year-old breaks both legs, falling from the helicopter while being rescued... An infant is mauled to death by the family dog... A man has sex with a Labrador, in a public toilet... Research reveals that 11% of 14 year-old boys pay prostitutes for sex.

SHANGHAI. After midnight. It's open season in the lobby bar. The hunters become the hunted. Predators stalk their prey with ruthless efficiency. You're mourning the passing of Yue-na. Her number and any chance of seeing her again was taken by the laundry gods. This is what happens when you don't check the pockets of your jeans before washing. You end up alone in the bar of the Holiday Inn at 1:30am with a bowl of wasabi nuts for company, watching prostitutes ply their trade for entertainment.

A young woman sits next to you. She hangs her gym bag on the hook beneath the counter. She orders a drink. Long Island Iced Tea. You settle into your third oo fourth bourbon and consider a trip to The Hamptons. She asks if you'll mind her bag while she goes to the washroom. She doesn't trust the girls in here.

Who would?

Uptown Girl returns. She thanks you for your vigilance.

Happy to help, ma'am. All part of the job. To serve and protect.

She buys you a drink. Are you waiting for someone? she asks.

No. Business trip. Leaving tomorrow.

She's been working out at the health club. Just having few drinks here and then going home. She has a busy day tomorrow. She wants to know what you're doing in Shanghai.

You give her the shampoo story.

Really? I have been a model. I was a shampoo girl, for local brand.

You could almost believe her, although it was probably a few years ago, when perms were in vogue. She's no Yue-na but she's no Miss Kim either.

You buy her a few rounds of drinks, wear out the conversation and call for the check.

Time for bed.

You walk to the elevator, push the button and wait. The doors open. You enter, insert your room card and press your floor.

Uptown Girl steps into the lift.

You're here too? Thought you'd just been to the gym.

She smiles and watches the doors close. She makes no move for the control panel. She must be staying on the same floor. What were the chances?

The doors open. Ladies first. She exits. You follow. She drops her pace and walks with you. Like she's escorting you to your room.

Nice hotel, she says.

Yes.

New.

Yes. They're still finishing parts of it.

You arrive at your door. Well, this is me. She stands by while you awkwardly fumble with your card. Good night. You slip the card in and out of the lock unsuccessfully. You grin embarrassingly.

Maybe I try, she says and takes the card from you. She slides it in and out effortlessly, in one fluid motion. The lock whirrs and clicks. The little LED light goes green. She turns the handle and pushes open the door. Time for bed, she says with a smile and enters your room, sliding the keycard into the light slot with a degree of familiarity.

Oh.

You could try and explain the misunderstanding. That *time for bed* was a personal statement, not an invitation or rhetorical question. You could do that. Or you could just see what happens. She's already here. It would be rude to ask her to leave. She's been so helpful. You wouldn't want to hurt her feelings.

The gym, it soon becomes apparent, is not the only method she has employed to maintain youthful looks and well turned figure. There are discoloured cicatrices beneath the areola of her bosom. The upholstering is full and firm. The quality of the stitching leaves much to be desired. Her nipples are on the cant, seemingly sewn to the south, in perpetuity. You can't help but think how painful that might be in a heightened state of arousal.

Noticing your curious appreciation of her *objets d'art* she proudly informs you she's had some work done on the windows to her soul too. A nip and a tuck to her optical lids to give them a double fold. The blepharoplasty is demarcated by thin white scars.

It's very popular, now. See. Not expensive. Two-for-one.

The price-point is self evident and was perhaps the most attractive part of the procedure.

Complicit in her self-regard, you collude in a braggadocios display of *arselins coup* and *fandango de pokum* before the vanity mirror. You cannot meet her eyes any more than you can look into your own. On a path to mutually assured self-destruction you cannot stop yourself. This Sino-babylon is beyond your own morality and you're beyond caring. You've poured your spirit down the drain. Filling the hole. Feeding the hole. One bourbon, one scotch, one beer, one prescription, one boondoggle at a time.

Protect your slopes. Tau pei, no way. Best food for diabetes. It's not just an airline, it's Israel. Step aboard a Gulf Air 747 and step off in any one of 14 countries. Why? Just because. It is, are you? Hair so healthy it shines. The legend lives on. Some people just know how to fly. Gives you the edge. Environmental pollution starts with you. The quiet fire. A rather unusual experience. More than a car, it's an invention. Arrive in better shape. After all, there's Heineken. Come fly the friendly skies. It reflects a man's good taste. Feels like Sunday. Expressions of you. The ultimate choice. Purity since 1903. You can be sure of Shell. We love to fly, and it shows. Living the Towngas way. If you flaunt it, you obviously haven't got it. It's your choice. He's so XO. Nothing else will do. You're in safe hands. Install a residual current circuit-breaker. The corporation is dead. Long live the federation. Being seen makes us happy and dressing is fun! This! Looks groovy! Taking mainstream of this moment, I wish to be dandy and adventurous! Now! A fuller personality than anyone's, more cute than anyone's. Cuteness at it's best! Where do you put your standard of cutie? I'm putting it around here. We're amazed that this cafe is run by mentally handicapped people. We're happy to continue our patronage. We are Hong Kong. City of life.

IT'S LIFE, JIM, BUT NOT AS WE KNOW IT. Hong Kong or abroad, you bounce from one soulless, meaningless encounter to the next. If it's Tuesday it must be Manila. Wednesday Jakarta. Bangkok on Thursday. You're finished with your meetings and done with your clients.

The night is not through with you.

Soi 33 is populated with bars named after Renaissance painters. Girls mill about in Victorian corsets and gowns, their beauty far from Rubenesque. Statuesque. You're up to your Bosch in Botticelli. Michelangelo a go-go. All Titian and Assumption Of The Blessed Virgin Mary. Your local Venus Of Urbino suggests a Feast In The House Of Levi.

Thai Double-cheeseburger Deluxe.

Sisters Of Mercy. Madonna And Child. In The Garden Of Worldly Delights, The Count Of Orgaz is buried deep. Six feet under.

Bury the corpse. Fill the hole. Feed the hole.

You have dreams. A recurring dream. Your teeth are crumbling. Falling. Falling to pieces. Brittle chalk and powder on the pillow.

What is this quintessence of dust?

What a piece of work is a man, how noble in reason, how infinite in faculties, in form and moving how express and admirable, in action how like an angel, in apprehension how like a god!

A snail crawls across the edge of a razor. You're shot with a diamond bullet through the forehead. You're Willard. You're Kurtz. You're falling through space and time. Hit the bottom before you wake and you're dead.

You almost suffocate in your sleep.

Your face rolls into the pillow. Your body convulses. A last, desperate gasp slurches you back from terminal slumbers.

Sitting in the dark, sweating, hyper-ventilating, you panic. You can't remember where you are.

Is this the dream within the dream?

Is this you, or are you someone else?

6. YEAR OF THE RAT

XI-SHI RINGS. Once. Twice. She is the postman. The postmistress. She will deliver. She wants to catch up. Dinner. Drinks. It's been a while.

Is that wise?

You'd be stupid not to.

She waits by the side of the road, dressed in Lycra. A white Spandex tube. Strapless. Sleeveless. There couldn't be any less. It looks like she rolled it on.

Fou siu fei gei.

She's burning the aeroplane. Cantonese phonetic tomfoolery has *burning clouds* sound the same as *seductive*. An attractive woman burns the aeroplane. *Fou siu fei gei.* Coincidentally, the colloquial term for masturbation is *dar fei gei.* Shooting the aeroplane. Clearly there's a strong correlation between air travel and sex. Twin jets or flying solo.

She glides in and lands gently in the cabin of the Alpha. Perfume floats in the air. Allure. Nectar of the goddess. Your spirits soar.

You drive to Mount Olympus. Two fallen angels dining on The Peak. She tells you her husband is away. He spends more time offshore than in her fragrant harbour. The marriage hasn't been perfect. They've had problems. She might've rushed into it. Maybe she wasn't ready. She really wants to be a better wife. Adjust her behaviour. She still has problems with men and drawing the line. Blurring the line, between being friendly, flirting and foreplay. She has a problem with one guy. He's a constant distraction.

Which guy?

You.

Oh.

It's still open, she says. It didn't finish. It didn't end. It didn't end on her terms. People need endings. She doesn't have an ending. She's tried everything. She went to the *feng shui* man, to improve her Marriage Luck. There was an elaborate $5,000 ceremony. He put all her problems into a turtle and released it into the ocean off Lamma Island.

You try to suppress a laugh.

Such a cruel thing to do to an innocent turtle. What did it ever do to her? Was the ceremony a success?

I'm here, aren't I?

She's moving to Australia next week. They're moving together. She doesn't really want to go but she has to try. It might save her marriage. Maybe being far away from her problems will help.

You wish her and her turtle luck.

She wants to go to the beach for a walk. You drive to Shek O. Sit on the sand. She leans her head on your shoulder. She'll miss Hong Kong. It starts to rain. You run to the car. You'll take her home.

Not yet, she says. She wants to talk.

You find a carpark with ocean views, overlooking the past, on The Point Of No Return. You sit there alone, together. She wanted to talk. You're too scared to speak.

How long you going to sit there? she asks.

You apologise and start the engine. You'll take her home.

Turn it off, she says. You didn't let her finish. How long are you going to sit there, before you kiss me?

You lean over, place a hand on her cheek and press timorous, chary lips upon hers.

Osculation. Escalation. Elevation.

It's Jack Nicholson and Jessica Lange. Frank and Cara at the Twin Oaks Tavern. It's a scratch that needs itching. Hand to cheek to chest. Breast. Your Car Luck is turning the corner. You drop the top. She slips your clutch and grinds your gears. Alternator. Flux capacitor. Lubricator. Cam shaft. Valves. Plug and piston. Crash position.

Bury the corpse. Fill the hole. Feed the hole.

You're subliminally manipulative, she says. You have a way of getting her to do what you want and making her think it was all her idea. You're not sure you put this notion in motion but you're happy to own it and drive it home. You have no idea how this fits in with the plan to save her marriage but it's not the time or place to discuss it.

Keep you eyes on the road and your hands upon the wheel.

She manoeuvres. Changes lanes. Into the driver's seat. Car pooling. Tailgating. Fender to fender. Tender. Rack and pinion. Power steering. Veering. Torque and tension. Suspension. Cruise control.

I've missed you.

It's true. The scent of Allure. The comfort of the estranger. Her viscous heat. Deliberate, controlled, she repeats her incredible motion. Over and over. The world begins, ends and begins again. Hyper-real. Unreal. The interior pulses. You're driving blind.

Shift. A change in ratio and rhythm.

You kick open the door. Swing out of the vehicle. Her legs bind. You throw her on the bonnet. Unfurl her on the hood, like Frank and Cara would. On the kitchen table. Willing and able. Come inside me, she whispers. Or was that don't come? You're struck deaf and dumb. She looks at you, demanding. Pleading. Manic mechanic. Oil and grease. Release.

Breathless bystander. Crash victim, splayed across the engine. Her naked chevron. She laughs and lifts her eyes to yours. Giggles at her wanton mores.

Is that what you call closure?

There's your ending. Happy?

Headlights on the horizon. Approaching traffic. You bundle her into the Alpha. A police wagon prowls by. Guilt by association.

Is there a problem, Officer?

You drop her at the front of her apartment. She kisses you on the cheek and says thanks. Like you've just opened a door and helped her with a few shopping bags or been a good friend. Thanks for listening. Thanks for being there. You wish her luck and hope things work out. She walks into her building and out of your life.

Probably for good.

The monthly trade magazine arrives on your desk in the morning. A legendary English adman passes judgement on your work.

Mentally inadequate, crossing the invisible taste line below which you just don't go. Puerile. Horrific.

Terrific. Is he talking about the ad or the person that created it? Last year's work or last night's abomination?

A shark kills two fishermen off the beaches of the New Territories... Patten criticises local and mainland politicians for listening to billionaires whose principal concern is that they should go on being billionaires. He uses his last policy address to accuse them of secretly lobbying Beijing to reverse his government's decisions.

NEW YORK, AGAIN. It's a city, according to Lydia Lunch, that fears and embraces it's own reflection. Like you. A gruesome portrait of Dorian Gray. Decay, mortality, failure and fraud, trapped inside a negatively charged environment. Your screams drowned out by the next drink, the next drug, the next fatuous encounter.

Slow death in the afternoon.

Your ears, nose and throat are blocked. You spit into the sink. Grab a tissue and blow. Pants, meet shit. You spend two days decomposing in a hotel that was thrown up and crapped onto the pavement.

The trip home is turbulent. Restless. Sleepless over Seattle. One Valium. One Zoloft. One Wellbutrin. Three bourbons. You dig on Ellroy. The Big Nowhere. Cooze. Bennies. Old rumours. New facts. Killer shakes. Dexies. Spooks. Toss the joint. Brace him. Cooze. Cooze. Coooooooze. The darkness, the big sleep, it never comes. You repeat the exercise. Ease off the liquor. Desperate for escape. A few more milligrams.

Shazam.

You're on the couch. No memory of leaving the plane or the trip through Customs. No idea how you made it home. You wake in the middle of the night. You walk around the darkness and try to work out where you are. Who you are and what you do?

What did you do?

You remember your name and begin to re-assemble your life around that. You wanted a mission and for you sins they gave you one. Brought it up like room service. Hong Kong. Shit. Still only Hong Kong.

Sai-ming's parents are sure he'll be home by Mother's Day. He isn't. Still they stay in Shenzhen, waiting. Like they have been every day, since September last year.

XI-SHI IS BACK from Australia. She couldn't stand it. Too many Australians. Funny that, being Australia and all. What was she expecting? She wants to know if you'll do some freelance work. Take a couple of briefs. Sure, you say. And wonder who is subliminally manipulating this situation.

You meet at her office. The boardroom. Empty and alone. Together again. Allure. She sits on the conference table. Short skirt. It hurts. She flirts. Echoes of the past. That night, our last. Outcasts.

What are your rates? she asks.

They're reasonable. Open to negotiation. Special price for her. Whatever the client can afford. Whatever she thinks you're worth.

A pound of flesh?

With compound interest.

You'd better take these briefs then.

Knees part. Her carnal art. Basic instinct. Sharon Stone. Catherine Tramell. Under her spell. A flash of lace. Embrace. Take the briefs. Claim your pound of flesh. Boardroom manoeuvring. Machinations, heavy with mephitic odours. Corporate raid. Hostile takeover. The minutes of the meeting. Fleeting. A knock at the door. No time for more.

Unfinished business.

The assignment. Her pet project. A no-brainer. You fax it a day later. She calls to say thanks. A favour in the bank. Can she buy you a drink? Maybe dinner? One good turn deserves another.

Unfinished business.

The restaurant is small. She makes it smaller, tighter, as she recounts her trip Downunder. She got bitten by a dog, you know. A dingo? No. She hikes her skirt, peels the top of a stocking and reveals small scars on her thigh. The wounds that time won't heal. Reminders that your past is real. Kisses come and go, wounds remain. You reach across and gently trace them with a surgeons hand. Exploration. Investigation. Examination.

Does it hurt?

Only when I laugh.

You order a few more drinks. Facilitate the mutual manipulation. She's confused. It doesn't look like it. She knows exactly what she's doing. She feels like she's having an affair but isn't. Perhaps you can help her with that.

Sure.

What are your rates?

Standard. A pound of flesh. Compounded with interest.

She downs another vodka cranberry. She's getting drunk. She'll need help getting into bed if she has one more. She'll be all over the place.

Another round?

Make it a double.

She takes your paw in the taxi. Fingers interlocking and laying in her lap, like dogs. Loyal. Always looking up. First into heaven, before the rest of us. You're looking for a way out but you're in too deep. Unfinished business. Where to from here and what happens next?

How's that Husband Luck panning out?

He's away. He's out of town.

Oh.

The taxi stops. You say goodnight. Bemused, at sea, she studies you for traces of insanity. Does she need some help getting into bed?

She steps out.

You give the driver $50 for a $25 fare. No chance of change. She reaches in, prises you out and streels you along. The Divine Tragedy begins.

Through me you pass into the city of woe.

She is Virgil. She is Beatrice. Fugitive, ephemeral at the gates, ascending the terraces of Purgatory.

Abandon all hope, ye who enter here.

All is repudiated in the master bedroom. A hotbed of vice. Mephitis seeping from the walls. Virtue and propriety, tossed with t-shirts, skirts and silks to the floor. Sacrificed to the mores of the ruling atman. Cooze. Heaven and hell on high heels and hosiery.

A portrait in the attic sneers.

Her husband smiles from across the room. Lit beneath the bedside lamp. Dark suit. Carnation in his lapel. A photo.

What's up, Bro?

The day of their wedding. His eyes are blind to the ceremony here and now, as you violate his marriage. Take his naked wife up the aisle. Her bouquet fallen before you. She sucks your name between cranberry stained teeth and pulls you deeper into her crimson maw.

What's up, Bro?

Revenge. A dish served smouldering. You could dine on this all day, just not tonight. Not here, in front of him. You take a moment. You take your clothes and you retreat down the passage.

Footsteps in the hall.

Her silhouette sways in the wynd, against the walls. What are you doing? she asks, *sotto voce.*

I don't know.

Come here.

The power of Christ compels you.

It's been said that once your mind has been stretched by experiences of a certain intensity it can never go back to its old dimensions. And it is this conquistador of the psyche that lures a man into evil, not his enemy or foe.

The hidden persuader wrests the reins.

A moth to her flame. Shuttle Tydirium in the beam of her Star Destroyer. Obnubilated. Her sinuous motion. A wife's devotion. She turns on you and turns you inside out. Come inside. Or did she say don't come? No time for clarification on this one. Fornication makes deaf mutes of all.

Bury the corpse. Fill the hole. Feed the hole.

Down the long shadows of shame, mystified eyes peer from the darkness at the end of the corridor. Maria the maid, investigating the noise. As her employer takes you to the cleaners and nails you to the floorboards.

I like the smile in your fingertips,
I like the way you move your hips.

It's raining buckets outside. You walk home. The filth is swept and sluiced from the streets. Trash is dumped, compacted and hauled away.

I like the way you look at me,

Everythin' about you in bringin' me misery.

It's late in the afternoon when you walk into Mulder's office. His desk is on the right. You drop into the couch opposite.

I've been looking at those layouts-

Mulder is not behind his desk. There's an old man there. 80 or 180, it's hard to tell. He's wearing a grey Mao suit. He stands there, rifling through papers, looking for something. He raises his bald head and, just as you make eye-contact, he disappears. Dissolves. Beamed up. Now you see him, now you don't. Pffft!

Gone.

You're not sure if you saw what you saw. You're trying to work it out when Mulder enters. He walks around his desk. Stands where the apparition stood. You okay? he asks.

Hmm? Yeah. Good. Fine.

What's up?

Nothing, just, you know.

Is there something you want to talk about? Something you want me to look at? Review?

Hey? Oh, no. Doesn't matter.

You back out of the room, slowly, and walk the corridors of The Agency like a ghost. Ana walks right through you.

Hey. Hey, Richard.

Hmm?

Everything okay?

I think, I just, you know. Don't be scared or anything, okay. It's pretty weird but I think I just saw a ghost. In Mulder's office.

You tell her the story. She hangs on every word. Either that or she's wondering if you've been toveling her bowl of Bob Hope's blifter.

You've seen him! she exclaims when you get to the bit about the vanishing Manchurian.

Apparently everyone knows this guy, or knows of him. He's like the Howard Hughes of The Agency. Always there, watching us all, but never seen. Until now. You're the first to make contact. The *gweilo* and the poltergeist. Of course. It all makes sense now.

You remind her that, technically speaking, you're not a complete *gweilo*. You're half Chinese. A ghost in the shell.

Exactly, she says. You walk between two worlds! That's why he chose to reveal himself to you!

She tells you how Kitty was working late one night. She could hear someone typing on the other side of her cubicle. She called out but got no response. The typing continued. She called again. And again. The typing continued. She stood and looked over the partition. The typing stopped.

No one was there.

Everyone has a story like that. A close encounter of some kind.

Baldrick lived with his grandma for a while. She would regularly claim to see a headless woman in the hallway. The neighbours pets always seemed to die in mysterious circumstances. Jumping or falling out windows. Getting caught in the washing machine and drowning with the next load.

Hong Kong suffered many atrocities at the hands of the Japanese during the war. A lot of restless spirits were roaming the territory.

China had spectres in spades.

Ana was in a Nanjing hotel. Late at night she was awakened by a high-pitched ringing in her ears. She couldn't move. Paralysed. Immobilised. It was like she was being held down by someone. Something. Five minutes. Ten minutes. It didn't make her scared. It made her angry. She started shouting at whatever it was to leave her alone. Go away. She swore at it. Cursed it. Then, as suddenly as it started, it stopped. The ringing in her ears ceased. The restraints were released. She stormed around the room, pointing to where she thought the ghost might be. Shouting. Commanding the spirit to leave. She went down to reception. She asked The Manager to move her to another room. He didn't even ask what was wrong with the one she was in and why she wanted to move in the middle of the night He just asked which room she was in.

Oh, that one.

No questions. No doubts. Move out. It happens all the time. She's never taken a corner room in a hotel since. That's where the spirits converge.

The mainland wife of a man killed by a metal pipe, when it broke loose from a shop awning during a typhoon two years ago, is finally told her husband is dead. They often went weeks without speaking to one another but even she'd started to suspect something might be wrong... Windsurfer Lee Lai-san wins Hong Kong's first, only and last gold medal at the Olympics in Atlanta.

XI-SHI CALLS. More freelance. Another pound of flesh? Kind of, but not really. No interest. Are you sitting down?

She's pregnant.

Congratulations. That's great, you felicitate. Or is it?

It might be yours.

Oh. Well, wow. How about that? Wait 'til your husband finds out.

More surprising than the news is your reaction to it. You're actually pretty happy. Happier than her, it seems. She doesn't want it. Can't have it. Not now.

Well, you're not going to have it now, you remind her. Give it some time. It might grow on you. Maybe you'll feel different in nine months.

Five months. She's in the second trimester.

Oh.

There are 25,363 abortions performed legally in Hong Kong every year. Xi-shi wants one of them.

Justice divine has weighed: the doom is clear,
All hope renounce, ye lost, who enter here.

The procedure, this late in the game, is more difficult. The Doctor has to induce the birth and make the body reject the baby. Contractions begin but the foetus hangs tough. Xi has to stay in hospital overnight. You spend it beside her, as she writhes in pain. Her phone rings.

What's up, Bro?

She tells him a girlfriend is having problems with a boyfriend. She's going to stay the night with her. And call him tomorrow.

History doesn't repeat but it sure does rhyme and can carry a tune.

By mid-afternoon, next day, she's still with child. Labour intensive. The doctor opts for surgery. Invasive. Xi loses a lot of blood. You drive her home when she is discharged. Return to the scene of the crime. You help her undress. Fold her clothes on a chair. Slip her into a t-shirt and put her to bed. She makes a call. You sit beside her until she falls asleep. It's Frank and Cara's last stand. Her hand holds onto yours. Last rites. People need endings.

Sorry.

So am I.

Maybe you both are, for everything.

Is this what you call closure?

Charles and Diana divorce... China endures rain the likes of which has not been seen for a hundred years. Five million soldiers join with farmers to stop the Yangtze from bursting its banks. Hundred die. Thousands are left homeless.... 40 people die and more than 80 are injured when a building on Nathan Road catches fire. A news helicopter, covering the blaze from above, fans the flames. Twenty-two women and children, huddling by a window, burn to death. Four men leap sixteen floors into inflatable mats.

THE STATUE OF QUEEN VICTORIA is vandalized by a local artist. He chips off her royal snoot and douses the regal crown in blood. His personal protest, he says, against the city's dull colonial culture. He is awarded twenty-eight days at Her Majesty's pleasure.

Art for art's sake is the philosophy of the well fed.

In The Forever Lounge, three young girls are making themselves hard to ignore. One is on her third trip to the phone at your end of the bar. She places her cigarettes beside your pint. She's written *hello* on the pack.

You buy her a drink.

Angel is going to a party with her friends. Candy and Kitty. You can meet them later if you want. She gives you her number. She asks what you do.

Commercials.

What's that?

The things that interrupt the shows on TV. Commercials. Shampoo. Beer. Toothpaste. Sanitary napkins.

Advertising!

Yes. Sorry. Yes, advertising. What do you do?

Study.

What're you studying?

Everything.

Everything?

Yes. Math. Science. Geography. History. English.

She's studying at high school. You try to stop beer from exploding out your nose and squirting out your eyeballs. She can sense your discomfort and proudly reassures you with the knowledge that it's okay, she's fifteen.

Oh, well, that's okay then. If you're Roman Polanski.

Given most girls lie about their age, you figure she's probably closer to thirteen. Coincidentally, this is also the number of years you will spend in jail if you pursue this any further. It could also be the number of bones an angry relative or member of the Sun Yee On triad will break, one at a time, if they catch you in here with her.

Where is this party they are going to, the school gymnasium?

You don't meet up with her. Ever. She calls frequently. Just the other side of midnight. Whispering into the phone. Asking if she can meet you. Common sense and cowardice prevail. You're through with being the catalyst for the sociopolitical experiments of others.

Self-imposed exile takes you to the Philippines. There's a hair care symposium you can hide behind.

You haven't seen this much deprivation, squalor and corruption since you peered into the deepest recesses of your soul. Or maybe that last trip to the far west of Xinjiang.

No wonder you feel at home.

Like you, everyone here is half something. Half Chinese. Half Spanish. Half Japanese. Half American. Half crazy. Half cut.

You catch up with Niña. Gracious as ever. Sitting in the atrium of her capacious home you can see who she gets it from. It's wired into the DNA of the entire family. The conversation turns to astrology and the occult. Small wonder Catholicism found its way, unimpeded, into the hearts and minds of the population. Filipinos want to believe in everything. And the power of song. The country enjoys a reputation as a paranormal hotspot. The confluence of cultures, no doubt. The Spanish legacy. There's a bit of a Gabrielle Garcia Marquez and an Isabelle Allende vibe to it. You tell her about the phantom of The Agency. She's not surprised. She's keen to take you for a walk in her garden. You hope that's a euphemism for more earthly delights.

It's not.

There are *duendes* in the yard and garden. Filipino leprechauns. Imps. Not everyone can see them but they are there. Sometimes they sneak into the car and ride around with you for the afternoon. They're not evil. They're naughty. Hiding keys is about as wicked as they get. In fact, according to those in the know, *duendes* don't do much at all. This gives them quite a lot in common with a great percentage of the mañana-loving population.

Niña's mother, Princess Grace of Metro, finds it fascinating. She could see it in you. It's your stars, she says. She declares you a Gemini. You don't want to be disrespectful but you feel obliged to correct her. No. Your birthday is February. Aquarian by birth. Gemini by nature, or behaviour.

I bet you're a ranter.

You're not sure where she's going with this.

Everyone deals with stress in a different way, she continues. I'm Cancer, I cry. Niña's on the cusp of Aries and Taurus. She screams and eats.

It's true, Niña's admits. I do. I'm a screamer.

Leos smoke, her mother asserts. Scorpios masturbate. Aquarians drink. Geminis rant. You're a Gemini. I can tell.

I don't mind a drink. Can't I be both?

It bet you were a Scorpio last night, chimes Niña.

Gemini, insists Princess Grace.

The conviction with which she states her belief is resolute. It taps into a dormant memory.

The family was going to New Zealand. Late 70s, early 80s. You needed a passport. No birth certificate could be found. Your name and date of birth were submitted to the Department Of Records. No one thought to look at the certificate before handing it over to the Passport Office. When the document was returned your date of birth had been recorded as June 4. It was written off as a clerical mistake. An amusing typographical error, quickly relegated and forgotten. The anomaly was corrected when your passport was renewed prior to this Oriental Oddyssey. Your *other* birthday had flown to parts unknown. A curiosity of a disregarded past.

Nina's mum revels in her vindication.

How long had you lain in the orphanage? There's only four months between February and June. You could've been a big baby. Switched at birth. A clerical error. These things happened all the time. It was the sixties. If you can remember them you weren't there.

It's absolutely better to be absolutely ridiculous and absolutely fabulous than absolutely boring.

Chairman Meow is conspicuous by her absence on your return. It's not uncommon for her to slip out the kitchenette window to visit the neighbours. The Landlady and a family on the fourth floor often feed her. They've even been known to cook for her. Nonetheless, after a few Meowless days, you wonder what has become of her. You ask The Landlady if she's seen the cat.

Yes, she responds matter-of-factly. We give it away last week.

Oh.

By given away she means they had the cat put down. Chairman Meow, it seems, had taken to urinating in shoes. The entire population of residents left them out front of their apartments before entering. Meow was never short on options. No one had nothing against cats, per se. It was agreed at the last tenants meeting, however, that slipping into their slippers and finding cat's piss in boots was not their favourite way to start the day. Chairman Meow, by overwhelming majority, was sent down. Earmarked for re-education. She had gone to England, to meet her maker.

Sai-ming's parents announce their intention to sue the government for

the loss of their son. $700,000 in damages. $600,000 in expenses...
A 19 year-old girl is reported to have had sex with thirty men a day,
every day, for three months. She'd been duped into believing she was the
high priestess of a religious cult, making preparation for the end of the
world. When it finally dawned on her that she was just a sex slave for a
prostitution racket, she filed a complaint against her captors. She sued
them for $200,000 in owed wages, calculated on the average number of
men she serviced every day, multiplied by $55.

THERE'S ONLY SEVEN MONTHS until The Handover. The one-horse race for Hong Kong's first Chief Executive is under way. Thirty-nine applicants were jockeying for position. Only eight qualified for selection. No one knows how the wheat was separated from the chaff but being a ridiculously wealthy, pro-Beijing businessmen didn't hurt your chances. Another mysterious, rigorous screening process sees half of them eliminated. The remaining four make it through to the bonus round, where they will be grilled by the Official Selection Committee. A Captain's Pick group of representatives acting in interests of the People's Republic.

Double Jeopardy. Political Motivations for 6.7 million please.

The final three are announced. It's a choice between the Hospital Authority Chairman, a Chief Justice and Knight of the British Empire, or a billionaire shipping magnate. The latter bears an uncanny resemblance to Rodney Dangerfield, in a Cantonese kind of way. He's also rumoured to have been delivered from bankruptcy by the Mainland government in a previous life. Although it's possible people may be confusing that with Easy Money, the movie he made with Joe Pesci.

No cheating. No gambling. No booze. No pizza. No nothing.

Rodney ends up with more than half the votes from the 340 who are allowed to go to the polls.

I don't get no respect.

The way my luck is running, if I was a politician I'd be honest.

You meet Mulder in Wan Chai, behind the velvet curtain. The Firehouse. It's not a bad place for a drink in the early evening. The expatriate beer monsters are still out to dinner or getting a skinful at places they can tell their wives about. Devoid of people and conversations to drown out, the music is low. It's one of the few places you can find a place to sit and enjoy a quiet beverage. The girls leave you alone, knowing you'll be gone by the wenching hour and not worth an investment of their time. They hang about their poles and slouch around the bar, pondering their reflections, waiting apathetically for Friday night to filter through the red drapes. They seem younger and more jaded than you remember. You also notice, in an attempt to stay en vogue and stimulate interest, they've traded the sexualized athleticism of aerobic leotards for the cut-price, Rabelaisian thrills of K-mart lingerie.

A tall, balding Deutschlander breezes in. Mid-fifties. Overweight. He takes a commanding position at the head of the bar, buys drinks for everyone and is soon swamped by giggling Filipinas. His bloated varicose face is familiar.

The Agency was launching a new ice cream. A premium brand to compete with Däagen Hazs. A heavy-hitting brand company, Acme, was brought in from Germany to design the packaging and consult on the marketing. One of the founding partners was airlifted in for the duration of the job. He was also charged with establishing Acme's inaugural Asian orifice in Hong Kong. Fritz was a nice guy doing a great job for loads of money. He had the respect of the industry, the appreciation of his colleagues and the love of a good wife.

It wasn't enough.

Tonight, Fritz has the obligatory gratitude of five hookers and a bar tab burgeoning like the national debt of Argentina. He's drinking for Aquarians everywhere, enjoying himself so much he's aging before your eyes.

You weep for Fritz's thymus.

Mulder shakes his head in deprecation. There's a type of person who just shouldn't come to this part of the world, he says. There's too much available to them. They go too far up the river. They lose the plot, their perspective and their compass.

Fritz recognizes Mulder and finds his way over. He re-introduces himself. He buys another round for the bar. The usual pleasantries are exchanged.

How's things? Busy? Sticking around for The Handover?

He lost his job a year ago. He was fired. He was having too much fun, apparently. His wife thought so too. She left him and took the kids. He didn't want to go back to Germany anyway. Who'd want to leave all this? he proclaims rhetorically, sweeping his arms around The Firehouse without so much as a hint of irony. That was probably made redundant too. Although he is German. He probably never had any to begin with. He does a bit of consulting now. When he's not too busy having a good time, all the time. Filling the hole in his life. Feeding the hole within.

You mention to Mulder, quietly, that it might be time for you to go. He agrees. He'll share a cab with you. Fritz motions toward the top of the bar, where his girlfriends are waiting. He asks Mulder if he'd like one. A take-away. One for the road. They're already bought and paid for. He doesn't think he can finish them on his own. His eyes are bigger than his mouth. Bigger than pretty much everything, he guffaws.

It's a very generous offer, Fritz, but no thanks.

How about *der Junge*. Maybe he'd like one.

Der Junge would not. *Der Junge* is almost full. Besides, he had one for lunch. But thank for thinking of him. Maybe some time later, in the past.

You leave thinking about all the things that can happen to a man. How it can all go spectacularly wrong. Not that it could ever happen to you.

Could it?

Never get out of the boat. Absolutely goddamn right. Unless you were goin' all the way. Kurtz got off the boat. He split from the whole fuckin' program.

You're sitting in a bar with Ana and Baldrick a few days later, reflecting on past glories. Van Morrison's Astral Weeks is liberating the Bose speakers.

In silence easy, to be born again,

In another world, in another time.

You take the top off your first beer, light a cigarette and are swallowed by silence. You fall into an audio vacuum. All sound simply drops out. Not just the stereo. Everything. Everywhere. Someone has pushed the mute button on the equalizer of life. People are moving their mouths but nothing is coming out. The ambient noise and sonic clutter have just evaporated.

Light washes over you, through you. Pure light. Incandescence. You're filled with it. Beyond weightlessness. It's like you've been stunned by life, as Lester Bangs would say. Overwhelmed. You're stalled in your body. Crippled by an enormous, brilliant moment. The world becomes two dimensional. You can see everything in front and behind. In one long, unbroken line.

You're standing on it.

Ana looks at you like you've just turned into a cluster of small spheres. Maybe you have. Her lips move. The sound gradually returns. Music. Voices. Sorry? you ask, cupping a hand to your ear.

Are you all right? You look like you aren't there, she says.

Maybe you aren't. You've been absorbed by the words of the song.

To search for love 'ain't no more than vanity.

You're not sure why these thoughts have come to visit. Maybe you've hit bottom and this is the epiphany. Maybe Van is right. Maybe love and the quest for its precepts is just some mutually exploitative exercise you feel compelled to undertake. Maybe you have to stop looking for it and just wait. Surrender. Surrender to it. Let life invade and conquer. To the victor will go the spoils. You'll probably never get over AJ, you just have to get on with it. Maybe it's time, in spite of all indications to the contrary, to begin liking instead of loathing. Transfer energy into strength, instead of violence and cruelty. Act rather than react.

Oh.

That night you sleep for six hours. It feels like sixty. At the office, in the morning, Ana is the first of many to tell you how different you look.

Different how? Sick? Fatter? Is something wrong with my hair?

Just different.

Great. Things are going to be different, again.

At the Christmas party thrown by a local production house you're approached by a West Indian woman. She's got a Grace Jones look in her eyes and a big Baron Samedi vibe. Bwa-ha-ha-ha. Live And Let Die. She asks what you're doing here.

Having a drink.

Not the party. What are you doing here, in Hong Kong?

You tell her you're in advertising. A writer. She says she thought so and asks if you've read Psychotic Reactions. The Lester Bangs biography. You admit you have, recently. It inspired your choice of jacket for tonight. Schott leather. A la The Ramones. A la The Wild One. Marlon Brando. You wonder how she could possibly have known that. She laughs. A big, hearty, Jamaican laugh. Bwa-ha-ha-ha. New Orleans voodoo.

Art and life, man! she bellows. Art and life!

It's a little bit scary. And she doesn't stop there. She wants to know if anything happened last Thursday, about 5pm. If you experienced something unusual. If you felt that you weren't really in touch with yourself. Underwent some kind of sensory deprivation.

Uh-huh.

You look around, seeking an exit. This is freaking you out. It must show. She tells you not to worry. She sees people sometimes. They're unsettled. Imbalanced. She tries to help them. She sends them a moment of peace. And hopes it helps.

O-kaaaay. Alrighty then.

Right now you need help of a different kind. A rescue. An intervention. Extraction from this moment. Yet you can't walk away. You know this type of thing is supposed to be bullshit. But it did happen. She knows about it. She's the only one who knows about it. You didn't tell anyone. The Force is obviously strong with this one. She invites you to join one of her meditation sessions.

It is nothing but remaining in constant company of the ever-loving Bhagwati.

You're watching the news. A large fire burns somewhere in Germany. The transmission suddenly cuts to images of topless European women playing darts. It appears Bathroom Cinema is branching into pub entertainment and you've been selected for a free preview. The game has obviously been re-designed to enhance the viewer experience. Compared to watching all those other guys who play darts go topless, it's a more engaging spectator sport. Of course it probably contravenes a few broadcasting regulations. Not to mention the rules of conduct and safety guidelines as laid out by the World Darts Federation. They frown on partial nudity. It's a family game, after all.

The unscheduled break from regular programming is accredited to the station's technicians. They're protesting over the size of their pay raises. It makes all other forms of industrial action look positively redundant. You hope Cathay flight attendants bear this in mind when staging their next industrial action or walk-out. It would garner a lot more sympathy and public support for their plight.

In a display of solidarity for your industry brothers and sisters, you attend a sit-in. And adopt The Lotus Position. At Grace Jones' house. Deep in the Sananda, she pulls up to your bumper and asks if your palms are tingling. Can you can feel heat on them?

Yes.

You wait for her to tell you the way to a healthy state of mind is to drink a glass of your own saliva each morning. And swing a chicken above your head before going to bed at night. This will eliminate negative energy.

Sahaja Yoga and the Kundalini doesn't work that way.

Your right hand corresponds to the physical and mental state of being. It's starting to develop pins and needles. Your left hand is the emotional side of your psyche. And it feels like it is burning. As if being held over a yellow flame.

The Kundalini can heal this.

It's a remarkable revelation. And you can't help but wonder how Toecutter's one-handed, minor minion in Mad Max became a major force for enlightenment and spiritual well-being.

That there is Cundalini. And Cundalini wants his hand back.

Grace explains the difference between Cundalini... and the dormant energy that sits in the first chakra at the base of the spine. The Kundalini. Then she takes you through the mystic motions. You'll know when you've entered an enlightened state, she says. You'll feel yourself gently swaying from side to side, or moving in small circles. If you feel heat pouring from you palms, that's bad energy. Cold emissions are good. On a clear day it will fountain out the top of your head.

The left hand receives vibrations and the right hand passes seven times over your aura.

The revelations continue and, for some inexplicable reason, you're promoted.

Richard Tong. Creative Director. $95,000.

The average Hongky is thirty-four and earns one-tenth of what you're on. And there are bankers earning ten times that amount. Money has no value for people pulling that kind of freight. Small wonder they lose their way. Who needs a compass when everything you desire is brought within easy reach.

Raise your Kundalini before and after meditation.

Meditation classes introduce you to some of the most positive, sentient beings on the planet.

They're terrifying.

They invite you to a costume party. Sensational 70s. Discopocalypse Now. You opt for a white silk shirt, unbuttoned to the navel, and a couple of gold medallions. Tight slacks, flared. Lashings of pomade.

You are Leo Wanker. Trevor Dagg. Disco Stu.

Arriving at the eighteenth floor of a Mid-levels building you ring the bell of apartment B. Celebratory sounds come from within. There is laughing. Latin American music. It sounds like it might be okay. You'll just have to get past those first awkward minutes when you enter and everyone looks to see who's arrived and you have to self-consciously scope the room for someone you know.

The door opens.

You're greeted by the woman who probably gave birth to Salma Hayek. She's surprised to see you and amused by your attire. Her costume seems more contemporary 90s than retro 70s. Maybe she didn't know it was fancy dress, or just chose not participate. You look over her Hayekian shoulder. Salma and two of her sisters are sitting around the living room table. You begin to suspect you may be at the wrong apartment.

You check the door. 18B. The numbers and letters are right.

Mrs Hayek suggests you come in and call your friends. The skintight, satin sheen of your trousers left no room for mobile communications. They're barely managing to contain you. You keep your eyes on the floor as you walk to the phone, too embarrassed to make eye-contact with Team Hayek. You're sure you can hear them mocking you in Spanish. A call to Grace Jones reveals you do have the right apartment. You're just in the wrong building.

They're all across the road.

You inform your host of your typographical error and apologise for the interruption. Someone's lucky husband, with guitar in hand, says they're also having a party. He invites you to stay for a drink. You should be going but, well, how often to you get to be backstage at the Miss España Pageant?

Rodriguez puts a beer in your hand and introduces you to the rest of the family. You end on the couch with Faith, Hope and Charity. The three pillars of heaven. It's impossible to look at them without blushing.

The family patriarch appears.

Corn chips are no meal for a man, according to Grandma Hayek. She insists on fixing you something. You thank her but it's not necessary. Really. You'll be fine. Thanks.

Stop talking nonsense. How skinny you are. You need a good woman to take care of you.

Looking around you're sure she could arrange that for you too. The girls roll their eyes and begin the most delightful inquisition. Where are you from? What do you do? That must be so exciting. Where's your family? Do you have a girlfriend? After three beers and a bowl of paella you feel like you've intruded enough. As much as you'd like to spend rest of the night and the remainder of your life in their company, it's time to leave.

The descent from Elysium is long, lonely and paved with regret. Particularly once you arrive at the Discopocalypse.

The crowd looks like they've just come from Rick Moranis' party in Ghostbusters. They regard you in much the same way as they watched Louis Tully transform into Clortho.

You are the Gozer among them.

You gaze out the window at the sunny side of the street and wonder what they're doing in 18B.

Raising and tying up the Kundalini: The right hand circles the left hand, moving upwards and tying a knot above the head. Do this three times and on the third time tie three knots.

Perth. Christmas again. In your newly acquired state of enlightenment, however, you attempt a solo flight. Independent of drugs and alcohol. With only the Kundalini for companionship.

You leave Chuck Norris' house late on Boxing Day. You're walking home with Kurtis. You're about to cross the railway tracks. He grabs your arm and pulls you back, just as the Fremantle Express thunders by. You hadn't seen or heard it coming.

You gotta be more careful, warns Kurt. How will you survive on your own without me there to save your arse.

You get to his street. Smoke a cigarette at the corner. Say goodnight. Shake hands. See you next time. You go your way, he goes his. You watch him disappear into the darkness.

Balancing the left side: For tingling, heat or heaviness on the left hand. Hold out left hand to receive vibrations and put the right hand toward the earth. Bring vibrations from the right side to the left until both hands are cool. Hold the left hand out to receive vibrations and put right hand towards a candle flame.

You're back in Hong Kong and so is Sai-ming. No one knows what he's been doing for the last sixteen months. No one ever will. As an autistic mute he can't relate his ordeal to anyone. He was found in a factory dormitory. Hundreds of miles from where they tipped him into Shenzhen so many moons ago. His overjoyed parents are not surprised. They never gave up hope. They knew he'd find his way home.

Balancing the right side: For tingling, heat or heaviness on the right hand. Hold out right hand to receive vibrations and lift the left hand to the air. Bring vibrations from the left side to the right, until both hands feel cool.

New Year sees you in Manila. You're staying with Niña, despite the emotional conflict of interest. The tectonic plates of your mutual affection have subsided to a platonic state. So much so she's decided to introduce you to a friend of hers.

Janet Jackson.

This is the Janet Jackson of Love Will Never Do. Not the Janet Jackson of Rhythm Nation. You're thrown together at a bar and spend the rest of the night trying to get to know each other, above the doof-doof of dance tracks. This is the aural equivalent of eating spaghetti on a first date. It's a bit untidy and ends in a mess. You somehow find a way through it and are rewarded with a fantastic few minutes on her doorstep, and a promise of much more to come.

See you on New Year's Eve.

Niña takes you to meet another friend. You're more than willing to accompany her. She's batting 100% as far as introductions go. This one is different, she warns you. He's psychic. Not a stargazer or soothsayer. He sees everything. The past, the future. The inner turmoil. The chambers of the heart.

His name is Bong.

Midway through the introductions he stops and apologises. He's worried. He doesn't want to upset you but he has to tell you something. He can see your parents but they're not your parents.

You tell him to relax. You're adopted. Your parents are not your parents.

It's an impressive opening salvo from Bong. So impressive you forget to ask him which parents he was seeing. The ones that abandoned you, or the ones that adopted you. You probably could have got him to clear up the great birthday mystery too.

Aquarius or Gemini?

Bong gives the taxi driver directions to the party we're attending. He's never been there before but he knows the way. Niña hadn't told him the address. He wasn't even invited.

He just knew he was supposed to go.

The moment he walks in the house he starts sweating. Too much colour. He's seeing auras. People are not people to him. They're colours. He's red. She's blue. They're pink She's yellow, turning orange. Colours mean something. They signify if someone is in a climate of change, or radiating sex. If they're a closed book, or open to suggestion.

He starts pointing at people, discreetly.

That person is sleeping with her. She fancies him but he doesn't know. That man's wife is having an affair with that man's wife. All this and more is confirmed by independent sources over the course of the evening. It gives Bong credibility in spades. Giant steam-shovel spades. The type of spades that could dig up fucking highways.

Two women burst through the door.

They're flustered. Out of breath. Slightly panicked. They only live five minutes away but it took them an hour to get here. Rockets and fireworks were being shot across the streets. There was smoke everywhere. They didn't know if they were going to make it through alive.

Bong did.

They unleash a lot of firepower in The Philippines on New Year's Eve. For safety's sake you're advised to stand under an awning or inside the house at midnight. To avoid being hit by bullets and shrapnel returning to earth. On average 360 people are injured every year when gravity catches up with ammo discharged into the night sky at midnight.

Place feet in a bowl of warm water containing a handful of salt. Place a candle in front of Shri Mataji's photograph. Hold out both hands to receive vibrations.

It's time to stop running, Bong says with a consoling hand on your shoulder. You can leave the past but you can't leave it behind. The damage has been done. Stop crucifying yourself. Get off the cross, we need the wood. The scars of the physician and his unhealing hands will always be there, like the burns, the beatings and the betrayals. They're part of you but they're not all you are. They are wounds that time won't heal, reminders that your past is real. They don't define you. Others can't see them. Stop picking at them. Re-opening them. Leaning on them. Let life treat and mend them. Turn that negative energy into strength. You've filled the hole. You can climb out on your own now. Or let someone give you a hand.

At least he didn't say everything happens for a reason. People who say everything happens for a reason are usually the ones who haven't been molested as teenagers, watched a loved one die of cancer or been punched in the face after they said everything happens for a reason.

Bong sees a Chinese girl in your future.

She's younger than you. He can't see her properly because you don't know her yet. Don't expect too much from Janet Jackson. She's not for you.

And just like that it's over before it started.

Any hope of repeating those precious, burning moments of a few nights ago evaporate with his words. How could someone so right about everything be wrong? Sure enough, when Janet arrives, it's on the arm of a boyfriend. He's tall and handsome. He's American. No, really. You couldn't make this stuff up. Usurped by the USA again.

Everything happens for a reason.

Midnight arrives.

The bullets fly and the full metal jackets fall. Plips in the pool. Thucks on the pavement. Clanks on the awning. Dings on the cars.

You get a kiss from Nina as the ammo rains down.

It's a shot through the heart but it's an awakening. It's the diamond bullet in the forehead. Kurtz's command has been terminated with extreme prejudice.

She knows, that's why she did it.

She knows, that's why she smiled.

The next morning you sit in the atrium, drinking coffee, listening to the Cocteau Twins. Niña's twin Siamese cats are basking in the sun by the window. One is grooming the other. Licking its coat.

That's all you're looking for, you tell her.

A place in the sun?

Someone to lick me.

On the short flight home you wonder when Bong's mystery girl will come out of hiding and reveal herself.

Once you have experienced the joy of self-realization and felt a cool breeze on your hands, one should understand that this is a precious gift which should not be wasted. One should stabilise it and allow inner yoga to work through one's being.

Sahaja Yoga renders a hidden bonus. Something they didn't tell you in the brochure. With self-realization comes an elevation of sensory perception. Heightened faculties. Auto-erotic stimulation. You can will yourself to a state of arousal and gratification. Send the testosterone, dopamine, serotonin and oxytocin coursing through your veins to the g-spot in your brain. Wet daydreams. Tantric ejaculation. Getting in touch with your inner Scorpio.

Look Mataji! No hands!
You're not sure what Kundalini would say about such things but decide it's all part of the healing process. Being at one with yourself. Finding peace of mind within. Burying the corpse. Filling and feeding the hole with positive energy.

Hold your palm upwards, as if asking for a blessing. See if you can feel a cool breeze on your hands. If so you are a realised soul and in good health.

Her smile lands like a breath of wind on your brow. A puff of air. It's a cat's paw on your soul. It came up in the express elevator, drifted through the lobby and arrived in reception. A special delivery just for you.

Bang.

She leads the dead. *Yun say yun.* Like the head of a funeral procession, throwing money into the air, to garner the attention of the ghosts. Distracting them. Allowing the procession to go by undisturbed. The ability to attract and distract is like that of a beautiful woman. She leads the dead. *Yun say yun.* She awakens the dormant sociopath. Arise Lazarus. You react and act on your instincts. Search and seek. You wanted a mission and now, for your sins, you've got one.

Yling.

She works on the fifteenth floor. She's part of The Agency's team for China. Instead of faxing copy down you deliver it. Just for a chance to see her. You request to work on accounts she handles. So she has to brief you.

Yling is a cultural mongrel just like you. She was born on the Mainland and moved to Hong Kong in her early teens, before finishing her education in Los Angeles. She impresses you with her charm, elegance and acumen. You impress her with your theories. Conspiracy Theory. Relationship Theory. Film Theory. Communication Theory. Mao Theory. Thierry Mulger. Actually, she doesn't think much of your theories. She thinks they're stupid. She laughs out of politeness. And to give you Face.

One afternoon, after a meeting in Tsim Sha Tsui, the two of you decide to get something to eat. You walk along the street. It starts to rain. You huddle under an umbrella. Together.

You give thanks to The Weather God.

Later in the week she invites you to lunch, to meet a few of her friends. It has to be a test, to see if you get the social seal of approval.

At an Agency dinner, and the ensuing karaoke session, you strategically position yourself next to her. You leave at the same time. Just to ride in the elevator with her and stand next to her on the street. To hail her a cab. If people knew how hard you worked to organise these little coincidences it would give them grave cause for concern.

When she works late you work late. You volunteer to take on accounts other people run a mile from. Just to be in her proximity. To be on her CC list. Be part of the agenda. What time is the meeting? Shall we meet up before and have some lunch? Can I give you a ride home? Do you want to go for a drink?

Serendipity by design.

A tourist is killed during the Lunar New Year Parade, when a float careers out of control. Thirty-one are injured.

7. YEAR OF THE OX

YOU CHIP AWAY AT YLING'S DEFENCES. Question the commitment of her boyfriend. Sew subtle seeds of doubt. He stayed out all night? Oh, I don't know if I'd leave you at home all alone while I went out with the girls from the office. All night. The two of you have been together six years? That's a long time. No talk of marriage, after all these years?

You start to meditate upon her beauty, excessively. Inborn suffering, check. The desire to carry out all love's precepts in her embrace, check. It's all getting very Capellanusian again. You position yourself near her at Agency functions and events. Manufacture reasons to have her explain something to you. Feign ignorance. Find excuses to drop something down to the fifteenth floor. People know something is up. She's the only Account Manager you don't argue with. When clients reject or mess with work they send her to give you the news, and brief in the changes. They start calling her Mrs Tong. By the time The Agency celebrates its 10th Anniversary everyone is convinced the two of you are dating. Even though you aren't. Not outside the theatre of the mind.

Karaoke.

You're sitting next to her, as usual. Someone puts on My Hong Kong. And there you are. The Occidental Tourist. Falling in and out of love. Yling blushes on your behalf. The guy to her right passes you her hands. Feel these, he says. They're the softest things in the world. Like freshly baked bread rolls. They've probably never worked a day in their life. You can't let them go. Awkward.

Can I have my hands back please. I have to go.

Me too.

You offer to drop her home, again. She accepts. Tonight, however, there's a change of plan.

I'll drop you home, she says.

You're sitting in your corner of the cab, silent. Daydreaming. Scheming. She asks what's wrong. You tell her nothing, really. You're just thinking about things. Stuff. You're not sure if you should tell her. It's nothing really. What if she misunderstands and gets angry?

She knows where you're trying to go and helps you along. She throws you a line. She tells you not to worry so much about things. If you feel like doing something just do it. See what happens.

Act don't react.

The cab pulls up outside The Forever Lounge. You say goodnight and quickly kiss her on the cheek, hoping to get out before she realises what you've done. She takes your hand in hers. Those incredible hands. She says maybe you should drop her home. And she launches the scud.

Her surface-to-air smile.

You walk through the garden. Podium Level. You sit on a bench in a dark corner. She puts her earthly delights upon your lap and tempts you for thirty-seven minutes. She smells like a baby, only not as milky.

Born when she kissed me, died when she left me, lived while she loved me.

See you tomorrow, she says.

You walk home on air. Rising from the void. You can see your light come shining from the East. Any day now, you shall be released.

☰

Cogito ergo dim sum. Descartes

YLING PICKS US UP IN HER BMW. It has 4,985 kilometres on the clock and still smells brand new. She drives us around to Repulse Bay, which is much nicer than it sounds. We're having lunch, with her friends.

It feels kind of wrong. We're a bit embarrassed about the white-anting. Being entwined with her while she still has a boyfriend. We've had our lunch cut once or twice. It's not a great feeling. Still, better to be on this side of the cuckold than the other. We ask after the condemned man.

I broke up with him this morning, she says casually, like she's just nipped down to the shops to get the papers.

Oh.

We change the subject. Leap over the pregnant pause. Compliment her choice of shirt. Versace?

Yes, she responds, impressed with our ability to recognise designer goods at a glance.

We've become a bit of a fashion victim. A side-effect of our prolonged fixation upon her. To ingratiate we replicate. We're tragically hip. Style without substance. We buy our clothes from the same stores. We've traded shiny shirts for Gucci and Prada. Alexander McQueen. Comme des Garçons. Paul Smith. D&G. Miyake. Yamamoto. Versace.

Yling also creates the need for a new apartment. She doesn't see the same quaint, inner-city charm as we do in a six flight walk-up. It's too much hard work. By the time she gets to the top she's too tired. The stairs wear her out. If we want her to come around she insists we move to a building with an elevator. She expedites the process. She sources the apartment, negotiates the lease and facilitates the move. Within two weeks we're comfortably ensconced in an 800 square-foot flat. Fourteen floors above North Point. Harbour views. A five minute walk from her place. Three, if we're in a hurry.

We off-load the Alpha. Give it away. To Baldrick. There's no parking bays at our new digs and Yling has given us the keys to her BMW anyway. It's a much sweeter ride. Even if it is only a 3-series and a bit of a girl's car.

Meanwhile... China admits that mainland patriarch, Deng Xiaoping, is dead. It's suggested he actually died months, possibly years, before, so long had it been since he was last seen. The People's Congress was waiting for an appropriate time of stability to announce it... 26% of students at a local kindergarten are diagnosed with tuberculosis.

YLING LIVES WITH HER MOTHER. We're told to call her Aunty, as is the local custom when it comes to other people's parents and taxi drivers. It will be years before we find out her real name. She speaks Mandarin, Cantonese, Japanese and Indonesian. Along with obscure Oriental dialects like Hakka. And Scorn, the ancient international language of disapproval. Aunty's English, however, is as good as our Chinese. And by good we mean rubbish. We communicate with her through a combination of mime and tone-deaf sino-soundbites. Yling says watching us converse is like a chicken talking to a duck.

Gai tong gnarp dong.

Everyone we know can converse in at least three tongues, including the maid. We are the exception. Yling finds it hard to believe someone can live in a country for this long and not pick up a remedial, working knowledge of the vernacular. We try to explain that languages aren't really our thing. We lived in Australia for twenty years and, like many people downunder, still struggle with English.

Aunty fears for her daughter's safety. She isn't sure she should be in a relationship with a *gweilo*. They're dangerous, she says. Yling has to convince her that not all foreigners beat up women and throw them from apartment windows after they've been drinking. We're not sure if this is the general public perception of foreigners or an urban myth peculiar to her upbringing. It must have been quite a neighbourhood where women were tossed from windows likes sofas, dead dogs, cans of tuna and empty bottles of beer.

Our mother harbours some bewildering preconceived notions too. This becomes apparent when she finds out we're dating a Chinese girl.

Oh that's wonderful! You used to be such a racist!

This, we are quick to point out, is not true. There's a difference between playground name-calling and being a xenophobic, card-carrying brother of The Klan. We weren't serious about it. It was half-hearted humour. Like making fun of someone because they had a big head, a bowl haircut or wore their pants too high. We didn't know how hurtful it could be. It was ignorance disguised as racism. And what a brilliant disguise it was. We were half-Chinese ourself. It wasn't bigotry.

It was irony.

Did we or did we not befriend Koki Takeuchi and sit next to him in class for a year? Don't forget Naomi Chan either, and my appreciation for the astonishing legacy her ancestors bequeathed unto her. If was okay to reduce Australians to Aussies, British to Brits and Scottish to Scots, was it so wrong to call someone from Pakistan a Paki? Or refer to people from Japan as Japs? Aborigines as Abos?

Yes is was, actually. Still is. It's not what we say, it's how we say it.

We see more overt racism in Hong Kong than we ever did in Australia. Like many things even the bigotry was casual there. Here it's institutionalized. We don't even have to look outside The Agency. Our new boss is Hong Kong Chinese and openly declares himself a racist. He apologises for it like it's something beyond his control. As natural as a bodily function. He even ranks ethnic groups in order of preference. Hong Kong Chinese hold down the coveted #1 spot, just above Taiwanese, Shanghailanders and Singaporean Chinese. Indians are on the bottom, below Filipinos. Mulder asks where he ranks Australians.

Just above the British.

In a Wan Chai disco, Anglo Saxons, Templar Knights and Freemasons get in for free. Locals are charged $150. Indians $300. Mongrels like us get in for $75 but we get a coupon for a free drink as well. The door policy for women is governed more by sexism than racism. Most are judged to be of one color. Pink. Their cover charge is open to negotiation. Although ladyboys often complain about being charged twice.

Meanwhile... an undercover policewoman, posing as a Japanese tourist, is charged $1,500 by a taxi driver for a trip that would normally cost $150... A suicide bomber explodes next to The Forbidden City.

BOWEN ROAD stretches from the high-rent areas of the Mid-levels to the back end of Happy Valley. It's pleasant and peaceful. People can run there without too much fear of becoming roadkill. Kids play. Many walk their dogs along its leafy paths. Lately, however, someone had been poisoning the pets of the rich and famous. Pooches were dropping like flies after eating tainted meat left in the curbside shrubbery. Even The Governor's terrier had fallen foul of the Bowen Road Baiter.

The Preliminary Legislative Council was wishing a similar fate upon its owner. Patten had forbid them from holding a function at the taxpayer's expense.

Use the means at hand to inflict the maximum amount of wounds, death and destruction on the enemy in the minimum amount of time.

Rodney Dangerfield and his cronies head across the border to Shenzhen instead, with money borrowed from China. For a bunch of billionaires they seem remarkably light on funds

Yling takes us to see Lai Ming. Leon Lai. The King of Canto-pop. It's one of twenty-five consecutive performances he's giving at the 10,000 seat Colosseum. It's quite spectacular in a late 80s way. We can't help but recall the last time we went to a concert here. With AJ. How lives were changed forever that night. How they were changing now. Holes have been filled and fed in ways we couldn't imagine back then.

Lord knows when the cold wind blows it'll turn your head around.

On Sunday we go to *yum cha* with the family. Our weekly fix of *siu yook*, *soi gau*, *char siu bau*, *har gau* and *xi long bau*. We even develop a taste for some of the weird shit. Although we draw the line at duck tongue, chicken feet, cow stomach and pig blood.

Yling's mother, overcoming her prejudice, adopts us. This is done more out of fear than anything. Yling's sister threatened to marry a black man if she didn't lighten up.

Aunty starts cleaning our apartment while we're away for work. She cooks for us and leaves food in our refrigerator, fulfilling the prime directive of all Chinese women.

Make sure everyone has enough to eat.

There is an innate desire to feed people, all the time. Everyone has it. Aunty. Yling. Ana. Even the shampoo girls. If we don't eat they get annoyed. Or worried. We're not eating right. We're not respecting our stomach. Those of mixed parentage are the same. Whatever traits are gained or lost as a result of cross-pollination, the food-provider gene remains intact. The paternal DNA. It not some subservient social residue, a Draconian kitchen imperative, or a case of obligation versus free will. Nine, nineteen or ninety years of age, it's just one of those things. Like the way they always make sure we're warm enough and wearing the right clothes.

We must respect the weather.

Respect is important. Respect your elders. Respect your superiors. Respect your stomach. Respect the weather. Respect the past. Respect respect. It's quite different, almost opposite, to the respect we grew up with. Out of respect for the weather we wore shorts, irrespective of the temperature. Our Prime Minister would respectfully pat reigning monarchs on the bum. Another was held in the highest regard for his ability to consume a yard of beer faster than anyone else on the planet. We honoured our mates by ridiculing, humiliating, abusing and embarrassing them at every opportunity. In consideration of public figures we invented Tall Poppy Syndrome, to stop them getting too big for their planter box. If they were pumping themselves up, acting a bit beyond their station, we'd cut them down and deflate their ego.

Respectfully disrespecting people was the cultural norm.

Meanwhile... the world's largest water-harnessing project gets underway with the damming of the Yangtze River. 1.3 million people have to find somewhere to live. There's no news footage of people chaining themselves to trees or militant lesbians shouting slogans. There's fireworks and dancing to celebrate this glorious achievement... Factory workers in Hong Kong consume chicken and duck feet contaminated with human excrement, causing a small outbreak of cholera... A new strain of flu takes flight. H5N1. Chicken Flu. Three die.

WE ATTEND THE ANNUAL JUNE 4 VIGIL in Victoria Park with 55,000 others. Yling doesn't want to go with us. She's never been before.

Why go now?

Who knows what we'll be allowed to do next year? We should remind ourselves of these precious freedoms we take for granted.

No one is going to lose anything, she reminds us. China is not the enemy. When trouble comes everyone will turn to China for help.

Trouble? What trouble?

Financial trouble. You never ask your parents for money?

We call Baldrick, pack an esky full of beer and decide to make a candlelight night of it. He wants to know what we think will happen after.

We can go to the pub. We haven't been to The Forever Lounge for ages.

Not after this. After The Handover.

We tell him it'll be a huge success. They'll do it on a regular basis. Make it like the Olympics. Countries will be able to bid for Hong Kong every four years. China, justifiably, goes first. Then, after their inaugural tenure, the IMF or some arbitrary body can decide who is to become the next host or proprietor. They can keep, say, 17.5% of the GDP they make during their term. Those in the running will have to submit a comprehensive proposal. They'll be evaluated on more than just fiscal initiatives and results. A social and environmental agenda will be required. Eventually the city will be listed on the stock market. They can float it. Maybe even tow it. Moor it off the coast of the host nation like that floating Jumbo Seafood Restaurant. Or the rubbish that sits in ships off every port, waiting to be unloaded. It gets towed from city to city until someone agrees to let them unload it in their country.

Meanwhile... 278 Vietnamese refugees walk out of a detention centre when the Supreme Court rules the Government has no right to keep them there.

THE HANDOVER kicks off with Beethoven's 5th. The symphony is used to drown the voices of protesters gathered out the out front of the main venue.

What are they protesting about? The deal is done. No one is going to change their minds about it.

Like most people we just want it to be over. It's all we've heard about for seven years. We can only imagine what it must be like for those who've had it hanging over their head for fifteen. We're so incredibly weary of it as a topic of conversation. As an excuse for doing nothing, and for not doing something.

Let's wait and see what happens after The Handover.

We're sick of camera crews and their probing lenses. Journalists shoving microphones in our faces, asking what will be different post-Handover.

Well, hopefully, there'll be a few less reporters.

We watch the events unfold on TV. Dignitaries arrive. The PLA arrives. Tanks arrive. It's hard not to caught up in the emotion of the event as Old Blood & Guts stands in the rain at Government House.

You're never beaten until you admit it.

The British flag descends for the last time.

Always take the offensive. Never dig in.

The trumpet plays The Last Post.

All glory is fleeting.

Patten, the last Governor, boards HRH yacht accompanied by Prince Charles. He sets sail with wife, family and surviving dogs, out of Hong Kong. Out of the media. Out of the way, as far as Beijing is concerned.

The Welcome Home ceremony, on the other side of town, is a different story. Mainland officials rub their hands with glee. Rodney Dangerfield warms up the crowd then passes the mike to President Jiang Zemin, who looks like he just got the keys to the mint.

Maybe he did.

Next day, everyone heads out to the new airport. Chep Lap Kok. They've decided to open it, officially, about six months too early. Like a bad omen for life under the change in administration it's a total balls-up. The centrepiece of Hong Kong v2.0 has faulty information displays. Luggage is lost. Phones are not connected. Flight delays abound. There are security lapses. Families who went out just to have look are found wandering on the wrong side of immigration without boarding passes, passports or the slightest intention of travelling anywhere but home. Computer failure forces the suspension of all cargo operations for weeks. Piles of rotting fish and vegetables are left to fester on the tarmac.

Welcome to China. Have a nice day.

We're having lunch with Yling and Aunty in Stanley, by the ocean. A storm is brewing. Signal 8 is hoisted. Two boys are swept off the rocks in front of us. A man runs out of the pub and dives into the water to rescue them. We rush to his aid. He brings one in safely and goes back for the other. The boy makes it to shore on his own.

The man is never seen again.

Meanwhile... Princess Diana is killed in car crash. Her funeral garners more attention and gets better ratings than The Handover... Gianni Versace, the patron saint of Tai-tais, ladies who lunch and other women who ignore their husband's affairs, is gunned down in Miami... Mother Theresa dies... The arse falls out of economies all over Asia. They call it Financial Flu... A drunk plainclothes detective ploughs his car through the lunchtime crowd in Central, killing three... Six men attack a food vendor with lead pipes the roast pork he sells is too bony... Michael Hutchence, lead singer of INXS, dies in a bizarre masturbation accident... 104 are killed when debt-saddled pilot sends a SilkAir flight from Singapore into a suicidal-homocidal dive.

WE ARE REBORN as a chicken. *Fei Gai.* Fat Chicken. Our skinny legs and meaty chest remind Yling of Foghorn Leghorn. We're *Ah-fei. Gai-gai.* Depending on how she feels about the whole brevity thing.

We've kind of stopped celebrating Christmas and its long-standing War On Poultry. It's just a few extra days off. An excuse to lie in bed. Then go out for some serious consumerism.We eat. And eat.

We eat anything.

If it has legs and it's back to the sky we'll eat it. Except for the table and chairs. A meal is not just a meal. It's an event. The menu has to be discussed at length. Amongst ourselves. Then with a waiter, who may exercise her right to invite someone else into the discussion. A manager. To bring a degree of formality to the conference.

Every meal is sacred, every meal is great,
If a meal gets wasted, Aunty gets quite irate.

We stop by a *dai pai dong* on the way to the office to get breakfast. If we eat it there we'll be late for work. We take it away and eat it at our desk. That way we can chat with colleagues as they arrive and watch them eat their breakfast, or talk about the breakfast they just ate. We eventually start work by mid-morning, attempting to finish the things we were supposed to do yesterday. Until it's time for morning tea. We walk to the pantry, stopping along the way, asking others what they're doing for lunch. We'll have to leave early to avoid the crowds. When we get back we're too full to work. We have to rest a bit. Answer a few e-mails. Return a few calls. Then make plans for afternoon tea. We eventually get down to the day's tasks by 4pm, provided we're not too distracted by the thought of dinner. Where will we go? What will we have? We return to the office after the meal to tidy our desk and ask colleagues if they want to join us for *siu yeh*. Late supper. We get home just before midnight, in time for a bowl of soup. *Yum tong*. We watch a bit of TV. Programs about food, usually. Then we go to bed and dream of all-you-can-eat seafood buffets. If we didn't stop to consume and talk about five meals a day we'd have everything done by 6pm. We could complete a day's work during the day. There just isn't enough daylight hours between meals. It's one of the reasons Hong Kong appears to be a 24-hour city.

It takes that long to feed everyone.

The other is a little-known relative of Deng Theory, Mao Theory and Conspiracy Theory.

Folding Bed Theory.

In the 50s, due to poverty and a general lack of space, people had to set up their beds in the evening. They had to dismantle them in the morning, to allow space for other things. Like eating, walking around in our pyjamas and watching television. They didn't want to lose face and let others see how poor they were, so they reversed the process. They started setting up beds in the morning, to fool those who might be looking in their windows. Folding Bed Theory might also explain why we work late into the evening and seem to be asleep during the day.

We often mistake working long for working hard.

Yling takes us to Lantau for a BBQ with her *pungyau*. It's not far from The Big Buddha. And right next door to the prison. We sit a few meters from the razor wire, under the gaze of twenty convicts. It's a Cantoberration of the traditional barbecue concept. More like a Peanuts cook-out with Snoopy and Woodstock on a stick, than Paul Hogan shrimp-on-the-barbie. We sit around the fire with a long two-pronged fork and spear fish balls, squid, chicken wings and wieners. We coat everything with honey, thrust it into the flames and hope salmonella doesn't survive the experience.

Meanwhile... a woman on a dialysis machine gets hooked up to carbon dioxide instead of oxygen... Surgeons remove a girl's Fallopian tubes instead of her appendix... A nurse pumps two litres of milk congee into the lungs of an 88 year-old woman. Medical records say she died of pneumonia.

WE'RE IN CHIANG MAI for the annual scalp summit. We bite into a blueberry muffin and our throat explodes. It swells up and looks like we've tried to swallow a grapefruit. We can't ingest anything. Liquids only.

It must be cancer.

The Thai doctor tells us it's an abscess and prescribes pills. Each one is the size of a small banana. He tells us to take one, twice a day, even though he knows we can't swallow anything.

It's cancer, for sure.

The doctor in Hong Kong doesn't know what it is. He's pretty confident it's not an abscess. This is the *modus operandi* of most modern medicine. Whatever they tell you it probably is, it usually isn't. Better to tell you what it probably isn't and work back from there. Do more tests. Prescribe more medicine. See what happens. So lacking in general consensus and confidence are they, every hypothesis is issued with a recommendation to ask someone else. Get a second opinion. Generate streams of revenue for their brothers and sisters in alms. It's hard to imagine any other business operating this way, successfully. Imagine telling your clients you're not sure what you're doing and recommending they see someone else. You'd be out of business by Tuesday. All these years of probing and investigation and the human body is still a mystery. A visit to the doctor remains a biological bug hunt and crapshoot. Specialists provide a very precise and expensive form of guesswork, working in very narrow fields of speculation.

Needless to say, my experiences at the Hippocratic hands of others may have jaundiced my view and shaken my faith in paramedical pundits.

Do we have to keep taking these extremely large tablets? you ask the medical maven. They're really hard to swallow.

They weren't not to be ingested orally, he replies. They were supposed to be inserted anally. They're suppositories.

Oh.

We have cancer of the throat and now, quite possibly, cancer of the rectum too. We're riddled with it. The doctor says he'll have to operate to find out what the giant lump is. We tell him one of those enormous ass-pills we've been stuffing in there probably got stuck and won't go down.

The idea of going under the knife doesn't thrill. With the number of mistakes being made in hospitals these days we'll probably be mistaken for an organ donor and have our vitals erroneously harvested. Be cut into handy fun-sized bits for reassignment. The bits that aren't black with cancer, that is.

After three sleepless nights we check-in to hospital and await our execution. Out of boredom and exhaustion we finally manage to fall asleep. Until a nurse wakes us up for a blood test. We fall asleep. A disorderly disturbs us for an x-ray. We return to the room and doze off, only to be woken for lunch. We sleep briefly and are woken for a urine sample. After a three-minute nap the Matron wakes us and asks if we're tired. Our chart says we're continually napping. We tell her they're just disco naps. It's actually one sleep that is constantly interrupted. She asks if we need anything to help us sleep.

Yes. It would help if you could all leave me alone.

Try to get some rest, she says. You'll feel better.

We fall asleep as per her instruction and, unsurprisingly, are soon woken by a doctor. He has twelve interns in tow. Why do you sleep? he asks, as if it were a round of Mastermind.

I'm tired.

Why are you tired?

I don't know. I'm just tired.

Dr Kildare notices the uneaten lunch on the table. Why do you not eat?

I'm not hungry.

Why are you not hungry?

Because I'm not fucking hungry, Quincy. Because fucking look at it. It's fucking crap. And what the fuck are all you doing in my fucking room anyway?

The bizarre sleep-deprivation experiment has left us in no mood for stupid questions from uninvited guests. Terrified, twelve interns and a doctor vacate the room.

We start crying. A nurse asks if everything is okay.

We tell her everything is not okay. We're insanely tired, upset and scared. Hasn't anyone told her? I'm dying of cancer and tomorrow they're going to make me the biological diorama in some fatal medical experiment.

She straightens a sheet, smiles and tells us not to worry. She'll take care of us. We try to believe her.

Can I have a sponge bath now?

She laughs. Leaves. And takes her eternal optimism with her.

It won't be all right. We have cancer and we're going to die. The Big Sleep awaits. Maybe then they'll let me rest in peace.

Dead me are heavier than broken hearts.

We haven't felt this doomed in quite a while. Not since our last trip from

Shanghai. It was during a typhoon. Signal 8. We'd flown straight into it for two hours. Bouncing, shaking. Incessant turbulence. It made the wings bend. Like when you hold a pencil between thumb and forefinger. Then wobble it up and down and it looks like it's made of rubber. The wings were doing that. Wings aren't supposed to do that.

Are they?

We tried to distract ourself with a magazine. The pages opened on an ad for the airline. Two pilots, seated in the cockpit, were looking over their shoulders and smiling at the camera. They were giving us dear readers the thumbs-up.

Change will see us through.

Oh, well, that's just great. Surely they're relying on more than change to get us through. A little skill, hours of training and cutting-edge safety technology will come into play at some point. Wouldn't it? Perhaps they could start by facing the right direction and looking out for incoming missiles. And what does that mean anyway? Change will see us through. Through what?

They're flying on a wing and a prayer.

We'd heard a story about an instructor who was training Mainland pilots. They weren't too bad apparently. This is a ringing endorsement. Not too bad. Like there are plenty worse and none good. These Top Guns could all get the plane up and down with varying degrees of competency. Except one. He gave the impression he'd never flown a plane before. He seemed totally out of his element. Someone from the airline came by and asked the instructor how this batch was doing. On the whole, he said, they weren't too bad. Except for one guy who looks like he's never flown a plane.

Shen? He's not flown a plane before. We're short on pilots and have to draft from the military. Shen is a helicopter pilot. Very skilful. He's never missed a target.

As flight KA801 prepared to belly-flop onto the Kai Tak tarmac there was scant comfort to be found in Dragonair's recruitment policy. They'd never put a chopper pilot in charge of an airbus, would they? Was this the change they were talking about, the change that would see us through?

At less than five hundred meters from impact we could see people in their apartments, looking out their windows. Some were laughing at our airman's folly. Some stared in abject horror as the wings collapsed and metal peeled from the fuselage. The madman was popping rivets outside my seat. We pitched violently to the left. The plane rolled forty-five degrees. Engines whined into overdrive and we lurched back into the sky. Tears welled. The hostess, sitting on the other side of the exit row, facing us, averted her eyes. Trying not to notice us.

Why? we asked her, crying. Why? Why do they do this?

That tipped her over the edge. She started to lose it. She began to weep. And there the two of us were, sobbing, hysterically. A stereophonic nervous breakdown. Then The Captain made an announcement.

Good evening ladies and gentlemen. Apologies if things are a little bumpy at the moment. As you may have noticed we hit a rather nasty crosswind there and had to abort the landing. We'll go into a holding pattern for a few minutes, circle around and have another crack at it.

Abort? Have another crack at it? Surely he has more precise, technical and reassuring terms at his disposal.

We touched down, twenty nerve-wrecking minutes later. Everyone, including the hostess opposite, burst into spontaneous applause.

A swift and fiery demise, streaking across the sky like a post-modern roman candle, was infinitely more appealing than the death by a thousand cuts that was waiting for me in the operating theatre.

If the tumours didn't get me the surgeons would.

Our confidence in physicians, it's fair to say, is shaky at best. We've lain awake all night in fear of the final indignities we'll be subjected too while under general anaesthetic. Before we take that long, last walk toward the light.

Nurses and a few curious observers get things under way in the early hours. They help us into regular-issue paper underpants and a backless smock. Considering what we were paying for the pleasure of this near-death experience you'd think something a little more *haute* would be afforded to us. Where are the Prada pants, Thierry Mulger thermometers, Chanel colostomy bags, Bulgari bedpans, LV loofahs and Gucci gowns?

Pre-op drugs are administered and, suddenly, the colours of the outfits make sense. They load us on an express gurney to hell and spirit us down the corridor less travelled, through the departure gates to a holding pen.

Past the point of no return.

Good morning, says the Doctor, examining the left side of our throat. A final check. These things have been known to go away overnight.

These things. What does he mean *these* things? What things? The reason we're here is because nobody knew what this *thing* was.

Yes! he proclaims. See! It's gone!

Amazing. A tumour the size of Macau just got up and walked away. Overnight. He's so happy and pleased with himself it seems almost a shame to tell him he's looking on the wrong side. The lymphoma, that is so big it can be seen from space, is on the right of our neck.

Really? Well so it is. Of course. My right, your left. You're right, my bad. Good. We'd better get on with it then.

We're wheeled in and lifted onto the slab like a side of malignant beef. They spread our arms wide.

Crucifixion? Good. Out the door, line on the left, one cross each. Next.

They wire us up and plug us in. Johnny Mnemonic. The black shakes. If you lose the head you're fucked. Come to Jesus. A woman attempts to tap a vein. She stops suddenly. Uh-oh. AJ used to make the same sound, just before she broke something.

Uh-oh? *Uh-oh* what?

Nothing, she says sharply. Just shut up will you. I'm having a bad day.

She's having a bad day? Ours isn't going swimmingly either. Someone runs across from the other side of the theatre. I'll do it! We never find out what it is she was struggling with.

It's Jesus time.

Opening our eyes in post-op we see, on the gurney beside us, an old man. He's just lying there. Covered in blood. Mouth agape. No sign of life. *Dues ex machina.* We bolt upright, screaming. Halt sinners! If I wanted the silicon dug out of my brain I would have gone to Mexico City! I want a full restoration. I want it all back! Two nurses run over. Hold us down and sedate us.

Cranial drill and a pair of forceps. Sino-logic 16.

We return to our terrestrial shell. If that was a dream what figment of our imagination is this? Two disorderlies are driving us to the recovery room, banging through swinging doors. They probably moonlight as mini-bus drivers.

They err in vision, they stumble in judgment, for all the tables are full of vomit and filthiness, so that there is no place clean.

Things don't start making sense until the next day.

We wake to find Yling beside us. Delicately balanced on the edge of the bed. She smiles and points to the specimen jar on the side-table. There's a solid white thing, about the size of a cigarette butt, rattling around the base.

Our tumour, the calcium deposit.

Running a swollen tongue along the bottom of our palette we find stitches. Eight of them. The nurse enters and we ask when we'll be allowed to leave.

What did the doctor say?

What doctor?

The doctor hasn't been to see you?

No.

You came out of surgery yesterday.

I know. I was there.

The doctor should've been to see you by now.

You'd think so, wouldn't you?

If this wasn't one of Hong Kong's better hospitals we might be getting a little worried by now.

Meanwhile... a casualty in road accident gets four litres of the wrong blood... A receptionist gets a flu shot at lunch time and dies on her way out of the clinic... A patient complaining of heart problems dies when the doctor, attempting to remove some bone marrow for diagnosis, inserts the tube thirteen centimetres wide of the mark.

MONEY CONSUMES US. It's all we think about. We don't really understand it but we know it's the answer to all our problems. 35% of teenagers believe it can buy happiness. 25% will do anything for it. To me, money is a god, says one. Only 5% would consider donating money to charity.

Fears of Hong Kong developing into a welfare state are unfounded.

Few feel any connection to their past, or shared history with the People's Republic. The Four Olds of Ideas, Culture, Customs and Habits might have been hunted down during Mao's Revolution but it's like they never existed here.

Why do so many of us find it hard to see ourselves in the world and why is our only connection to it money? We're obsessed by it and the making of it. Money, food and sex. The triple pillars of our existence. In that order. We can criticise people who deal in it, like we can criticise those who deal in sex or food, but we can't denounce the substance itself.

Money don't get everything it's true, what it don't get I can't use.

According to a survey, Filipinos and Indonesians are the happiest people on the planet. Japanese and Hongkies are the most miserable.

Meanwhile... only 19% of Hong Kong teenagers identify themselves as Chinese. 54% refer to themselves as Hong Kongers. 9% say they're Hong Kong Chinese. 18% say they don't have an identity.

WE'RE CHINESE BUT WE'RE NOT. We fled to the barren rock and furtively fuelled Jardine's opium trade. Our past forsaken, our future forfeited with colonial chirographatures. Yet without the European influence what would Hong Kong be?

Guangzhou.

Ours is a refugee mentality, in a way. Survival. Short-term gains. Our houses are cluttered with small portable things that, as Theroux said, can be thrown into a suitcase at a moments notice. Knick-knacks. Gold. Jade. Money. We don't even worry about furniture. It comes with the house. The black vinyl couch. Beds. Tables. Stuff like that. We don't own a lot of large things that are difficult to transport. Except for the homes themselves. Profit-turning symbols of semi-permanence.

An eighty year old woman died. She owned four apartments, yet she slept under the stairs. The flats were filled with thirty tonnes of garbage. She had a hundred umbrellas.

Ours is a KFC culture. Instantly digestible. Immediately forgettable. A mystery. We idolise false gods and collectibles. We bay at the twin moons of commerce and greed. The Hong Kong Special Administrative Region is possessed by the devil in a free-market cheongsam. Gambling and speculation are our Olympic events. The only thing better than making money is winning money. It's often the only means to improving our end. To fight our fate and improve our fortune. We can't change what we're born into but our luck could shift anytime. We could win $300 million by simply picking nine horses from three races. It's no coincidence there's a racetrack in the heart of the city.

Happy Valley. Wednesday nights.

We sit high in the stands with 39,996 professional punters. Drinking cheap beer. Eating hot dogs. Making lazy wagers. We put $500 in a kitty. Whoever goes to buy the beer takes 20% and makes selections for the next race. It's cheap entertainment. Win some, lose some. The guy in front bets the farm on the same horse as us. It's encouraging. Maybe we've made a shrewd bet.

The horse is either still running, or they buried it out there.

We've lost a few hundred bucks. Our unfortunate friend has done his kids out of an education, or a home. If he's swimming in debt, with the loan sharks, he may have gambled his life away. The average working class wage is somewhere between eight and ten thousand dollars a month.

He lost $17,000 on one race.

For the first day of the year, to get things started on a lucky note, we drop $1.29 billion on the track.

After a dinner party, as soon as the meal is finished, the plates are cleared. Green felt is rolled across the table. We play an oriental spin on 21. Blackjack with tiles. Sixteen of them. Eight stacks of two. Bets are placed behind preferred piles. Trump the dealer and win. We make $10,000 in ninety minutes. Not bad for a night's work, we think.

We quit while we're ahead.

A week later we run into the host and ask him how the evening panned out. Were there any other big winners?

Victor won $80,000.

Eight thousand?

Eighty.

Eigh-*teen* or Eigh-*tee*?

Eigh-tee.

Holy Buddha. Who lost?

Paul. $105,000.

I thought you guys were friends.

We are. He doesn't have to pay until next week.

Meanwhile... 1.4 million chickens are slaughtered over three days in an effort to contain the bird flu. Six people die and thousands swarm to hospital emergency wards. Alektorophobia sets in. Hundreds of parrots, budgies and other pet birds are abandoned. Government workers attempt to stuff live poultry into large plastic bags, to be gassed. Until they run out of gas. Bags are left to jump around, with half-dead chickens climbing out of them. Thailand, Japan and Taiwan tell citizens to avoid travelling to Hong Kong. Australia considers quarantining people from the HKSAR. The World Health Organisation contemplates isolating the entire territory... Peregrine Investments becomes the biggest victim of the financial flu and takes a $3 billion swan dive. It's feathers plucked by a $2 billion loan to Steady Safe Taxi Company.

8. YEAR OF THE TIGER

YLING BUYS US A WATCH for our February birthday. IWC. It's New Lucky Watch status is short-lived. We lose it within a week. It falls or is lifted from our wrist in Causeway Bay. If only we'd replaced its conventional strap with one of those infrangible Velcro ones.

I knew you we're too young for a watch like that.

We aren't sure how to break this $25,000 piece of news to her. Best to meet out the front of Gucci, just in case we have to do some major sucking up and apologizing. Retail counselling is the best way to begin the healing of a fractured relationship.

She can immediately tell something is wrong. We're wearing our heart on our sleeve. Our enormous forehead sweats guilt. There's no use putting it off. We tell her we've done a bad thing. She has to promise not to get too angry but we'll understand if she does. This opening salvo has her worried and thinking the worst. Whatever that may be. Infidelity? Disease? End of the sale season? We tell her we've lost the watch.

She seems nonplussed at first. We can see the cogs of her mind turning behind her eyes. Then the news sinks in. And she smiles.

Is that all!

She jumps up and gives us a hug, like we've won a prize. Maybe we have. She thought we'd done something really bad.

It's just a watch.

Later, watching her sleep, we marvel at this beautiful freak. How she found something other than luxury goods and the accumulation of wealth to care about. Her friends would be appalled

How she could refer to an IWC Chronograph as just a watch?

We watch the Miss Chinese International Beauty Pageant. It's shot on location in Xiangjiang Safari Park. The girls pose in miniskirts alongside bears with metal rings through their noses. The bears, that is. The girls don't have rings in their noses, yet. Tigers are whipped and made to jump through hoops of fire. One contestant, when asked what she hopes to do in the future, says she want to get a job in animal welfare.

Meanwhile... to encourage participation in a local election, a jeans store offers discount coupons to anyone who fills out a ballot... A 10 year-old boy drowns in a pool while two lifeguards are on duty. One claims he wasn't sitting in the chair which affords him a view of the pool because it was wet. Comfort is important to his job. The other says he was busy talking with other swimmers in another area of the pool. He saw the boy at the bottom of the water but thought he was playing.

WE WALK WITH A SENSE OF PURPOSE, real or imagined, during the week. We dawdle on weekends, and after work. Weaving our way up and down the pavement, along the street and around the mall. When someone thinks they can zig, to overtake us, we zag.

We go to work on Sunday to prepare for Monday's presentation. We do a lap of the office to see if anyone else is there. And check up on The Agency Apparition. A young Suit is sitting at her computer.

Hey Wanda. What're you doing? Busy?

Not really. I didn't have anything better to do.

Nothing better to do than sitting in the office on a Sunday. Playing computer games. The air-conditioning isn't even on. Is this better than a walk in the park or a movie? Having afternoon tea with friends? Watching TV? Shooting yourself in the face with bazooka?

We persuade her to go shopping.

She's been wanting a camera for some time. She goes to one of those duty free shops in Kowloon, even though every shop in Hong Kong is a duty free shop. There's no tax on anything, except for alcohol and cigarettes.

The salesman phones the warehouse and gets them to send over a new one. The wrong camera is delivered. It's a more expensive model. Coincidence? What are the chances? Realizing she's about to be conned into spending more money she reminds him she doesn't want that one. He says she should take it. It's better. She says she doesn't want it. She wants the one she asked for.

The guy hits her on the head with a phone.

He's probably trying to sell her that too. He pushes her and berates her. He bullies her. She doesn't really approve of his methods but, in an effort to avoid further assault, she takes whatever he's offering. When she asks for a receipt he punches her. Then throws her out the door.

Meanwhile... senior government officials declare the World Cup to be a good anti-depressive drug for the gloomy economic situation. Being allowed to gamble on it, legally, would be a better one. If we want drugs we can go to the basketball courts in Wan Chai and get a drinking straw full of heroin for $20... The fishing industry is decimated by a red tide... At his annual eye test a minibus driver is declared legally blind... Three women and two children are found dead in an apartment, after giving their feng shui master $13 million. He told them if they drank his special potion, laced with cyanide, they'd live to be a hundred... The Post Office decides to stop putting the Dalai Lama on stamps because his face is not recognisable. They replace it with an image of Amelia Earhart.

WE ARE RENAMED. Relaunched. Rebranded. Same shit, different wrapper. We're *Tong Wei Cheuk*. Tong can mean sweet, as in nice or kind. It can also mean soup, or cold. So, you know, we've got that going for us. *Wei Cheuk* is a phonetic representation of Richard. It means outstanding or extraordinary. Great. Put them together and I'm Extraordinarily Nice, Outstandingly Sweet or Exceptional Soup. Depending on how you are with the translation and interpretation thing.

We're lost in transition, at Heathrow. Disembarking. Some guy hits Yling in the head with his backpack. She takes off after him, a blur of brand statements. *Haute* pursuit. We've never seen her designer shoes move so fast. Still, her little luxury-clad legs cannot carry her close to her quarry. We ask what she would've done if she'd been able to catch him.

I would give him The Face.

This is the preferred weapon of irate pedestrians and disgruntled drivers. The Face is a close relative of The Pout. It's a grumpy black-faced expression that resembles that of an onery chicken hawk. It's a sure-fire way of letting others know they've done wrong and you're greatly vexed by their actions.

Come on, you big balooka. Get up and fight. Put up your dukes, you schnook. Are you coming quietly or do I have to mess you up? Come on. Let's start something. What's the matter? Ya chicken.

We go the Notting Hill Festival with 249,998 others. We've been there for six and half minutes. We turn around. Bam. There's Niña.

What're you doing here?

Everyone has to be somewhere.

We're on our way to a wedding in Italy. Tuscany. Old friends, new lives. Isabelle is there too. She tells us she's also getting married to an American.

No, really. At least she waited a little longer than the obligatory three months, after our break up before she pledged allegiance to the flag and did one for The Gipper.

Meanwhile... A woman discovers her husband is having an affair with a Shenzhen prostitute. She throws their two sons, and herself, out the 14th floor window. The husband returns to his mistress with the media in tow. They film him telling the woman his wife is dead and asking if she'll to spend more time with him now... Nine die when man straps explosives to his chest and detonates them in a Guangzhou train station.

AMONG THE PROSTITUTES, foot massages, fake Prada bags and exploding commuters of Shenzhen is the Aloha Cafe. A painting of Waikiki's Diamond Head, circa 1972, covers an entire wall. Like the famed fried egg sandwiches of Honolulu, the *darn gee* here is worthy of the paradise that is Guandong province. The Hawaii and Riviera of the East rolled into one.

The *yin yeung* is not too shabby either.

Think of the best cup of tea you have ever had. Now think of the best cup of coffee you've ever had. Now tip them both into the same cup. You're half-way to appreciating the bicultural, bicaffeinated, biuretic beauty of *yin yeung*. Ask politely and the good people of Aloha Cafe have been known to blend an avocado into it, for that extra smooth taste.

We stop at Aloha every time we're in the neighbourhood. At least once a week under the current regime of hair care. One afternoon, while savouring the delicate flavours of our *darn gee* and considering the radical notion of an iced *yin yeung*, our eye is drawn to the building site opposite.

A man stands atop a ten-meter brick pylon. It is the last remaining structure in a block of razed rubble. Armed with a sledgehammer he attempts to knock the pylon out from under him. Life imitating the art of Chuck Jones, Friz Freleng and Hanna Barbera. He's the hapless coyote, the cat, the dog, the duck, pig or Fudd engineering his own demise. Chopping or sawing the branch, exploding the cliff or bridge, until it falls away beneath him.

On the train home we sit next to an old woman. She vomits into a plastic bag every fifteen minutes, for two hours. Morning sickness at three in the afternoon? Guangzhou withdrawal symptoms? Pre-Hongkong anxiety? Or just the effect we have on woman these days?

Clearing immigration at the boarder we indulge in our love of queues.

The longer the better. Size matters. The only thing we love more than a good queue is a queue fucked-up beyond all recognition. A sprawling, unwieldy queue seemingly without beginning or end. Multiple queues. Like the ones here in customs. At supermarkets, banks and cake shops. Queues we can share with the family. We can put one person in each line, see who looks like getting served first and then all move across to that one at the last minute. We'll queue for anything. Especially if it's out the front of McDonald's and miniature Snoopy figurines dressed in a variety of national costumes are involved. We'll stand there for hours. Waiting. Every day for a month. Apart from bragging rights and completing the set, a rare Japanese Snoopy could fetch $300 on the black market. Not bad for an initial investment of $6:50 and 1,200 man-hours.

Queues are to be honoured and respected. Obeyed. Do not disregard or underestimate their power.

News that Disneyland will be heading East is met with great joy, fervent celebration and much anticipation. SinoDisney? CantoDisney? The queues at Mouschwitz will be myriad and legion. The legend of the line king lives.

Meanwhile... eighteen die when a bomb goes off in Zhejiang... A bridge in Wuhan blows up, killing sixteen... A suicide bomber in Beijing kills four.

WE BUY A CAMERA, making it through the experience without being assaulted, too badly insulted or fleeced. We want to capture the contrasts on the streets of our island home. More artsy than fartsy, we shoot things in black and white. Off-centre and out of focus. Sometimes on purpose.

We go to the Sitting Out Area, in the back streets of Wan Chai where gnarled men play checkers.

We're surprised to find Chinese people don't actually play Chinese Checkers. The Chinese Checkers of our youth, with the coloured glass marbles and the inscrutable man with the Fu Manchu moustache on the box. Another myth busted. It's like finding out Singaporeans don't eat Singapore Noodles and Thais don't really dig on rice in pineapples. Proper Chinese Checkers is a serious game of strategy. No one dares to speak. A crowd of twenty or thirty stand around, silently observing the game. They look at each other from time to time. They nod, knowingly, like it's the most important thing in the world. Maybe it is.

Beside them, on the basketball courts, kids shoot hoops. At the sidelines, heroin addicts nod-out on discarded vinyl sofas. They buy their gear in the stands for $20 a throw.

Everyone is playing the game of their lives.

We board the Mid-levels Escalator. The longest escalator ride in the world. It runs from the heart of the CBD to the tip of The Gweilo Projects. We're angling for a shot of the open air butcher in the street below, as he stands amongst his pork products, smoking a cigarette. Raw ham hangs from the ceiling.

God speaks to us.

It's just as we've always feared. God is a woman with a speech impediment. A lisp. She's dealt herself a savage hand, some might say, and gone the full Elmer.

Be vewy vewy quiet. I'm hunting wabbits.

We would wike to wemind passengers it is iwwegal to take photos on the escawator, sayeth the Lord via an overhead speaker.

God has been watching on closed circuit TV. She's waiting at the end of the escalator. Grey pants, short-sleeved white shirt, blue tie. She demands we suwwender the fiwm fwom our camewa.

Why?

It's iwwegal. Sowwy.

This is a public area, we protest. The photos are for my personal use. You can't take my film. I'm a tourist. This is what we do. It's kind of our thing.

We're not sure where to go with this argument now. We've played our hand. Deployed our ace. Once you declare yourself a tourist you will live or die by that defence as if, somehow, being a tourist is an excuse for everything.

Sowwy. Bweach of weguwation. Secuwitty.

In Fudd we twust.

At least She's polite and somewhat contrite. Compunctious. We frequently meet people like this and, while they don't all have speech impediments, they're rarely sympathetic to our plight. There's probably a correlation between the two. Those who struggle better understand those who struggle to understand. Arseholery is inversely proportional to a the severity of their impediment. Most authority figures have an unwavering commitment to The Rules. No interpretation is allowed. No initiative can be shown. No discretion permitted. No explanation tolerated. No correspondence will be entered into. The judge's decision is final.

What we got here is... failure to communicate.

We're obsessed with hygiene. Once upon a time, if the eye couldn't see it then it is was clean. *Ngan buk gheen wei gon tzang.* Now we shower before and after work. Bed is bookended by bathing. We wash our feet upon entering the home. Clean our hands and mouth at meals. We brush our teeth four times a day. We'll eat the crutch out of a duck but we won't look at food that falls on the table. The floor is a forbidden zone of filth, despite being vacuumed, washed and waxed every day. Those who choose not to observe the same exacting standards are viewed with suspicion.

Meanwhile... Daniel Tsui wins the Nobel Prize for Physics. Hundreds of eager parents besiege the kindergarten he attended and attempt to enrol their children... Only 250 people storm the box office for Celine Dion tickets. Perhaps that explains the long face.

YLING TAKES US TO SEE KWOK FU-SHING. Aaron Kwok. The bonny Prince of Canto-pop. Live. It's fun in a Soft Cell and Erasure kind of way.

The following day sees one of many festivals held throughout the year. It's hard to remember which is which. They nearly all involve a day off work, food and setting things on fire. Not necessarily in that order.

Chung Yung, the Festival Of Ancestors, is in Autumn. It's a close relative of Spring's better known Ching Ming. Gravesweeping Day. As the name suggests, to honour our deceased relatives, we sweep around their graves. Dozens end up being airlifted off rural mountains when incense, *gum un yi tzee* and other flammable offerings start fires in remote golgothas.

The cremation of paper houses, cars, VCRs, beds, other domestic products and luxury items is not limited to these occasions. Most neighbourhoods are equipped with incinerators. Roughly the size of an average TARDIS, they're also responsible for transporting things through time and relative dimensions in space. To dearly departed relatives. By oxidising a Mercedes, a yacht, a plasma television, a Zegna suit or a duplex we can improve the standard of living of the dead. Bits of burning paper sometimes escape the incinerator, igniting a small shop or setting fire to a hawker cart of ersatz Ralph Lauren shirts and yea, verily, there is much rejoicing in the netherworld.

The Gates Of Hell open in the seventh month of the lunar calendar. Spectres storm the earth. This is *Yu Lan*. The Hungry Ghost Festival. We leave healthy portions of rice and fruit on the side of the road. It's an odd place for them to eat, given our obsession with hygiene. At least it gets them out of the house. We only do it once a year. No wonder they're hungry. Maybe if the Kitchen God got off its deified arse and cooked something once in a while they wouldn't be so rambunctious. Granted, the Slightly Peckish Ghost

Festival doesn't quite have the same ring to it and maybe the Dietician God frowns upon snacking between festivals. To keep them all happy we burn some Devil Money, in case they want to order-in.

The Mid-autumn Festival takes place in September, depending on lunar machinations. It's also known as The Lantern Festival and is one of the biggest, most eagerly anticipated of them all. Lanterns, naturally, abound. Candles are lit. Mooncakes are eaten.

The mooncake is more a hockey puck than a pastry. It's the size and shape of a tin of shoe-polish, with much the same nutritional value. Beneath the unassuming, baked exterior lies the indigestible horror of sickly-sweet lotus paste. Inside that, at its core, is an egg yolk so salty kidneys explode, arteries petrify and blood pressure erupts before it's even unwrapped. They're banned in certain agricultural districts for fear someone should inadvertently drop one and the saline levels poison the earth for all eternity. Each contains the caloric equivalent of four Mars Bars. A single bite delivers two-thirds of our daily fat allowance.

Mmmm... mooncake.

Many children choose this time of year to immolate, using a colourful combination of electrically charged plastic lanterns and red wax candles. The torching of parks and gardens is an optional, albeit popular, pastime.

Summer kicks off with The Dragon Boat Festival. Teams of competitive locals and enthusiastic expatriates attempt to paddle through the territory's clogged waterways, burning calories under a blazing sun. The snack *du jour* is sticky rice wrapped in a vine leaf.

Buddha's birthday is in May. We're faced with the same old dilemma every year. What do you get the deity that has renounced everything?

Thanks to The Handover, and our return to Mainland sovereignty, we now get to enjoy Chinese National Day as well. This brings the annual number of firework displays we must endure to three. Four if you count the firework festival in neighbouring Macau. It also affords us the rare opportunity to reflect upon how fortunate we are to be back in the bosom of the Motherland and celebrate the bountiful harvests of communism.

Lunar New Year is perhaps the mother of all celebrations. Chinese New Year. CNY. Almost a million people depart Hong Kong during this period. 16% of the population. 70,000 cross the border into Shenzhen every day. The city slows down for 48 hours. Across the border, the entire country stops for the best part of a week or more.

Golden Week.

In our house the happy and prosperous strains of *Kung Hei Fat Choy* are augmented with choruses of *Gong Xi Fa Cai*. We put on our lucky red jacket or Cosby sweater, load Aunty into the car and do a circuit of The Island. *Hung Dai Wan.* The Big Lucky Lap. It's one of the many ways we can bring wealth and prosperity to the year ahead. And it gives us something to do after lunch.

Afternoon tea is served with a little rubber snack that will help us grow taller, metaphorically speaking, and should garner us a promotion.

It's also important, at this time of year, to make as much noise as possible. Even more than usual. Firecrackers, drums and cymbals are all employed to scare the living bejezus out of ghosts and evil spirits, and fray the nerves of the living. Taxi drivers have two-way radios and stereos cranked up to eleven. They shout above them, rather than turning them down, when phone calls or conversations regarding directions beckon.

The living must suffer for the dead.

It's not a good time of year to buy shoes. In Cantonese the word for shoes is the same as the sound we make when something goes wrong. *Hai*, like a sigh. And we wouldn't want to start our year on the wrong foot.

We have to be careful with the *hai* thing all year round. Go wrong with the Nine Tones Of Canto and you can end up in all sorts of phonetic ass-hattery. *Hai* can mean shoes but it can also mean crab, or vagina. *Gau* can mean nine but it can also mean dead, dog, penis or cake. For monosyllabic Australasians it can be quite a challenge. Especially when ordering nine dead dog's dick cakes.

Gau gau gau gau gau, m'goi.

CNY is also where Kjeldsen's Butter Cookies and Fererro Rocher chocolates, the official snacks of the season, are re-gifted to friends and relatives. There's a tin of biscuits that has been circulating in our clan for two or three generations now, passed from family to family, like a quilt.

Last but not least are the all-important red packets of cash. *Lai see*, or *ong bao*, depending on where you went to school. Married couples are obliged to surrender money. Bosses and employer have a fiscal obligation too.

Kung Hei Fat Choy! Sun Tai Gihn Hon!

By limiting your public appearances, and deploying children strategically, it's possible to recoup more than you outlay. This is probably the reason more than a million flee the territory at this time. Better to spend the money on ourselves than improving the fortune of others, and spending time with distant relatives.

The end of the Chinese calendar is marked by the Winter Solstice. *Dong Zhi.* It's the shortest day of the year, revered and feared in equal measures. There's less time between meals, but one of them involves a family reunion.

Meanwhile... rumours that a chain of cake shops is about to go under see thousands descend upon the stores. Customers demand to redeem $450 million worth of gift certificates in one day. The company is forced to honour the vouchers and subsequently goes broke... A man threatens to disfigure his wife with acid, and chop the arm and legs off their daughter, if she doesn't give him $200,000.

LYING FACE DOWN ON THE PAVEMENT, the beggar bangs his head on the ground. A collection plate in front of him accepts coins from those sympathetic to his cause. He begs in Causeway Bay on weekends because the money's better. During the week he's a hawker in Tsim Sha Tsui, selling fish balls.

Who knew fish had testicles? I know I learnt the hard way.

The woman who shakes her red plastic cup by the Star Ferry takes home between $50 and $200 a day. She's applied for social security but isn't eligible. She has sons. To qualify for government assistance she has to prove familial negligence. And that needs an affidavit. Unfortunately the affidavit will cost $800 and she doesn't have that kind of money. That's why she's begging. We take up a quick collection at the office, on her behalf, only to discover the affidavit is useless anyway. She doesn't know where any of her children or step-children live.

Ragman has been roaming Queen's Road and Causeway Bay for 27 years. He's wrapped in a smattering of cloth and bandages like a decrepit Boris Karloff. Lying flat on his back with his hands buried in the tatters of his clout he gives a credible performance of someone in the throes of an epileptic fit. We throw $20 into his plate and hope he can soon afford medical treatment. Yling tells us he isn't busking or begging. That plate is just dish he uses to collect the scraps of food he pulls from the bins for meals. And he's not suffering a seizure. He's pleasuring himself. Shooting the aeroplane.

Dar fei gay.

If only we had a dollar for every time we've brought down an aircraft with the human howitzer.

Every time one of these Lancasters fly over, my chickens lay premature eggs.

Has much changed since The Handover?

We don't really know how to answer that question but wouldn't mind a dollar for every time we've been asked that too. Apart from an obvious increase in tolerance for masturbating in public, it's hard to say.

There's a sign behind the concierge at The Sheraton that wasn't there before. *Goods will be condemned after 14 days.* All the Royal red postboxes have been painted purple and green. As much as some would like us to believe, the current financial crisis has more to do with overseas markets than the return to Chinese rule. The red menace that weighs most heavy upon us is debt.

The city probably looks a bit more Chinese.

Parts of Hong Kong are starting to look like suburbs of Guangzhou, architecturally. Maybe there's a few less *gweilo* about but that's not necessarily a bad thing. Many of them have crossed into China's fields of opportunity.

Perhaps the most obvious change is the number of Chinese visitors we see roaming the streets and squatting on the curbs. They smoke and spit with impunity. Trawling malls. Struggling with turnstiles at the MTR. No respect for the sanctity of queues or the protocols of line formation. The men all seem to wear a variation on the same grey suit. They probably got them with their Entry Visas.

We've heard, from a reliable source, there's been a biblical increase in the number of prostitutes. Like the Jews out of Egypt they have crossed the desert and spilled into the promised lands of Mong Kok, Sham Shui Po and Wan Chai.

I heard one of the four creatures say with a voice of thunder, Come. I looked and behold, a white horse, and he who sat upon it had a bow. And a crown was given to him, and he went out conquering and to conquer.

There used to be an old guy selling jade and other talismans out the front of our building. Now he and his milk crate are gone. He was arrested and fined for illegal hawking. It was his only source of income. He only made between $30 and $200 on each item. He was lucky if he made one sale a day. Often he only sold one item a week. He refused to pay the $1000 fine because he didn't have the money. He was summoned to court. The judge ruled against him and confiscated all his merchandise.

The old man set himself on fire. Right there, in the courtroom.

He poured petrol over himself. Struck the flint on his antique Zippo lighter, the one with the portrait of Mai engraved on the side and pfft, just like that, he was gone.

Meanwhile... a twenty-four year-old nurse injects herself with rat poison... A medical student, discussing her exam worries with her mother and grandmother, gets up from the kitchen table, walks to the window and jumps twelve floors to hear death... A group of parents condone the use of the drug known as Ice by their children. They sleep better, it keeps them off the street and, after taking it, they have a lot of energy for chores and homework... A nine year-old fails a school test and leaps from his bedroom window. A girl hangs herself in the living room when her parents impose a 10pm curfew. Traffic accidents take 262 people a year. 870 take their own life.

AND JUST LIKE THAT, PFFT, HE'S GONE. By his own hand. Kurtis. Like Ian Curtis and Kurt Cobain before him. Kurtis, who's been so close to death with us so many times. When we fell from the tree. When we nearly drowned. When we almost got hit by the train. Kurtis was there to save our life. Yet we couldn't be there for Kurt when he fell into the void. We weren't there to pull him up, pull him back or out of the way. Away from his private apocalypse.

He broke from them. And then he broke from himself.

It's devastatingly surreal. We take a leaf out of Kurt Vonnegut's book and try to look at it from a non-linear, Tralfamadorian point of view. See all the moments of his life at the same time. Like a range of mountains. They're always there, all the time. Beginning, middle and end. Kurtis only appears to die at this one point. He's still alive in the past. In all those other moments. They're always there. We can see them and be in them whenever we want. If we look at that one time, when he died, we'll see he's in bad condition. Everywhere else, however, he's fine.

We gather Yling and all our Tralfamadorian resolve. We board a plane for Perth, and Kurt's funeral.

What're they gonna say about him? That he was a kind man? That he was a wise man? That he had plans?

Kurtis was always there when we went back. This time he's not. Not really. His body is there, at the funeral, but that's about it. At that moment he's in a bad way. Two hours later he's just fine. We resurrect him. We bring him back to life and he has a great time, all his great times, in one afternoon. We've never been confronted by our own inevitable mortality before. Not like this. It isn't like the hundreds of deaths we've endured on planes, or that time we had cancer and died on the slab in the operating theatre.

This death is real. Unreal. Hyper-real.

It heralds revelry and drunkenness. Grieving and sobriety. Feasting and fasting. Remembering and forgetting. Our heart orders anguish and pain, the brain serves up adrenaline to counter the trauma and anger. To rouse and tranquillise. We laugh and cry, often at the same time.

Death is invigorating, life affirming stuff.

We take Yling to Fremantle, to Rotto and to the pub. We leave her standing with Chuck Norris, Spicoli and Alby Mangles while we order a round of drinks. A fight breaks out. We see Yling standing in the middle of the mayhem, holding her glass. She's smiling, oblivious to the five beasts throwing punches around her. She's never witnessed violence before and has no idea of how violent and painful it can be. It's an abstract concept, like it's not happening at all. We take her to one side. Ask her how it started and what she was thinking, just standing there, as it blew up around her. She said she didn't know what to think or do. It didn't seem real.

It's like it was happening to someone else.

Meanwhile... Big Spender kidnaps the sons of Hong Kong's eminent squillionaires. He demands $1.3 billion and $600 million in ransom. A new World Record. It's not revealed why one is deemed to be worth twice that of the other. Le grand dépensier collects it in person, proving he is also holds the world's biggest set of cajones.

WE'RE ASKED TO VOTE for the annual Clean Public Toilets Casting Award. In some ways it's no contest. In others it's quite a challenge. Clean public toilets are a shallow pool. The one at the bottom of Lan Kwai Fong isn't bad. It does, however, also function as a meat 'n greet supper club. Impromptu show 'n blow sessions can be observed from the cheap seats in the stalls. The performance-art cum glory-hole vibe could be seen as somewhat counter to claims of cleanliness, in a puritanical sense.

In our guise as Regional Creative Director we visit toilets all over the length and breadth of Greater China. Guangzhou once a week. Shanghai once a month. Beijing every eight weeks. Taiwan two or three times a year.

All in the name of hair care.

We haven't been this hair-involved since the halcyon days of the mullet. We're away from the office so often only a few at The Agency even know who we are or what we do. They're not alone. We ask ourselves the same question with constitutional regularity.

What are we doing here?

There are places in the PRC that redefine the word bleak. Parts of Guandong. Xinjiang. Wuhan. Harbin. Outback Beijing. Now imagine them in the bleak mid-winter. Probably not the sort of places you would associate with the glitz and glamour of television commercials.

Yet there we are.

Seventeen hours a day, for six days. Sub-zero temperatures. No studio heating. The worst people-to-ablutions ratio in the history of advertising. 175:1

Two hours into proceedings on Day One, someone decides to redecorate the washroom, the one only washroom, with their stool. Seriously. Shit has been smeared wall to wall, floor to ceiling. It's left that way, to fester, for the remainder of the shoot. If the proprietors are aware of the Clean Public Toilets Casting Award they clearly don't give a shit about it or the thousands of dollars of filthy lucre up for grabs. They seem quite content trudge out to the tundra, into the frozen wastelands of untamed China and commune with nature.

We decide it's easier just to stop eating. We get by on a diet of distilled water and Coca-Cola. The breakfast of champions.

Our biggest concern is not how many shots we're going to get through that day, or if we'll have time to cover a few more. We don't care if the talent has gone to bed early to ensure there's no bags under her eyes, in preparation for her close-up. Our chief worry centers around suppressing the urge to purge the detritus. At least in KL, when the going got tough, we could get going to the hotel. It was only fifteen minutes away. There is no such luxury on the road to Yanquing.

Things are not much better back at the lodge.

A testament to Qing Dynasty modernisation there's no doubt it must have been quite something before electricity. The outhouse sits fifty meters down the garden path, across a paddock. When we inevitably suffer a debilitating gastric event, courtesy of the evening goulash, we have less than a minute to make it to the honey pot.

Setting foot into the yard we realise we're not the only one of God's creatures desiring absolution. Our torch searches the ink and discovers a drift of pigs moving toward us at speed. They seek the divine slop bucket and, in a way, we're the Holy Grail. We trip down the path and battle our way to the thunderbox, slamming the door on their snouts.

The exorcism begins.

Squatting over the gaping trench of the latrine we unleash an unholy torrent of effluence.

Be gone from this creature of God! Be gone! In the Name of the Father, the Son, and the Spirit! The power of Christ compels you!

There is a chorale of indulgent grunts and enthusiastic squeals at the rear of the chapel, where our porcine brethren have congregated for the

Eucharist. Their hairy nebs probing, protruding between the wooden wall and earthen floor. Tonguing at our hell-bound sacrament

Take, eat, this is My body which is broken for you:
Do this in remembrance of Me.

Not everyone is as economically active in agriculture and tilling the land as we are. Thirty million have left the farm. Or, to look at it another way, the population of Australia is unemployed and pursuing a career elsewhere. Many get no further than the world's oldest profession.

How ya gonna keep 'em down on the farm,
After they've seen Paree'?
How ya gonna keep 'em away from Broadway,
Jazzin around and paintin' the town?

A stable of fillies is being run out of the outback *auberge*. Their owner, operator and trainer calls us at 11pm. Massagee? asks the elderly woman. Massagee? You want massagee?

We think it's one of the crew. The Hairstylist with the questionable sense of humour. Sure. Me want massagee. Yeah. Love me long time massagee. Send two. Me want double massagee party.

There's a knock at the door a few minutes later. We're expecting The Hairstylist and a six pack of Yanjing Beer.

We're greeted by two teenage girls.

Even in the pale glow of hallway globes we can see they're wearing too much make-up and not enough clothes. Their bare arms and legs are decorated with lesions, bruises and scars. We apologise and try to send them on their way. They don't understand or pretend not to. They enter the room and sit on the bed. We give them two hundred yuan from our wallet and attempt to usher them out. Except now they've accepted your cash as a deposit on services yet to be rendered. They begin to undress and tug at your robe. Panic mode. We do what most people in marketing do when faced by a seemingly insurmountable problem.

We throw money at it.

This is probably the kinkiest night they've ever had. Someone throwing money at them, paying to watch them get changed. If this is a stitch-up it's world class. The only thing worse than colleagues or crew seeing them enter your room would be if they saw them leave.

They'll never want to see a rake or plow.
And who the deuce can parley vous a cow?
How ya gonna keep 'em down on the farm,
After they've seen Paree'?

For the rest of the shoot, every evening at 11pm and every hour thereafter, the phone rings.

Massagee?

We lie awake, unable to sleep, as *fille de joies* canter up and down the hall procuring womb service. Delivering massagee. With no book left unread, or television to watch, we pick up the Guest Services Directory.

To accommodate the visitors privately or transfer the rooms or beds is not permitted. Poultry or other pets are forbidden to bring into the hotel. Easy-fired, explosive, poison, x-ray and other dangerous goods are forbidden to bring into our hotel. And not allowed to make firework in the room. Don't be allowed fighting, gambling, hopping hoolism and play dirty, audio and video in the room.

As a guest in their country we're in no position to complain or criticise. Nonetheless, it's obvious that at least four of their rules are being violated. Maybe more, depending on your definition of hopping hoolism.

Meanwhile... nine out of ten Hong Kong women think it's customary for men to visit prostitutes when on the mainland.

SUB-ZERO TEMPERATURES mean Tiananmen Square is devoid of people. Except for patrolling soldiers or the occasional dim-witted, undeterred tourist. The emptiness adds dimension to its infinite acreage. A huge portrait of Mao looks down upon us, warily. Silent and solemn as we read the rules posted on a statue.

4. No Joking.

The Forbidden City looks like it did in The Last Emperor, minus the colour and carousing. Sadly there is no sign of Joan Chen. We try to get a photo of the concubine's quarters. Fresh out of Camera Luck and Tourist Luck a soldier materialises. He informs us we are not allowed to take pictures in The Forbidden City.

Why not?

It is forbidden.

He offers to take a photo for us. 20 yuan. Extortion, it seems, is not *verboten*. As a communist, this comrade's understanding of capitalism, entrepreneurial spirit and the need to grease the wheels of commerce is commendable. It's a trait very much in evidence across the length and breadth of the Middle Kingdom.

A man is not a man until he's been to The Great Wall.

It's been said there are only two man-made objects visible from the surface of the moon. One of them is 21,000 decaying kilometres of tamped earth, stone, brick and wood.

The other is Jennifer Lopez's ass.

Standing upon the former, wishing it was the latter, we feel small and insignificant. Introspective. We ponder the eternal question.

Is this where they took that photo of Wham! in 1985?

At sunset, The Wall and surrounding countryside is bathed in gold. It really is quite a sight to see. Many photos are taken at various shutter speeds and F-stops. A haggard crone, who was probably there when the foundation stones were laid, has been hounding us from pillar to guardpost.

Postcard?

No. Thanks.

Postcard?

No thanks.

Postcard?

No.

Postcard?

No!

Postcard?

No thank you!

It's a classic strategy. The war of attrition. Keep pestering and pushing. Eventually, just to be rid of you, people will purchase. You will bore and nag them into submission. Brands use it when devising media schedules. Hookers engage it when cold-calling your room at 11pm and every hour thereafter. Hawkers too.

Postcard?

Oh all-fucking-right then. Give them to me. All of them.

On a separate excursion we're led to the Ming Tombs. The ones that aren't available to the public. They haven't been restored and maintained. They've succumbed to the elements and budget cuts, picked over by fortune hunters and fallen into disrepair.

The Republic also guaranteed to protect the Imperial Tombs in perpetuity.

We jump the fence and try to climb to the top of one. We scale a fissure that's opened across the middle. We get stuck halfway and temporarily become part of a Ming Tomb, as one with the Emperor and his Concubines. It takes half an hour for the courtesans of our court - The Hairstylist, The Cameraman, The Producer and The Gaffer - to rescue The Shampoo King.

Meanwhile... Big Spender is arrested in Guangzhou. His family insists he's just a businessman. A flamboyant, thieving, kidnapping, murdering businessman. Justice is swift. There's twenty minutes between verdict and execution. Relatives arrive at the courthouse, to say good-bye, and are handed his ashes.

NEW YEAR IS RUNG IN and wrung out at a restaurant in Causeway Bay. Many of Yling's well-to-do friends are in attendance. Including Sally. Miss Hong Kong, Number Three. Second runner-up. The sheerness of her Dior blouse is matched only by the keenness of her intellect. Celine jeans appear to have been sprayed on, forcing her to stand for most of the evening. The joint declaration has more give in it than those pants. A Gucci handbag hangs from her elbow in much the same way she drapes from her boyfriend's arm.

Two must-have accessories of the season.

As we sit there, judging her appearance, it appears as if she's about to say something. Then she changes her mind. She puts a hand to her mouth, perhaps to stifle a gastric reflux. Summoning all the grace and poise of the third-most elegant woman in the Special Administrative Nether Regions, she takes a step back and cowers behind her man.

Swiftly and surreptitiously she opens her bag. And pukes into it.

She closes it with snap. Takes a napkin from the table and dabs at her mouth. She attends to her hair and straightens her blouse. She leaves the building. Boyfriend in one hand, designer-clad vomit in the other. It's been many years since we've witnessed such an impressive display of social regurgitation.

We'd have to go all the way back to the summer of '88.

We were in a club with Kurtis, the ghost of New Year past. He was fine-tuning the stereo, in the parlance of the time. Dialing up the magnetism. Hoping to storm the charts and get himself into heavy rotation with a couple of Chantoozies. Midway through his charm offensive he turned to us.

Watch this, he whispered from the corner of his mouth.

Retuning to his story, he regaled the unsuspecting divas with his plans to drive around Australia in a van, solving mysteries. Without warning, and for reasons known only to Kurt, foamy beer began to surge from his mouth. While he was talking. He wasn't spewing it, throwing it or projecting it. The strange brew just flowed from his mouth, like lava, as he spoke. If the young women had any appreciation for the kind of control, planning and commitment this type of performance takes they didn't show it. And then, just like that, it stopped. He turned off the tap and stood there, grinning, like the Cheshire Cat that kecked the cream.

As Sylvia Plath said, there is nothing like puking with somebody to make you into old friends.

Meanwhile... a motion is filed to outlaw preselection of a child's sex after 90% of births leveraging this method are found to be male... A man buries his 14 month-old granddaughter alive. He was hoping for a grandson. He reports her death. Suspicious officials exhume the body. They can hear the infant crying as they dig. The grandfather has to be restrained from strangling her when she is brought to the surface... The mistress of a 54 year-old man demands $6,000 after consenting to sex. When he refuses she stabs him, 51 times, with a steak knife. He offers her $100,000 to take him to hospital and she refuses. He dies.

ALL THE MAJOR CITIES OF CHINA are positioned like product. They come equipped with superlative slogans, like those found on license plates. Western Australia, state of excitement. Idaho, great potatoes. Delaware, it's good being first. New Hampshire, live free or die.

Beijing is the most grandiose. Shanghai, the most extravagant. Hangzhou, the most feminine. Suzhou, the most exquisite. Nanjing, the most sentimental. Chengdu, the most laid-back. Dalian, the most masculine. Wuhan, the most trivial. Chongquing, the most impatient. Shenzhen, the most lustful. Zuhai, the most romantic. Xiamen, the most cosy. Taipei, the most dangerous. Hong Kong, the most tough and uncertain. Xian, the most ancient. Guiyang, the most corrupt.

We take a tour of homes in Guangzhou, the most confusing, in search of consumer insights. If we view enough people in their domestic habitat we'll be able to think up new ways to make them buy shampoo and conditioner.

Our first host has recently been married. She proudly shows off her cisterns, faucets and free-standing air-conditioner. These are not euphemisms. They are the spoils of matrimony. No toasters, salad bowls, cutlery sets, glassware or panini makers from the department store gift-registry here. Her bathroom exhibits an incredible range of foreign haircare, cosmetic and beauty products. All manner of bottles, jars and tubes from international brands. Strangely, they're all empty. They've been strategically placed, like souvenirs from a foreign land, to show us how urbane her tastes are. To impress us with her spending power.

The Client takes us to Highest Ranking Wild Flavour Restaurant, for a laugh. We can't possibly be here to eat. The menu is amok with fox, cat, dog and python. Rat, apparently, is their signature dish.

Rat. The other *other* white meat.

More than an exotic delicacy, rat is a cure for baldness. It will turn grey hair black. It can repair kidneys. It's also one of the few meats that doesn't taste like chicken. We're ashamed to admit we don't have the courage to investigate the rodent's innate flavours and try Rat Sushi. In our defence, however, we don't eat regular sushi either. We play it safe. Rat Simmered With Black Beans. It tastes like simmered black beans, only rattier. The Client orders their celebrated rice dish. Ratso Rizzotto.

The two basic items necessary to sustain life are sunshine and coconut milk. Didya know that?

In some ridiculous triumph of optimism over Pteromerhanophobia we find ourselves aboard a twin-engine plane, bound for Lombok. The aircraft, dips, rolls, banks and rattles. We grip the arms of our seat. One of them comes away in our hand. We wave it around. The forlorn hostess collects it as if it were an empty plastic cup, rather than a vital piece of infrastructure.

We make our final approach. The cockpit door swings open. The pilots are arguing. One of them is holding what looks like an instruction card. He's pointing at it excitedly. Angrily. The other is shaking his head in denial, contradiction and disbelief.

They're flying *a la carte*.

We celebrate this year's birthday, our February birthday, like it could be our last. Given we still have to make the return flight that could be closer to the mark than any of us care to admit. Certainly closer than our Captain came to hitting the runway.

In a remote bar we discover a forgotten tribe of expatriates. They've been away far too long and have lost all contact with reality. We're thinking Marlow, The Congo and The Company. Kurtz. Joseph Conrad's Heart of Darkness. They reek of the worst aspects of colonisation and are decades old before their time. Decrepitated by isolation, alcohol, nicotine, syphilis and masturbation.

You don't have to be Papillon to know what rubbing one out eight times a day can do for your complexion.

We seek refuge in a luxury resort. Hiding, sleeping, eating, drinking, fishing and swimming. Not necessarily in that order or at the same time.

All too soon it is with a heavy heart and misgiving mind we return to Lombok International Airport.

Better three hours too soon than a minute too late.

Our flight is scheduled to depart at 10:40. We check-in early and wait until 10:45. There is no boarding call or board of information. We inquire after the status of our flight at the Merpati Air counter. We have to make a connection in Bali, to make it to Singapore for a flight to Hong Kong. This might seem to be an unnecessarily risky flight plan but then so was the alternative.

Garuda.

We're informed the 10:40 flight departed at 10:25. Everyone was on the plane, waiting for us. The Captain decided to go. You pointlessly protest the logic of this. Are passengers supposed to guess the time of departure? Can we just get on the plane when we feel like? She knew we were sitting there, why didn't she say something?

We thought you were waiting for the next flight.

When will that be?

We're not sure. We can't find the pilot. He's been sick.

It's Merpati and we'll cry if we want to. Die if we want to. You would cry to if Merpati happened to you.

The 11:45 eventually departs at 12:15. We arrive at Bali's Domestic Terminal at 12:50. A mad sprint to International sees us standing before the Singapore Airlines counter at 12:53. It is unattended. The gate is closed. We let rip with the international distress call of exasperated travellers.

Fuck!

A small smiley face pops up behind the counter.

Can I help you, Sir?

We explain our predicament and the need to make the flight. The plane is probably still at the gate. We'll be in so much trouble at work if we miss it.

He picks up a walkie-talkie, mutters something in Bahasa and hands us a boarding pass. Follow me, Sir.

Smiley leads us through a door, behind the counter and takes us straight to the plane. No customs. No immigration. On one hand it restores our faith in humanity. On the other it fuels our apprehensions regarding airport security and flight safety.

We make the connecting flight in Singapore and are soon knocking back vodka tonics in Cathay Pacific's incident-free aircraft. The last leg. The homeward stretch.

We feel desperately for our fellow passenger who suffers a heart-attack at 30,000 feet. Yet we also find a certain comfort in it. This is the one bad thing that happens on every flight.

And it didn't happen to us.

We can relax. The chances of screaming across the sky in a twisted ball of fiery metal have been greatly reduced. Practically eliminated. The number of small children on board also makes us feel pretty good about our chances of survival. There's a lot of them. Little kids have a lifetime of luck ahead of them. They've hardly had a chance to use any of their quota. Get on a plane packed with old people and you're pretty much fucked. They've run plumb out of luck. They shouldn't even be buying a green banana.

Our Birthday Luck holds up pretty well too.

Returning home we find Yling has bought us a present. A watch, from Cartier. Pasha.

I knew you were too young for a watch like that.

Time is what we crave the most but have used the worst. And lost time can never be found. Still, it does change everything. It heals wounds, except that something deep within which is always surprised the change it brings.

We ask Yling a question.

Why?

You lost the other one, remember. Better not lose this. Everyone needs a good one.

Why *me?*

Who else was I going to give it too?

Not the watch. Us. Why choose me?

She searches our face. At first we think it's because she's surprised by the question. Then we realize it's because she's surprised we don't know the answer.

You looked like you were broken, she explains, as if it were the most obvious, natural thing in the world. I wanted to make you better. I thought I could fix you. Or have some fun trying.

9. YEAR OF THE RABBIT

THERE ARE MORE THAN 150,000 domestic helpers in Hong Kong. Most come from the Philippines and are available in a variety of makes. Maid to order. Custom maid. The employment agency sends us a list of models and optional extras. Buy now, while stocks last. Government sanctioned human trafficking. We can get one that cleans, or one that cleans and cooks. One that cleans, cooks and looks after our children. One just to take care of an infirm relative, or a dog. One that cleans, cooks, cares for the kids and will service the master of the house. One that cleans, cooks, cares for the kids, services the master of the house and his brother.

All for less than $5,000 a month.

Regardless of pedigree, for the first year of employment, 90% of their salary will go to the agent. To inspire devotion and commitment to the tasks at hand we take away their passports. This is a deterrent and incentive. If they want to see their passport and their family again they won't steal things or run away from their responsibilities. They'll carry our children's bags to the bus stop, come to *yum cha* on their day off and feeds the kids, take them to the toilet, clean up after them and play with them.

While we read the paper.

It's true there is an ever-present danger they might eat our babies or put one of them on a spin-cycle in the washing machine. But it's a small price to pay for effectively outsourcing the development of our children.

If an amah does step out of line, or accidentally damages our silks with the iron, we are sometimes left with no choice but to beat them with a stick, scald them with boiling water or force them to put their hands upon the board so we can burn them with the iron.

It's a difficult job but someone has to do it.

Meanwhile... a maid repeatedly bangs her head against the wall of her employer's apartment. The mere sight of water terrifies her which, for someone who spends their day cleaning and washing, must be a living hell. After three visits to the doctor her illness remains undiagnosed. She

*dies, three weeks later, of rabies... A woman sues her maid for $168,258.
She claims the domestic helper fell asleep when she was supposed to be
caring for her son. The boy had consequently suffered second degree burns
in an accident. The mother was also in the flat at the time but insists the
boy was her amah's responsibility.*

THE ROAD IS DESERTED. Shanghai. Three in the morning. We're on our
way back to the hotel. There's a woman on a bicycle up ahead. The driver
doesn't see her. He's turned to face us. He's attempting to explain something.
We try, unsuccessfully, to warn him of the impending collision.

The taxi ploughs into her.

She bounces off the windscreen and lands on the road. The taxi runs
over the bicycle before coming to a stop. The driver is unaware of what has
happened. He just panicked at the sudden noise and hit the brakes. He sits
there, stunned, staring through the crack in the windscreen.

People file onto the street. Like rats from a drainpipe, there's ten, twenty,
thirty of them. One hundred. We urge the driver to get out and see if the
woman is okay. He has no idea what we're saying. He exits the vehicle and
inspects the hood for damage. He either hasn't seen the woman lying at his
feet, doesn't care or has assumed her to be dead. The health of his vehicle
is his primary concern.

An unintelligible murmur rises from the crowd of rubberneckers. The
roadkill wails. The driver walks across to her, tentatively. He attempts to lift
her. She howls like a wounded banshee. It frightens him. He drops her onto
the road. She screams. The volume of the assembly increases. He addresses
them. They turn their attention to the back of the taxi.

Accusing eyes peer out of the darkness, in our direction.

It appears this accident is our fault. We have visions of being dragged
from the cab, like that truck driver in LA, after the cops who beat Rodney
King were acquitted.

We open the door and stand on the street.

Neighbourhood Watch contracts around us. The tone of their Mandarin
suggests things might get worse before they get better. The police will arrive
soon and then we'll really be in trouble. They'll take us to the station for the
rest of the night. They'll expect reparations for the experience. We decide
to do what any red-blooded man would do. The same thing we've been
doing all our life.

Run away.

We try to maintain a little dignity and integrity, at first. We walk off. The crowd, unfortunately, walks with us. We walk quicker, moving at a canter. The crowd keeps pace. We turn a corner and run like the clappers. We have no idea where we're going. It's Shanghai. It's three in morning. We're being pursued by an angry mob with pitchforks and burning torches.

There's no justice like angry mob justice.

Two blocks ahead we spy a beacon. The castle gates. Safe harbour. It is The Hilton.

Any port in a storm.

Meanwhile... ten Falun Gong practitioners gather in Beijing and begin breathing exercises. They're arrested and carted away. Respirating without a permit... China states that if Taiwan does not agree on reunification, it could lead to a military invasion.

IF IT'S TUESDAY IT MUST BE TAIPEI. We're observing focus groups. An attempt to find out what women aspire to. Sartorialy, tonsorialy, socially. Judging by the obvious lack of contemporary fashion sense the answer appears to be something from the 80s.

Taiwan is home to some of the most ensembley challenged people we've ever seen. And, remember, we've been to Mandurah. We've seen Wuhai.

The power goes out, completely, for two days. The focus groups are cancelled. We spend the night smoking by candlelight in the lobby bar of the hotel. Drinking warm beer. Reminding anyone who'll listen what happened in New Zealand last year.

The US were developing a weapon, in the Antarctic. It could blast the atmosphere above a particular location with an electro-magnetic pulse. This would render everything in that area useless. The same month this weapon of mass destabilization was due to become operational, Auckland mysteriously found itself without power for two weeks. The closest city to the Antarctic, and the base where the weapon was developed, was without electricity. Not for one or two nights. For two weeks. It was only a matter of time before the technology was tested on a real target. No offence, Auckland, but you know what we mean. The blackout in Taipei also happens to coincide with an election.

What are the chances?

Things escalate beyond the obligatory threat of conflict or sabre rattling wargames in The Strait. PLA garrisons in Hong Kong are put on full alert. Electronic Warfare Units are moved to the Mainland coast. Techno-geeks from both sides lay siege to each other's web sites.

I loved it when you nuked Las Vegas. Suitably biblical ending to the place, don't you think?

We arrive home and fall into bed. It feels different. Like it's not our bed. We pull back the sheets and find a new mattress.

We call Yling.

Turns out her mum bought us a new mattress. She thought we were too big to be sleeping on that old one.

Meanwhile... careless grave sweepers start 383 fires during the Ching Ming Festival... A policeman is killed when a woman, diving out the 32nd floor of her apartment, lands on him... A bomb goes off in front of a Tsim Sha Tsui department store.

NATO BLOWS UP THE CHINESE EMBASSY in Yugoslavia. Three die. It was an accident. The map they had of the area was an old one, given to them by The CIA.

Who did the CIA get that map from?

Conspiracy theorist suggests China is suffering an internal crisis of confidence. Millions are starving and unemployment is at a record levels. More layoffs are expected by the day. The 10th Anniversary of June 4 is just around the corner. Something like this could be just what the spin doctor ordered.

A dose of national pride to distract the masses.

Students are bussed into the US Embassy in Beijing, two hundred at a time. It is a constant, organised stream of unrest. Each group is given an hour to yell, throw stones and hurl paint. A fresh batch is then rotated in. If caught empty-handed, at the front lines, they're sent to the back where soldiers are distributing projectiles.

We demand compensation for this barbaric act.

After a few days, the wheels of diplomacy roll in. Negotiations begin with a call for China's expedited entry into the WTO, and trade sanctions to be dropped. Within a week, life in the capital returns to normal. For everyone except CNN.

Beijing is quiet, too quiet.

They broadcast images of peak-hour gridlock, juxtaposed the deserted streets around the Embassy. Nothing unusual or uneasy in that. The streets around the embassies are always deserted.

An uneasy calm has settled over the city tonight.

We drive to The Client's candy factory. It's deep in the forsaken countryside. The city deteriorates before our eyes. Each minute is like a step back in time, except the buildings get older and crumble. People live in shacks of tin and stone. They squat in squalor beside the road.

A Mars a day helps you work rest and play.

Have a break. Have a Kit-Kat.

Catch the rainbow. Grab the rainbow. Taste the rainbow.

We shoot a series of soda-pop commercials in Ireland. And are touched by the Blarney Stone. We feel like we're grounded there. Connected. Maybe we're half Irish. The locals seem to think so. The shoot goes well. No days are lost to rain. Must be the luck of the Irish.

The client hates the ads.

They're not what they were expecting. This suggests they were predisposed to a certain outcome, or had some clairvoyant vision of what they were supposed to look like.

Why wasn't that shared with us at the pre-production meeting?

We have to re-shoot them at The Agency's expense. There's a possibility we may lose the account. Or get fired. Redundancy doesn't sound half bad. It would earn us a $500,000 golden handshake, maybe more.

Typhoon Dot howls into town.

We're playing mahjong when she arrives. It's as close as we get to a night on the tiles these days. We're not up to Canto-speed, however, and are a constant source of frustration for Yling and her friends.

We play slow. And win.

The TV is monitoring Dot's progress through the archipelago. Every half hour a journalist is blown across camera in a downtown location. Segments are intercut with images of umbrellas being turned inside out by gusts of wind and bamboo scaffolding swaying in the wind. Trees are torn up. Neon signs are brought down.

Suddenly there is a late-breaking report.

Ambulances and fire trucks screaming across an airstrip. A plane has flipped on the tarmac at Chep Lap Kok and burst into flames. All but three walk off the packed airbus and live to tell their tale, repeatedly. On every channel.

The Weather God is in a vendetta kind of mood.

Typhoon York barrels in shortly after. It's our first Signal 10 in sixteen years. Newscasters dig deep into the archives and broadcast footage from the last time the penultimate warning was hoisted.

Our bedroom window pops.

It's blown in at three in the morning. Rain streams onto the bed. A wind-tunnel, suitable for the testing of military aircraft, establishes itself in the hallway. We check other windows in the apartment and learn that ten out of thirteen are not sealed properly. We spend the next six hours wringing towels and emptying buckets.

Driving through Wan Chai in the morning, Revenue Tower and Immigration Tower have suffered a similar fate. To the power of ten. Windows are shattered across all floors. The road is covered in glass, tax returns and immigration files. It's like the aftermath of some anarchic ticker-tape parade.

An earthquake hits Taiwan. 7.6 on the Richter Scale.

Rodney Dangerfield sends a team to help clear the rubble. It takes thirty-six hours to assemble the squad and one hour to get there. The sixteen men are returned to sender upon arrival in Taipei. They arrived too late. They had a bad attitude.

Rodney insists the decision to send them home was not a politically motivated insult to the Motherland. The episode is praised as a remarkable achievement.

We pass the hapless heroes in the airport.

We're on our way to Los Angeles to shoot another shampoo commercial. We checked in twelve hours before, requesting a seat in the upper deck. Business Class. Stepping aboard we discover our place has indeed been reserved. Right beside the toilet. Seems the chair is broken too, incapable of performing the most rudimentary of functions. It won't recline and the footrest collapses. The toilet is looking like a more comfortable option. Naturally, we complain, but the aircraft is full. There's nowhere else to sit. Three cabin attendants, of ascending seniority, take turns apologising. They tell us there's nothing they can do and leave us to endure fourteen hours of misery. Upright and awake. Every time we come close to dozing off someone goes to the toilet. They open the door and, if the light doesn't disturb us, the vacuum-suck of the flying dyke does.

Prior to landing a well-meaning hostess apologises again, on behalf of the airline. She offers us a US$25 Duty Free voucher. Twenty-five bucks, for half a day of torture. We thank her for the offer and explain how we don't really want a voucher. She insists we take it. We insist we have no need for it.

We really want you to have it, she says.

We really want you to leave us alone, we reply.

Her superior returns ten minutes later. She makes a final push for absolution. She apologises and suggests that, if we don't want a Duty Free voucher, perhaps we might like a miniature model of a Cathay Pacific 747. She pulls it out from behind her back, where she's been hiding it, so as not to spoil the surprise. She seems to think we're a six year old child who might be impressed by such a thing.

Just what we need. A permanent reminder of The Flight From Hell.

We laugh and look around the cabin for the candid camera. Surely this must be a joke. She offers the little jet to us again. Thrusts it toward us sincerely. Playfully. Like she's spooning mush to an infant.

Here comes an aeroplane! Open wide! Nom nom nom!

We say it's lovely but, really, we don't want anything from her or the airline. If we didn't want a $25 voucher what on earth makes her think we'd want that trinket?

Sir, please. The airline insists you take it.

Madam, please, we insist. Take the plane and shove it up the airline.

Meanwhile... a slab of concrete falls from the sky and kills a woman standing in a market stall... Twenty men burst into a Yuen Long pub and attack four others with choppers, water pipes and wooden poles. One dies... A 24 year-old man assaults another for making a pass at his girlfriend in a Lan Kwai Fong night club. He ties him up for two days and beats him with a baseball bat. Then takes him to the dump, covers him with paint thinner and sets him alight.

OUR NEIGHBOURS are renovating their apartment. The floor has been resurfaced. It's covered in varnish. The decorator warns the women not to light candles or joss sticks until it's dry. Ignoring his advice they continue with their daily worship. A rogue joss stick ignites the floor in a flash. It takes the decorator with it. Just like that.

Pffft!

Waiting for a taxi, on the way to work, a dormant mini-bus kicks into life. A giant carcinogenic mushroom swallows us whole.

The buses are out to get us. All of us.

A double-decker overturns on the Wan Chai off-ramp, injuring fifty. Another collides with a mini-bus in Central and gets six. Two are nailed when a taxi is rammed in Aberdeen. A schoolboy is run down in Pokfulam.

Sixteen are injured in Sheung Wan. An old man is mowed down on a Mid-levels sidewalk. A double-decker bus, three tour buses and a motorcycle pile up in Mong Kok. Another pins a 69 year-old woman to the ground in Stanley.

An account manager at The Agency decides to sue the driver of a mini-bus. She claims a collision he orchestrated has made it impossible for her to wear high heels. Her career, like her fallen arches and the front end of his vehicle, is ruined. She's limited to shoes with flat heels. This has impeded her career prospects, in terms of outfits she can wear and delivering against key performance indices.

With altitude comes attitude. The higher the better. Heels empower a woman. There is pleasure in their pain.

We drive to lunch on Sunday. Every third person on the street is carrying at least one case of Coca-Cola. Two supermarket chains are having a price war. The first shot has been fired across the bow of the world's favourite beverage. Cases of black gas are discounted by ten percent. It's not much of a saving, to be honest. Still, it's enough to make people believe they'd be crazy not to buy it. Even those who don't like Coke think it's too good to pass up. No one wants to miss out on a bargain. Besides, we can always sell it on, at a higher price.

Coke, like the multitasking rat, is more than just a refreshing beverage. We can glaze chicken wings with it. Toss it into a salad. If we bathe in it we'll become more virile. Heat it up and it's a cure for the common cold. We can use it to clean brass and silver. Let's face it, when we see what it can do for precious metals it's a wonder anyone drinks it at all.

Coca-cola. It softens hands while you do dishes.

In Thailand a senior executive of Hong Kong's biggest bank is arrested in a Pattaya hotel room. He's been making deposits and withdrawals with 12 year-old boys.

Dipping into the pool at our hotel we notice a small Japanese man by the deep end. He looks like Doraemon's Nobita Nobi. He's swinging his arms and stretching his legs. His wife stands beside him like a subservient Sailor Moon. She hands him his goggles. He snaps them onto his head, dives in and begins swimming laps of the small, twenty-meter pool.

Sailor Moon walks to the deep end. She slips into the water and promptly sinks to the bottom. Nobita Nobi swims right on by. Over her. She claws her way to the surface, arms flailing, sucking air and water. She's in over her head. This is obvious to all except her husband, who continues swimming laps.

We dive in to rescue her, thrilled that all those episodes of Baywatch are finally going to pay off.

In her state of panic Sailor Moon is a major handful. Bringing her to the surface is only slightly easier than keeping her there and piloting her to the side of the pool. She flounders mightily.

Her husband continues to swim laps.

We push her up and out of the water. She lies there like a beached baby seal, honking chlorine onto the paving. We get her a towel and help her into a chair while her husband continues to swim comical laps.

She frowns and walks, unsteadily, to the edge.

She throws her towel at him. He stops, mutters something and removes his goggles. She shouts at him. He is shocked then embarrassed and, finally, humbled. He exits the pool and walks over to us. He bows and recites ancient Japanese words of gratitude.

According to our wafer-thin knowledge of Eastern culture, this means Sailor Moon now belongs to us. Her life is ours to do with as we like.

We decide to dispense with tradition.

It would be too difficult to sneak her through customs let alone into the apartment. We've already exceeded our baggage allowance anyway. The twelve kilos of bird nest, shark fin and durian that Yling's mother has put on her wish-list have taken care of that.

Meanwhile... a cure for cancer is found on a street corner in Sham Shui Po. It only costs $50,000 and looks like a box of elastic bands... One woman pays $50,000 for a cure for The Millennium Bug. She isn't sure if The Bug is a physical ailment or a computer virus but she's convinced she can resell the pills for a profit. She buys 400 tablets of Gelusil Plus... $700,000 worth of advanced electrical components are purchased in the belief they can solve all Y2K related problems. Electrical engineers reveal them to be unlabelled AA batteries... For sixth months a woman allows a Qi Gong Master to fondle her breasts and genitals. She believes it's part of the cleansing rituals he's prescribed to remove evil spells and drive out bad spirits. It's only when she starts meeting him at Villa Victoria and he asks her exorcise his demons that she becomes suspicious and has him charged him with sexual harassment.

WE'RE HAVING PROBLEMS with a few cleansing rituals of our own. We've shot nineteen shampoo commercials in twelve-months.

We're responsible for just one of 240 brands in the market. And, it's fair to say, the heady realm of haircare is warping our view of the world. The follicle follies. The never ending parade of slow motion shots. The Swing. The Flip. The Flip Wilson. The Curtain. The Harp. The Peacock. The Double Harp. The Half-peacock. The Triple Garlic. The Yanni. The Suplex. The Duplex. The Over-easy. The Benedict. The three-day discussions on Brand Character, insights and defining what elegant means to Chinese consumers. We begin to feel we're part of some cosmic joke and shampoo commercials are the punchline. We see a nice beach or an exotic location. A photograph from someone who was lucky enough to take a vacation.

That looks like a nice place... to shoot a shampoo commercial.

Interesting *objets d'art*, nice furniture and simple, stylish clothes. A photographic technique. A special effect. Look at the hair. The make-up.

That would look great... in a shampoo commercial.

An attractive girl graces the Sunday papers, walks by on the street or is working in a bar.

I wouldn't mind having her... in our next shampoo commercial.

We hear something. A turn of phrase, an idiom or an analogy. An anecdote. A myth. A scientific experiment.

I wonder if we can use that... in a shampoo commercial.

There is travel, per diems and a backdrop of beautiful women. Yet it's become an academic, joyless and imperious task. An endless procession of 30-second nothings that challenge no one.

Lester Bangs would not be amused.

We'd be interested to hear his views on the High Priestess of Canto-pop too. Sammi Cheng. We've come to see one of the twenty live performances she's commanding at the 10,000-seat Colosseum. To check out her wardrobe and hairstyles. The lighting.

A large group of fans have gathered out front of the venue, pre-show, to practice arm-waving. It's been scientifically proven that most of us have no natural sense of rhythm. The sequences can take a while to button down. In addition to the traditional left-right-left-right movement, there's the revisionist left-right-right-left. If we want to change things up, for more uptempo tunes, we can invoke left-left-left-right, or right-right-right-left. At our own peril. The margin for error is exponential when attempted, live, in real-time conditions. Throw in a fluorescent glow-stick and things can quickly get out of hand.

Anyone feeling well proceed to right exit for assistance.

We figure this message has been projected onto the wall by The Fun Police. Part of Hong Kong's ongoing program to stifle the arts and stop people from having a good time. It had once been suggested audiences at outdoor concerts should be issued with gloves, so their clapping wouldn't be too noisy. Bands could dispense with speakers altogether. The music could be piped to people through headsets plugged into each seat. Just like sitting at home, listening to the CD. Through headphones. It's perfectly fine to operate a jackhammer on a Saturday night, or sing Chinese opera outside someone's window for three hours on a Sunday morning. A little music for two hours in the evening, however, infringes upon civil liberties.

Anyone feeling unwell proceed to right exit for assistance.

A school survey reveals most students believe a meal of bananas, milk and Corn Flakes is the best thing to have for breakfast. Even though seventy percent of students don't actually eat breakfast, are lactose intolerant and prefer soy-milk.

It's what they think they should be eating.

We interview some Mainland women in search of consumer insights. We're looking for magic moments between a mother and child. Something we can exploit and use against them. To emotionally blackmail them into buying more milk to go with the Corn Flakes they're not buying either. We hear stories of apology notes, breakfast in bed, kids helping out in the kitchen and many other endearing efforts undertaken by the Little Emperors.

Your child actually does things like that?

Oh no. I would just like it very much if he did.

We're waiting to clear Immigration on the way back from Shenzhen. Two men in front are asked to open their bags. A quick search uncovers a number of boxes full of grasshoppers. Fighting crickets. They're being smuggled in for illegal cricket-fighting tournaments.

Meanwhile... a policeman gets caught with a night club hostess, in his car. The 23 year-old agreed to have sex with him after he promised to buy her a mobile phone.

ARTHUR MILLER may have been referring to 1960s America when he wrote of a system pouring its junk over everybody and marooning individuals on little islands of commodities, but he could just have easily been talking about Hong Kong in the 90s. Buying things we don't need with money we don't have, to impress people we don't know or like.

We don't have a life. We have a lifestyle.

We wear phones around our neck, a sad badge of upwardly mobileness.

The phones that give us tumours and cancer. Brain, breast or testicular, depending on where we carry them. We buy earpieces to reduce the risk and walk around hands-free. Tourette's Syndrome for the masses. The hearing-aids channel radiation directly to our grey matter and leave 3/4 of the population unable to hold conversations at normal volume.

Once upon a time there was only 180,000 chunky, brick-like devices. Phones were so big we needed two hands to pick them up. Immobile phones. By October 1999, five million of us are GSM-ing, dual-banding, WAP-ing telecommunicators.

At the cinema we hear Greensleeves while Kevin Spacey pleasures himself in the shower. Waltzing Matilda when that creepy kid sees dead people. Jingle Bells plays when Matt Damon caves in Jude Law's head with a paddle.

During The Insider, one guy takes a dozen calls despite constant shushing from his neighbours. When it happens again six of his companions turn on the shusher. They beat him for interrupting their friend's call. We get the usher, an officially sanctioned shusher. He waits up the back of the cinema for the phone to ring again. When it does he goes down the aisle, leans over and asks the guy to turn it off. The great communicator stands up and punches him, for not respecting his right to free speech.

Free speech means the right to shout 'theatre' in a crowded fire

For our 20,000km Anniversary Yling suggests we move apartments. She's found us a better one. It's two blocks further back from the road, halfway up the hill. Only two hundred meters from her place. In fact, it's the apartment she grew up in. It's so quiet we can hear a man vomit six floors below.

Our girlfriend has become our landlord.

With every move, we're brought closer to the family. Into the inner circle. The circle of trust.

It's a glorious time to be Chinese. Eight of the world's ten most polluted cities lie within our borders. Langzhou, on the banks of the Chlorine-yellow River, holds down the coveted #1 position.

It's the Golden Anniversary of the PRC.

Celebrations are peppered with speeches emphasising progress. Appearances tell a different story. There are moments when we wonder just how far we've come and how far we have to go.

In the background we see The Forbidden City.

Twenty-four emperors of the Ming and Qing Dynasties reigned there. The Sons of Heaven grew and multiplied there. Thousands of years of Chinese culture is housed in 9,999 buildings spread over 720,000 square meters. The Boxer Rebellion ended there. The Last Emperor was born there. Now, it seems, Confucianism and Maoism have been traded for consumerism and materialism. We can get a Tall Double Skinny Decaf Latte there.

Starbucks has taken up residency in The Imperial Palace.

President Jiang Zemin looks more like Mao Zedong, presiding over the festivities. Rather than celebrating fifty years it's like stepping back half a century. The massive parade of military might. Missiles, tanks, goose-stepping troops. If it wasn't for the liberal use of primary colours it could be a 1950s newsreel. Floats trundle along like the homecoming parade from Animal House. There's scientists in lab coats, splitting atoms.

Science and technology are the primary productive force.

Men in dirty overalls work on an oil rig. Peasants in traditional garb look like contestants in some humiliating game show. The importance of agriculture is highlighted by children dressed as stalks of wheat. Others wear lampshades on their heads and wave flowers.

Advance the modernisation of agriculture.

There's troops of boys on unicycles, performing stunts. A battalion of men in Hugo Boss suits wave magic wands. More than one hundred leggy models strut by.

United no one can divide us.

In Hong Kong we're dividing and conquering ourselves. Batches of oyster sauce are withdrawn from supermarket shelves when it's discovered they contain three times the safe number of carcinogens.

There's a safe number of carcinogens?

The shark liver capsules we've been taking to improve our health and beauty have too many polychlorinated biphenyls in them.

This is a bad thing.

The owner of the Stinky Tofu shop, next to Yling's office, is summoned to court for polluting the environment. It's a step in the right direction but probably has little to do with the smog that settles over the city. Visibility is reduced to one hundred and seven meters. For weeks. The pollution index soars to 174. Twenty-six points below the number at which canaries drop off their perches

Rodney Dangerfield gives his third policy address. He promises to improve the quality of air and water. This is on the day every air-monitoring station in the territory reads high or dangerous, and our main water supply is swarming with e-coli.

Barney, the Killer Whale at Ocean Park, dies of lung disease. And he only comes up for a breath six times a day. Officials blame his pack-a-day smoking habit.

Tempting fate, and hoping history doesn't repeat itself, 5,000 Falun Gong practitioners turn up in Tiananmen Square and engage in meditation exercises. The movement is outlawed. It's a threat to national security.

China gets an early Christmas present. Macau. This is the political equivalent of sorbet. A palate cleanser for cadres between courses. After filling their boots on Hong Kong, before they make a meal of Taiwan.

Pre-millennial hoarding makes typhoon-raids on supermarkets and 7-11s look positively pedestrian. We spend the end of the century waiting for the Millennium Bug to bite.

On our way to High Tea at the Shangri-la, people are waving placards. They're throwing rocks, bamboo sticks and flower pots. Fruit and paint. Street signs. A park bench. Police fire pepper spray in an effort to quell the riot.

The Riot Of Abode.

The Court Of Final Appeal has decreed children of Mainland parents, born in Hong Kong, can stay. The problem is Rodney has asked Beijing to reinterpret the Basic Law. Just to make sure the decisions of the Court Of Final Appeal are actually final. The judgement is re-interpreted. Overruled. Overturned. Like the flower pots, street signs and park bench out the front of the High Court, opposite the British Embassy.

One country, two systems.

There is a lot of talk about interpreting The Basic Law and civil rights from one side. And a lot of talk about the interpreting The Basic Law and civil rights from the other.

One country, no systems.

The sad truth is some people are dying to get into Hong Kong. And others are dying to get out of China. Fifty-eight mainlanders were found dead in a shipping container in Dover. A failed attempt by snakeheads to smuggle them into the country.

Meanwhile... after being abducted and sold to mainland farmers, 35 children under the age of six are handed back to their parents. One kidnapper admits to stealing at least 60 kids, some as young as twelve months.... 52 drug traffickers are executed in one afternoon... Dotcom Lau is born.... A woman flies into Hong Kong to collect her grandmother from hospital and is told she's already been discharged. Strange, considering grandma is supposed to be dead. Enquiries lead her to the HK Funeral Home where she's told grandma has already been cremated.... The SPCA visits Hamsters Shop and finds a dead rabbit in a cage. They inform the owner the animal is dead. She replies it's not dead, it's sleeping. And is subsequently charged with an additional 826 counts of cruelty to animal... 150 tons of trash are left on the grounds of Victoria Park after the Lunar New Year Flower Festival. An extra thirty-one garbage trucks are needed to remove it all.

10. YEAR OF THE DRAGON

WE'RE GRANTED THE RIGHT OF ABODE. Unlike our Mainland cousins we need only to have completed a seven year tour of duty to attain Permanent Resident status.

It's not as simple as it sounds.

First we must be awarded Unconditional Status. This means submitting a 16-inch deck of personal information. It takes three months to process. Once this Unconditional Status has been confirmed, and we agree to the terms and conditions, we can go for Double Jeopardy Permanent Residency.

For reasons known only to a handful of high-ranking civil servants, this requires the same 16-inch deck of tax returns, letters of employment, bank statements, high school diplomas and video library memberships to be re-submitted. You'd think, as they're already familiar with the material, the gatekeepers would be able to expedite the process on the second time around. Unfortunately this would contravene the mandatory three month minimum imposed on all government inaction. The suffering it would cause within the corridors of power is unconscionable. It used to take half the time. One of the great things about having two systems, however, is you get to embrace seventeen new levels of bureaucracy as well.

When the time comes to collect our new and improved status symbol, we're running late for the appointment. We make the near-fatal mistake of telling the cab driver to put the petal to the metal.

Ho fai, m'goi.

He attempts to secure pole position at next month's Macau Grand Prix. Every car we hurtle toward is the one that will send us skidding, screaming, careering into the ER. We avert our eyes and take cover behind the pages of Fight Club.

You are not your job. You are not a beautiful and unique snowflake. We are all part of the same compost pile.

We hear rubber clawing pathetically at bitumen. Carnage is imminent. A dramatic demonstration of Newton's First Law unfolds in bullet-time. A body in motion continues in motion, with the same speed in the same direction, unless acted upon by an external force or Keanu Reeves. Our body continues in motion, slamming into the back of the front seat. We drop into a pile on the floor and hear the muffled sound of fender upon aluminium panel. The taxi jerks to a halt. We brace for aftershocks. They never come. A few near-miss skids and honking of horns is as close as we get to a second wave. Peeking over the seat we see the snout of the taxi crumpled against the rear of a mini-bus.

I am Jack's smirking revenge.

Behind, four lanes of peak hour traffic is trying to squeeze through the one that remains unclogged.

Project Mayhem.

The cab driver leaves the vehicle and engages in the ancient tradition of standing around and apportioning blame. He lights a cigarettes and waits for police while we sit there, rubbing our neck, wondering if they'll give my PR status to someone else if I'm not there to collect it.

What if our application was among the records blown across town by Typhoon Victor?

The meter climbs from $20 to $40 to $60 and beyond. Immigration Tower is two-hundred meters away on the other side of the expressway. It lies across five lanes of traffic. Our window of opportunity closes in ten minutes.

We make a run for it.

Hurtling from the cab we leap over the concrete divider and charge blindly into oncoming cars, almost causing a few accidents of our own.

Sprinting down the sidewalk, we see an old woman tipped out of her wheelchair and onto the pavement. A guy, who is clearly a few tiles short of a mahjong tournament, grabs her handbag and scampers away.

Like Carl Lewis pursuing a personal best we hurdle over the ah-por. Someone yells out something about a purse and needing help. People see us running, clutching our manbag. A guy lunges at us. We sidestep and execute a perfect blind turn around him.

It is thirty seconds to closing when we land on the eighth floor of Immigration Tower and secure our new ID Card.

There is no fanfare. No handshake from the Chief Executive. No commemorative durian. Nothing. Quite a disappointment really. A bit of a non-event. Still, we proudly make our way back to the office. A full-fledged, card-carrying member of the Hong Kong Special Administrative Region.

Meanwhile... the government takes an unlicensed pet monkey from a ninety year-old man. It's his only source of income. 11,000 sign a petition, *supporting the monkey's Right Of Abode. Mainland spouses and children of Hong Kong residents would welcome even a fraction of the support extended to this close relative of the human race... Taiwan welcomes a new President. The first non-Kuomintang one since Chiang Kai-shek established the Party in 1945... A three year-old boy is made to sit on a stool, on top of a chair, on a mahjong table, in the middle of a room. Punishment for not speaking English properly. He falls off and cries. His stepfather beats him and leaves him on the floor. He slips into a coma and dies.*

THE WIFE OF THE AGENCY'S REGIONAL CEO and a busload of expatriate women are held hostage. They were on a tour of the New Territories and stopped to take photos of a historic village. A group of men approached them and demanded money. When none was forthcoming they held the ladies at bay. One of the captives called police on her mobile phone. None of the women could tell them where they were waylaid. It takes two hours to find them, and several thousand dollars worth of appeasement, to see them safely home. So much for the US policy of not negotiating with tourists.

We can't allow the world's worst leaders to blackmail, threaten, hold freedom-loving nations hostage with the world's worst weapons.

We get a call from The Agency's TV Producer. She's in Bangkok on a family holiday. They were playing golf. When they got to the 17th tee a retired General tried to play through. She wouldn't let him. She gave him a serve of Cantonese obscenities. He ignored her and marched on.

She winged a ball at him.

Back in the clubhouse, police were waiting to arrest her. She had to issue an apology. And by apology they meant massive financial transaction. She refused and, along with her husband and son, was taken to the station.

She used her one phone call to contact us.

She's scared and rightly so. We well remember the bodies of fifty Chinese tourists that were found in a Thai jungle, murdered for their watches, jewellery, credit cards and traveller's checks. Done-in by policemen.

Even in the Land Of Smiles there are septic teeth.

We go to Hong Kong's finest and tell them the story. They say there's nothing they can do. We ask The Officer what he will do if something happens tonight. What will he do when the papers find out he knew what was going on and did nothing about it?

He calls Interpol.

Unfortunately, Interpol is only open 9-to-5. Anyone who gets fucked outside office hours is fucked. Too bad we didn't keep in touch with our friends on Soi 33. We could've called in the carnal cavalry and had them take care of the Bangkok Peelers. We end up contacting a Thai producer we worked with the year before. She goes to the station and negotiates the cost of the apology down to an acceptable level. When the Shampoo KIng talks, people listen.

Before a Cat will condescend, to treat you as a trusted friend,
Some little token of esteem is needed, like a dish of cream.

Attendance of the June 4 vigil in Victoria Park is noticeably down. It has nothing to do with Rodney Dangerfield's request for us to lighten up on the anti-China sentiments.

There's a $300 million trifecta to be won at the track.

In Central, police baste protesting students with pepper spray. The City Of Life becomes a city of civil unrest.

City Of Strife.

1,200 doctors protest the restructuring of the medical profession. 2,500 homeowners call upon the government to stop interfering in the property market. 1,300 social workers are against lump sum payments to non-government organisations. 15,000 voice concern over the pace of civil service reforms. Whether the reforms are happening too quick or too slow is not clear. A small group hits out at the Urban Renewal Authority, over compensation for land retrieved by the government.

We have dinner at the Secret Crab Restaurant, tucked away in one of the minor arteries of Causeway Bay. It's like a crustacean speakeasy. Unpublicized. Unlicensed. Illegal. We enter a small, regular-looking *dai pai dong* and request a table for six. *Luk wei, m'goi.* The guy looks around to see if he's being watched. He tells us to wait. A young woman ushers us out into the street and marches us down an alley. To a small door in the wall. She knocks twice. The secret knock. It opens an inch, closes, then pans wide.

The room has no windows.

There's a row of fluorescent tubes in the ceiling and eight large, round tables beneath them. A dozen people at each. They're getting medieval on chilli crab. Mounds of them. They're being torn apart. Christaceans to the lions. No conversation can be heard. Just the raw cracking of shells and sucking of claws. An occasional belch.

They are all but stomachs, and we all but food; They eat us hungrily, and when they are full, They belch us.

We pitch for a dotcom business. In the wake of all the recent internet bubble burstage it's the last of an endangered species. The job started as a simple bit of freelance. Easy money. Then The Agency CEO met The Client at a cocktail party. He told him The Agency could solve his marketing problems and, in a metaphysical twist of fate, we end up pitching against ourselves. We have to develop two sets of work for the same piece of business. One on behalf of The Agency. One for ourselves. We guess this is what they mean by a win-win situation. A conflict of disinterest.

We lose, to ourselves.

The work we developed for The Agency wasn't deemed as effective as the work we developed for ourselves.

Gemini rising. Niña's mum would be thrilled.

As we sit there contemplating the existential implications of losing to oneself, and ponder our *raison d'etre*, an explosion rocks the washroom.

Smoke billows from the toilets.

The cubicles had just been sprayed with insecticide. An unknowing art director went in to give birth to a concept and, as many are want to do, lit up a smoke.

Blammo!

HKSAR Government Health Warning. Smoking causes respiratory diseases.

Alarm bells ring inside the building. Tocsins sound in our head. What if that had been us? Would anyone care? As far as The Agency goes we no longer feel like a necessary evil. We feel like we're not even necessary.

I am the shit and infectious human waste of creation.

The Agency would probably want us to stay but they don't really need us. We're like that guy from The X-Files. It's good if he's there but the show goes on without him. Maybe we're too comfortable. Bored. We just sit there at our desk. Stranded, though we're all doing our best to deny it. The bullshit piles up so fast we need wings just to stay above it. Maybe we need to get the flame-thrower out. One last time.

We do what everyone else does when their life lacks meaning and they're looking for a little clarity of mind.

We shop.

White t-shirts from Calvin Klein. Black t-shirts from Paul Smith. Levis. Prada shoes. Gucci sandals. Back to basics. Designer basics, of course. We haven't gone completely mad.

The mall does its best to convince us we have.

What they call the second floor is actually the tenth floor. The first floor is on the ninth but the eighth floor isn't the ground floor. It's Upper Ground. Beneath that is Lower Ground 1, then Lower Ground 2 and, finally, the Ground Floor. There's a Mezzanine level somewhere in there as well. It all makes sense once Yling explains that developers can charge higher rent for Ground Floor shops.

Our perception is their reality.

Meanwhile... a man loses his job at Correctional Services for having two packets of peanuts in his locker... A government secretary resigns because the work was driving her insane with boredom. She writes a memo to colleagues, offering tips on how to kill time: 1)Take long lunches. 2)Fill kettles all the way up so they take longer to boil. 3)When people ring, hang up and then call them back. 4)Perfectly align everything on the top of the desk. 5)Drink lots of water so you'll have to go to the toilet more often. 6)Walk slowly... Sixty-five drown when a bus plunges into the Liujing River... Ten die when their coach dives into a Sichuan lake... A Guandong bus rolls down a ravine, killing thirteen... Twenty-six bodies are pulled from the wreckage in Shangxi.

SHAMPOO CLIENT ISSUES A CHALLENGE to The Agency. Brand relaunch. It's no big deal. We've known about it for a while. We've got a killer presentation planned for two weeks. One that will make The Client very happy. It's guaranteed to please and will test through the roof in Wuwei. All The Agency has to do is smile and nod. Promise to put the best people on it. And leave the rest to us.

Others have agendas of their own. Points to prove. Positions to justify. Behind our back they're putting together an alternative presentation. We offer to help. Give them the benefit of our five years on the account. We're all on the same team.

Aren't we?

We work until 5am, pulling the campaign together. On our own. Making it idiot-proof. In the morning we go from the office to the train station. Our boss gets there late. We miss the Guangzhou Express. We have to take a regular train to the border and walk across to Shenzhen, then catch the local train to Guangzhou. We miss that too and must complete the journey by bus.

No time for *darn gee* and *yin yeung* in the Aloha Cafe.

One of the Horsemen Of The Apocalypse is moonlighting for the Guangdong Bus Company. He takes us to the fender and soft shoulder of death half a dozen times. By the time we get to the client's office we're fried. Shampoo Client looks just as anxious. The complete world of hair care is in the room, via teleconference and video conference. London. New York. Tokyo. Singapore. Manila.

Only two ways home. Death, or victory.

Our presentation goes well, like we knew it would. Only better. The other stinks and sinks, like a smelly stone. It's kind of gratifying in a way. Annoying in another. Part of us will wish it had gone the way of the pear.

It would've been our ticket out.

We have two hours to stew on it. To think about the previous weeks. The double-dealing. The back-stabbing. The politics. The e-mail sent to us by mistake, laying the foundation for our final ride in the great glass elevator. So hard to believe, after eight years, this is what it's come to.

There were times when I would've have fired me. This is not one of them. Not now we've turned the corner and entered a brave new world.

There are things known and there are things unknown, and in between are the doors of perception.

It gives us the shits. It's worse than Visine in the coffee. If you don't know what that means put two drops into your next cup of java and see what happens.

We stop by the Stress Reduction Centre at lunch time and whack a big, blonde, female mannequin with a stick. It doesn't help. By the time we get home we've thought ourselves into a rage. Yling wants to know what's wrong.

You sound angry, Fei-gai.

I am. I want to quit.

Uh-huh.

On Monday. Fuck those guys.

Good. Quit. It will be best for you.

I will!

Good.

Fine!

We wake up angry. Why wait 'til Monday? Tyler Durden was right. Advertising has us working jobs we hate so we can buy crap we don't need. We've been raised by TV to believe we'll be billionaires and popstars even though we know we'll never be. It's like we've got on a plane and, instead of waking up in a different time and place, we've woken up as a different person.

I am Joe's bitter and twisted half-brother.

We construct a resignation letter Mario Savio would have been proud of.

There comes a time when the operation of the machine becomes so odious, makes you so sick, that you can't take part anymore. You have to throw your body upon the gears and upon the wheels, upon the levers and just make it stop.

The void is no longer churning. It's as full as a toxic tick. We've fed it and indulged it, piled it high and stacked it tight with despair, desperation, degradation, depravation and dissipation. We can almost clamber out.

We salvage what's left of our integrity and, just like that, pfft, we're gone. Out of the shampoo business. Into the Richard business. We may not end up happy but we'll be fucked if we're not going to try. Freedom, after all, is the ability to make choices and accept responsibility for the choices we make.

Martin Luther King said that. Or was it Bono?

Meanwhile... the former Vice Chairman of the National People's Congress is sentenced to death after being found guilty of corruption... To celebrate their first year of being officially outlawed, Falun Gong members stage a protest in Tiananmen Square. Soldiers and plainclothes detectives descend upon them and cart them away... A cancer patient sets fire to his house, and mother, because he doesn't want her to be sad and lonely after he dies... Police find the head of a girl stuffed inside the head of a Hello Kitty doll. She was held hostage and tortured by three men for a month. One says he asked the others to stop beating the girl because her screams were upsetting his young son. He admits to disembowelling the teenager but says it was the other guy who sawed off her head and skinned the corpse. Lawyers for the defence claim the girl died of an overdose... A 52 year-old man is found lying on the floor of his apartment, head caved in. A neighbour didn't approve of the mirrors the guy had placed over the entrance to his flat, to improve the feng shui and deflect bad luck. He stormed into the apartment while he was watching television with the family. And brained him four times with a hammer... Mainland residents seeking Right of Abode take their protest to Immigration tower and demand ID Cards. One tips paint thinner over the floor and sets fire to it. An Immigration Officer suffers third degree burns to sixty percent of his body. So many people are injured that the hospital runs out of skin to graft.

DESPITE BEING UNEMPLOYED, and having no discernible income for the foreseeable the future, we're able to sign off on a $10 million loan for a new apartment. All the bank wants to see is our last two financial statements.

It's a nice place. Or, it will be, when they finish building it. Forty-eight floors above the city. Panoramic harbour views. A rooftop garden. Space for a proper barbecue. No fear of falling objects. Outstanding *feng shui* prospects.

We set a course for adventure and step aboard Star Leo.

320

It's a floating trailer park. The Sino Love Boat is making another run, to Vietnam. It promises something for everyone. And by something we mean gambling, gambling and gambling. Captain Merrill Stubing upgrades us to The Presidential Suite. It's up the bow, beneath The Bridge. There's an entrance hall, living room, bedroom and jacuzzi within. It might even be bigger than the nonexistent apartment we've just purchased. It's a welcome retreat from the maddening monotony of pleasure cruising. The only alternative to gaming is the buffet, and the disco a go-go on the Galaxy Of The Stars deck.

Macarena. YMCA. The Birdie Dance. Thank-you! Goodnight! You're the best audience we never had!

First port of call is San Ya. A big island at the bottom of China. It looks like it recently lost a war. Maybe it did. We're taken to the shell museum. Over 1,500 shells! On the way back to the boat we stop by to the famous dried fish shop. We buy a year's supply of dried fish, dried squid and dried coconut. Then it's on to Vietnam. Seventy-five clicks up the Nung River. Above the Lo Mung bridge.

Lieutenant Kilgore was right. Charlie don't surf. Charlie sells postcards, tacky souvenirs and Graham Greene paperbacks.

We embark on another group-tour of duty. Get off the boat. Get on a bus. Get off the bus. Walk around. Get on the bus. Get off the bus. Eat something. Get back on the bus. Get off the bus. A souvenir market. On the bus. Off the bus. Photo opportunity. Back on the bus. Back to Star Leo. Willard knew what he was talking about.

Never get off the boat. Absolutely goddamn right.

We take our seats for the Gala Dinner. It's in the Japanese restaurant. Six of those who are supposed to be at our table sit at another table. They're in the casino, too busy losing a quarter of a million dollars to eat. It's no big deal for them. And not really a big deal for us. Except waiters bring their meals to our table anyway. Four of us have to finish ten seaweed salads, twenty portions of sushi and ten pork cutlets.

The highlight of the evening is The Baked Alaskas On Parade.

It's a culinary extravaganza. A dozen half-Baked Alaskas, stuck like pigs with sparklers, file into the room and are paraded around by Filipinos in kimonos. Twangy Japanese music blares from speakers in the ceiling. Everyone claps along, out of time, while the kimono dragons take the baking, parading, sparkling Alaskas to each table for that all important photo opportunity. By the time they get to us the sparklers have petered out. The Alaskas are baked beyond recognition, looking every inch like they've passed through the other 49 states to get here.

As we disembark Star Leo for the last time, staff gather at the gangway to bid us farewell and make sure everyone leaves. We notice all the waitresses have legs like billiard tables and wonder if that's mandatory for employment, or simply an occupational hazard. The result of years spent bracing against the elements, while supporting trays of cocktails, and taking Baked Alaskas on parade.

Captain, I don't know how you feel about this shrimp, but if you'll eat it, you never have to prove your courage in any other way.

We make one last trip to Thailand to film our parting shot in the world of hair care. The Big Bangkok Blowout. Four commercials. Eight shampoo girls. Three weeks. Five days of shooting. A fortnight of waiting. Edits will have to be done. Morphs will have to be rendered. Images generated. Colours graded. Music scored. Final cuts approved. We have plenty of time to ourselves. To sleep. Swim. Read. Biographies. Stanley Kubrick. Woody Guthrie. Don Simpson. Janis Joplin. My Dark Places, James Ellroy. No Logo, Naomi Klein. We go to The Banyan Tree twice a week. Body scrubs. Body wraps. Body glazes. We step out of the treatment room one afternoon, naked and covered in honey. We look and feel like a Christmas ham.

Got any pineapple rings?

We get facials. Massages. Saunas. Spas. Colonic irrigation. Dine at some of the world's greatest restaurants. French. Italian. Nouveau and traditional Thai. We go and see local bands. Kickboxing tournaments. Muay Thai. We hang out in a nightclub that's a mecca for amputees. The place is crawling with amputee prostitutes.

Who knew there was such a big market for such services?

We watch TV. Sit around. Lie around and get around, loaded on some of the world's greatest skunkweed. It's kind of like being a rock star, without the coke and blowjobs. We think about nothing and everything. About what to do next.

There's really only one thing to do.

After 32,793 kilometres we know we just have to keep going because we can't imagine going on without her. She pulled us from the darkness and put us back together.

We call one of Yling's friends. The Gambler. His father owns a jewellery shop. We tell him we want to buy a ring.

Engagement ring? he asks excitedly.

A diamond ring, for her birthday.

Engagement ring?

We meet for dinner with six others. A good cover for clandestine ring ordering. At one point during the meal The Gambler suggests we go to the toilet. He pulls different types of rings from his pocket. We pull pictures of rings from ours. Together we design a ring, in the toilet. This is birthplace of our first-ever plan, 33 years in the making.

We fly to Florence.

Yling is not well. She has some kind of flu. She asks us to rub her back with a bottle cap. She takes off her shirt and we see a dozen red welts running parallel to her spine. Like she's been beaten or whipped. We ask what happened. She says her mother did it.

What?

She laughs and explains that, when she gets sick, she needs to get the air out of her back. A coin, a bottle cap or the lid off a tin will do. Something with a blunt end. It gets dragged across her back and lets the air out. Figuratively and maybe even literally. It makes her feel better but leaves giant, red skidmarks in its wake.

It's effect is immediate and we are soon laying siege to Prada, Gucci, Ferragamo and Versace.

Part of our elaborate and cunning plan is to have Yling walking by the Trinity Bridge at midnight. This is where we will propose.

We've convinced ourself we could be half Italian. That would explain some of the super-sized quantities of Catholic guilt we carry around. This move is designed to appease that and please half our forbearers. Yling being Chinese should palliate the other half, unless they're racists. Of course, recent exploits have suggested we could also be half Irish. So we're going to Dublin tomorrow. Just in case.

We have to tick all our ancestral boxes. Real or imagined.

Before we get too ahead of ourselves we have to get Yling to the middle of that bridge. She has no idea why it's so important. We've been roaming the streets of Florence all day and half the night. She's tired and just wants to return to the hotel.

Just come out to the bridge.

Why do you want to go on that bridge? It's not even the tourist bridge.

Let's take a photo.

We took a photo this afternoon. Why do we want another one?

The view. At night.

You can't see anything. Come on, let's go to bed.

Let's just go out there, take a photo and we'll go straight back. Promise

I don't want to.

It's pointless to argue and, not wishing to ruin the moment, and lose first-mover advantage, we pull out the box that's been burning a hole in our pocket for 72 hours. We open it and offer her the contents.

She stands there looking at our one carat proposition.

She's trying to work out what's happening. The cogs are ticking over. She bursts into tears and throws her arms around us.

We go back to the hotel, shed our skin and get things started. Doing our bit for the national average as we go.

Studies have shown we lose our virginity at the age of nineteen, and have 5.1 sexual partners. We engage in sex eighty-four times a year. Each time lasts approximately 12.3 minutes. This make us the worst fuckers in the world for the second year running.

I am Joe's shrinking groin.

75% of men bang the gong out of lust, compared to 34% of women. 56% make luuurve. 4% do it out of a desire to have children. That leaves 6% getting it on for some other undisclosed reason. Money? Designer goods? Real estate? None of us rock the pagoda with procreation in mind. Only 5% of men feel sexy whereas 16% of women do. It's a realistic figure. Popular opinion would have us believe the city is awash with insatiable nymphomaniacs, whereas everyone knows only about 16% of the population. Only 2% percent of us enjoy being spanked. There is no data available for the number of people who were molested in their early teens. Which is hardly surprising. No one really wants to know about that sort of thing.

Do they?

Meanwhile... a mentally ill woman is kept in a 170x60cm steel cage for two years... In Urumqui, an army truck explodes in the middle of rush hour traffic. 60 die, 180 are injured. The government donates $280,000 to the families of the dead. $1,500 each... A man takes legal action against Pizza Hut for doing him out of the $50,000 First Prize in the Hong Kong Salad Bowl Stacking Contest. The winner was from Macau and Macau, as everyone knows, is not Hong Kong... Despite an obvious loss of press, judicial and academic freedoms, Hong Kong is awarded Free-est Economy In The World for the 7th year in a row... The Bowen Road killer's ten year leash on terror continues as another dog dies after eating meat laced with insecticide.

LIKE ALL GOOD THINGS our run of unemployment comes to an end. Baldrick finds us a job at a small advertising agency. Three afternoons a week. The CEO is the same guy who hosted the party where AJ met Mulder ten years before. Small world. No wonder I nearly fell off.

Things are going to be different, this time.

We take an 80% drop in salary, for starters. This sounds like a lot of money but, when we factor in an 80% drop in hours and there's not a shampoo account in sight, we figure we're coming out in front.

Yau cheng yum soi bau.

If one has good feelings for another, even drinking water alone will fill your stomach.

We go to Los Angeles for a wedding. Not ours. Then it's on to Las Vegas to see Wayne Newton. We even wing over to Dallas and stand on the grassy knoll. Inspect the book depository. See the Zapruder film and ponder the magic bullet.

Back and to the left. Back and to the left.

Walking through the car park, on our way to Euro Christmas, we see a Honda Civic filled with smoke. An unconscious woman is in the passenger seat. There is a tin of charcoal beside her. We smash the window with a fire extinguisher, open the door and pull her out. A bottle of pills falls onto the concrete. We notice she's also slashed her wrists. And yet she's still breathing.

When it's not your time to go, it's not you time to go.

More people have committed suicide this year than in the previous three years combined. Every ten minutes someone jumps off a building, hangs themselves, or inhales carbon monoxide from burning charcoal. Forty percent of them are teenagers. One in five think suicide is the way to solve problems.

Like Rent Boy said in Trainspotting, sometimes it's shite being Cantonese.

Choose life. Choose a lifestyle. Choose a career. Choose a wife. Choose a mistress. Choose a big television, a luxury car and compact disc player. Choose skin whitening, breast augmentation, hair colouring and double eye-lids. Choose weight loss, hair gain, low fat, no-MSG, abalone. Choose whiskey. Choose Cognac. Choose fixed interest repayments. Choose your friends. Choose LV. Choose Cartier. Choose Gucci and Chanel. Choose mind-numbing, spirit-crushing game shows. Choose McDonalds. Choose KFC. Choose Hello Kitty. Choose property speculation and day-trading. Choose 18-hour days. Choose the sex of your baby. Choose schools for the selfish, fucked up brats you spawned to replace yourselves and fight over your estate before you're even dead. Choose your future. Choose life or, if it's all too hard, choose not to choose life. Choose something else. Choose Panadol. Choose charcoal. Choose gas. Choose a rope. Choose a rooftop. Choose a hammer. Choose a meat cleaver. Choose Pepsi. The voice of a new generation.

Meanwhile... a woman returns home to find her brother unconscious and the apartment filled with gas. She tries to shut it off and accidentally hits the ignition button. The flat explodes... A man locks himself in his home and threatens to commit suicide. His father asks the Fire Department to break down the door. He's told it will cost $4,000, a standard non-emergency charge. The father thinks that's too expensive and haggles, as if buying fish at the market. Technically speaking as a life is at risk. It is an emergency situation. The firemen concede to his argument and break down the door. Too late... An elderly paper collector stabs a women over re-cycling rights to a cardboard box... Swedish pet detective, Ikea Ventura, is brought in to track down the serial killer who's done-in 16 canines, and poisoned dozens more, on Bowen Road.

WE GET PINS AND NEEDLES IN OUR ARMS when we lie down. If we bend a certain way or pick up something at an angle, the right side of our neck goes into spasms. We suspect this is more than likely a result of Project Mayhem and the near-life experience we endured in that taxi.

I am Jack's screaming lumbago.

Yling takes us to see her uncle. He's a chiropractor. He takes a cursory look at our spine, runs his hands across our shoulders and says C5 and C6 are not aligned properly. He sends us for an x-ray. To check for fractures.

The radiologist confirms the diagnosis.

Each week Uncle spends forty minutes massaging our back and neck. Then five minutes snapping it into place like a Rubic's Cube that's three moves from completion. The sound of our spine cracking is horrifying and hilarious.

A pace for everything and everything in its place.

Meanwhile... developers dump rotten pork and other noxious items in a New Territories village. Electrical wires and drainpipes are interfered with. As part of some black magic ritual, eleven poles, each with seven scissors attached, are erected in public areas. Two houses are demolished when the owners go on holiday. Others receive threatening phone calls.

WE MOVE ONTO THE FORTY-EIGHTH FLOOR of Yling's new apartment, secured with our fraudulent loan. Our new home. Her mother and sister become our flatmates.

Eventually we'll enjoy impressive harbour views. The exterior of the building, however, is not yet complete. We'll have to make do with sweeping vistas of bamboo scaffolding and panoramic green safety netting, for six months.

Meanwhile... 309 die in a Henan disco inferno, on Christmas Day... Two planes, conducting flight safety tests, fall out of the sky and hit the same village, on the same day. 15 airmen and six ground-dwellers are killed... Five Falun Gong members set fire to themselves in Tiananmen Square... As part of a campaign to rid the streets of crime and warn potential offenders ahead of the Lunar New Year holiday, Beijing executes twenty-six criminals.

11. YEAR OF THE SNAKE

BEIJING ISSUES ANOTHER WARNING about the poisonous tumour of Falun Gong activities in Hong Kong. Rodney Dangerfield is asked to invoke Article 23 of the Basic Law, an anti-subversion clause that will effectively outlaw the sect in the HKSAR as well. He doesn't but he tows the party line, condemning the movement as more or less an evil cult in nature.

More or less than what?

Apart from being highly inflammable things rarely escalate beyond breathing exercises. They're like the Scientologists of the East, minus the celebrities and spaceships. They're a quasi-evil cult. The margarine of evil cults. The Diet Coke of evil. Just one calorie. Not evil enough.

Upholding Civilisation. Opposing The Evil Religions.

At the Evil Cult Exhibit in City Hall all the biggies are represented. America's Branch Davidian, 80 dead. Japan's Aum Shinrikyo, 12 dead and thousands poisoned. Uganda's Restoration of the Ten Commandments, 1,000 fatalities. Falun Gong, 100 killed. Although 93 of them were in police custody at the time. The Cult Of Personality is strangely absent, despite having been responsible for more deaths than Hitler and Stalin combined.

The International Olympic Committee arrives in Beijing, blinkers on, to evaluate the city's suitability to host the 2008 Olympics. They're not there to assess the country's human rights record or the political situation. Everyone knows the Olympic Games has nothing to do with politics and even less to do with a celebration of humanity. Their chief concern centres around plans to stage beach volleyball in Tiananmen Square.

Citius. Altius. Fortius.

In Central a man stands out front of Hongkong Bank and strips down to his underpants. He holds up a placard. No one has any idea if he is protesting or bragging.

Legal rights are inborn, mine are too.

Nana Mouskouri sounds like the name of a Greek death cult and, in a way, probably is. She's headlining the Hong Kong International Arts Festival. Thousands wonder if that also counts as an infringement on their legal rights.

Love is like a butterfly, a rare and gentle thing.

We need a few drinks to get through the show. Unfortunately, like many Hongkies, our tolerance for alcohol has dwindled to less than half a dozen drinks. We go out after and, awakening the dormant Aquarian, get embarrassingly drunk. We misplace our manbag. Our wallet, keys, passport, cheque book and $3,000 in various currencies was inside, along with a copy of Time's Arrow.

The city does things to people who live in it.

We go to the temple and make an offering to the Lost Property God. If he returns our satchel and its contents we'll give up drinking. The following morning a guy calls and says he found it in a taxi.

We honour our vows and get on the temperance rickshaw.

Meanwhile... a teacher with an interest in a catering business is jailed after poisoning student lunches with arsenic. He was trying to frame and discredit a competitor... In protest against the Trade Effluent Surcharge, a restaurateur sets himself on fire... 500 pigs die of foot and mouth disease, while 2,152 other animals become infected... A primary school explodes, killing 42. Residents claim the building was also being used as a fireworks factory. Higher grades made barrels, lower grades attached fuses. Officials admit the school was only used to make fireworks, until 1999. This was the work of a mad bomber, who took enough fireworks and gunpowder to level a building to the school.

WE'RE WATCHING Lock, Stock And Two Smoking Barrels on HBO. Yling wants to know why they've dubbed out all the fucks but left in all the cunts.

Cunt is ruder than fuck, isn't it?

We explain there are undoubtedly those who would agree with that statement. Maybe the cunts went by unnoticed, to untrained ears, hidden beneath the incomprehensible cockney brogue.

Guns for show, knives for a pro.

Out of nowhere two cunts climb in our forty-eighth floor window. The bamboo scaffolding that covers the eastern facade has given them access to every apartment. It's a common *modus operandi* for breaking and entering. There are even posters in the lobby alerting us to the danger. Reminding us to keep windows closed. We just didn't think that meant we had to do it while we were at home.

One of the invaders holds a knife.

Figuring he must be a pro, we lock ourselves in the bathroom with our mobile phone and call the police. Their response is quick. The burglars are still rooting around our drawers when The Peelers arrive. They attempt to escape the short arm of the law. One jumps out the window, loses his footing and falls to his death.

Meanwhile... a policeman investigating a noise complaint in a Kwai Chung housing estate is shot five times, with his own gun... During a random ID check in the street, a man pulls out a gun. He shoots one of the officers in the face and the other in the chest... A young girl accidentally injures a boy at the playground and is made to run naked around the park, twice. The mother of the injured boy then asks for $2,000 in reparations. To save Face, the boy must also be allowed to beat up the girl.

WE PICK UP A GYM MEMBERSHIP. In an effort to shed some layers of our winter coat we embark on a running, swimming and general exercising program. A commotion erupts in the female changing room. Maybe there's no hot water in the showers. Or someone has stolen someone else's shampoo.

A man is dragged out.

He's wearing a wig, bra and skirt. Suspicions were aroused when women noticed he'd been sitting in there for hours, masturbating, while they washed and changed.

They watched him masturbate for hours?

Across town a happy nude year really comes into its own at the busiest intersection in Central. Paparazzi swarm around a young Japanese woman as she unbuttons her blouse, scoops out her left breast and tweaks the nipple. Pandemonium ensues, the likes of which has not been seen since the public transport pink-seat rampage of '91. The more things change the more they stay the same. Photographers fall over each other, jockeying for position in an F-stop frenzy. It turns out she's not a secretary making the most of her lunch break. She's the star of such contemporary porn classics as New Sister's Underwear, Virgin Memorial, Reverse Soap Heaven and Female Molester Plan. Sexy Tennis School 2: Sexy Golf School. She's on a promotional tour. Other highlights include falling out of a nurse's uniform at the hospital. Dressing as a student and fellating a banana in the University cafeteria. She was removed from Legco when she attempted to raise more than few queries at question time.

The general election for the new Chief Executive was being discussed. They were going to be hold it on a Sunday until members of the Committee suggested people might want to go away for the weekend, or have to play golf. The election would interfere with these plans.

LIke Winston Churchill said, the best argument against democracy is a five minute conversation with the average voter.

Meanwhile... four separate explosions tear through factory dormitories in Hebei. Over 100 are feared dead. Police declare it to be the work of The Factory Bomber, a deaf 40 year-old man already on the run for murdering his lover... A 20 year-old woman buries her five year old sister and three year old brother, alive, to claim the family home.

THE DALAI LLAMA GOES TO TAIWAN. China accuses him of using religion as a pretext to engage in the practice of splitting China and colluding with Taiwanese separatists. Others believe it's just an excuse to stay in the $10,000 a-day Presidential Suite, so he can renounce all its worldly pleasures.

Some see His Holiness as the incarnation of Avalokitesvara, the Buddha of Compassion. He's *Jetsun Jamphel Ngawang Lobsang Yeshe Tenzin Gyatso. Holy Lord, Gentle Glory, Compassionate, Defender of the Faith, Ocean of Wisdom.* To Rupert Murdoch, he's as a very political old monk shuffling round in Gucci shoes.

And by their loafers ye shall know them.

An April Fool's prank goes horribly wrong when a US spy-plane collides mid-air with a Chinese jet-fighter and is forced to make an emergency landing in the PRC.

Chicken wing politics and media spin soar to new heights.

China demands an apology to protect its sovereignty and dignity. The US has confused right and wrong again. Displayed an arrogant air, used lame arguments and made groundless accusations.

The US denies any impropriety but sends someone to make a purchase from the Tianjin Apology and Gift Centre anyway.

We say sorry for you.

The TAGC was established with these types of situations in mind. To profit from the complicated business of contrition. It's a process made more complicated by the fact apologies were never really packed into our cultural baggage, as they invariably result in someone losing a great deal of Face. Now we can just pay someone to lose it for us. They'll visit those we have wronged and present them with an apology and/or gift on our behalf.

George W Bush adds a nice personal touch with a handwritten note, using all the colours of his favourite crayons.

Mainland media twist the words of the apology and turn it into a full-fledged grovel. The interpretation invokes much stronger language than was originally submitted. *Daoquianxi* and *zhiquian* are potent expressions of apology. The letter handed over by the US Embassy used the much weaker *wanxi*. This is more an expression of condolences. Still, as far as 1.3 billion are concerned, it's as good as the US bending over the table and taking it up the tradesman's entrance on national TV.

Carry the battle to them. Don't let them bring it to you. Put them on the defensive and don't ever apologize for anything.

The Campaign Against Superstition gets underway, just in time for the Ching Ming Festival. Mainlanders are urged to remember their ancestors on-line instead of incinerating paper money, joss sticks and half the countryside. The cyber-homage is expanded to include computer cremations, to help reduce the amount of undeveloped land being wasted by profitless cemeteries. Due to a slight misunderstanding, however, computer stores experience an unexpected surge in demand for CD burners.

One on-line cemetery has ten thousand tombs available for immediate occupancy. As soon as someone works out how to intern a relative in one.

Meanwhile.. 25 immigrants are killed on a bus in Guangdong when a policeman detonates a bomb he's carrying... The charred remains of a Hong Kong democracy activist, and retailer of gay pornography, is found on the steps of a Guangzhou police station... A man sexually abuses his eight year-old daughter because he didn't want to go to a prostitute. The court finds him not guilty on six counts of incest due to the fact he didn't completely penetrate her.

MORE THAN ONE HUNDRED COUPLES camp out at the marriage registry, hoping to secure a particular, auspicious date for their nuptials.

June 16 is deemed to be particularly lucky.

Throwing auspicion to the wind we decide to get hitched at a nice little castle in Ireland. This is part foolish romantic notion, part homage to our self-determined roots.

It's also part of an escape plan.

Neither of us, including Yling's mother, want to be subjected to the rigours of a traditional Chinese wedding. What we lose in quantity of guests and red packets of cash we'll make up for in quality of attendees and Guinness.

A man takes the plunge off a building outside our office. Ironically, he lands on the roof of an ambulance. It had been called to the scene when someone saw him step out onto the ledge.

He lives.

A few days later he is presented with a bill for the damage he caused to the emergency vehicle. He refuses to pay. The reason he was trying to top himself was because he has no money. He didn't call the ambulance. If they hadn't come he would've landed on the pavement and died. The vehicle wouldn't have been damaged and no one would be in court. The judge concurs with his line of reasoning. Case dismissed.

Our man in Mongolia is not so lucky. He attempts to sue the manufacturer of some thermal underwear he bought. He says the product doesn't deliver against the claims made in the advertising. *Keeps you warm, even in space!* His $4,000 suit is rejected. The judge calls him stupid for believing in advertising.

Everyone has a gripe.

Generation-Y is fast becoming Generation-Whine, in advance of the Fortune Global Forum. Two hundred Falun Gong practitioners convene upon the Convention Centre and execute a co-ordinated attack of breathing exercises, protesting the Government's refusal to grant visas to 60 of their brethren. Five hundred people seeking Right Of Abode stage a sit-in. Anti-globalization protesters a march on the venue. Even the April 5th Action Group turn up. This prompts many people to ask one very important question.

Who the fuck are 5-4 Action Group?

They waltz around with a black coffin on their shoulders. *Butchers power stinks for 10,000 years.* When The Peelers move in to take it from them the charade devolves into something akin to the end credits of The Benny Hill Show. Police chasing protestors chasing police chasing protestors around the park.

The Bird Flu comes home to roost.

Government workers descend upon wet-markets and march 500,000 foul off to the gas chambers. Media outlets label it the Poultry Holocaust. Government officials suggest the number of befallen fowl has been greatly exaggerated and are immediately labelled Poultry Holocaust deniers. To pacify the souls of the slaughtered, and atone for this sinful search and destroy, Buddhists release hundreds of fish into the ocean. Floods and typhoons are forecast as punishment if these rituals are not held.

They too are destined to die, as they were born to be eaten. Killing them in such a mass quantity goes against the natural cycle of life. The sin is going to affect Hong Kong and must be compensated for. The lost souls must be pacified or there will be more disasters to come.

It's not clear if the monks are referring to the chickens or the fish. Most of the latter are an exotic, non-indigenous species. Many are unable to adapt to their new environment and swiftly die. It begins an endless series of rituals designed to pacify lost souls, and compensate for the sin against the natural cycle of their existence. With fish stocks running low some release flights of birds instead. Other unleash squadrons of turtles. Complaints from animal welfare groups regarding all the animals being sacrificed to honour these customs are told they are taking an unnecessary short-term view of an eternal quest for peace. The animals died for a good cause and will be rewarded for it in their next life. Conservationists join in the chorus of disapproval for all this unchecked atonement. The rituals are a threat to native animals. At least four alien bird species have been introduced to Hong Kong as a result of them.

Macau also joins in the first great poultricide of the millennium when the virus is found in two pet geese. More than forty thousand birds are slaughtered as a precautionary measure.

We come down with a bit of a fever as well. Maybe *Fei Gai* has Chicken Flu too, quips Yling. We go into hiding, like Anne Frank, hoping the homicidal avian Nazis pass us by. A vigorous bottle-top treatment sees our temperature subside and we're back on our chicken legs in no time.

With more than a million birds in the ground, and the H5N1 menace temporarily at bay, the government returns to the important business of denouncing Falun Gong.

Rodney Dangerfield compares the self-immolation of two Gongers in Tiananmen Square to the 1978 mass suicides in Jonestown. Although 912 more people actually died there from drinking tainted Kool Aid. Not the practice of better health through meditation and breathing exercises. It's not clear what makes this group of crackpots such a threat to society or why their delusion is more dangerous than others.

Perhaps they're worried about a mass hyperventilation.

No mention is made of the two pensioners who went into the Social Security Appeal Board, doused themselves with lighter fluid and set each other alight, or what that might be related to.

Meanwhile... in the wake of the spy-plane fiasco, the sale of arms to

Taiwan and the Dalai Lamma's visit to Washington, Jiang Zemin confirms what the West has suspected for some time, declaring President Bush to be logically unsound, confused, unprincipled and unwise in the extreme... Operation Strike Hard notches up its 1,000th execution since firing its first shot across the brow of corruption, two months ago. Triad gangs in Sichuan threaten to execute one hundred students in protest against the persecution of their employers.... The complete set of Tin Tin comics are launched in Chinese... Tin Tin In Tibet is retitled Tin Tin In China's Tibet.

AN E-MAIL FROM ISABELLE informs us she's pregnant. She's expecting twins late June. Geminis in Gemini. Niña's mum would be beside herself.

Is this what we call closure? .

We run into Kelly. We haven't really seen him since that awkward dinner with Xi. He asks if we've heard from AJ lately. Not since she moved back to Australia, we admit. She's probably up the duff and wondering if she should tell us about it.

So you've heard then?

We have now.

Is this what we call closure?

Returning home just after midnight we find the Mahjong Family has settled in for another session. They've been playing for eight hours. We watch TV in the bedroom and fall asleep. Waking at 3:37am, they're still hard at it. We give Yling a break, jump in for a few rounds, then go back to bed. The morning comes and the girls have powered through the night. They've got their second wind. We have a meeting. We say good-bye and tell them we'll see them when we get back. The quip gets a lukewarm response. Either they're tired or they don't think we were joking.

The familiar rattle of times is there to greet us as we approach the door at 2:30pm. The rise and fall of laughter that usually accompanies it is absent.

Inside we can see why.

The ladies are slumped over the felt, blindly swirling ivory around the table. They've hit the wall. The game is officially declared over an hour later.

We go the annual Tiananmen Square vigil with 39,998 others who remember not to forget.

Meanwhile... Snoopy mania spreads to Guangzhou. Hundreds camp beneath the golden arches. Queue-jumping and hoarding results in chaos.

*Windows are broken. Students arrive more than an hour late for classes
Police are called in to restore order... Four cases of cholera are reported.*

THE NUMBER OF DOMESTIC HELPERS has grown beyond 220,000. That's
three times as many as that first Sunday we walked through Statue Square,
ten years ago.

Is Hong Kong wealthier or just lazier?.

The population explosion echoes across all walks of life. Our ecosystem
is now home to record numbers of Snapping Turtles. The Tiger Shark Of
Turtles. The most fierce turtles in the world. Snapping at their heels are bales
of Terrapins. Not the fiercest turtle in the world but the most enthusiastic.
These abandoned pets are destroying the habitat and crowding out native
wildlife faster than a soul-pacifying monk.

We can't help but wonder if Xi's promiscuous spirit turtle has anything to
do with the proliferation of half-shells.

We ask her about it when she calls. She's got another project she'd like us
to help her with. We're not sure if we can. She says she'll make it worth our
while and we have no doubt as to the veracity of her statement. It's just that
we're getting married and our dance card is kind of full. Indefinitely.

Congratulations. That's kind of what I wanted to talk to you about.
Wedding invitations. I'm getting married too.

Great minds think alike.

Idiots seldom differ, she counters. I've got a baby due in October.

Is this what we call closure?.

As if we need a reminder of what happens when you even think about
breaking a few commandments, it starts to rain. And rain. Seventy millimetres
fall in an hour. Three hundred millimetres over the next twelve. It rains
all week. Nonstop. Biblical rain. Noah Chan, of the Tsim Sha Tsui Chans,
starts work on a copy-ark. Cramming it with two of everything. BMW. Gucci.
Prada. Rolex. Mistresses. McHappy Meals. The queue stretches halfway to
Guangzhou.

*And it came to pass after seven days, that the waters of the flood were upon
the earth.*

Aunty's birthday is upon us. We buy her a fruit basket. You can't go wrong
with a fruit basket. Any occasion. Birthdays, funerals, get well, thinking of you,
congratulations on your new born. Good luck. With thanks. Fruit is gender-
neutral. All ages, all religions, race colour or creed. Everyone loves a fruit
basket. Aunty is a fruit Nazi. She presides over a fierce frugivorous regime.

Jackfruit diplomacy. Forcing it down us like a Strasbourg goose. Oranges. Apples. Chinese Pears. Grapes. Grapefruit. Dragonfruit. Longans. Lychees. Bananas. Mangoes. Mangosteens. Mandarins. Pineapples. Prickly Pears. Durians. We handpick a discriminating selection. Easy-peezy lemon squeezy. Stumbling only at the last gate.

Durian.

Buying a durian is another of those seemingly innocuous things we like to turn into events. In addition to holding a Masters Degree in Carpology we need to know which costermonger specializes in this particular produce.

Durian is a completely different discipline.

Protocol dictates we must allow him to recommend one first. We accept it, looking him in the eye as we do. A sign of sincerity and intent. We shake it. Then shake our melon. We allow two or three more durians to catch our eye. We give them a waggle. When the fruit is ripe the pods of flesh inside should be slightly loose. Not too loose. If they're too loose the fruit will be over-ripe. Determining the appropriate level of looseness is a skill that takes years to hone.

You have much to learn, young Skywalker. Size matters not. Our ally is the Durian. And a powerful ally it is. Life creates it. Makes it grow. It's energy surrounds us. Binds us.

Once we've found The One we push a few of the green spikes. To see if they bend. Slightly. They should not bend over. Really bendy ones are no good. The dark side of the durian are they. More seductive it is. Start down the bendy path and forever will it dominate our destiny.

Consume us it will.

When making a durian the centrepiece of your fruit basket it's important to pair it with mangosteens. Durian is *yit hay*. Heaty. Mangosteens are *hon leung*. Cooling. To maintain the culinary yin-yang, and our biological balance, we need one to cancel out the other. Unfortunately mangosteens are out of season. Aunty will have to drink water from the durian shell instead. It has the same cooling effect.

Remember, a Jedi can feel the Durian flowing through him.

To prove it's capable of staging an international event, Beijing has The Three Tenors perform in The Forbidden City. Twenty days before the host of the 2008 Olympics is announced.

We stood beneath an amber moon, and softly murmured someday soon.

One hundred thousand turn up, including a contingent of opera buffs and official brown-nosers from the HKSAR. For those of us not connected enough to get them at the taxpayer's expense, tickets cost $3000. Each. Ours afford a view of a giant video monitor. A partial view of a giant video monitor. We're fifteen rows back and the seating only allows us to see the top of it. Once the concert starts, and everyone stands up, all we can see is backs. We get a great view of the giant video monitor during the intermission. When everyone sits down. The commercials for Chinese medicine and tea blasted at us are spectacular failures.

Getting out of The Forbidden City, back to our hotel, takes longer than the concert itself. The efficiency that was so much in evidence when students were being bussed in and out of the US Embassy is noticeably absent.

Meanwhile... a man stabs his boss to death because she won't give him time off to watch Manchester United play football on TV... After rescuing two girls from being raped by seven men, a boy is beaten and stabbed to death. His parents sue the girls for $64,000... Officials deny a village has been quarantined because 60 residents have been diagnosed with cholera. The cholera epidemic is under control, they say. It's not an epidemic. Eight cases in one month is only an outbreak... 14 Falun Gong followers commit suicide in prison.

TYPHOON DURIAN SWINGS BY. No, really. Typhoon Durian. It might sound like they're created on a whim but there's actually quite a complicated system in place for the naming of typhoons.

Fourteen members of the Northwestern Pacific Ocean and South China Sea Region Typhoon Committee submit ten names each. The Regional Specialized Meteorological Centre in Tokyo then arranges the names in random order. This set of 140 names is quite irregular. They are from different nations and districts. Some take an obtuse approach, as adopted by rock-stars and Hollywood couples when it comes to naming children. Others go full-nerd. They include names of people, animals, plants, astrological phenomena, places, mythological figures, jewellery and fruit.

It's believed Rodney Dangerfield uses a similar, random process, when handing out Hong Kong's Birthday Honours. The Grand Bauhinias. The OBEs of The Orient.

On the fourth anniversary of the HKSAR he awards most of them to our wealthiest men. Which is only right. They helped make the archipelago what it is today.

One of the leaders of the 1967 riots also gets one. He was a pro-Beijing union leader who helped lay siege to Government House and attack all things British. Fifty people died. He's honoured for his services to the community and labour, welfare and union affairs. The rest of the list reads like a who's who of who's got influence with the eight-hundred member Election Committee. The same Election Committee who'll be deciding who gets to hand out the Grand Bauhinias next year.

Typhoon Utor drops in for a whirlwind visit and collect it's award for being the best typhoon since Typhoon Dot. We're all sent home from work. Two hundred flights are cancelled. Busses and trains stop running. Mini-busses and taxis treble their fares and take the extortion of a stranded public to fantastic new heights.

By taking Hong Kong's Gross Domestic Product ($1,300 billion) and dividing it by the population, we figure that Utor costs us $500 each. Not including taxi fares.

The Legislative Council approves the Chief Executive Election Bill. This is the rules for the next election. One amendment allows Beijing to remove the Chief Executive at any time, in accordance with The Basic Law. A small group takes to the streets, in accordance with The Basic Law, and protest this. They unfurl a banner containing 30,000 signatures. It is adorned with eight little durian motifs.

All HK people enjoy the right to choose a durian which they think smells good. If we do not choose our own durian, we doubt whether it has a good smell.

One pro-Beijing Legislator responds. Dictatorships usually arise out of democracy, he says. And the most aggravated form of tyranny and slavery come from most extreme liberty.

Worrying his message may be going over the head of the average voter he invokes a simple analogy.

Not many people know how to choose a good durian. It's better left to those who know how to choose a good durian. And the 800 members of the Election Committee know a good durian when they shake one.

Apparently we can also take comfort in the knowledge that, if the EC has any doubts as to the quality of our durian, Beijing will choose one for them.

Meanwhile... officials amend their previous announcement. 11 Falun Gong attempted suicide in prison. Only three succeeded... The cholera count hits double figures... A man is arrested and faces the death penalty. For transporting 16,280 bibles into Fujian... A young boy is kidnapped. His parents pay a $1.4 million ransom. Three days later his body is found in *the New Territories. A twelve year-old girl and two fifteen year-old boys are arrested and charged with kidnapping, extortion and murder... A 66 year-old man refuses to pay $5:60 in overdue tax and is beaten to death, by the taxman... A Henan man sells his year old son, to pay a restaurant bill.*

WE WIN THE OLYMPICS. That is, Beijing wins the right to host them in 2008. But what's theirs is ours. One country, two systems. No one loves a winner like Hong Kong and, like our Mainland cousins, we believe it's the answer to everything. A timely solution, a good explanation and sweet vindication.

To celebrate we reinterpret the Right Of Abode judgement, again.

Children born in Hong Kong, of one or more Mainland parents, are allowed to stay. This is good news for 2,300 kids and their families. Bad news for adopted children. They have to go. Whether this means all of us adoptees, or just our Mainland siblings, we'll have to wait and see.

Meanwhile... in a serious blow to China's One Child Policy, it is revealed that thirty percent of mainland condoms fail strength tests.

WE FALL OFF THE WAGON. Our bachelor party rehearsal goes horribly wrong when, out the front of the pub, one small step for Melon ends up being one giant fuck-up for Melonkind.

Even the sidewalk is out to get us.

Martin Amis was right. The city does things to the people who live in it. Does most things, perhaps, to the people who shouldn't be in it.

We fall and try to stand up. We fall down again. We've had a few drinks. We might be drunk but we're not paralytic. Everyone thinks we are because we can't stand up unassisted. We hobble around for the remainder of the evening.

'Tis but a scratch. I've had worse. It's just a flesh wound. I'm invincible. The Black Knight always triumphs.

By the time we get back to the forty-eighth floor our ankle is the size and colour of a large eggplant. And someone is trying to hammer a blunt nail through it.

We cry. A lot.

Yling takes us to hospital. An x-ray reveals a broken ankle in two places. Never missing an opportunity to humiliate patients, the doctor decides a prostate examination would also be appropriate. We're somewhat reluctant, given what happened last time we dropped our trousers for a medico. Yling can sense the fear and see the sweat forming on my brow. On the other hand, being Chinese and acutely sensitive to bargains, she thinks only a fool would turn down the opportunity to get something, anything, for free. Regardless of the attendant discomfort. She offers to stay and support us. We tell her that's not necessary. There are some things a woman shouldn't have to see.

Your fiancé getting a prostate exam is probably one of them.

We lie on the examination table facing the wall. The Doctor presses deep into the Kyber Pass. He says not to be embarrassed and warns us that it's common to feel aroused and get an erection during this procedure.

We thank him for his consideration and tell him it's highly unlikely we will be deriving any pleasure from this experience.

Not you, he replies. Me.

Oh.

It occurs to us, at this point, while we might not have had much luck with women our strike-rate when it came to medical professionals was pretty close to one hundred. At least I could claim this one on insurance.

Does that hurt? he asks probingly.

Kind of.

Can you describe the pain?

It feels like someone's got their fist up my bum.

We're given a fibrecast and crutches to keep us company for eight weeks. The healing process mostly consists of sitting around, protecting our prostate from further invasions and watching a lot of television.

Baywatch is back, again.

The gritty, real-life adventures of lifeguards is heading into uncharted waters, patrolling the exotic shores of Hawaii. Hard as it is to believe the producers of Baywatch Hawaii have found a way to surpasses its predecessor in terms of picture quality, gratuitous cleavage and side-boob. The Baywatch Hawaii theme song has also been masterfully re-orchestrated. Contemporary island rhythms have replaced the LA-rock riffs.

We watch every episode of The Simpsons. Twice.

Hey Apu, got any breakfast cereal for guys with syphilis?

The population will increase by 680,000 over the next ten years, bringing our numbers to 7,280,000. That figure is based on the assumption people like us will still be here in a decade. And the chances of that are slim.

Aren't they?

We'll be leaving soon.

Won't we?

We said something like that once before and here we are. Ten years later. Sitting in our ivory tower. Engaged to a Chinese princess. We'll have to take her with us. Her mum and sister too.

7,279, 996.

Down below a 73 year-old man is sitting out with his friends in the local Sitting Out Area. Another septuagenarian limps over, pulls out a meat cleaver and hacks him to death.

7,279,995.

On the day our cast is removed we get a reminder from The Fates of what happens to people who don't keep their Prohibitionist promises and imbibe in the demon liquor.

A 34 year-old expatriate gets out of a taxi after a night in Lan Kwai Fong, trips, hits his head and dies on the pavement.

Yut sut tjuk sing cheen goo hun.

Once a person falls down, he will regret it for life.

7,279,994.

We learn to walk again. Yling drives us to Stanley for a shuffle along the beach. We're sitting on the steps at about six in the evening. The water boils with hundreds of people. An alarm sounds and panic floods the coast.

Sha yu! Sha yu!

We scan the chaos. Something is moving through the water. It's about twenty feet long. Five or six feet wide. No fins break the surface. Those closest to shore scramble to safety. Those out deeper make for the rafts. A lone swimmer continues with his backstroke. He's wearing earplugs. His head is submerged. He's blissfully unaware of the shadow closing in on him until it passes beneath him. He feels it. He sees it. Panic stricken he swims for the beach and collapses onto the sand. People clinging to the rafts point toward the shadow as it surfaces half a dozen times then disappears.

The Leisure and Cultural Services Department declares it a false alarm. It was a school of fish or a trick of the light. Sparkling, they call it. This sounds like something you do before stepping onto a float at Mardi Gras.

There are more fearsome things lurking in the shallows of restaurants. Raw seafood in thirty-one of 350 establishments fails hygiene tests.

I never drink water. Fish fuck in it.

Our apartment block is terrorised by The Door Curtain Arsonist.

Door curtains are just like regular curtains. They hang over the entrance of our apartment, behind the security grill. They afford us some privacy while, at the same time, allowing cross-ventilation and cool breezes to circulate through the flat in the summer months. It's an elegant drapery for a more civilized age. More than twenty have been set ablaze in our building alone.

Freedom is the open window through which pours the sunlight of the human spirit and human dignity.

The third Saturday in September is National Defence Day. It's an important day for many Chinese, particularly the next generation. They need to be reminded that the world is plagued with constant regional conflicts and the threat of hegemony. In the past hegemony was a euphemism for Soviet domination and frequently associated with communism. Now it's a thinly veiled reference to the growing influence of the United States on global events. This is not to be confused with Pokemony. A euphemism for the dominance and influence of Japanese popular culture.

Taiwan is told that if it reunites with the Mainland, under the One China Principle™, it will be allowed to select its own political and administrative leaders, keep its government structure, continue using its own currency and retain its armed forces. It can maintain its status as a separate customs territory too. It's quite a liberal approach to reunification.

Two countries, two systems.

The City Of Life falls under the auspices of a tropical depression and monsoonal malaise. A young woman suffocates her six year-old son then jumps to her death. A postman in Lai Chi Kok, a twenty-eight year-old man in Tin Shui Wai and a fifty year-old woman in Wong Tai Sin suffocate on charcoal fumes. Two men jump to their deaths in Tuen Mun. A seventy-three year-old woman leaps off a building in Happy Valley and another hangs herself.

Not bad for a Wednesday.

7,279,985.

Two planes crash into the twin towers of the World Trade Centre in New York. Another hits The Pentagon.

After fifteen years of negotiation, The Second Long March comes to an end and China gains entry to the WTO.

A man sells his father to his brother for $10,000 to clear his debts and pay back the $7,000 he borrowed for treatment of a sexually transmitted disease.

Hey Apu, got any breakfast cereal for guys with syphilis?

Ten Hong Kong tourists drown when a bus dives into a Sechuan river.

7,279,973.

Twelve years after Tiananmen and four years after The Handover, the media war on terrorism rages. Like his father before him George W Bush continues the family tradition of war-mongering, bombing what's left of Afghanistan forward to the Stone Age.

Our mind wanders back to the day we arrived here in Beijing's backyard. That first assault.

What's changed? What's stayed the same?

We limp out to Chep Lap Kok. Bruised but not beaten. No longer running away from something, we're sallying toward something. On our way to Ireland, to get married.

To start something.

It's a typical October day. Not much in the way of humidity. Twenty-five to thirty degrees. And yet temperatures boil.

A group of youths beat a thirty-seven year old man to death with a folding chair when he tries to stop them teasing his girlfriend.

7,279,972

In an act of road rage a driver loses control of his truck. It topples over on Tuen Mun Road and spills its load. The street is flooded with durian.

Firemen break into an apartment and find a young woman lying on her bed, arms around her infant son. A pot of burnt charcoal sits on the floor.

The Bowen Road canine killer notches up victim eighteen.

7,279,970.

We make our way through the airport. A couple, returning from Taiwan beat the crap out of four women who jump the queue in Immigration. They're killing each other to get in here. One cycle of violence beginning as another ends.

Just another day in paradox.

Forget it, Jake. It's Chinatown.

We clear Customs. Take Yling's hand and walk away.

Departures.

POSTLUDE

Did you write this? You call it a confession? This is nothing but a list of dates. A child's fairy tale.

What did you want me to confess?

By Order of the Supreme People's Court, the war criminal Aisin-Gioro Pu Yi, male, 53 years old, of the Manchu nationality and from Peking, has served 10 years detention. As a result of remoulding through labour and ideological education during his captivity, he has shown that he has genuinely reformed. In accordance with Clause One of the Special Pardon Order he is therefore to be released.

- The Last Emperor

ME&MY
POTATO

One man, two worlds
and a baby.

RICHARD TONG

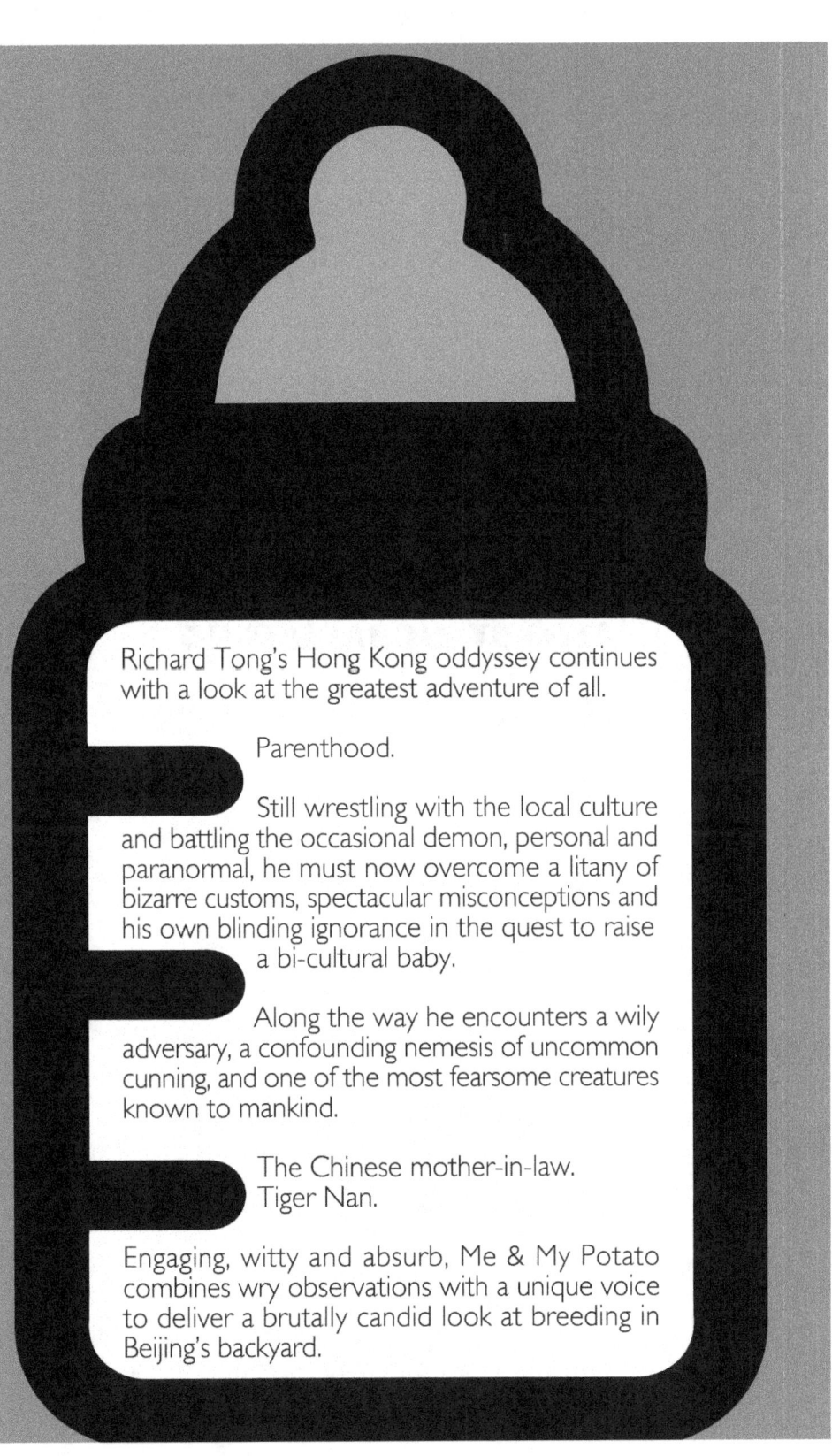

Richard Tong's Hong Kong oddyssey continues with a look at the greatest adventure of all.

Parenthood.

Still wrestling with the local culture and battling the occasional demon, personal and paranormal, he must now overcome a litany of bizarre customs, spectacular misconceptions and his own blinding ignorance in the quest to raise a bi-cultural baby.

Along the way he encounters a wily adversary, a confounding nemesis of uncommon cunning, and one of the most fearsome creatures known to mankind.

The Chinese mother-in-law.
Tiger Nan.

Engaging, witty and absurb, Me & My Potato combines wry observations with a unique voice to deliver a brutally candid look at breeding in Beijing's backyard.

ALSO BY RICHARD TONG

Discover the Neon Noir world of Jack So

BITCH ON HEAT

RICHARD TONG

1987. Jack So is a hard-boiled, not-so-good Samaritan and single father. When a bombshell drops into his lap, it sets off a journey through the simmering, Neon Noir™ shadows of Hong Kong.

I'M OFFERING YOU ALL I CAN, JACK.

THAT'S NOT WHAT I'M LOOKING FOR.

THEN LOOK A LITTLE LONGER. AND HARDER.

Navigating perilous curves in pursuit of an ancient artifact, he soon discovers the past is not finished with him, yet. History still has some harsh lessons for Jack So to learn. And history, when it comes unbidden, can be a bitch.

AVAILABLE IN
HARDBACK, E-DITION AND PURE PULP

SHE'S GONE...

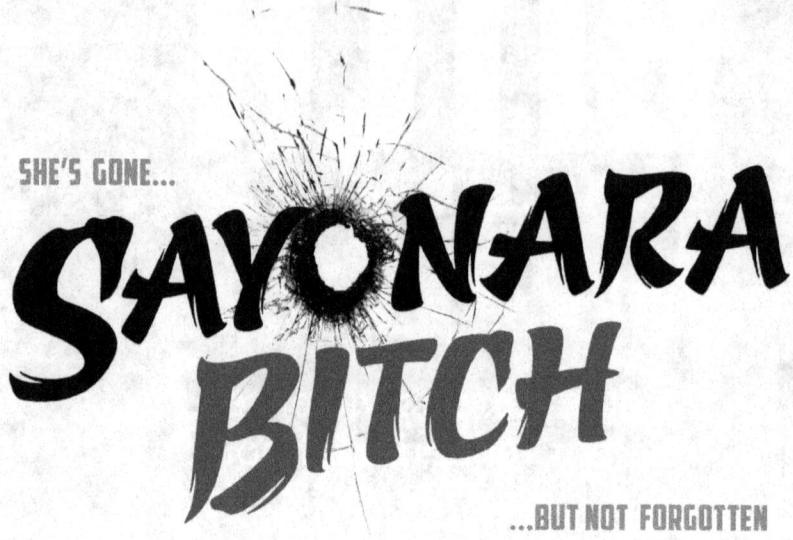

SAYONARA
BITCH

...BUT NOT FORGOTTEN

RICHARD TONG

1988. Jack So is a not-so-good Samaritan and single father. When a benevolent beer spills into a brutal bloodbath, a wave of violence washes over the murky Neon Noir™ shadows of Hong Kong and dumps Jack in the deep end.

WHAT DO YOU WANT, JACK?

MORE THAN YOU'VE GIVEN. AND NOT AS MUCH AS YOU'RE OFFERING NOW.

YOU CAN HAVE IT ALL, IF YOU WANT IT BAD ENOUGH.

HIRE ME OR FIRE ME, KOKO. OR THIS IS AS FAR AS WE GO.

MAYBE WE SHOULD GO SOMEWHERE ELSE.

Setting sail in search of a sultry seductress with an incendiary secret, Jack finds himself all at sea, rubbing shoulders with society's most celebrated, salacious and unscrupulous. Some home truths, he soon discovers, are better left unsaid. You can't bury the past if it's not dead. And sins of the father can be a bitch.

AVAILABLE IN HARDBACK, E-DITION AND PURE PULP

www.ingramcontent.com/pod-product-compliance
Lightning Source LLC
Chambersburg PA
CBHW061925170626
46813CB00006B/2306